THE ROSETTA MAN

CLAIRE McCAGUE

EDGE SCIENCE FICTION AND FANTASY PUBLISHING
An Imprint of HADES PUBLICATIONS, INC.
CALGARY

The Rosetta Man

Copyright © 2016 by Claire McCague

EDGE SCIENCE FICTION AND FANTASY PUBLISHING
An Imprint of HADES PUBLICATIONS, INC.
P.O. Box 1714, Calgary, Alberta, T2P 2L7, Canada

The EDGE Team:
Producer: Brian Hades
Editorial Manager: Ella Beaumont
Editor: Ron Bender
Cover Artist: Erfan Nuriiev
Book Design: Mark Steele
Publicist: Janice Shoults

ISBN: 978-1-77053-124-6

EDGE Science Fiction and Fantasy Publishing and Hades Publications, Inc. acknowledges the ongoing support of the Alberta Foundation for the Arts and the Canada Council for the Arts for our publishing programme.

Canada Council   Conseil des arts
for the Arts   du Canada

Library and Archives Canada Cataloguing in Publication
CIP Data on file with the National Library of Canada
ISBN: 978-1-77053-124-6
(e-Book ISBN: 978-1-77053-094-2)

FIRST EDITION
(20160804)
Printed in USA
www.edgewebsite.com

Publisher's Note:

Thank you for purchasing this book. It began as an idea, was shaped by the creativity of its talented author, and was subsequently molded into the book you have before you by a team of editors and designers.

Like all EDGE books, this book is the result of the creative talents of a dedicated team of individuals who all believe that books (whether in print or pixels) have the magical ability to take you on an adventure to new and wondrous places powered by the author's imagination.

As EDGE's publisher, I hope that you enjoy this book. It is a part of our ongoing quest to discover talented authors and to make their creative writing available to you.

We also hope that you will share your discovery and enjoyment of this novel on social media through Facebook, Twitter, Goodreads, Pinterest, etc., and by posting your opinions and/or reviews on amazon and other review sites and blogs. By doing so, others will be able to share your discovery and passion for this book.

Brian Hades, publisher

"You have to know everything about squirrels.
Because they know everything about you."
— Bill Adler, Outwitting Squirrels

Prologue

Wellington, Present Day

The possum invasion was a serious problem. Millions of alien, Australian brush-tailed possums were munching through New Zealand's bush, forest, and farmland. This guaranteed continuous research funding, which Harry Hatarei appreciated. It suited him to study an immediate threat to his home islands. That said, the problem had been around for a hundred and seventy years, and Harry wasn't cruel enough to solve it.

He pulled open the heavy middle drawer of his filing cabinet and sank a chipped coffee mug into the birdseed piled in it. His paper, which used road kill data to track possum populations, had been rejected and correcting it would require painful statistical contortions. The Maori professor preferred to tackle his research like a rugby fullback — fiddling with numbers put him up the wall. Outside, the sun was pressing fingers of light through the cloud cover of a damp August day. He tossed the birdseed out the window of his cramped office in the biology department.

The phone rang as birds fluttered from the tree shading his window. He answered it immediately. "Harry, here."

"It's Ben. Do you have time?"

"Paperwork is quicksand," Harry answered. "Save me."

"I'm tracking some critter sightings up by the Carter Observatory." Ben was a local park ranger often tasked with trapping pest-possums. "All the reports are strange. Folks swear that they've seen a couple of red pandas or wallabies or baboons, but the zoo has rattled all their cages and they aren't missing a thing."

"You've got a problem if people can't tell a primate from a kangaroo," Harry noted.

"There's a fellow who thinks he saw two baby moa birds. Half the height of an ostrich instead of twice as big," Ben replied. "If it's a prank, the people making the sightings aren't in on it. I'm starting a grid search."

"I'm on my way." Harry hung up. Digging the keys for the biology department's animal transport truck from his pocket, he headed for the parking lot.

It took a handful of minutes to reach the hill that lifted a swath of green in the heart of Wellington. He turned onto an access road for official park vehicles and pulled off beneath a stand of possum-infested trees. Locking the truck, he hiked the trail to where Ben was organizing the search. A wiry bystander, who was loudly insisting the extinct moa bird had been resurrected from DNA fragments, greeted Harry enthusiastically, hoping for an expert ally. Harry pledged an open mind and extracted himself to join the grid search. After four hours, he asked Ben to call if anything dropped from the trees and headed back to where he'd parked.

Blackbirds burst from the underbrush as he approached the truck. The doors on the box canopy were ajar and a glint of metal caught his eye. The padlock from the cage in the truck was on the ground, open and undamaged. He glanced around, figuring someone had tried to rip him off. Tugging the door, he let it drift open, looking to see if the department's shovel was still in its mount.

A glimpse of movement made him leap back. Two porcupines were hunkered in the cage. While Harry grappled with the incongruity of porcupines occupying his truck, their quills changed color, taking on the dark blue of pukeko birds. The skin beneath the spines was rust red. The one closest to him looked through the bars of the cage with pupil-less yellow eyes. Its oddly-knuckled fingers were wrapped around a short length of fallen wood, gripping it as any climbing mammal might. It turned the branch in its hand and then passed it to the second creature.

Harry stepped forward, bracing a hand against the door frame of the truck canopy. "You're not a possum."

Chapter One

Ten Days Later

Estlin Hume was ignoring the squirrel on his bedside table. The squirrels in the closet and under the bed were easy to ignore — they'd settled and were dreaming quietly — but the one on the table wanted to place a hand on his pillow. It wanted to line a nest with his dark hair. Any violation of the *no squirrels on the bed* rule would force Estlin to get up, fetch bricks and chicken wire, and deal with the latest security breach. So, he was trying not to think about the squirrel because thinking about squirrels only encouraged squirrels to think about him.

The cell phone on the bedside table buzzed. The squirrel became a projectile, leaping onto the window curtains. Estlin's nerves jumped with it. He jerked against the bed, as though waking from a dreamed fall. The phone hit the floor as he fumbled for it with fingers that felt like they were the wrong size.

Squirrels bounded around the room. One of them bounced against the windowpane. The others scattered and climbed, collectively forgetting that they'd broken through the eaves of the old farmhouse and gnawed a gap from the attic into the closet.

Estlin grabbed the phone, checking the display. The caller ID was restricted. "Hello?"

"Lyndie! Are you home?"

"Harry?" Estlin recognized the voice immediately. Harry lived on the other side of the world and never paid attention to time zones.

"Are you home, Lyndie?"

"I'm in bed." Estlin sat up, leaning against the headboard. He raised a hand to quiet the squirrels.

"Good, you're home. I assumed you were home. He's home!" Harry called out.

Estlin reached for the lamp, needing light. "What time is it?"

"It's nine o'clock here. What's that there? Late or early?"

"Both." The old wood clock on the wall suggested it was two a.m.

"I've got a job for you." Harry was professor and possum expert who often sidelined with other species — work that ranged from rat control to contracts with wealthy individuals who could afford a specialist when their exotic pets seemed depressed. "An exciting job."

"I don't like exciting jobs."

"Yes, you do."

Estlin slid under his light blanket and contemplated the rain damage on his ceiling. His last working holiday with Harry had cost him too much. He accepted the medical bills, but the officious denial of the expense forms Harry made him submit to Victoria University had irked him.

"I can't afford your jobs," he said.

"This one pays. Forty grand for five days, plus travel."

Estlin froze. He lifted the phone from his ear and wondered why Harry was calling from an unlisted number. "What kind of job is this?"

"The kind where we don't talk about it until you're down here."

"Species?"

"Can't say," Harry answered. "Lyndie, you can't miss this. Pack now — don't pack — grab your toothbrush. Your ride is on its way."

"Forty grand?"

"No camels. I promise." Harry hung up.

Estlin looked at the phone. The squirrels regarded him expectantly.

"I'm leaving," he said and rolled out of bed. He pulled on a pair of jeans, slipped his wallet into the back pocket and dug through his underwear drawer for his passport. Stopping at the window, he heaved it open, propping the sash with a stick he kept on the window sill. "All of you, out. Out!"

The squirrels did not want to go. It was a constant side effect of his extreme, involuntary empathy with animals. It made him a useful assistant for Harry, but otherwise complicated his life. When he asked them directly, the squirrels said he was tasty, filling, warm, soft, smelly, furry and shiny. These were truthful answers, but incomplete. The squirrels didn't have a sensory or conceptual symbol for what it was they liked about him. He was just *shiny*. He was so shiny that they gathered from miles around to find out what was shiny and stayed to bask in the glow.

This caused problems. He'd been expelled from three universities and one veterinary college. He'd given up on urban and suburban living because among every set of neighbors there was a kind, tree-loving soul — a concerned citizen — who watched in horror as a horde of bark-stripping squirrels killed every tree in an expanding death zone around him. The tree-lovers were compelled to phone municipal bylaw offices, wildlife conservation societies, animal welfare, and the police. This was problematic, especially as the issue was never resolved by fines or injunctions. Several of the offended parties had ultimately turned to their gardening sheds, where sharp implements lined the walls. Estlin did not like having axes swung at him. Having been assaulted with gardening tools on three separate occasions, he couldn't dismiss the events as freak and unlikely happenings.

People prone to making helpful suggestions usually felt he should get a cat, not realizing that this would only lead to untold levels of carnage.

He'd tried houses and high rises and lost every damage deposit. He'd camped in a condemned mine — a low point — and had lived on a cabin cruiser for a record six months until it sank. When he inherited the farmhouse from a reclusive uncle, from his first view of its peeling paint and sagging deck, he'd seen the beauty of the place. The isolated house on the southwestern edge of Alberta was next to a provincial park and miles from the nearest active farm.

It wasn't perfect. Work was hard to find, the squirrels still gathered and every storm stole shingles from the roof. But he didn't have to worry about being hacked to death by an irate neighbor whose sanity had been gnawed away by the tree-rats.

At thirty-three, Estlin accepted his lack of ambition. His squirrel affliction made keeping a job impossible, so he'd never linked his happiness to advances on a career path. Now, he owned twelve acres of wild grass. If he could keep the roof above him, he might be able to live an unremarkable life, perhaps even get a dog, if he could find one willing to ignore squirrels.

"Out, now." Estlin pointed at the window. The squirrels tipped their heads and thought about it. He glared at them. "Out."

Bright stars and the quarter moon cast dim light on the flat expanse of tall grass. He heard the distant rumble of prairie thunder. The rumble broke into a grating roar as a bright floodlight swept over the house. The squirrels shot out the window and galloped across the roof as a Harrier jump jet did a wheels-down, dirty pass taking three shingles with it.

A blast of heat swept into the room. Estlin yanked the stick from the window, letting it drop closed. The Harrier turned, then inexplicably paused, hovering on the raw power of its downward directed engine, before descending vertically into his backyard. The deafening engine swallowed and whined as it shut down. The canopy slid back.

"What the—" Estlin stepped away from the window and grabbed a green T-shirt from the floor. He pulled it on and leaned forward to look out again. The pilot was climbing from the cockpit.

Running to the hall, he nearly killed himself careening down the stairs, his feet ahead of his brain. In the kitchen, he stopped to check reality. The Harrier was still in his yard. He stepped into the sandals on the kitchen mat and opened the back door. The pilot was on his deck with her hand raised to knock. She was smiling and her cropped brown hair was spiked in odd directions. *Helmet-head*, Estlin thought, *is sexy*.

"Lyndie Hume?" she asked.

"Yes," he answered. "Estlin, actually," he added, correcting the nickname that only Harry inflicted on him.

"I'm Flight Lieutenant Verges, Royal Air Force." She removed a black glove to offer her hand.

"Welcome to Canada?" He smiled weakly, trying to meet the strength of her handshake.

"I'm hitting all the air shows." She slipped her hand back into her glove, adjusting the Velcro cuff of her olive flight suit. "Are you good to go?"

"That's a Harrier," he said.

"An old T.10 trainer, yes, sir," Verges agreed, lifting her chin with pride. "We've taken most of them out of service, but there's still nothing like it."

"And you're my ride?"

"Yes, sir. I got pulled from a repositioning flight to give you a lift."

"Does that happen?"

"Never," Verges grinned at him. "It was a real test of the guidance system finding your corner of nowhere. Are you ready?"

No, he thought. "I haven't packed."

"There's no room for luggage."

Harry, Estlin realized, had said not to pack. Harry, apparently, was an unbelievable bastard. "I need to make a phone call."

"We're chasing the clock, sir. My orders are to get you to Whidbey at all speed."

"What-where-when?" He could smell the engine exhaust. The Harrier was radiating palpable heat. Estlin was drawn off the deck towards it. "Where?"

"The American Naval Airbase on Whidbey Island." Verges paused, squinting at him. "Have you had any experience in tactical aircraft?"

"No. None. *None*." He wanted to be completely clear on this.

"We're breaking rules tonight." Verges was serious, her brow pinched. "If you wanted a joyride, you'd get eight hours of training and a flight suit. This isn't a joyride. They want you on the coast five minutes ago."

"What's going on?"

"I'm flying you to Whidbey Island," she answered.

"Right." Estlin cautiously touched the narrow step ladder extending from Harrier's fuselage below the cockpit. The question of his willingness to fly off with no notice and no answers wasn't much of a question. Harry had called, and he'd do whatever Verges asked because she was offering to take him somewhere in a Royal Air Force fighter. "How do I...?"

"Climb up." Verges placed her hand on the ladder directly beneath his, standing close, exuding confidence. "Step onto the seat and then down. Don't touch anything."

He climbed and Verges followed him. She reached in and swiftly buckled him into place. "The release for the belt is here. Don't touch it. Don't touch the stick, the throttle, the switches. Don't touch anything. Don't touch anything marked in red. Don't touch things marked in yellow, either. The eject is here. Don't touch it. Hands off at all times. If something happens, I'll punch us out. Nothing will happen. We'll go up. We'll go fast. We'll make a runway landing at Whidbey. Headset. Helmet." She handed them to him and brusquely corrected his fumbling. "The sick bags are there. Don't hesitate. Don't miss."

Verges tapped Estlin's shoulder and pointed at the cluster of concerned squirrels that had gathered beneath them. "Are those pets?"

"Not exactly."

"The engine can melt asphalt."

"Oh." Estlin lit a fire in his mind. He imagined the ground burning brightly. He imagined the heat and the smell. The squirrels scattered.

"Did you just—?" Verges stopped short.

"No," he said.

She looked at him with the spark of excited realization in her eyes. It was a rare reaction to Estlin's oddness. Most people blinked and looked away when the squirrels danced around him.

"Ready?" Verges asked.

"Not really."

Verges checked his harness again. "You're ready," she said and closed the back half of the canopy over Estlin, pressing it firmly down before she climbed into the trainer's lead seat. Estlin contemplated the dials, switches and levers surrounding him, particularly the stick between his legs. It was placed and shaped in a way that made him want to wrap his hands around it. He flexed his fingers and curled them back towards himself.

"Radio check." Verges voice sounded directly in Estlin's ear as the forward canopy slid into place and locked. The engine was already roaring. "Respond, please."

"I hear you," he answered, hoping there wasn't a switch he needed to press. His hands were sweating.

"Remember to breathe," Verges said. "Here we go."

The plane lifted off, then jumped forward. Estlin pressed his hands to his knees and drew a sharp breath as the Harrier rapidly accelerated. There were two display screens directly in front of him. Everything else was a stick, a lever or a switch. The dark beyond the windows was disorienting. He swallowed and his ears popped.

"You all right?"

"Ye'h." His answer barely escaped his throat.

"Keep breathing," Verges instructed.

— « o » —

The doorbell woke Sanford. He'd stretched out on the couch during the late news and lost some time. His cat complained when he sat up. He assuaged it with the gentle press of one hand as he found the remote and turned off the muted television. On his way to the foyer, he peered through the curtains on the front window. The street was empty, but a dark sedan was parked in the driveway. Sanford opened the door.

"Professor James Sanford?" A man wearing military fatigues was standing on the front step. The soldier's age and the rank on his shoulders indicated several years of service. His green eyes were alert and engaged.

"Yes?"

"Sorry to wake you. Please read this." The soldier handed him an envelope.

Sanford fumbled a pair of reading glasses from his shirt pocket and unfolded the single page letter from the Department of Defense. It offered him a position to consult on broadband electromagnetic signals from space through participation in an international panel. Transportation, accommodation, and reasonable expenses were promised and immediate relocation required. The letter indicated that the University of Washington was required to grant him leave and could not penalize him for his departure in service to his country. The language of the passage, and the surge of patriotic pride it inspired, both surprised Sanford.

"May I come in? I'm Sergeant Malone."

Sanford was a physicist, and his living room reflected two weeks of the most intensive research of his long career. His wife, Millie, had died eight years past, and the living room had fallen far from her standards for company. He looked at the letter again. "Yes, of course."

Malone stepped through the doorway and evaluated everything in view with a few swift glances.

Sanford realized he'd let a complete stranger into his house. "Do you have identification?"

"No," Sergeant Malone answered. "You've read the letter. Any questions?"

"No." Sanford had not expected this opportunity. His publications gave him a presence in the field, but he lived in a small house adjacent to the university where he kept a small office. "I mean, yes, questions—"

"I can't answer them." Sergeant Malone went to the coffee table and picked up a pen. It was resting with the notes and printouts that had consumed Sanford since the Burst. "I can't even tell you where we're going until you sign."

"Going?" Sanford was taken aback.

"Immediately means now." Sergeant Malone offered the pen.

"Oh." Sanford had been fixated on the Burst. He'd worked until his cat complained of neglect. The solution required radical thinking. Sanford's theories were so radical he hadn't yet ventured to share them.

"Is there a problem?" Sergeant Malone asked. "Clearly, you understand what this is about."

"This is all signal data," Sanford answered, "pieces of the puzzle collected by receivers around the world. It wasn't a microquasar. I assume you know that. But it wasn't a nano-quasar, either. The White House statement suggesting it was some crazy miniaturized version of a natural phenomenon makes us look like idiots."

The mysterious origin of the electromagnetic pulse was sinking in the nightly news cycle. The media alternately assured and alarmed the public. Official statements from the government fed conspiracy theories while scientists gathered every fragment of the raw signal and set to work. Sanford's work focused on the energy signatures that a completely hypothetical type of interstellar event would emit. If he was right, deep space emissions that everyone assumed were from natural celestial objects would take on new meaning. "I accept." He signed and handed the document back.

"I'll be taking you to the airbase immediately," Sergeant Malone said. "You need to pack."

"Airbase?"

"Your flight leaves tonight."

"How long will I be gone? The term starts in two weeks. I need to make arrangements for my courses. My cat...." Sanford picked up Teddy. *Could he go? Could he leave this instant?*

"The cat's not coming."

"Teddy doesn't travel." Sanford did not mean to sound as affronted as he instantaneously felt.

"He's a Persian, right?" Sergeant Malone offered his fingers to the cat. Teddy refused to sniff them. "You can leave a key and call a neighbor when you get to New Zealand. The university will receive a letter, but I expect you'll want to call them tomorrow."

"New Zealand?" Sanford knew that many prominent scientists had dropped out of on-line discussions. Several of them had cited government contracts as they excused themselves, but numerous academics had vanished without explanation. Offices were abandoned, phone calls went unanswered, and courses in quantum decoherance, relativity, and radiative processes in astrophysics were foisted on new faculty members.

"At the airbase, you'll receive your contract and non-disclosure agreement. You'll sign them before you step on the flight."

"Yes, of course." He wasn't relocating down the coast or even heading east. He was flying to the far side of the world to *consult.*

"Dr. Sanford, pack now."

Chapter Two

"We'll be on the ground in three minutes."

Estlin's appreciation for Verges' voice had grown throughout the flight. It had pulled him back to himself when his vision had tunneled and grayed. She had steadily told him how best to keep blood in his head, how best to tie off a sick bag, and how if they flew west fast enough they could drop a time zone and, by-the-clock, arrive five minutes before they left.

They were over the mountains, dark peaks rising through a field of clouds. He'd glimpsed a stretch of highway and few small towns, but now the stars and moon had his attention. "Great sky."

"Say again?"

Verges query brought him back to the cockpit and all the displays before him. Estlin checked the altitude, the easiest instrument for him to read. They were steadily descending. "Sorry, I was admiring the stars. It's a great sky."

"Yes," she said. "Tight turn coming."

Estlin curled his toes, gripped his knees, braced his shoulders and breathed. The runway was beneath them, brightly lit amongst the shadows of the coastal mountains. They turned over the water, dropping speed and altitude to deftly touch down. Estlin wondered if they'd beaten the clock and realized he'd left his watch at home next to his cell phone. The canopy opened letting in a blast of fresh air as they taxied past a row of light grey combat aircraft precisely parked on the tarmac with their wings folded. The snub-nosed planes had wide cockpits, seating two across with two more behind under a second canopy. Each one had twin engines tightly mounted in a sharply narrowing fuselage and an unusual bulge high on a single vertical tail fin.

"What are those?" Estlin asked.

"Prowlers. For electronic warfare," Verges answered. "They intercept and interrupt enemy communications."

The Harrier turned toward a massive gray military cargo plane waiting on the tarmac. Its wingspan exceeded the open hangar doors behind it. Ground crew surrounded the transport plane and scurried to the Harrier as they rolled to a stop a hundred yards away.

The ground crew immediately pushed steps alongside. Estlin handed the sick bag to someone who clearly didn't want it. He unbuckled the harness and waited until Verges offered him a hand. He almost lost one sandal climbing up onto the seat, but a strong pull from Verges kept him balanced. She placed a hand on his shoulder as he stepped onto the aluminum stairs.

"You okay?" Verges asked.

"I'm good. Thanks for the ride." Estlin followed her to the tarmac, feeling wobble-kneed and awkward. He caught her hand again. "Verges, you have a great job."

"I know." She smiled, squeezed his hand and let go.

The hairs on Estlin's arms rose. He realized that he'd met someone extraordinary, allowed all opportunity to talk to her fly by and, essentially, puked in her car.

"Mr. Hume, I'm Sergeant Pollock, loadmaster on the *Cascade*." The airman had close-cropped, white hair and sun-baked skin. "You'll be riding with us to Wellington."

"That's a Cascade?" Estlin asked.

"It's a C-17 Globemaster. When they're that big, we name them like ships." Sergeant Pollock pressed a clipboard stacked with forms into Estlin's hands. "You need to sign these."

"What's this?" He glanced at the forms, reading nothing as he realized Verges was escaping. "Wait. Wait!"

Flight Lieutenant Verges stopped. The ground crew paused to watch them.

"Thanks again. That was—" Estlin ran out words.

"My job," she said. "Take care."

"You, too." Estlin watched Verges stride off toward a nearby hangar. His shirt was clinging to him and the Pacific wind was damp and cold. When he crossed the equator, summer would become winter. He wasn't prepared, and he didn't even know Verges' first name.

"Sir, you need to sign the forms."

"What are they?"

"Contract, non-disclosure agreement and waiver," Pollock answered. "You're our last passenger. We'll be underway as soon as you sign."

An American military letterhead dominated the contract. Estlin felt airsick again. "I'm sorry. I need to make a phone call." He was certain Harry wouldn't have asked this of him. But Harry hadn't asked. He'd hung up without saying a damn thing.

"We're wheels up in two minutes. You're either on or you're off, and you're off if you don't sign. The door closes now."

"Lyndie?" A woman was approaching from the hangar. She had straight black hair, Asian eyes, and a New Zealand accent. Her blouse and slacks were both impeccable and practical for travel. A black bag was slung over her shoulder.

"Estlin, yes, hello," he answered.

"I'm Yidge Lee, special envoy with the New Zealand consulate." She handed him two curling sheets of fax paper. "Harry said you'd need these."

Estlin read the first page. It was a consulting contract hand-written in Harry's looping scrawl, committing him to work for Harry studying the behavior and zoosemiotics of a recently discovered species for one full-time/over-time week for NZ$40,000, transportation and accommodation provided. Estlin signed it without hesitation.

The second page, also hand-written, was titled *Preliminary Non-Disclosure Agreement.* It read:

> *When I arrive in New Zealand, I (Lyndie Hume)*
> *will sign a massive non-disclosure agreement*
> *full of legal jargon and dire warnings that reflect*
> *the concerns of project collaborators. The non-*
> *disclosure agreement will apply to everything I've*
> *learned and done since Harry Hatarei called and*
> *offered me the most incredible consulting job ever.*

Estlin signed. He handed the pages to Yidge and the clipboard to Sergeant Pollock.

"You need to sign these, too," Pollock insisted.

"You're mistaken," Yidge said firmly, taking the contract and flipping through the pages.

"Everyone signs, ma'am," Sergeant Pollock insisted. "No one boards without papers. Sensitive issues may be discussed in-flight and—"

"Do you expect me to sign these?" she asked.

"You're excepted, of course," Sergeant Pollock answered. "He's not."

"He can't sign these," Yidge said.

"I've got orders."

The sergeant was grim-faced and decades older than Yidge, but she held her ground, and quietly expressed her opinion of his dilemma. "Too bad."

"We delayed our departure for you."

"Mr. Hume is needed in Wellington. I won't leave without him. If you insist, I'll arrange alternate transportation. I can reroute an Air New Zealand 747. But they've run out of tarmac in Wellington. A parking spot is being held for me," she said, hefting the bag on her shoulder. "If you want to forfeit it, go ahead, but you'll land in Christchurch."

Sergeant Pollock's expression darkened. "I'll request a clarification." He took a few steps back and got on the radio.

"What's going on?" Estlin watched Yidge, who was watching Pollock.

"They'll sort this quickly," she said, not breaking her gaze.

"A Harrier landed in my yard."

"I was willing to wait until morning, but they're cranked about flying tonight. They considered whipping an F-35 across the border for you, but the Harrier was closer."

"Why me?"

"Harry thinks you can help us." Yidge smiled. "He knew I was flying back tonight, and it would be the quickest way to get you. I can't say why. It has to wait until we're in Wellington."

Pollock broke off his radio conversation. "Mr. Hume," he yelled. "You can board."

"Go," Yidge said. "I'll follow shortly."

— « o » —

Sanford had a new idea. It was actually a variation on an idea he'd already had, but it had potential. Unfortunately, the closest pencil was buried in a suitcase that Sergeant Malone had secured to the deck of the cargo plane with a pair of ratchet straps. Two hours later, the C-17 Globemaster was still on the tarmac on Whidbey Island.

They'd driven to the Naval Air Station with absolutely illegal speed. He'd been hustled through the paperwork in the hangar and out to the C-17. Restricted to one suitcase, Sanford had loaded his papers and notebooks first. He'd have to free the suitcase to dig them out, which would be fine unless the wait was suddenly over, which Sanford suspected could happen at any moment or in any number of hours.

He expected more scientists to board. So far, he'd only seen the pilots and a twelve-man tactical team. The hold of the C-17 was a wide open space. Four lengthwise rows of seats were locked to the metal flooring at the front of the cabin. He'd chosen a seat in the last row with the expansive cargo bay behind him. A single cargo pallet was tied down and covered with a green tarp.

A man in his thirties stood in the doorway looking lost. He was rail thin, unkempt and clearly not military. He didn't look like he'd been dragged from the halls of academia, either, though Sanford found that harder to judge every year. Sergeant Malone had stepped off and none of the soldiers aboard offered the man any direction. Sanford waved. The fellow nodded and came down the aisle, dropping into one of the inward facing seats lining the walls of the C-17.

Sanford offered his hand. "James Sanford, theoretical physicist."

"Estlin Hume." The man shook hands absentmindedly. His eyes swept past the tarp covered equipment to the closed tail ramp. "No windows?"

"I know," Sanford agreed, though flying blind felt appropriate considering the circumstances. "Are you a scientist?"

"No."

Sanford was perturbed by this closed response. "What do you do?"

Estlin seemed to find this a difficult question. "Pest control," he said, finally.

"Pest control?" To Sanford, this was an obvious and disappointing evasion. "Bugs?"

"Bigger. Furry." Estlin leaned over to Sanford. "Do you know what's going on?"

Sanford hesitated. "No."

"You, too?" Estlin settled back in his seat. "Weird."

"Very strange," Sanford agreed. He'd hoped to spend the flight dissecting common theories about the signal and introducing his own ideas. Instead, he would spend the next fourteen hours sitting with a rodent hunter. "Have you been to New Zealand?"

"It's the land without squirrels, and I got kicked out." Estlin smiled wryly. "I tried to take a holiday, picked up a job, landed in hospital, and got expelled for working without a visa."

Sanford didn't know what to do with this information.

Estlin's roving gaze found a focus and Sanford realized that the enigmatic Asian woman from the hangar had boarded. She was in her twenties, he thought. He'd noticed her because she appeared out-of-place and yet at home on the military base. He'd caught himself staring when she released her straight black hair, letting it fall to shoulders, then pinned it up perfectly without the aid of a mirror.

She crouched to stow her bag under the seat next to Estlin. "Sorry for the confusion," she said. "They got their wires crossed."

Her accent surprised Sanford.

"Have you met Yidge?" Estlin asked. "She's with the New Zealand consulate."

"Professor Sanford, I presume?" Yidge shook his hand. "There was a bit of a muddle. They wanted Estlin to sign a copy of your paperwork."

"Strap in. We're rolling!" Sergeant Pollock yelled as he secured the forward door. The loadmaster came aft to check that the civilians on his flight had found their seat belts. "Welcome aboard. Emergency exits are forward and immediately behind you. Wait for direction. Toilets are forward. You can walk around once we're level. Please keep your hands and feet inside the aircraft at all times."

The engines were cycling, their heavy thrum resonating in the open hold of the aircraft. Pollock glanced over his shoulder and then refocused on them. "Stay clear of the cargo. Respect my other passengers. They're working. If you have an issue, you talk to me."

Pollock went forward to take his seat in the nook beneath the ladder to the cockpit level.

"What can you tell us?" Sanford asked Yidge, raising his voice above the din as the C-17 taxied to the runway. "Are the military running everything? Why New Zealand?"

"I can't say," she said.

"No in-flight briefing?"

"I'm sorry to disappoint you."

"It's maddening," Sanford said, "these attempts at secrecy, considering the world witnessed the event."

"What?" Estlin interrupted. "What event?"

"The flash. The EMP. The Pulse." Sanford used his lecturing volume against the engines, but the question remained in Estlin's eyes. "The Rosetta Burst. The electromagnetic pulse that turned the moon blue for sixteen seconds."

Estlin's look of confusion persisted.

Sanford wondered what the man was doing on this flight. "It made the news."

"Sorry," Estlin answered. "My TV died."

"Internet? Newspapers? Radio?" Sanford asked, but Estlin denied every manner of modern communication. "Where are you from?"

"They landed a Harrier in my yard a few hours ago. I don't think my neighbor noticed."

Sanford gripped the armrests as the C-17 leapt off the runway. The heavy lifter was minimally loaded and gained altitude at a steeper pitch than commercial flights.

"When did your TV die?" Sanford asked.

"About two weeks ago."

"The burst was an intense electromagnetic pulse from space," Sanford explained. "It didn't damage ground-based electronics, but communication satellites were affected. Most service interruptions were temporary."

"It's why the world noticed," Yidge added.

"Can you tell me why he's here?" Sanford asked Yidge.

"No."

"Harry called," Estlin interjected. "He told me to grab my toothbrush because my ride was on its way. He didn't say it would be a *Harrier.*" He mimed a vertical descent. "I forgot my toothbrush."

"I'll get you a new one when we land," Yidge said.

Estlin looked distinctly uncomfortable with this offer.

"It's my job," she continued. "I make sure that Harry gets what he needs. He needs you. You need shirts and shoes." She looked at Estlin's sandals. "And socks. I'll arrange for the basics. If you need anything specific, just ask."

"What about me?" Sanford asked.

"I don't know where you're going," she answered.

"Oh." Sanford felt like he was sitting in the wrong place. He glanced over at the soldiers. The flight had leveled and they were all up and unpacking gear. He wondered what would require immediate attention on such a lengthy flight. "Can they tell us anything?"

"I doubt it," she said.

Sanford realized that Malone and the other soldiers were unrolling sleeping bags in the cargo hold.

"That's a great idea," Estlin said.

"Do you want one?" Yidge asked.

"Really?"

"I can get you one." She lifted her black bag as she rose to pursue the loadmaster.

"She likes her job," Estlin said.

Sanford leaned into the aisle, trying to guess what skill or knowledge had gained the man a seat on this flight. "You want to sleep?"

"I didn't pack a book." Estlin shrugged.

"Why are you here?" Sanford had to ask.

"Harry offered me lots of money."

"How much?" Sanford realized the rude question would not be answered and waved off any response from Estlin. "It's been a very jarring evening. Can you say who Harry works for?"

"Victoria University, usually. But tonight, I really don't know."

Yidge returned with a green sleeping bag procured from Sergeant Pollock.

Estlin stood to accept it. "Thanks."

"No problem," Yidge said, taking her seat.

Sanford couldn't help but notice that, while he didn't want a sleeping bag, he hadn't been offered one.

— « o » —

Estlin held the canvas sleeping bag and felt like he was standing on a precipice instead of preparing to lie down. He was tired enough to feel a clumsy softening of the connection between his brain and fingers. If he didn't sleep, he'd be useless by the time they landed and who knew what use Harry had intended for him? Harry had told someone something to get him on this flight.

He dropped his borrowed gear haphazardly alongside a soldier who was tying his bedding to the deck with military precision. His neighbor had a scar on his hand that extended to his wrist then vanished under the cuff of his sleeve. The surname Malone was printed above his breast pocket.

Estlin thought about introducing himself, but the man's focused actions and lack of eye contact conveyed a kind of active disinterest. He wasn't acknowledged nor was his choice of deck space denied, so he unstrapped the sleeping bag and let it unroll, toeing it into an approximate orientation.

A sharp whistle drew his attention in time to catch a small packet Malone tossed at him. It contained earplugs. The man turned his back as Estlin nodded his thanks.

Estlin stepped out of his sandals. Vibrations from the engines thrummed through the soles of his feet as he crouched to open the sleeping bag. Malone silently unlaced his worn black boots and planted them on the deck, deliberately blocking the floor level eye-line between them. Estlin stared at the boots and their broken laces, adjusted his earplugs and fell asleep.

— « o » —

Harry checked his watch as he hiked up the stairs to the boardroom. It was 7:09 a.m. After years dealing with academic committees, he didn't usually regret being late for a meeting, but Major General John Stodt, commander of the New Zealand landforce, started and ended his briefings precisely on schedule. When the project was handed to the military, Harry had been angry and wary. He hadn't expected the mix of soldier and administrator he found in Stodt. The man consulted then gave orders that immediately moved equipment, men, policies, and fences.

The briefing was underway. Harry met Stodt's eyes as he entered, but did not interrupt him with an apology. He glanced around the room and took his seat next to the Major General. Chinese Ambassador Huo sat at the far corner of the table, reserved and unreadable. The Russian next to him always looked sympathetic. The Brit was concerned. The Australian was absent. The American, Edmund Dontis, was angry.

Dontis had arrived with polished teeth, a diplomatic passport, and the title of American National Science Attache. Harry knew he was neither a diplomat nor a scientist. Dontis was well fed and had the tailored suit of a moneyman. He favored the seat directly to Stodt's left, presenting himself as a grand *facilitator* for the project.

The other seats around the table were filled by some rotation or lottery that Harry had insisted on without having time to ever find out how it was implemented.

"The Frankfurt incident has drawn a regrettable amount of attention," Major General Stodt continued. "We've suspended all chartered flights into Christchurch, in part to accommodate traffic redirected by the runway closure here. We thank you again for the passenger screening measures and travel restrictions you have imposed."

"Mainstream media will broadcast your secrets around the world within a day," Dontis announced. "It would be better if, when everyone comes looking, the story is no longer here."

"Secrecy was a temporary security measure," Stodt answered. "We all need to prepare for the impact of increasing public awareness."

"You can relocate them to your airbase or offshore to our facilities," Dontis continued. "The risk amplification of keeping them in your capital city—"

"Their actions speak for them, Mr. Dontis," Stodt responded. "They chose the place."

"If the Pacific impact marked their arrival — and we cannot assume that the incidents are related—"

"You keep an open mind." Harry's sarcasm was ignored.

"If the impact marked their arrival, they simply avoided densely populated areas and heavily defended airspace," Dontis said. "Geography put them in your backyard. That's not a choice."

"By your words, they made a geographic, demographic or geopolitical choice. A South Pacific splashdown doesn't immediately equate with them turning up in our downtown park. This wasn't the closest island, nor the nearest port of call, and yet they are here. The reasons for it may become clear."

"Russia appreciates the systematic dissemination of critical information and respects the risks New Zealand accepts for us all." Dr. Kybnakov, the Russian representative, let his accent draw out each word. "Should events force relocation, we hope that New Zealand will remain the host nation. If this is not possible, we have a suitable biomedical facility on the Kamchatka Peninsula."

"The *George Washington* has arrived," Dontis said. "This situation requires the exceptional security and infrastructure available aboard a carrier."

"You were told to keep the carrier out of our territorial waters," Harry interjected.

"Right of innocent passage," Dontis answered bluntly.

"Your carrier will draw protesters and cameras," Major General Stodt replied. "It'll turn the present chaos into a circus."

"You've had the most catastrophic security breach imaginable. This is a circus." Dontis stood and left the room.

Stodt continued the meeting without hesitation. "Dr. Hatarei, how is it?"

"Declining — if we judge its condition from its body temperature, coloration and level of physical activity." It amazed Harry how quickly one could become the world expert in something in which the world had no experts. "The changes are consistent with the first separation."

Ambassador Huo spoke quietly from the far corner of the table. "You are certain it is a terminal decline?"

"I can't be certain," Harry answered. "My bet is that in two days it'll be in terrible shape. I don't know what happens the day after that."

Major General Stodt ended the meeting, and Harry followed him to the adjacent office.

"They chose us?" Harry asked.

"Every day, you tell me that they communicate through their actions," Stodt answered. "This is where they are. They arrived on foot. They arrived unarmed — two of them, not twenty, not a hundred. They took a walk in a park, drawing just enough attention and no more."

"They climbed into a cage," Harry added. It had made his choice to transport them easy.

"And they chose this island and this city," Stodt added.

Harry tried to imagine what would have happened if they'd turned up any other way, anywhere else. "I see your point. What happened in Frankfurt?"

"UFO hunters chartered a flight. They weren't permitted to board, and it turned into a brawl," Stodt answered. "Miss Lee is on her way back. Your expert is with her?"

"Yes."

"The answer-man you failed to mention until yesterday."

"Like I said, he's off the grid, but he's the best I've ever met. We'll know if he can help us the moment he steps into the room."

"Take him directly in," Stodt said.

Harry nodded sharply. The project was in a free fall. He didn't think it could get any worse, but knew that was just a deliberate lack of imagination on his part.

Chapter Three

Dust motes danced in the light, swirling up from the hardwood floor of the farmhouse. The ceiling brightened, drawing Estlin's eyes to the window and the blue sky beyond it. He was lying in a sleepy daze when the floor dropped. It felt like the foundation had given way and a sinkhole was trying to swallow the house. He slid across the floor, falling toward the window, now directly before him, defiantly showing open sky.

He woke as the C-17 leveled out of a turn. He'd stretched out and slept without a thought to how far turbulence could throw someone in a cargo hold. The deck space next to him was empty. Wriggling out of the sleeping bag, he found that two loose straps were tethering it, top and toe, to the deck. Looking for Malone, he found him aft, playing cards with the white-haired Sergeant Pollock.

Estlin stepped into his sandals and decided to join them. They glanced at him as he approached, broke off their conversation and separated, Malone leaving Pollock. It made Estlin feel unpopular.

"How long did I sleep?" Estlin asked, pulling out his earplugs.

Sergeant Pollock shrugged, gathering the cards and tucking them into his pocket.

"How long have we been in the air?"

"Six hours, twenty three minutes," Pollock answered. "You're a heavy sleeper."

"Did you tie down—"

"Securing cargo is my job," Pollock said. "There's a cooler full of sandwiches forward by the stairs."

"Thanks."

"They brought you in from Alberta," Pollock said. "North or south."

"South," Estlin answered. "Right on the border."

"Too bad," Pollock said. "The only bit of Alberta I know is up near Fort McMurray. My brother's a bush pilot. I've spent time on the northern runways."

Estlin nodded. "Sandwiches?"

"The blue cooler," Pollock answered.

Estlin wandered forward. Yidge was curled across a few seats, asleep, using her black bag as a pillow. He took the seat next to Sanford, who was occupied with a notebook and pencil. The equations were surrounded by continuous curving figures with arcs nested in larger arcs. Of all the sketches on the page, only one was recognizable to Estlin. It was a cat with a single curling whisker drawn across the two curving lines forming the head and body.

As a student, he'd judged his professors by their pets or lack thereof. It told him where their minds were open and where they were closed. "You have a cat," he said.

"What?" Sanford was confused until Estlin gestured to the drawing. "Yes, I do."

"Nice. What's that?" Estlin pointed to another simple sketch, one that looked like a sharp curving blade.

"The shape? It's an arbelos."

"This Rosetta Burst, it's been big news?"

"The media think, or have been told to think, that two weeks ago the Earth's orbit intersected with an extraordinary pulse from a microquasar," Sanford said. "They've got it wrong."

"How do you know?"

"A microquasar is a radio jet emitting x-ray binary. I'm certain it wasn't one of those because we'd be dead," Sanford explained. "It was too close. And it was a completely different signal. I call it the Rosetta Burst because its distinct frequency signature could unlock a new language in astrophysics."

Malone was a few rows ahead, eating a sandwich and watching them intently.

"Do you know him?" Estlin asked.

"Sergeant Malone? He picked me up," Sanford answered. "Did you sign the confidentiality forms?"

"No."

Sanford closed his notebook leaving his pencil amid the pages. "You aren't American, are you?"

"Canadian."

"And you're not a scientist. Pest control, you said. You're an exterminator." Sanford slid sideways, moving away from Estlin. "Was that a euphemism?"

"I don't even kill bugs," Estlin clarified. "Harry's rats were on the wrong island. I talked them into relocating. It was illegal to release them, but I couldn't trap them under false pretenses." Estlin shut his mouth. The truth always got him in trouble.

"I should rest." Sanford tucked his notebook against his armrest until he was practically sitting on it. "I'm sure we'll be busy once we land." He leaned back, though the seats didn't recline at all, and closed his eyes.

"Sleep well," Estlin said, deciding to find a sandwich. He caught a whiff of himself and wondered if Pollock had spare deodorant.

— « o » —

The four engines reversed as the Globemaster braked. Estlin kept his fingers laced together. Across the aisle, Yidge smiled brightly as Sergeant Pollock took up the intercom, announcing their arrival in Wellington.

"Stay in your seats until we're at a full stop." Pollock ignored his own order, jogging down the aisle to crouch next to Yidge. "Miss Lee, your escort is waiting. He's going with you?" Pollock asked, pushing a thumb towards Estlin.

"Yes, thanks," Yidge answered.

"What about me?" Sanford asked.

"Stay in your seat until we complete this business." Sergeant Pollock braced a hand against Yidge's seat as the taxiing aircraft stopped. "Grab your gear," he said. "I'm dropping the ramp."

The engines shutdown, and Estlin was startled by the quiet. His ears had acclimatized to the solid noise during the long flight. He followed Pollock, standing with Yidge as the single cargo door raised and morning light streamed into the plane. As the ramp dropped, he saw a black SUV parked on the tarmac, flanked by two silver BMWs.

"What's this?" he asked.

"Secret Service," Yidge answered. "A girl could get spoiled. I've been to twenty-eight countries in the last eighty-six hours and met everyone's most select security."

Estlin looked at her in confusion. The tactical team formed up around them.

"If anyone *lost* me or my cargo, Harry promised to exclude them from the project," she said. "It'll make sense soon."

The ramp touched the ground, and Sergeant Pollock gave them a nod. The tactical team escorted them, stopping at the base of the ramp where they were met by local security and a customs officer.

"She's officially yours," Sergeant Malone said when the customs officer stamped Yidge's passport. "Drive safely." The Americans marched back into the C-17.

"Mr. Estlin Hume, do you have your passport?" the customs officer asked.

"Yes." Estlin dug his passport from his pocket.

"Canadian citizen arriving via the United States."

"Yes," Estlin agreed.

"You've been granted an unlimited work visa." The customs officer stamped the passport without examining it. "Welcome to New Zealand."

"Off we go," Yidge said, opening the side door of the black SUV.

"Go where?" Estlin asked, taking the seat next to her.

"Stone Street." She placed the black bag at her feet. "It's not far."

The convoy drove through a gate in the chain-link fence surrounding the airfield. The cloud deck was high, and the streets familiar from Estlin's previous visit. Four blocks later, they turned at the studios clustered on Stone Street. The escort vehicles parked and the SUV proceeded through the gates.

"A movie studio?" Estlin had imagined a more ominous or isolated destination.

"I'm a production assistant and translator," Yidge said. "When the project moved here, they needed a few in-house people. I did a biology work-study term with Harry five years ago. He recognized my name. Instant job."

The SUV stopped at a newly installed eight-foot fence topped with razor wire. This gate remained closed, but Harry stood next to it. He sprang forward to open the door of the SUV.

"You jackass," Estlin said. "A Harrier! You call that a *ride?*"

"A hell of a ride." Harry's smile was twisted by an impressive rugby scar. "Did you get my note?"

"He signed them!" Yidge laughed and gave him the handwritten pages.

"Perfect." Harry grinned. "And how was your round-the-world?"

"Different," Yidge answered. "Like you said, I gave everyone a slice more than they were promised. The long half is now one fifth, but I kept the base intact."

"Good girl." Harry patted her shoulder and steered them on towards the gate.

Estlin followed him. "What's going on?"

"I can't tell you yet."

"Wha—?"

"Not until you sign in. Trust me. It's worth it."

"I don't like surprises."

"Yeah, you do." Harry waved to the four guards at the next gate. "Jervis, our Yidge has returned and this is Lyndie. You're expecting him."

Jervis nodded. "Do you have ID, Mr. Hume?"

Estlin handed over his passport.

"Twin Butte?" Jervis asked, noting the details.

"Alberta."

"Thank you, Mr. Hume." He returned the passport, and gestured to a nearby guard who unlocked and rolled open the tall chain-link gate.

"Jervis has a photographic memory," Harry said. "He just memorized your passport. Tomorrow, you'll forget his name, and he'll know your birthday."

"This is a lot of space," Estlin said. The high white walls of warehouses and sound stages lined the access road.

"I thought we'd just use Studio C. Now, we have three studios, the production offices, and we're about to pick up the Kong Stage."

"This is my stop." Yidge pointed to the entrance to Studio B, a converted warehouse with tall brick walls supporting a peaked iron roof. "Good luck."

"Why do I need luck?" Estlin asked.

Yidge waved and disappeared into the studio. Estlin followed Harry to the gate in another chain link fence which surrounded the smaller Studio C. The gate was opened for them.

"Did you clone a dinosaur?" Estlin asked. "Are you building an ark?"

"Forms first."

The Studio C access door took them into a narrow security room. Sign-in sheets hung on the wall. A picture of Estlin with Harry was pinned next to them. Harry handed him a heavy clipboard.

"All of these?" Estlin asked.

"Contract. Non-disclosure. Medical. Intellectual property. Allegiance. First born." Harry gave him a pen. "Two copies of each."

"Unbelievable." Estlin dropped the clipboard on the table and started signing. "Should I be reading these?"

"Probably," Harry answered.

A soldier sat squarely at a desk, watching them. Behind him, three soldiers manned a deck of monitors. AV carts were wedged around them to supplement the permanently mounted security monitors.

Estlin scrawled on the last page. He lifted the clipboard, offered it to Harry then withheld it. "You'll tell me what's going on?"

"Better. I'll show you." Harry took the clipboard and traded it for a security pass with Estlin's picture laminated into it.

The soldier at the desk rose and unlocked the door. "The room is clear. Your entry has been approved."

"Come on," Harry said.

They entered a multipurpose space adjacent to the main studio. The large loading doors were sealed with multiple locks. The single door next to them was unlocked and opened by the pair of soldiers stationed there.

Estlin tried to walk forward confidently. Centered on the floor of the vast studio space was a plexiglass enclosure thirty feet wide and eighteen feet high. A schoolyard climbing fort was anchored to the floor inside it. Wooden ladders spanned the remaining space on different angles at different heights. Cameras surrounded the enclosure and lamps shone down from the lighting grid above it.

"Those transmit on a closed circuit to Studio B," Harry said. "We have a small direct contact team and a large outside observation group."

"What...?" Estlin approached the cage. Something was hanging from the monkey bars. It seemed oddly out of focus, as though his eyes couldn't believe what they were seeing. He took a step forward to look at it, then immediately backed up three paces. "What is that?"

"You can see it?" Harry was watching him closely.

It was definitely an *it*. It had long, dark reddish-blue limbs and a short, wide, prehensile tail. "The alien thing dangling in the cage? Yeah, I see it."

"I thought you would," Harry said. "Most have trouble seeing through the illusion."

"Illusion?" Estlin took another step forward. "What do they see?"

"Monkey's, lemurs, leopards — all sorts of things," Harry said. "Exotic animals, though. Nobody sees that and imagines it's a dog."

"Does it fool the cameras?"

"Not at all."

"Creepy." Estlin let out a long breath. "Your eyes catch it, and your brain gets something else."

"Unless it wants you to see it," Harry said. "That's why I thought you might—"

"Does it work when it's asleep?" Estlin asked. The illusions were either a conscious manipulation or an unconscious defense mechanism. "Does it sleep?"

"It has rest periods. But if someone is close enough to look at it directly, it's usually awake."

"And it's a.... What do you call it?"

"Waetapu."

"Your grandma called me that, didn't she?" Estlin said.

"Waewae tapu," Harry answered. "It's Maori for rare visitors. Visitors from far away. The kind one has responsibilities towards. Its name is Wae, now. The other things you could call it just didn't fit."

It slowly unfolded an arm, the spiky structures on its shoulder rising as it reached to take another handhold.

Estlin couldn't take his eyes off it. "Are those spines or fur?" he asked.

"Both. Sharp but flexible. It gave us one. The best labs in the world now have a slice. Yidge took it around."

The waetapu swung off the bars and landed on its hind legs, dropping to all fours. It examined its new visitor with startling bright yellow eyes. Estlin blinked. He felt something shift behind his own eyes. The waetapu blinked. It bounded towards the plexiglass and went vertical so completely that only the slightest forward drift brought it against the clear wall. It stuck — limbs spread wide, fingers and toes spread wider. It had three or six fingers on each hand depending on how you counted. Each digit split into a pair at the first knuckle. The palms were deep purple.

Estlin's vision was blurring, his gaze was drawn to Wae's yellow eyes.

"Are you okay?" Harry placed his hand Estlin's shoulder.

"I'm...." *Confused,* he thought. "Fine."

"You're crying."

"No, it just...." Estlin rubbed his eyes, they were wet. Eyes closed, the image of the room before him remained clear in his mind, then sharply changed. He saw himself in the room, looking bright, pale, and thin. The room tipped. Estlin's body jerked, the sensation of falling towards the enclosure was so convincing. "I need to sit."

He sat back on his heels and pressed his fingers to the floor, trying to ground himself in the sensation as the reversal of perspective faded.

"Lyndie?"

"I'm okay." Flickers of yellow and orange disrupted his vision. The waetapu slid from the glass to the floor to crouch like Estlin with its fingertips touching the concrete.

"The floor," Estlin said. The floor was cold — an impossible icy cold. He knew he shouldn't trust the sensation, but he did. "Hot blooded?"

"What?" Harry crouched next to him. "What did you say?"

"I think—" Estlin lifted one hand, and the waetapu echoed his gesture. "Are its fingers warmer than mine?"

"Why?"

"Is that a yes?"

"Yes," said Harry.

"This shouldn't work." Estlin rubbed his fingers on the unyielding concrete. "There should be complete miscalibration. It feels cold; I smell burning bread. Touch to touch? Perception of temperature? Wow."

The colors intensified, flecks of yellow and orange dominating his field of vision. He imagined a dark canvas. It was promptly filled by two glowing spheres — one orange, one yellow — two strong bright eyes. The colors were pure, but there was the unmistakable sense of orange in the yellow and yellow in the orange. Estlin closed his eyes, then opened them again. It made no difference because what he was seeing he wasn't exactly seeing — colors and shapes writ large across the room.

"Lyndie?" Harry's voice had its own color in the dark. "You need to keep talking."

"It's showing me...." More words brought more colors. Estlin couldn't see what he was supposed to see. "Quiet," he said. *Quiet* was pale blue. "Quiet, please." *Please* was red. He didn't expect *please* to be red. The word-colors faded. The spheres were pulsing with strong and bright life.

"Lyndie...?"

Estlin held up a hand to ask again for silence. The orange sphere hovered directly in front of him, then it was drawn away, taken somewhere beyond his vision. He closed his eyes trying to look for it, but only the yellow sphere remained. The yellow sphere lost the orange that gave it depth and life. It bled color until it was clear, then it fell through the black, struck another plane of black and crumbled into shining dust. The dark became an empty dark. Estlin shuddered and opened his eyes. The waetapu was watching him.

"There are two of them," he said.

"You're sure?" Harry asked.

"The other one has orange eyes," Estlin answered, certain.

"They're almost identical. The only difference is the eyes." Harry took Estlin's hand and pulled him to his feet, "Wae and Waewae."

"Cute. Where's the other one?"

"It was stolen."

"Stolen?" Estlin felt vaguely sick.

"It was here with Wae, and then it wasn't."

"That is not good. I don't think it can live without the other one."

"We know." The voice came from the door behind them. Estlin turned to see a senior New Zealand army officer striding across the studio floor.

"You know?" Estlin looked at Harry.

"This is Major General Stodt. He's in charge."

"Welcome to the project, Mr. Hume," Stodt said.

"We know they can't be separated because we tried it," Harry explained. "The impact was immediate, starting with a drop in body temperature. Its skin tone and eye color changed within a day. Within four days, they were both in crisis. We didn't know why. I thought it could be the air, the water, the light or lack of suitable food. We put them together again because we thought they were dying. They immediately recovered."

"When was the other one taken?" Estlin needed to know.

"Two days ago," Stodt answered. "The cameras failed and we found the guards asleep. I have one witness." Stodt pointed at Wae. "I need to know what it knows. Harry says you're an expert in animal behavior. He said that you would read meaning from its gestures. I didn't see it gesture."

Estlin wondered how much Harry had told Stodt about him. "Others have seen weird things, right?"

"Not like that," Harry answered.

The waetapu flexed each limb, watching Estlin with an intensity that made him queasy.

"Alien," he said. *"You have an alien."*

"Yes," Harry said with a modicum of sympathy. "Surprise?"

"Yeah." Estlin's brain dried. There were questions he should be asking. He looked to Harry for help and received a shrug.

"I need to know who broke in here." Stodt was blunt. "Time is critical."

"I think it's dying," Harry said. "If it dies, we lose all our answers."

Estlin wondered if the alien received ideas as clearly as it sent them. He considered the cameras recording everything and knew Stodt wasn't the only one staring expectantly at him. He needed to get on with it.

"I'm going to sit." Estlin walked toward the enclosure, separating himself from Harry and Stodt. "Don't you guys believe in chairs?"

He sat on the floor a few meters from the enclosure. The waetapu had provided a starting point. He imagined a dark canvas, his focus breaking as he tried to formulate a question. Wae swiftly scaled the ladders to stand high in the enclosure.

"Alien in cage," he said and imagined two spheres.

"How will you—?"

"Quiet would be good," Estlin said, the dark still dark. "Sorry. Earlier there was this…. When it was doing its thing and you spoke, the words turned into colors. It got really psychedelic. So, quiet," he said, and quiet was blue.

He focused on the spheres — orange and yellow. He couldn't match the colors from before. He couldn't mix colors without making a new shade and there was no sense of scale, but still he imagined the spheres and tried to offer the image.

The waetapu snatched the symbols and they flared to life. Wae rewrote Estlin's simple objects into complex signifiers, each a layered mixture of colors from center to skin. The surfaces were textured. The objects had weight and shadows, layers of meaning he couldn't understand. He felt the weight of the objects placed back in his own mind. The symbols were given to him to maintain and manipulate. They were so detailed he could barely manage it — he knew he wasn't managing it. *The difference between a rectangle and a dictionary,* he thought. But it didn't matter how bad his accent was, they were communicating.

He placed a dark wedge between the spheres, pushed them apart and crudely drained their color away. He tried again, this time letting the colors fade of their own accord as the spheres were separated. He repeated the action making the wedge the focus. He gave it limbs, creating a stick figure as simple as his hollow spheres. He gave it a depth of emptiness, space waiting for details, shadows waiting for light. The waetapu took the figure and made it deeper and darker, a figure of empty shelves.

"It knows," Estlin said, his voice distant in his ears.

"Knows what?" Stodt was close, his words were black on black. "Knows who?"

"Yes." He took the question-figure from Wae, reformed it and sent it back, ready to be filled. The waetapu responded.

It was an explosion, a concussion, a compression wave smashing the softest parts of his brain against bone. It felt like a mind was being forced into space that wasn't free for it. The signal flooded through, leaving nothing but pain. His eyes were burning. He couldn't shout. He couldn't think. The alien understood its message hadn't been received. Estlin tried to refuse, but the answer thumped in his head again. He tried to yell, to break Wae's attention. The whisper-echo of the question slid into his brain, followed by the answer. He felt it short circuit and disappear along with everything else.

— « o » —

Physicists from around the world were assembling, and Sanford had been abandoned at the airport. After Hume was hustled off the plane, the tactical team had taken more time, unloading their cargo with the help of Sergeant Pollock. Sanford had waited patiently for the loadmaster's attention. Finally, Sergeant Pollock had unstrapped his suitcase and pointed at the terminal.

Clearing customs without a flight number or airline ticket had been impossibly difficult, and then suddenly, strangely easy. He made his stateside phone calls from a public phone in the international arrivals area. His neighbor accepted responsibility for Teddy. The departmental office at the university had not received any letter about his departure, and the department chair wanted more answers than Sanford had to offer. He stood next to the phone and considered who to call next. He was now certain that he should have stayed with the transport plane, but there was no way to get back to it.

"Sanford, perfect, you made it." Ben Boxley was striding across the terminal, sunglasses in pocket and briefcase in hand. The young professor maintained a lean physique and stubbled beard, and he was the rising star of physics at CalTech. Sanford had crossed paths with the man at the international conferences that occurred in San Diego and Seattle every spring.

"Boxley, I was beginning to think I'd been forgotten." Sanford offered his hand. "Are you my ride?"

"Ride? No, no." Boxley missed the handshake to flash a boarding pass at Sanford. "I'm heading for home. I've been here four days and that's enough. I need to get back to the group. You're replacing me."

"Sorry, I was rushed onto a flight last night," Sanford said, "and given so little information. I still don't know where I'm going."

"They don't brief anyone in public spaces." Boxley clapped a hand on Sanford's shoulder. "The real brains have assembled at Lawrence Livermore, but we need a man here on the international panel. That's you. Listen and take notes, get Sarah to transcribe all the relevant bits of discussion and send them to us stateside. If you have any bright ideas, for god's sake, don't talk about them, just write them down and tag them onto the files you send us."

"Who's Sarah?"

"One of my graduate students. Young, but she can handle the notation. She'll get you up to speed. Don't expect too much. Everyone is playing their cards close on this, but we need to keep an ear on the ground here. Thankless work, but it has to be done." Boxley checked his watch. "Grab yourself a cab. Keep receipts. Sarah will take care of those, too."

"Wait! Where am I going?"

"Stone Street Studios," Boxley said with the tone of a tolerant lecturer. "The physics crowd has moved into the production offices. They've got simulations running on the hardware used for movies effects. It's crazy. And they have an issue with people coming and going. I mean, they've got bunks on site. I took a hotel room. I suggest you book one now if you can find one, but do what suits you."

Boxley checked his watch. "I've got to go." He grabbed Sanford's hand and shook it, before striding passed him. "Keep receipts!"

— « o » —

Harry knew that introducing Estlin to the situation would reveal his unusual talent via live camera feed to a room full of people. Those people had already been entrusted with the biggest secret ever, but the project was rapidly approaching critical mass. The secret would inevitably explode and then seven billion people would want all the details. He'd considered how complicated things could get, but hadn't imagined that it could be catastrophically bad until Estlin shuddered, jerked, and fell back, pale and silent.

Stodt was close and quick. He caught Estlin under the shoulders and kept his head from bouncing on the concrete floor. The Major General deftly shifted from a crouch to his knees, setting Estlin's head down with care.

"He's out," Stodt reported, pressing two fingers against the pulse point on Estlin's neck. He looked directly into the nearest camera. "I need Dr. Mir now."

"She's on her way." The answer crackled back from speakers above them.

Harry crouched and tapped Estlin on the cheek. "Lyndie?"

"Does this happen?" Stodt asked.

"Never." Harry took hold of Estlin's ear and gave it mean pinch. Estlin twitched, opened his eyes and squinted at the rafters.

Harry leaned into his line of sight. "Hey, Lyndie."

"Hey," Estlin answered quietly.

"You fainted."

"Yeah." Estlin sat up a bit, rubbing his ear. "That hurt."

"Did it answer?" Stodt asked.

"Yes. No, I—" Estlin pressed his fingers against the bridge of his nose. "It answered. I got the question right. It knew what I was asking. I thought I'd get an image but it tried to shove who they were into my brain."

"It knows?" Harry looked over to the enclosure. Wae had climbed the plexiglass and was watching intently.

Estlin shook his head. "It wasn't in bits and pieces. It was one everything. It was too much."

"You can explain that in a minute. We're leaving now." Stodt pulled Estlin to his feet.

Harry took hold of his other arm. "Good idea."

They crossed the floor with Estlin between them. Estlin tried to shake them off after a few steps, but Harry kept a grip on him as Stodt used his security pass to open the door. There was a chair next to the guard station.

"Chair," Estlin said, and sat in it. He put his head down.

"You all right?" Harry crouched next to him.

"It tried to tell me who they were," he answered. "Not what they look like or smell like, but what they're like inside their head."

"Good," said Stodt.

"Not good." Estlin leaned back in the chair to look at Stodt. "It wasn't an answer I could keep."

"It must've left an impression," Harry suggested.

Estlin covered his eyes. "Imagine having the memories of every breakfast I've ever had shoved into your brain in a single burst. That was not good."

The door from the studio offices swung open and hit the wall. Dr. Mir arrived in a breathless, professional sprint. She dropped into a crouch next to Estlin, taking hold of his wrist. Satisfied with the look of her patient, she released his hand to slip her military backpack of emergency gear from her shoulders.

Dr. Mir had spent decades alternating between private practice and service in the reserves, until retiring from the civilian half of her career. She liked her coffee black and deftly performed all the needle work on the mandatory physicals that had recently become part of Harry's life.

"Lyndie, this is Dr. Mir," Harry said. "Trust her."

"How long was he out?" Mir asked.

"A few seconds," Stodt answered.

"What's your name?"

"Estlin."

"And the date?" She flashed a light in his eyes.

"The fourteenth?" Estlin paused. "Or fifteenth? I'm not concussed. I crossed the date line last night."

"Fifteenth," Harry answered.

Dr. Mir straightened and addressed Stodt. "I want an MRI."

"No, thank you. No." Estlin was halfway out of the chair.

Stodt planted a hand in his shoulder. "Sit."

"I'm fine," Estlin insisted. "I'll be fine. Harry?"

"A brain scan," Dr Mir insisted, "as a precaution."

"No," Stodt answered.

"We might learn—"

Stodt cut her off with one shake of his head. "He stays. The semiotics and cartography teams want a session with it. We'll give them an hour." Stodt pointed at Estlin. "You'll rest, and we'll reassess the situation. Dr. Mir, escort Mr. Hume to his accommodations. Harry, you're with me."

"I slept on the flight," Estlin protested weakly. "You said you'd explain."

"I will," Harry promised. He had to follow Stodt.

"Harry?" Estlin pleaded.

"Later." Harry tried to read Stodt from the set of his shoulders. The man had disturbingly good posture.

Stodt held the door to the office access hallway, directing Harry to precede him. In the hallway, Stodt stopped and let the door drop closed behind him.

"What was that?" he demanded.

"Progress?"

"He's a psychic?"

"No. Not exactly." Harry

"You better tell me exactly what you should have told me before you flew him here."

"He can tell you if a rabbit is hungry." Harry regretted the analogy — rabbits were always hungry — he tried again. "Lyndie can count the bats in a cave without a flashlight, but if there's a human in the cave full of bats, he doesn't know unless the bats tell him."

"The bats tell him?" Stodt drew a hand across his forehead. "What the hell does that mean?"

"I don't know how it works, but he's got a *sensitivity*. He can figure out what an animal is thinking. But with us? Nothing."

"Us?"

"Humans."

"That makes less than no sense."

"When he was three or four, he was diagnosed with severe atypical autism. When he was twelve, something very bad happened, and he was cured."

"Cured?"

"He said he was catatonic for a while and then, *better*. He thought the trauma might have killed a few brain cells. I've seen him do unbelievable things. Last time he was here, he talked a colony of rats off of Matiu," Harry explained. The island conservation area in Wellington harbor was a refuge for native lizards and bugs that were vulnerable to the rats introduced by years of shipping traffic. "Lyndie was here when I heard there was a problem out there. We borrowed a boatload of humane traps. He slept on the island two nights, and the rats left with him. No bait and he didn't catch anything he didn't want to catch."

"There's a limit to the number of impossible ideas I can absorb in a week." Stodt looked weary. "Dontis wanted a private conversation this morning. The Americans bent over themselves to fly your man here. I thought they were accommodating us. Truth is, they are aware of Mr. Hume and his *limitations*."

"What?"

"Yidge said they tried to get him to sign a contract. She called them on it. They claim that it was a miscommunication, that the flight crew thought he had to sign the same paperwork as the other scientist aboard."

"Why?"

"You tell me. You sent papers for him. You must have suspected something."

"I wasn't sure he would board a second military transport without some reassurance from me."

"That's all?"

"That's all." Harry could think of only one odd American connection. "A year after we met, he flew to Chicago and let an autism researcher run a bunch of brain scans. Two weeks later, he came back looking like death warmed over, but he said they didn't find anything."

"Find out if there's more we need to know. And Harry," Stodt looked him dead in the eyes, "you break my trust again, and you're out."

Harry accepted this with a nod. "I didn't expect that much, that quick. I didn't expect it to drop him."

"I thought the damn thing had killed him," Stodt paused. "If I let him back in there and he strokes out, we'll have a serious problem. This becomes a completely different game."

Harry agreed with a nod.

"Think about the people that have been in the room with it." Stodt was grim. "According to your man, it knows what they like for breakfast. We need to rethink our security protocols."

"What about Lyndie?" Harry asked.

"The critter likes him," Stodt answered. "He walked in and its body temperature jumped three degrees."

"Did you see its eyes?" Harry knew Stodt couldn't have missed the color shift.

"We'd proceed on that alone." Stodt paused, considering. "One hour. Yidge can bring you a camera. Have him talk through whatever that was. Then you're in again. Stay with him. Get us answers."

"It likes him."

"I hope he signed the fucking waiver."

Chapter Four

Pylons blocked the entry lane to Stone Street Studios. A pair of guards watched from the gate as the taxi driver hauled Sanford's suitcase from the trunk. Sanford opened his wallet and realized he should have used a bank machine at the airport. Negotiating the currency exchange flustered him, and he neglected to collect the receipt.

Pulling his wheeled suitcase, he approached the security guard at the gate. "I'm Doctor James Sanford. I've just arrived."

"You're not on the list," the guard responded.

"You didn't check."

"I know the list," the guard answered. He was clean-shaven and had military manners despite the private security uniform. "I know who is arriving and when they are arriving."

"I was delayed at the airport. Could you check—"

"Woods," the guard called to his coworker in the nearby booth, "is there a James Sanford on the list?"

"No, sir."

Sanford felt a pang of despair. "But this is Stone Street. Boxley said I should come here."

"There's no Boxley on the list, either."

"I'm a physicist. I flew here on very short notice."

"You've got the wrong gate. If you're with the theory group, follow the fence and turn at Park Street. You're looking for the post production studios."

Sanford looked at the block of high fencing. "Could you just call—"

"Sir, you aren't on our list. I can't do anything for you."

Sanford grabbed the handle on his suitcase and turned his back on the guard. His eyes were prickling. He needed to get to wherever he was supposed to be and sit down. In the meantime, he put one foot in front of the other, found the cross street and bumped his wheeled suitcase over the curb to follow another fence line. Leaning against that chain-link fence was an African man who, Sanford hoped, could offer more precise directions. The black man watched him approach, taking the occasional drag on his cigarette.

"That's a big suitcase," he said.

"I'm looking for the post production offices."

"You're looking for the project. Are you joining us?"

"Theory group?"

"That's us. I'm Bomani." The man shook Sanford's hand with a firm grip.

"James Sanford."

"James, you're lucky. You've missed the morning meeting. Every day, the same argument. It's all noise." Bomani raised a hand to sweep up the sky. "That extraordinary light. The stars have spoken and our ears are full of muck. Nobody knows anything. They cling to little ideas. They run big simulations with bad math."

"How many people in the group?"

"Too many. Not enough," Bomani shrugged. "It's like a three-headed dog trying to decide where to piss."

"You have a theory?"

"About the Burst? You think my ego complains? I have no theory. I'm not that smart. But I know quantum decoherence and knot theory, and I know bad math."

"How long have you been here?"

"All week." Bomani leaned against the fence. "I was in Auckland working on a doctorate. I have a doctorate, but — *knot theory* — there is no work, so I need another doctorate. I get a phone call from Malawi. And I think it is a joke, the president of Malawi calling me. But he says there is a project here studying the Burst, and he wants me to come and represent my country. So, I am here, knee deep in slop. The bigger the group, the deeper the hole." He crushed his cigarette. "What are you?"

"Physicist."

"American," said Bomani, wagging a finger at Sanford. "Good. That Boxley needed to go home."

Bomani reached out and grabbed Sanford's large suitcase, lifting it off its wheels. "I'll take you to Sally. She organizes all of us. She'll give you a pass, a bunk, the works." He hefted the suitcase, curling his arm to carry it high over his shoulder against his back. "You got a library in here?"

"I didn't have much time to pack."

"Lucky thing."

"I brought all the data." Sanford didn't mention the layer of textbooks beneath those printouts.

"Do you have anything I haven't seen?" Bomani asked.

"Probably not."

Bomani waved at the gate attendant. "This is Sanford. He's replacing Boxley." The gates parted, and Bomani set off towards the nearest entrance. "The movie computers are fantastic — lots of parallel processing — but, most interesting, is what they've got hidden in Studio C."

"What do you mean?"

"Did you see the harbor on your way in? It's a parking lot, every different flag flying. Something made a big splash — maybe a rock, maybe some satellite brought down by the pulse, maybe a piece of whatever went bang. All these ships were out searching and now they're here. Easy math. One plus one. Studio C, I'm telling you, they've got something in there."

— « o » —

Harry hiked the steps to the door of a white movie trailer. They'd picked up the rental on six trailers a day ago and had towed two alongside Studio C. He'd flagged one for himself and Lyndie. His name was pinned to the door, but he hadn't been in it or caught any of the sleep he needed. He stacked the coffees he was carrying, tapped on the door and pushed it open. Estlin was sprawled on the couch opposite the door, all limbs and bone. Dr. Mir was leaning against a nearby chair.

"Harry." Estlin sat up.

Harry passed him the coffee. "How're you feeling?"

"I'm fine."

"Are you?" Harry looked from Estlin to Dr. Mir.

"I have a headache," Estlin said. "Not too bad. She won't leave."

"Without diagnostic imaging, I fall back to direct observation," Dr. Mir responded. "And time devoted to collecting a detailed patient history is never wasted."

"Thank you," Harry said. "I can stay with him. We have things to discuss."

"I'll see you later," Dr. Mir told Estlin. "Ask for me if your symptoms change."

Harry waited until the doctor left the trailer and closed the door. "Headache?"

"Quiet throb. It's nothing."

"Not nothing. That was a lot more than I expected."

"Yeah, thanks for the warning." Estlin sank back into the couch. "*Alien.*"

"You got past the disbelief faster than anyone I've introduced to it."

"I don't have to trust my eyes." Estlin pressed a finger to his temple. "I can tell it's not movie magic."

"They broke into my truck a week and a half ago," Harry said.

"What?" Estlin looked at him.

"I was in a park downtown. They broke into the truck and waited for me." Harry settled on the arm of the couch. "I knew no one would believe it. I told outrageous lies to get people into the room with them. You know my uncle is the minister of foreign affairs? I got to the top of the food chain right quick."

"Seriously?"

"I had the prime minister in my lab. The minister of civil defense and emergency management threw up in the sink." Harry mimed this with unnecessary vigor. "The visual tricks truly hammer some people."

"And they put you in charge?"

"The general runs the show. They kept me for the care and feeding. I'm trying not to bugger it up, but we almost killed them in the first week."

"How the hell did you lose one?"

Harry shifted on the arm of the couch. "We have no idea."

"You have an idea."

"Everyone has a motive." Harry gave a frustrated shrug. "It's clever, and it can pretend to be your neighbor's cat if it wants to. I can't figure how you'd get one anywhere if it didn't want to go. Then you say Wae knows exactly everything about who snagged its mate. I really want that answer."

"Sorry. Colorful, suggestive light show followed by brain damage." Estlin sipped his coffee. "How did it react?"

"I don't know. I was watching Stodt catch you," Harry answered. "Do you think that will happen again? I can't have you in there if all you do is turn a whiter shade of white and fall down."

"It was like stepping in front of a freight train."

"You are not reassuring me."

"Let's assume it's smart enough not to do that again, because that was the end of the conversation, wasn't it?" Estlin sank into the couch. "Aliens broke into your truck. I can't even...." He waved a hand in limp circles above him. "This changes everything."

"I thought it would," Harry said. "But people are people. Let's say you tell us who stole its buddy. That's a small question compared to a potential alien invasion. But now it's the only question, the life or death question."

It was a relief for Harry to have someone in his corner. "I'm sorry I didn't get you here sooner. From day one, I was trying to think of a way to swing it. You're not exactly accredited. Then we lost one, and there wasn't any time to think about it. I said we needed you, and you were on a plane."

"How'd you get them to throw so much money at me?"

"I didn't." Harry hadn't planned to talk about this so soon.

"Harry?"

"We lost one and I thought: How much would I pay to have you here?" Harry decided to offer up the full truth. "And how much would it take to make you jump and not ask why. That contract is with me."

Estlin gave him a long considering look. "You figure I'll talk you down."

There was a knock on the door.

"You're closest," Estlin said.

Harry opened the door and found Yidge on the stairs.

"Stodt wants Mr. Hume in the enclosure room," she said. "It's on the partition again. It assumed the exact position and posture it took when Estlin arrived."

"Damn thing communicates well enough when it wants to." Harry tossed the last of his coffee into the sink. "You up for this?"

"You're paying me really well," Estlin answered.

— « o » —

Jeanette Goff listened to the bare metal hangers on the closet rail tap against each other as the ship rocked. The knock on the door offered an insistent counterpoint to the tuneless chiming of the hangers. Gray morning sun was seeping through the curtained porthole. Rising, she padded barefoot the three steps across the cabin and realized that the ship was rolling far less than it had the night before. Binding her red hair back from her face, she opened the door and squinted at Nia's bright smile.

Nia was the cook's assistant on the Greenpeace icebreaker, *Arctic Sunrise*. Despite its name, the ship was on a three-month patrol of Antarctic waters. Jeanette had a temperamental stomach, and this made having a friend in the galley important, but Nia was a challenge. The young Chilean volunteer was always pressing Jeanette to try new things. Yesterday, she'd prepared a spicy bean dish.

"Forgive me yet?" Nia asked.

"I've never been so sick."

A strong chop had developed through the evening, and the round-bottomed *Arctic Sunrise* really moved. Aware that Jeanette had spent the evening expelling her dinner, Nia had stopped by after closing the kitchen, bringing her a glass of juice. Jeanette's stomach agreed that a rinse cycle was an excellent idea. At five a.m., she'd disarmed her alarm clock as a second dose of Gravol put her out.

"Blame the ship, not the food," Nia said.

Jeanette's squint narrowed.

"Forgive me later," Nia said. "Get dressed. You have to see this."

"See what?"

"You have to see it!" Nia said. "Get dressed! We need to get out on deck."

Jeanette changed quickly, pulling a blue windbreaker over her pajama top. "Did we catch up to the *Kaiko Maru?*"

The *Arctic Sunrise* was shadowing the *Kaiko Maru*, a harpoon ship for the Institute for Cetacean Research. The international moratorium on whaling did not outlaw spearing whales for research. Extracting slivers of livers and eyeballs and bones for study made the meat harvest legal even in absence of any scientific publications.

Jeanette was a marine biologist, unemployed because her postdoctoral research efforts had floundered. Jobs she took to establish her seamanship had proved that she spent too much time bending over the side. Now, she was volunteering in the South Pacific, learning to manage her motion sickness.

"Where are we?" Jeanette followed Nia up the steep steps from below decks. When the *Kaiko Maru* had veered away from a pod of pilot whales, *Arctic Sunrise* had followed.

"Wellington." Nia held the door for her. "Look up."

The entire crew was on deck, but Jeanette didn't need to join her shipmates at the rails. They were passing between two American destroyers. As they eased through, she gained a view of the crowded harbor. "Holy crap."

— « o » —

It was a spectacular bowl of Irish stew. Guiness served the broth well, but it was the thick sliced lamb that elevated the meal, and that had everything to do with being in a country where sheep out-numbered people. Sergeant Malone loved his job for the lamb, for the brief rain, for the sunlight shining through the window, and for the view this two-story pub offered not of roads or fences but of rooflines.

Malone's job was to develop and implement creative responses to complicated situations. This project had a hard deadline, one completely wild variable, and both the absolute requirement for stealth and the absolute impossibility of it. Wellington was full of eyes — organic and electronic — on the ground, in the air and in orbit. Casual dress didn't conceal the other protagonists in the pub. Malone wore a T-shirt and jeans, not to hide his background, but to reveal it. While everyone in the room read the scar on his arm, he read them by the speed at which their eyes moved.

There was no way not to be seen. If you made that the objective, your imagination would fail and all plans would collapse before they could muster. Malone's first act of imagination was to embrace being seen and, through overt visibility, to drive the assumptions of careful and casual watchers alike. He knew that those watching with the best tools would see through all misdirection. But advanced intelligence gathering required significant spending, and those who invested valued information. Malone knew they wouldn't bleat; they'd hold their cards for later play.

Chapter Five

The headache pulsing behind Estlin's left eye vanished as he stepped into the enclosure room. He hesitated.

Harry was watching. "What's wrong?"

"Nothing."

The waetapu was clinging to the plexiglass. A chair had been set in front of the enclosure. Estlin walked to it, and then took a few steps further. Wae reminded him of a squirrel — a big, spiky, blue-red squirrel with a gecko tail and no mouth. The squirrel-ness was mostly in the shape of its head, its mode of climbing, and the way it held its tail in a curl when it wasn't in use.

"Four limbs and a tail," he muttered.

"What?"

"For something completely foreign, it doesn't look as foreign as a worm or a jellyfish or a giant fungus."

"It's got ball and socket joints at the knees."

"That is disturbing," Estlin admitted.

"Shouldn't you sit down?" Harry stood behind the chair and crossed his muscled forearms.

"Right." Estlin took the seat and waited.

Harry had one minute of patience. "What's it doing?"

"Nothing," Estlin said.

"What are you doing?"

"Nothing." Estlin realized that he wasn't waiting for the waetapu; the waetapu was waiting for him.

"I'm burning money on your time," Harry said. "A little more effort?"

Estlin leaned back in the chair and tried to settle his thoughts. He imagined a pulsing blue field. It resembled the waves of a slowly shifting tide, and he tried to let the wave nature of the blue carry it across the room rather than consciously pushing it. He'd used the pattern before. It worked really well with horses and terribly badly with camels. It took a few minutes for Estlin to realize that Wae was echoing the pattern very quietly. Quiet was blue.

"It's apologizing," Estlin said, then corrected himself. "It's not really sorry. It's being cautious and unintrusive. I find it reassuring, which is likely its intention."

A yellow wave pattern was now lapping across the blue one. The colors were fusing together, enhancing each other where they intersected — yellow and blue combining without ever making green. The waetapu created the pattern, then passed it to Estlin to hold — to agree with — and he did his best to maintain it.

"How's it going?" Harry asked. The question was a splash of pink across the room.

"We're bonding," Estlin answered. "It's kind of a water-color experience."

"That's nice. Don't you have a question?"

"That last question went badly. I'm working on a better question. You had cartographers in here?"

"It didn't acknowledge the maps."

Estlin imagined the solar system and was immediately embarrassed by his lack of knowledge. He couldn't create planetary orbits with any realistic sense of scale. He couldn't remember how many moons were orbiting Jupiter and Saturn. He quickly pressed his focus to the planet with which he was most familiar and its single moon.

Taking an image from Sanford's description, he splashed blue across the moon then let gravity pull him past it, down to a pair of distinctive islands in the expansive Pacific. He had Wae's attention, especially as he planted a yellow fleck on the lower edge of the northern island. The waetapu took this idea, accepting it and re-rendering it, adding a blue fleck next to the yellow one.

"I'm blue," Estlin said. This wasn't the answer he was seeking. He didn't know how to add an orange fleck into the picture without localizing it. He was trying to add orange in an unfixed way when the waetapu broke the image. Wae jumped off the partition, climbed to the highest, deepest corner of the enclosure, and settled on a big branch.

"That's its sleeping perch," Harry said.

The door behind them opened and Major General Stodt entered.

"Have you an answer, Mr. Hume?" he asked.

"I'm still working on the question," Estlin responded, rising from his seat.

"I thought it understood your question."

"If I ask the same question, I might get the same answer. I don't know if it can separate what we look like from what we look like inside our heads. I'm trying to ask it where the other one is."

"Do you think it knows?"

"It knows where we are," Estlin answered. "We got that far."

"It may only know that its companion isn't here," Stodt replied. "The evidence suggests that their connection relies on proximity. You had the right question before."

"We just started—"

"You're finished for now." Harry pointed at the enclosure. The waetapu was folded up on the perch, looking more prickly in stillness than it did in motion. "It's been off its usual sleep cycle. It hasn't taken that perch since the other one vanished. We'll let it rest. You can tell us how it communicates, and we'll have every brain here thinking about how to get the answers we need."

"Let's step out." Stodt led them to the door. "Harry, I need you to take a meeting with Dontis."

"Now?"

"Now," Stodt answered.

"You're kidding."

"He's in the boardroom."

"Dontis?"

"He specifically requested you."

"Okay," Harry agreed. "Lyndie, did Wae want to check on you before catching a nap, or am I anthropomorphizing?" He caught Stodt's look and waved off Estlin's answer. "Yidge will arrange the debriefing. I'll be back soon."

Harry left them at the guard's station, crossing the studio's anteroom to the far exit.

"Where do I go?" Estlin asked.

"You stay here," Stodt answered. "I want you available as soon as it wakes. We'll use a camera for the debriefing. Any questions?"

Estlin had one. He didn't want to direct it at New Zealand's top army man, but he needed an answer nonetheless. "Is there a restroom?"

"Over there," Stodt answered, and turned to the guards on duty.

Estlin spotted the marked door. When he reached it, his head was throbbing. He paused, one hand braced against the door jamb. Across the room, Stodt remained at the guards' station, engaged in conversation. The headache was worth reporting, but a few steps toward Stodt, Estlin felt as if a cool breeze had washed the pain from his eyes out the back of his head. As he backed towards the restroom door, the pain returned, each pulse of blood pressing into the fine vessels of his brain. The experiment bore repeating. He walked part way across the room, then returned to the far wall and leaned against it.

Stodt looked over at him. "Mr. Hume, can I help you?"

"Uh, no." Estlin was pretty sure Stodt couldn't help him.

Stodt joined him anyway. "You were pacing."

"Yeah, I was just—" Estlin made a limp, dismissive gesture.

"Your hands are shaking."

He glanced at his fingers. Stodt was right. He shoved his hands in his pockets and hoped the tremors were a physical reaction to his realizing how thoroughly screwed he might be, as opposed to being another symptom.

"I have a headache," he said.

"Harry didn't tell me exactly why he needed you here. Regrettable, but he wasn't wrong. A week ago, I wouldn't have believed that you could exist." Stodt paused. "It's been a long week. Withholding information from me is a mistake that you don't get to make."

"I don't know when this headache started, but it vanished when I stepped back in the room with it. Over there, I'm clearheaded. Here, I'm smashed."

"You're staying with the pain," Stodt noted. "You want out?"

"No." Estlin wondered when Harry would be back. He needed a second opinion. "It could be nothing. It was a long flight. If it's masking a headache that I already have, that's not a problem.... You came looking for me."

Stodt acknowledged this with a nod. "Its vital signs dramatically improved during your first visit. We thought it was excited by the communication breakthrough. This time, its condition improved a few seconds before you entered the room. One of our observers just called to tell me that its temperature is fluctuating, and you're out here, pacing."

"Crap."

"You understand the magnitude of the situation?"

"I think I do."

"That thing could be a tourist, a castaway or an envoy from another world. We don't know, and everyone is getting very twitchy. What I can tell you is that, historically speaking, it's an incredibly bad idea to kill an ambassador from an empire that's larger and more technologically advanced than your own. I want it to live. I want to know why it's here. I want to know who took the other one. I think you can get me answers. But if all you can do is keep it alive a little longer by sitting in a room with it. I'll take that, too."

"Sounds reasonable."

"Good." Stodt checked his watch. "I'll have Yidge bring you a cot."

"A cot?"

"I think you should have a glass of warm milk and lie down."

"You want me to sleep in there?" Estlin didn't think he could sleep in a room with an alien and two dozen cameras.

"If it wants to talk, I'll have Harry with you as soon as it drops off that perch. But if nothing happens, I'll be happy," Stodt said. "It was resting for two to three hours once or twice a day, but it broke that pattern when we lost the other one."

"It's nap time?"

"It'll take you ten minutes to tell us what you can about how it's communicating, am I right?" Stodt asked for agreement and got it. "You don't need a dozen scientists trying to advise you on how to hold your next conversation; you just need time to think about it in a big, quiet room. We'll dim the lights."

— « o » —

"What are you doing?" Jeanette asked under her breath. Binoculars raised, she watched the French frigate *Moquese* receive visitors from a yacht. The *Moquese* was Wellington's first unusual arrival — a "scheduled stopover" that surprised the port authorities. Three men and a woman climbed a rope ladder from the yacht to the frigate. Jeanette added a note to the book in which she had transcribed every ship name, pennant number and port of registry she could see.

While her crewmates scoured the news and monitored radio communications, Jeanette was perched on the helicopter platform built on the stern of the *Arctic Sunrise*. She hoped her notes would complement those taken by Bjorn. He was in the enclosed crow's nest, which offered a complete view. There was enough traffic in the harbor to keep them both occupied.

It was a challenge getting an anchorage in the crowded harbor, but they were staying. The chief mate had taken a small group ashore in the *Green Meanie*, the largest RIB aboard the *Sunrise*. He'd reported that five icebreakers had entered the harbor the day after the *Moquese* had arrived: China's *Xue Long*, the HMS *Endurance*, then Russian, Chilean, and South African ships. Also at anchor were Chinese and Taiwanese freighters under Panamanian and Liberian flags, as well as trawlers, frigates, yachts, and — most remarkable — the two 500 foot American destroyers.

"Jeanette!" Nia called from the main deck. "We're meeting. Now."

Jeanette closed her notepad and followed Nia to the packed lounge. A couch was built into the corner with more seating along the opposite wall and a table in the center of the room where the crew took their meals in shifts. Captain Neil Arnot was standing at the table, surrounded by volunteers and crew. The captain was in his forties, the light blonde tint of his hair and beard already fading to gray. His chief mate's whistle cut through the room.

"Two weeks ago, shortly after the Burst, something splashed down in the South Pacific," Arnot began. "We don't know what hit the water, but we can make an educated guess. The Burst damaged a number of satellites. There are plans to de-orbit some of them and crash routes have been publicized. We suspect a secret satellite fell — possibly an uncontrolled de-orbit burn triggered by the Burst, possibly evidence of the illegal weaponization of space. The Burst itself may have been a test of a space-based weapon built to disable communication and navigation systems with electromagnetic pulses from orbit."

Jeanette considered the scale of weapon required to create a flash that would light up the moon and how many people would have been needed to design, build, and launch it.

"Whatever fell, wherever it fell, everyone is here. The Wellington port authority is accommodating all arrivals. We don't know why. We will find out." The captain paused, instilling the responsibility in the collective. "Last night, we passed an American Nimitz-class carrier, the USS *George Washington* deployed from Yokosuka, Japan. It is powered by two nuclear reactors and likely carries nuclear armaments. The American Navy has an absolutely strict policy of not discussing which of its vessels carry nukes. Therefore, the entire US Navy has been forbidden entry in New Zealand's ports and internal waters since New Zealand's Nuclear Free Zone legislation passed.

"The law forbids both nuclear weapons and propulsion systems. Nothing is to come within twelve miles of shore. The carrier is toeing the line here just fourteen miles out. The two destroyers in the harbor are part of the *Washington's* battle group. A letter submitted to the New Zealand parliament certifies that the destroyers are *nuclear free*. I don't know if this letter is worth the paper it's on, but the US Navy just broke its own biggest rule."

Davis, the third mate, arrived, slapping the door at the back of the room. "The carrier has crossed the line. It's in Cook Strait at the mouth of the harbor."

"Bloody hell," Arnot responded.

"The strait is a transit passage," Bjorn interjected. "The Americans will claim that they have the right of innocent passage, and they'll be right. The international rules of navigational freedom override New Zealand's laws."

"I don't care," the captain responded vehemently. "It's nuclear. This is a nuke free zone. Today, we tell every camera that we can talk to that the law's been broken. Let the lawyers tell them otherwise. Our response is: *No Nukes. No Loop Holes.* If the law can't keep them out, change the law." Arnot paused, collecting himself. "We were bombed. Pereira was murdered, because the French wanted to nuke an atoll on schedule. This law is the legacy of that loss, and we will protect it. We will blockade the harbor. We will call out for all who are willing to assemble at dusk. However many gather, we will use this ship to ensure that the *Washington* does not enter the port.

"This action presents significant risks to the ship and everyone aboard her. We may be boarded, arrested, impounded, or rammed. It's time to get off if you want off. If you don't feel you can be out here with us, go portside now. We'll need you to keep us supplied and informed."

The solidarity and excitement in the room was palpable. Jeanette's stomach twisted itself into a knot. A big piece of the puzzle was missing. "Why would the carrier enter the harbor?" she asked. "There's no room to maneuver."

"There's no tactical advantage to crossing the twelve mile line, either," Bjorn said, as though it were an explanation. "It should shut down their flight deck. If they're launching fighters, the right of innocent passage doesn't apply. But you can't expect their next move to make sense because they've already crossed the line."

"The threat of that carrier entering the port will draw a flotilla of protest vessels," the captain responded. "Blockading the harbor means nothing in, nothing out — no freight traffic, no fishing traffic, no inter-island ferry — not until that nuclear reactor leaves New Zealand's territorial waters. This puts incredible pressure on the government to respond to the American presence, and it will generate international pressure from all the countries with ships trapped at anchor."

"Xin will take the *Green Meanie* ashore," he added. "Anyone leaving has twenty minutes to pack. I need volunteers to speak directly to environmental groups and boat owners in

Wellington and beyond. We will work quickly and quietly. Keep off the radios please or this could end before it starts. I will call London. We meet again in two hours."

The captain left followed by his bridge crew.

Jeanette gripped the table edge. She knew she would stay aboard, but they were about to whack a beehive to see what would fly out of it. She'd never figured herself to be dumb enough to grab hold of that kind of stick.

— « o » —

It was a quarter past eight, according to the clock on the bookshelf. Sanford checked his watch to confirm that it was evening and not morning. He hadn't meant to sleep and now his back was aching. Sarah had photocopied her notes for him, shown him to the office and then retreated to write another summary for Boxley. It seemed the office had been hastily vacated and rearranged for him. The surface of the desk was clear, but the drawers were locked and pictures of smiling kids were stacked on a bookshelf. A filing cabinet and chair had been moved into the hallway to make room for the cot wedged alongside the desk.

Sanford stretched his back and shoulders, but the muscles remained tight. He'd moved to the cot to read the minutes from the morning meeting because he'd felt like he was sitting at someone else's desk. Sarah's notes had scattered to the floor. He braced a hand on the desk as he crouched to gather them. They had been frustrating to read.

Sarah's penmanship was clear, and her minutes were concise, but every idea presented at the meeting was overwritten by other relentlessly competing theories. When the discussion ventured in the direction of interstellar communications or man-made weapons, it was promptly yanked back to potential natural sources, including outlandish stellar phenomena.

He folded Sarah's loose pages into his notebook. Light was leaking around the edges of the heavy blinds. He was tempted to peek through them to definitively read the time of day, but a page with "KEEP BLINDS CLOSED" printed on it was taped to the pulley. Instead, Sanford cracked the door, and then stepped out of the office. The hall was lit but quiet. He picked a direction only to hear Bomani call from behind him.

"Sanford, you're up."

"Yes, yes," Sanford answered. "Almost."

"You were tired. I heard you snoring through the walls." Bomani patted his shoulder. "Come, I know where the good coffee is."

Bomani led him passed the nearby lounge and into a stairwell.

"I do know a few people working in knot theory," Sanford said as they descended.

"Academics," Bomani answered, dismissive. "There's no money."

"And you chose quantum decoherence?"

"The future that is now — quantum computing. When field effect transistors got small, there were guys who knew exactly where they'd hit the wall, where building anything smaller would make the barriers too thin and all the circuits would leak. They studied the wall, so they could know exactly where it was — this small and no smaller. They built devices with their design parameters pressed against the face of the wall." Bomani had the smile of one building toward a good idea. "Then someone said a leak is just a leak. I can build these so they all leak in exactly the same way. If they all leak the same, everything still works. Put a little fan on there, so the heat doesn't melt it, and you're good. Brilliant. The chips got smaller.

"Now the only way to get smaller is to go quantum, and decoherence is the leakage current of quantum computing," he explained. "When I finish, I go wherever there is money."

Bomani opened the door at the base of the stairs and held it for Sanford. "This place has everything: microwaves every floor, foosball here, rooms upstairs with whiteboards all around."

The foosball table was being put to enthusiastic use. "This is John Cutler," Bomani pointed to the nearest player, a blonde graduate student with Maxwell's equations printed on his shirt. "And that's Jakarta."

Jakarta was short and dark-skinned with darker hair. "Hello," he said, not looking up from the white ball shooting across the board. His entire body was engaged in the game as he tried to redirect it.

"Jakarta is from Jakarta," Bomani explained. "His name has twelve syllables so we don't use it. John's tracked the signal through every reflection on every receiver, especially the remote eyes on Mars and near Jupiter. Others dismiss receivers with no frequency range. There's no detail, but there is timing. All robotic spacecraft have atomic clocks. The data gets to us much later, but John went tripping through it all down to the microsecond. The Burst was from an off axis event."

"By off axis, he means off the ecliptic plane, below the Earth's orbit out around Neptune." John scored.

Jakarta scowled, retrieved the ball and threw it back into the game. The rhythm of his play was in his hips as much as his hands. "See me right now?" he said. "I am working very hard — hundreds of processors running. This is the hardest I have worked in my life."

"James, sit," Bomani said. "I'll bring you coffee. Want popcorn?"

"No, thank you." Sanford sat on the couch, opened his notebook, and braced it against his knee. As he sketched the solar system, highlighting Neptune, he realized that with a source that close, John's work could distinguish a radially symmetric signal front from a directed beam. It made him smile.

Bomani returned, placed a mug of coffee on the table, and looked at the notebook. "What's this?"

"An idea I've been working through."

Bomani picked the notebook out of Sanford's hands. He examined the page closely, then turned back three pages and worked his way forward. Sanford braced himself; his theories did not fit with anything else that had been discussed here.

"Is this...?" Bomani trailed off. "I don't understand this at all. You have to teach me. We should go upstairs. John, we're going to the white room. Sanford has something new."

John stopped toying with the foosball, scoring with a few swift moves. "Game point."

"No! I was distracted," Jakarta protested.

"Jakarta, you're coming, too," Bomani answered. "Time to work harder."

— « o » —

Harry glanced through the window on the boardroom door as he approached it. Dontis waited, his expression unreadable, his fingers flicking his cufflink. He rose as Harry entered.

"Dr. Hatarei." Dontis offered a seat at the table with a pointed gesture. "It's been an exciting day. I'm glad that Mr. Hume recovered swiftly."

Harry ignored the invitation, wary of Dontis' up-to-the-minute interest in Estlin. The man reminded Harry of a boa constrictor he'd met on the edge of a farmer's field. The snake, having swallowed a goat, had a disturbing bulge in its middle. A month from needing a meal, it still measured everything around it with unblinking eyes, evaluating potential prey. Dontis looked at the world the same way. The snake wasn't hungry, but it kept licking the air around him.

"You have a question for me?" Harry stayed at the end of the table with the open door behind him.

Dontis rose and crossed the room to pull the door closed. "I expect you'll keep this conversation in the strictest confidence."

"Major General Stodt sent me. He'll get a complete report."

"There is an asset we are bringing to the project," Dontis continued. "The creature's reaction to Mr. Hume suggests it responds to people with a specific brain abnormality. While we were transporting Mr. Hume, aware of his limitations, we arranged a flight for another sensitive individual. Utilizing this type of asset requires certain allowances — very reasonable allowances given the urgency of the situation."

"By asset, you mean a person."

"She'll be here in three hours. We want her and her personal physician granted immediate access to Studio C."

"Lyndie learned a lot in his first session. I'll give him every opportunity to get the answers we need."

"He has a peculiar and limited talent," Dontis replied. "He may not be able to acquire the critical information we need. Our asset is more sensitive and highly trained."

"I'll need her name."

"We require a level of anonymity be maintained. The number of observers would be limited and access to any electronic recordings would be heavily restricted."

"Excuse me?"

"She's a minor. Her identity must be protected."

"A minor?" Harry waited for Dontis to correct or clarify himself. "And you want to put her in the room with the alien that knocked Lyndie on his ass today?"

"Her abilities are significantly stronger—"

"So, it might hit her twice as hard?" Harry responded. "Do you have a note from her parents granting permission for this field trip?"

"Our doctor is her guardian."

"That sounds wrong."

"Individuals born with these rare neurological defects suffer natural psychological complications. They only reach their potential in the care of those with the knowledge and patience required to manage the side effects."

"Is that your way of saying she's a mental case?"

"Your friend can't receive impressions from his own species," Dontis responded. "It's a critical short-circuit. What makes you think he'll ever be able to process the information you want?"

"My answer is no."

"We are trying to help," Dontis said.

Harry found his sincerity underwhelming and remained silent.

"We want information as much as you do," Dontis continued.

"I'll tell Stodt that you want to bring in an anonymous kid with a mental disability," Harry said. "I'm sure he'll give the request the consideration it is due."

"Dr. Liev is an exemplary physician and medical researcher. I'll expect to hear from you shortly." Dontis snapped open his briefcase, withdrew a CV and handed it to Harry as he let himself out of the room.

Harry read the doctor's credentials as he walked to Stodt's office. Dr. Liev's American security clearance was listed prominently. Harry rapped his knuckles on the doorframe of Stodt's open office. Stodt admitted him with a glance, and Harry sank into the chair opposite the desk. Harry waited until the Major General closed the folder he was studying.

"Dontis wants to bring in a specialist," Harry said. "Someone like Lyndie, only she's a minor and maybe she's mentally ill." Harry straightened, crossing his arms as he got to the question that wasn't a question. "I'm not risking a kid on this, not with Lyndie already making progress. Not ever, actually. Dontis knows my answer, so he wants yours. How is it?"

"Sleeping."

"And Lyndie?"

"Asleep. You should get some rest."

"I know," Harry agreed. He also knew he'd need to find a meal before trying to sleep. "Dontis wouldn't give me the name of the girl, but I've got her doctor's pedigree. They're both coming." He handed the CV to Stodt. "Someone needs to look this doctor up because this problem will be at the gate in three hours."

Chapter Six

Estlin's roommate wasn't breathing, at least not audibly. The waetapu wasn't making any noise at all. Meanwhile, the cot creaked every time he shifted, and he'd spent twenty minutes thinking about ditching it to lie on the floor. The door behind him opened and closed. Estlin listened to the light footsteps crossing the floor and considered rolling over.

Yidge didn't speak until she stepped into view, the half-light shadowing her features. "You're not sleeping," she said.

"Could you?" Estlin asked.

"No. It took a few days," she said. It was a beautifully honest answer.

Estlin sat up, one hand pressed against his eyes. "I won't last that long."

"Do you need anything?" she asked.

"Where's Harry?"

"Asleep at his desk," Yidge answered. She was holding a form loosely at her side. Estlin could tell that she was waiting to inflict it on him.

"What's that?"

"Dr. Mir would like to access your medical records," she said. "As a precaution, in case any other *complications* arise."

Estlin waved for the form, negating any further explanation or pleading. He read it quickly and accepted a pen from Yidge. "I can give you doctor names and towns," he said. "You'll have to look up the contact details."

"My job," she said, taking the form from him. "Try to sleep."

— « o » —

"Look at that." Nia joined Jeanette, leaning on the rail of the *Arctic Sunrise* to gaze at the forest of masts. "Everyone shaking off their day-to-day to really do something."

The blockade had mobilized rapidly and with immense local support. Jeanette could tell that everyone had been waiting for an excuse to join the ruckus in the harbor. Several sailboats had Christmas lights strung from their masts, which, in the dusk, added to the sense of occasion.

"What are we doing?" she asked.

"You think we should let the Americans invade?"

"Nia," Jeanette released an exasperated sigh. "They're two miles closer than they should be."

"The footage of the *Kaiko Maru* has gone worldwide," Nia insisted.

Two Russian ships had run through the blockade before it was complete. The *Kaiko Maru* had followed with its horn blaring and loudspeakers warning them to move aside. Captain Arnot had not obliged and the ships had scraped hulls — the dramatic paint loss was captured on video and immediately posted to the web.

"We don't know why the carrier is here."

"This will make them tell us."

"No, it won't," Jeanette answered. "We'll make the news. We'll fill the void with noise. But the story isn't out here. It's over there somewhere." She pointed to the hills surrounding the inlet.

"It doesn't matter why they're here." Nia's indignant response reflected her steadfast belief in her captain and the cause. "That carrier is a nuclear war machine. Do you know how rare this water is, this place on Earth where it's forbidden? That's why we have to make sure the law holds."

Jeanette considered the harbor. "The French secret service bombs and sinks the Rainbow Warrior in Auckland, killing a Dutch citizen. A murder. An act of war. New Zealand, by treaty, is under America's umbrella of protection. Imagine what might have happened, if it had been in anyone's interests to fight?" Jeanette found it inspiring. Here, one ship sent to the bottom, one life lost, had created a pivot point that moved nations. It revealed the true character of the governments involved. Moreover, it had generated a powerful response in the larger population, like the sub-cellular reaction of an organism when the temperature rises. The nuclear testing had stopped, and legislation was pushed forward that not only banned nuclear warships, but made it illegal for any New Zealander to build, buy, design, own or sell components for nuclear weapons.

"We're sending a message," Nia said with a burst of open optimism. "And there will be even more of us in the morning."

Jeanette said nothing because this was the southern hemisphere, and she was certain that their perception of the situation and their response to it were both upside down.

— « o » —

Bomani closed the door. The white-topped table that filled the room was surrounded by white boards on every wall. He picked up a felt marker and tossed it to Sanford. "The floor is yours. Begin at the beginning."

Sanford went to the board, uncapped a pen and capped it again. "What if you created an infinitesimal connection between a distant point in space and this one?" Sanford said. "It's not a hole. It's an infinitely small point of contact, like a node or a nexus point connecting two locations in space."

"How?" John was an attentive student, and Sanford could tell he was seeking clarification, not dismissing the idea.

"Let's start with why." Sanford drew a single dot on the board. "What if you had this connection between point A and point B, a hole so small that the only thing you could slip through it was part of a photon?"

"Part???" All three asked the question at once.

The answer was central to Sanford's theory. "It's a node connecting two distant points. If you feed electromagnetic energy from one place to another while keeping it pinned to the node, the node keeps a small fraction of the energy wave at the point of origin. Imagine a loop of electromagnetic energy, sweeping out from the node and back to it, a coherent standing wave miles long with thousands of harmonics built into it. When enough energy accumulates, it's used like a counterweight to balance the equation as an object is transferred from one side of the node to the other. Energy is exchanged for mass."

"You what how?" John was lost.

Jakarta used a fingernail to lightly trace numbers on the tabletop, running equations by their orders of magnitude. "It's too much energy. The power required to move something the size of a shuttle would be insanely large. The signal was only a few seconds long. To inject and discharge that much energy, that quickly? That's not transportation, it's Armageddon; any mistake would be incredibly bad for the solar system."

Sanford was prepared for this argument. "There's no signal while the energy builds. No pulse. You can't see a laser unless something crosses its path and scatters the light. The energy can be trickled through for months. The beam is invisible until the inversion. The energy pours back through the node. The object is transferred as the loop collapses. A fraction of the light hits the object and — flash — for a moment we see it. And the energy isn't lost. It's not discharged. It's back on the other side of the node, ready to be reused."

Sanford knew when his ideas were being received and when they weren't. "Ever see a counter-weighted lift bridge? You can lift and drop a steel bridge using the energy required to run a couple of toasters." Sanford tapped the marker against his palm. "There would be losses. It might cost something to trickle the energy through the node and, of course, the energy that scatters off the object as it comes through is lost. But that's a small fraction of the power, the rest stays in the loop."

"You are a crazy man." Bomani spoke from his corner of the room where he flipped through Sanford's notebook, grinning dangerously. "How would you control it?"

"With a single node? You wouldn't." Sanford grabbed a marker, approached the white board, and drew his arbelos. "You need three."

Bomani joined him, looking again from the notebook to the board. He reached out and tapped each node. "Input, monitor, switch."

"A stabilizer," Sanford said, pointing to the central node, "that you can use to create an instability to trigger the inversion." He offered a small smile, shrinking a bit, and stepping back to give the idea its space in the room.

"You are wonderful crazy, Sanford." Bomani was all teeth and energy. "A space bridge. You really believe this?"

"Of course he does," Jakarta answered. "You've seen the signal. Harmonics on harmonics on harmonics. It is music. I looked at it and thought only God could strike such a chord. Give us the math."

"There are pieces missing," Sanford answered. "Some of it is simply beyond me." He picked up the marker again, turned to the white board, and began to write.

Chapter Seven

Estlin stopped in the hardware store aisle, curled his hands into fists, and tried to wake up. Groomed university grounds had been supplanted by wild prairie grass and now he was facing a row of ladders. This was a lucid dream. The old wooden ladders among the new aluminum ones had given it away. He leaned back, trying to fall awake, and found himself in the studio. Thick transparent walls contained him. Beyond the plexiglass, a shining figure stood over his own slumbering form.

"Wake up," Estlin whispered to himself.

The standing man had one arm extended, and there was an object in his hand. Estlin thought was a drill. It took effort to recognize the gun, and even then, it remained inert and abstract. Another bright figure dropped into view directly before him, startlingly close. Estlin slapped the enclosure walls, leaping back as he startled awake. He sat up, trying to dispel the dream. Reality bashed him in the face with a gun, crushing his cheek against his teeth.

Propelled to the floor, Estlin covered his head as he coughed a splash of blood onto the concrete. He'd slept surrounded by cameras and guards, not thinking that they'd already lost one of their valued guests.

The floor was cold. Face down, he could see the room. There were three men on the ground and one on a cable overhead. They were now dark forms in a bright space — one next to him, one at the door, and one by the enclosure. He peered through his arms at the black boots of the man standing over him. The man silently gestured a directive to the others before glancing down. Eye contact was followed by swift action. Estlin tried to scramble away as the air was kicked from his lungs. The man kicked again, flipped Estlin onto his back and planted a foot on his sternum.

Wae dropped awkwardly, twisting as it fell to land in a deep crouch. Estlin felt it drop and stretch its limbs. The room filled with grating noise. The pitch rose to an earsplitting shriek like a metal grinder, like the biggest grasshopper ever. Estlin grabbed the boot pressing down on him, but he had no air in his lungs, no strength in his arms. The gun swung round to discourage him.

A louder alarm joined the din. The pressure on his chest was released, and Estlin drew a sharp breath. He didn't keep it — a kick to his side drove the air out along with a fine haze of saliva and blood. He couldn't breathe. He couldn't yell. He stared into the dark space above, glimpsing motion, a man flying up on a line as the overhead lamps engaged, flooding the space with light.

Bullets chipped the concrete. The precise series of muffled retorts was overwhelmed by the sound of cameras shattering. The tripods surrounding him collapsed. Time restarted. He scuttled a few feet towards the exit, gasping and bleeding on the concrete. He was halfway across the floor when the door smacked open and six guards with automatic weapons spilled into the room.

"Get down! Down!" Jervis directed a gun at him while the others spread out.

Estlin raised his hands, blood slipping down his cheek. The alarm was screaming. Wae was screaming. The barrel of the weapon was a deep, dark hole. He couldn't gather a coherent thought.

"On the ground! Now!"

Estlin dropped, reacquainting himself with the floor. His hands were pulled behind him and secured in plastic bindings.

"What's wrong with it?" Jervis demanded, pinning Estlin's head to the ground with one hand. "Why is it screaming?"

Estlin twitched at the pain and the hand pressed harder.

"Secure!" The shout rang across the space and was echoed by voices from all corners.

Estlin was given a little room to breathe. He lifted his bruised cheek off the floor. "Four men," he said, "down through the roof."

The information was relayed. The alarm was silenced, but Wae's piercing cries continued.

"What were you doing?"

"Sleeping. I was asleep." Estlin felt the inch of understanding he'd been offered evaporate.

"Here?"

"Report!" Major General Stodt yelled from the doorway.

"There was a break-in. There's equipment on the roof. Our men are unconscious."

As Stodt approached, Estlin closed his eyes and rested for a breath.

"What's wrong with it?" Stodt continued to the enclosure, inspecting his charge through the plexiglass. Wae's cries had softened to a broken keening. Stodt came back and stood over Estlin. "Why is it making that noise? Is it injured?"

"No," Estlin answered. "It's okay."

"And you?"

"Four men. It saw them." He rested his head on the floor. "Armed. Combat fatigues. Black boots. No faces. They didn't say anything."

"Release his hands," Stodt ordered Jervis.

Jervis flicked out a blade. A moment of pressure was followed by the snap of plastic yielding. Wae was abruptly silent. It bounded forward and leapt onto the glass. It regarded Estlin with its intense yellow eyes, but made no other contact. It dropped from the glass and leapt around the enclosure, corner to corner. Estlin pressed his palms against the concrete and thought about getting up.

"Stay there," said Stodt. "Get Mir in here."

The command was relayed and the soldiers stepped back as Stodt crouched next to Estlin.

"How did you get to the alarm?"

"I didn't."

"The alarm was manually triggered from here." Stodt sounded certain.

"I didn't." Estlin looked to the enclosure. Wae had settled on its sleeping branch. "Could it?"

"Someone hit that panic button." Stodt gestured to the panel by the door.

"I didn't get that far. I got this far." Estlin pointed at the floor. "How did they get in here?"

"A non-lethal gas was introduced into Studio B. I think we lost all the eyes watching this room before we lost the camera feeds. This was a very sincere operation."

Estlin could attest to the sincerity of the guy who had kicked him in the ribs. The blood from his nose was drying on his face and hands.

Dr. Mir arrived and flashed her familiar light in his eyes. "Mr. Hume, did you black out?"

"No."

"Possibly," said Stodt.

"I didn't get anywhere near the door," Estlin insisted as Dr. Mir gently pressed his cheekbone.

"Track my finger," Dr. Mir said. "Good. Any other injuries?"

Estlin reluctantly lifted his shirt, allowing her to inspect the rising bruises.

She stood and addressed Stodt. "I'm taking him for a CT scan."

"He's not leaving the compound," Stodt responded, getting a grip on Estlin's arm. "We need him here."

Estlin left a palm print on the floor, quickly getting his feet beneath him as Stodt muscled him up. He wiped his hands on his shirt as Dr. Mir flashed light in his eyes again.

"I need to be absolutely clear," she said. "If you stay in this room, you're taking a completely unquantified risk."

"Isn't everyone?" Estlin replied.

The doctor took his hand again, her fingers on his pulse point, her eyes on his. "You reported auditory-visual synesthesia earlier — seeing sound as moving colors. While that can occur because of natural genetic differences impacting certain brain structures, sudden onset synesthesia is associated with strokes and temporal lobe epilepsy. I'm concerned that it has emerged as a contact side effect. I have no baseline information about your unique brain and, now that you've had a doubly eventful day, if a complication arises I won't be certain when the injury occurred."

"Mr. Hume, do you want to go to the hospital?" Stodt asked.

Estlin pulled his hand away from Dr. Mir. "No."

"Are you an idiot?" she asked.

"Yes," Estlin replied. "But, it's already complicated. There's a complication."

"Tell me," she said.

"It likes me, a lot, in a physiologically dependant way, co-dependent, maybe."

"What?"

"It does better when I'm close."

"He volunteered to stay," Stodt interjected.

"And if you leave?"

"Headache." Estlin tried to shrug this off.

"That's a complication." Dr. Mir dug a bottle of pills from her kit. "Painkiller and anti-inflammatory. I'll get an ambulance with an EEG in through the gate here. When it arrives, I get an hour of his time. I also want to know where the mobile CT unit is stationed and how quickly it can be recalled."

"Agreed," said Stodt.

Harry burst into the room in a barefoot sprint. "I was on the wrong side of the lock-out. What happened?"

"Break-in," Stodt explained bluntly. "They failed. We failed to catch them. He says the visitor is unharmed, but it was screaming when I got here."

"It was distressed," Estlin explained. "It can sing with those spines."

"Lyndie, you're a mess. You're sure it's okay?"

"It's resting," he said and realized that the guy with the gun hadn't shot him, hadn't flailed his ribs into his lungs, hadn't cracked his skull or smashed bits of bone into his brain. "I need out for a minute," he said. "I need to clean up. I need a minute."

"Go." Stodt was sympathetic. "Harry, go with him."

— « o » —

The whiteboards were crammed with text. Hours of exploration and revision overlaid Sanford's original efforts. Jakarta had stepped back to take it all in, reading everything the math said. John's arms were crossed, his brow furrowed as he struggled with the new concepts. Sanford knew from years of teaching that young minds weren't always as malleable as older ones. He noted that Bomani was dealing with the uncertainties well, but then the man's business was decoherence.

"You just pushed a three dimensional object through an infinitely small hole." Jakarta waved at the board, paced a short circuit, sat down and pressed his fingers into his hair.

"It's a nexus," Bomani corrected him. "John, what do you think?"

"I think my brain just leaked out my ear," John complained. "You realize your photons don't live in normal space. They don't travel here. They just show up when they hit things."

"Sorry," Sanford said. He sat next to Jakarta and started transcribing the new material, mostly Bomani's quantum knot work, into his notebook.

"I like this." Bomani tapped the board with the back end of the marking pen. "And this is fantastic. That is ugly." He wagged a finger at the lower right corner of the board. "That is like using a turnip to represent an orchid, but we will worry about it later."

"We've missed the evening meeting," John said.

"I didn't miss it at all," Bomani answered. "I need a cigarette. Sanford, you should come with me. Jakarta, you need to check on your computers."

"What? What time is it?" Jakarta glanced at his watch, leapt to his feet and raced out the door. A moment later, he returned to grab Sanford's hand and shake it vigorously. "James, glad to meet you. You can call me Su."

He turned to go, but Bomani stopped him at the door. "I could call you Su."

"No, Bomani. I am Sukarnotritapurnoma." Jakarta ducked easily under Bomani's arm and was gone.

"I need some fresh air," Bomani said. "Sanford, will you come?"

Sanford finished his notes and closed his book. "Sounds good."

John was still looking at the equations with an expression that suggested that he'd like to stop looking at them. "We'll never prove this," he said, turning away from the board. "I'm coming with you."

As they walked down the hall, Sanford had a thought. "How much dust is there in space?"

"About five particles per cubic centimeter," John answered. "Tiny particles, mostly silicates."

"Is that a lot?"

"Not really. It's enough to interfere with certain kinds of infrared astronomy. The Earth sweeps up about two tons of cosmic dust every hour. But that's because the Earth is big and moving really fast. Why?"

"This is like your laser?" Bomani interjected. "You think the beam would have lit up the space dust before it discharged."

"Anything intersecting this beam would be incinerated," Sanford answered. "I just don't know if there's enough dust out there to see it burning."

"The dust density is way lower off the ecliptic plane," John said, puzzling through an answer. "No, we wouldn't have seen it. You wouldn't see that, not unless you knew exactly where to look." John stopped. "You think your energy loop is building again." He turned on his heels. "I have to go. I have to reposition a telescope."

"John!" Sanford's yell stopped him. "By incinerate, I mean vaporize, atomize and ionize. The energy density will rip off electrons. You're looking for—"

"X-rays, I know." John took off down the hallway.

"Elemental high harmonics!" Sanford shouted after him.

"You are crazy, Sanford." Bomani clapped him across the shoulders. "But if you're the right kind of crazy, there will be fame and fortune."

They reached the lobby, and Bomani waved to the guard as they passed. Stepping into the night air, they walked along the fence a short distance to stand Bomani's place of habit. He lit a cigarette. "You think the universe is talking. You think someone pushed something here from a distant star." He looked over at the studios at the end of the street, box-edged silhouettes against a barely brighter sky. "Do you think there is a message in this bottle?"

Sanford didn't answer, but the beliefs were folded together. To believe the bridge had been built was to believe it was built to be crossed.

They were interrupted by a thin distant wail.

"Fire alarm?" Sanford asked.

"That's inside the fence. One of the studios. *The studio*, do you think?" The buildings were suddenly lit as if in answer. They could hear a helicopter inbound from across the bay. A man approached with such speed and intent that Bomani and Sanford automatically yielded, stepping back against the fence. Street light transformed him from a shadow, and Sanford recognized him immediately.

"Sergeant Malone?"

"The cat man! Hey, Sanford. So, this is where you ended up." Sergeant Malone stopped to stand at ease with them.

"What's going on?"

"It could be a drill. I'm on perimeter patrol. You know as much as me."

The light from the helicopter swept across them. Sanford made the mistake of looking straight up at it, only to shield his eyes, bright spots flaring in his field of view. Bomani, it seemed, knew enough to keep his eyes on the ground.

Malone watched the helicopter, and then stepped back from them. "I should get on with the job," he said, and turned to Bomani. "Can I see your ID?"

Bomani crushed his cigarette and drew a security pass from his pocket. While Sergeant Malone inspected it, Sanford unclipped his pass from his belt loop.

Malone waved it off. "Sanford, I know you. I've got to get on with the job. I advise you both to go inside."

The helicopter circled the studios, and Sanford realized that the alarm had been silenced. Bomani watched Malone go, his expression oddly closed and unreadable.

"Let's get inside," Bomani said. "You're hungry, aren't you? We should eat."

— « o » —

Harry swiped his access card and took one more look at Wae as he held the door for Estlin. Dr. Mir was crouched next to a pair of groggy guards. One of them was a foot from the alarm trigger. It was ridiculous and Harry was angry.

"You sure nothing's broken?" he asked.

"Sure enough," Estlin said. "I really hate guns."

"Why were you in there?" Studio C was Harry's domain. He couldn't believe he had to ask.

"Why do you think?" Estlin responded curtly. "Stodt suggested I stay close, considering how much it likes me."

"He told you," Harry said.

"Why didn't *you?*"

"I would have," Harry answered, following Estlin into the restroom.

"You should have." Estlin leaned over the sink, rinsing the blood from his face. "It kind of shifts the meaning of my last conversation with the damn thing!"

"What do you mean?"

"I have a headache."

"Concussion?" Harry asked. "You look like someone backed a land rover over you."

"No, I have a *headache*. In with Wae, I'm fine. I leave that room and my brain starts to hurt."

"You're serious."

"Oh, yeah." Estlin cradled his head. "And that's fine if it's my headache it's fixing. But remember how I said we were bonding? That might have meant more than I thought it meant because no one suggested it might ask me to be a walking life support system. I don't mind helping out, but I think I made a choice I didn't know I was making. So, now I'm your critter's roommate, which is great, except I just kissed someone's gun."

"I got out of the meeting. Stodt said you were sleeping and it was sleeping. I hit my office, planning to join you in the trailer." Harry had put his head down on his desk only to be woken by the alarms. "I try to sleep while it sleeps."

"That's not enough sleep."

"I know." Harry shrugged. The incident fall-out would occupy him for hours, and the pressure to move the project would again increase. It felt like the situation was shifting beneath his feet. The international collaboration they'd tried to forge was giving everyone enough access to assault the place. "What a hell of a first impression we're making."

"They avoided killing anyone. At what point do you think that changes?" Estlin leaned toward the mirror and inspected the shallow gash on his cheek. "The Americans had a tactical team on the C-17. None of those guys talked to me. We rolled out sleeping bags on the deck of the plane. The guy next to me planted his boots a couple of inches from my nose, and I thought *those are serious shit-kicker boots.*"

"And?"

"And I just got the shit kicked out of me."

Harry took in Estlin's full meaning. "Not good."

"Not good," Estlin echoed.

"You're sure?"

"It's stupid. The guy had broken shoelaces."

"Did you tell Stodt?"

"No," Estlin answered. "I might be wrong."

"Are you wrong?"

"No." He pulled off his bloodstained shirt and tossed it in the sink, gathering a handful of soap as he cranked on the cold water.

"I'll tell Stodt," Harry said. "I'll tell him you can't be certain and didn't want to speculate in a room full of cameras."

"Broken, bullet-ridden cameras. True enough." Estlin gave the shirt another violent wrench and threw it back in the sink.

There was a knock on the bathroom door.

"Coming in!" Yidge called to them as she entered with a bag of ice and a bag of clothes. "You okay?"

"I'm fine." Estlin accepted the ice, leaned against the counter, and carefully covered his face with it. "Bless you, Yidge."

"We'll be a few minutes." Harry took the other bag and politely kicked Yidge out. As the door fell closed behind her, he unzipped the bag and searched through it.

"She is so good," Estlin said from under the ice.

"She is." Harry pulled a black shirt from the bag. "Here."

Estlin dropped the ice on the counter, pulled the t-shirt from the sink, and twisted the reddened water down the drain. "Why am I washing this?"

"I don't know."

Estlin threw the wet shirt in the garbage, accepted the shirt from Harry, pulled it on and buttoned it.

"Take your pills."

"I have a thing about pills." Estlin eyed the bottle on the counter. "I had a bad reaction once."

"Did you tell Dr. Mir?"

"No. These are fine. The drug I reacted to was particularly esoteric — experimental, actually. But I don't like pills."

Years back, Estlin had spent days carefully propped on Harry's couch with a hoof-print on his chest, ignoring a bottle of prescription painkillers. "You don't get to be stupid today," Harry said. "Take them."

Chapter Eight

Estlin was reclining in the chair, his face covered by a sloshy bag of ice, his feet propped on the cot. The bruising across the bridge of his nose made his eyes feel hot, but the swelling was minimal. There were few people in the studio, considering the size of the space, but it felt crowded. Soldiers were posted in every corner and were searching the rafters for equipment left by the intruders.

Yidge had arrived with a bag of video cameras and light tripods to continue the documentation process while a technician inspected the damaged gear.

"What a waste," the tech said, nudging a shattered lens casing with the toe of his shoe. "This was senseless. They burned the transmission cables before they broke in here. Magnesium ribbon — hot, fast and localized."

"What do we do with the cameras?" Yidge asked, adjusting a new tripod.

"Get a broom and a bin and call your insurance company," the tech answered.

"Replace them first. The control room is blind. I can string some of these through a laptop onto a local computer network, but they want the closed-circuit cameras back as quickly as possible," Yidge said. "Harry's on his way."

"I'm back," Harry announced. "And I brought a present." He was carrying a massive sketchpad under his arm. He handed it to Estlin along with a pen. "While the linguistics team has enjoyed your descriptions of visual communication, they want you to draw it out for them, literally, as much as possible."

"Great."

"A move is being considered," Harry said. "No decision yet."

"I'm going," Yidge said. "Work to do."

"See you later," Estlin called after her.

"Mind if I take the cot?" Harry knocked Estlin's feet aside and stretched out.

Estlin looked at the corner of the enclosure and wondered why no one was repairing the damaged plexiglass. He was about to ask when he had another thought. "What does it eat?"

"It's funny," said Harry. "I'm too tired to make this funny. It eats wood — cellulose — it digests it with its palms. I found it with a stick in its hand, and, for days, I thought they were starving."

Estlin had noticed that Wae's palms were considerably darker that its fingers and arms. "Think of all the time we waste lifting food to our mouths."

Harry shrugged, and then proceeded with serious tones. "Do you know anyone else like you?"

"No," Estlin answered. "I think there are more, though. There's an association between autism and a lack of signal filtering in the brain. I think there must be a few kids that are like I was — tuned in to other people and trapped by the sensory overload. Imagine being in a room and feeling the hot-cold-itch of everyone's skin. That was me once, and because of it I can barely remember my mother. It's why I let Liev scan my brain looking for the glitch. If you could identify which wrecked little kids have my exact problem, maybe you could zap some small bit of their brains and help them."

"What was the name of your doctor?"

"Liev."

"Dr. Liev from Chicago. It's a small world after all," said Harry. "Was he a truly altruistic man?"

"*She* was a self-aggrandizing, doctor-god with serious research funding. But she believed in what I was and some of those giant-ego types really accomplish things." Estlin hadn't enjoyed his time in Chicago. After an afternoon looking at the architecture, he'd checked-in for his first night of brain scans and found out that the trouble with aggressive medical researchers was that when they don't find what they're looking for they *look harder*. Being Liev's prime specimen had stretched his spirit of altruism. "Whatever glitch I have didn't show up on her scans."

"Your doctor is coming. The Americans want to bring in a kid with your kind of special skills. She's the guardian."

"Fuck." Estlin dropped his bag of ice on the floor. "She gave me a hangover and hives trying to light up my brain with her drug trial."

"Do you want to be invited to this meeting?"

"No, Harry. I think I don't. You're not going to let her bring a kid in—"

"No." Harry's attention shifted to the waetapu. "Lyndie...?"

Wae stretched, hunkered on the sleeping platform and then leapt across the enclosure, landing high on a steeply angled ladder secured to the floor and roof. It curled its hands around the rungs.

Estlin thought about digestion and its natural conclusion. He drew a deep breath. "What does it smell like?"

"Nothing," Harry answered.

"What does this room smell like, right now?" Estlin pressed.

"The ocean," Harry answered.

"Like the beach at your grandma's place?"

"Lyndie, we're next to the bay."

"If you stepped outside, would the air smell as fresh?"

"Shit." Harry sniffed the air.

"When I arrived, it smelled like prairie grass in here," Estlin said. "It smelled like home."

Harry walked towards the enclosure, drawing a deliberate breath. "The smell just changed."

Estlin considered the light, distinctive scent. He couldn't place it. He wondered if that made his mind easier to push, that it wasn't starting with a sharply identified sensory input — not apple or cinnamon or fish, just a smell. Maybe the smell was part of the sensory tricks. Maybe they were all high. "You should get an air sampling thing in here."

"Gas chromatograph," said Harry. "We tried that. We should try harder. Bernie!"

"Yes, Harry?" The voice echoed from above them.

"Gas chromatograph," Harry responded.

"I heard," Bernie replied. "Any particular type?"

"The sensitive kind. Lyndie says there's a smell in here that we aren't smelling right."

"GC won't help. It'll tell you there are aromatics floating around, but nothing more. You want a GC feeding a mass spectrometer. The good ones aren't portable. I've sent air samples, but—"

"Bernie!" Harry interrupted. "You decide. Do your best, thanks."

Estlin spotted the microphone dangling from the rafters. He assumed the speakers were mounted higher up. "Can we order pizza on that thing?"

"Are you hungry?" Harry asked.

"Getting there."

— « o » —

"We got in. We got out," Sergeant Pollock said. "Two out of three objectives ain't bad."

Malone checked his watch. The rest of their team was still integrated in the security patrol and would return after the next shift change. "Close counts in horseshoes and hand grenades," he responded.

The older soldier laughed roughly and stirred two packets of sugar into his coffee. "What was he doing in there?"

"Sleeping," Malone answered simply. Their next round of intelligence would likely explain how and why his plan had collapsed, but it wouldn't change anything.

"It went off like a banshee when you kicked him," Pollock said. "Someone must've heard it."

Malone didn't think so. There was another variable he'd missed.

"Seeing it was something else," Pollock continued. He'd been on the fly line closest to the alien and charged with breaching the enclosure. "I looked in that cage — thought I saw a wolverine. Felt like I was a kid out in the bush where I had no business being. What's next?"

"We wait," Malone answered, "until they try to move it."

— « o » —

Wae was clinging to the glass, still as a startled deer. Several cameras were capturing the unchanging moment for posterity, so Harry was watching Lyndie. He could tell that whatever Estlin was pushing against wasn't moving. The silent conversation was revealed by the way Estlin's eyes tracked back and forth, as though he were watching a caged animal pace and not facing a stationary alien.

Harry knew Estlin's gift could look like a whole lot of nothing happening, especially when he introduced himself to a new species. He sometimes used touch, not to connect, but as a point of reference to navigate an unfamiliar nervous system where it could be hard to tell a sore stomach from a sore toe. Somehow Lyndie would sort it out using the feel of his own hand from the animal's perspective. This was a concept that Harry wouldn't have accepted if he hadn't seen it demonstrated. While Lyndie tried to keep his superpower on the down low, he constantly gave himself away, and that wasn't even factoring in the diligent attentions of his squirrel acolytes.

"Is it responding at all?" Harry asked.

"It keeps putting Waewae's color here."

"What?"

"This is simple. Dots on a map — yellow, orange, blue." Estlin pointed at himself for the last color. "But it's putting all of us here, which obviously isn't right. I tried expanding the map, to open up the possibilities. I've tried New Zealand, the world, the solar system and it keeps putting the dots here. I'm having trouble trying to get it to distinguish the past from the present using floaty color ideas."

"Lyndie, just ask the big question."

"Why is it here?" Estlin answered. "Where is it from? How did it get here?"

"Right. Any of those."

"The big questions might have big answers." Estlin approached the enclosure.

"Want to lie down?" Harry asked. "I could tuck you in."

"Shh." Estlin and Wae were making significant eye contact. He returned to the cot, grabbed the pad of paper, sat on the floor and started to draw. The sun blazed at the center of the page. "Mercury, Venus, Earth, Mars, Saturn, Jupiter—"

"Jupiter, Saturn," Harry corrected him.

"Then what?"

"Uranus, Neptune, Pluto or the Plutoids, whatever." Harry looked at Estlin's sketch with all the planets stretched out to the right of the sun. "Mars is on the other side of the sun right now, and so is Saturn. I've been to a lot of meetings."

Estlin corrected his drawing and then stared at the page. "Give me something," he said, scratching his pen on the paper. "Do you think I have to start on a bigger scale?"

"I don't know," Harry answered, looking over his shoulder. Estlin had drawn a non-planet in the midst of his solar system under Neptune. "What's that?"

Estlin looked at what he'd drawn. "It's an arbelos."

"Is it important?"

"There was a physics guy on the flight. He was drawing these — part of some theory about a signal from space."

"What theory?"

"It was physics. I didn't ask." Estlin kept tracing and retracing the three semicircles that created the simple structure.

"Why are you drawing it now?"

"It came to mind and—" Estlin looked up as Wae traced an arbelos on the plexiglass. "It might be important."

Estlin turned the page and drew a larger version of the arbelos, adding details until he put down the pen and stared at the complete picture as though it were completely foreign. "Huh."

A more structured shape was depicted. It was a duplicated version of the same basic form — the arbelos touching its own reflection at three points.

"I have no idea what this means." Estlin flipped between the pages. He shifted from his crouch to sit, leaning back to stare at the studio lights.

"There's no way, I'm drawing that," he said, gesturing at the rafters. "Sun, planet, planet, planets, not a planet."

Harry looked up, though there was nothing to see.

"It's a wobbly light thing. Pulsing." Estlin's eyes widened. "Something just flew out of it. There was a flash. It went right through me."

"That might be important," Harry agreed. "Anything more?"

Estlin pressed his fingers into the corners of his eyes. "No."

"Your physics guy. I need to know his name."

"Sanford. An American. Yidge met him, too." Estlin got to his feet, gathering the pages off the floor.

"Where are you going?"

"We should track this down."

"I think you should stay here with your new friend," Harry said.

"Oh." Estlin rocked back on his heels, seeming to once again see the studio confining him.

"Am I wrong?"

"No." Estlin pushed the drawings at him. "You should do it."

"I can send someone."

"But you can tell him what you need to tell him," Estlin said. "Quickest way to get someone in here, right? Especially now."

Harry had to agree. He accepted the pages.

"I want someone to stay with you. Bernie!" he called to the microphone hanging from the rafters. It was one of the few pieces of equipment not demolished by gunfire.

"He's in the lab." A voice replied from above.

"Get him," Harry answered. "Bernie has three or four degrees — astereotypic behavior, neurophysics, biochemistry — he's going to stare at you like you've got three heads."

"Great." Estlin walked over to the enclosure. "It's eating?"

Wae had a firm grip on the ladder. Harry thought he could judge its mood from the set of its spines. The ladders were his idea. The studio construction shop had built the enclosure and had sanded the old wooden ladders repeatedly to remove any traces of chemical treatment.

"It does that for several hours every day," Harry said. "There are grooves in its favorite rungs."

The intercom clicked. "Harry, it's Bernie. We've isolated six more ovoids. All appear identical."

"Good," Harry answered. "Get in here."

"What?"

"I want you in here."

"Now?"

"Now. You're going to sit with Lyndie while I step out."

"Oh, okay. Good. We need final word on where to ship the six. And Hodges wants you to call him. He's ecstatic because he managed to see something with his near field scanning optical microscope. And I pulled the GC-mass spectra for you.

Mostly mundane molecules, but we've got trace transition metals maybe a percentage point higher than you'd expect, and the carbon isotope ratios are wild and—"

"Bernie?"

"Yes?"

"Now."

There was a pause. "Okay."

— « o » —

Sanford brushed his teeth, his eyes drifting from his reflection to the mosaic tiles covering the walls of the communal restroom. He automatically sought the pattern in the shades of green. They were placed to give the impression of randomness, which made them deliberately not random. His first full day on the job would start in a few hours, and he would be wrecked by lack of sleep. The cot wasn't the problem. The nap had upset his internal clock, and his brain wouldn't stop ticking. He rinsed his toothbrush and closed the taps.

Stepping into the hall, it took him a second to reorient himself and turn towards his office. He rounded the corner and ran into John. John had a loaded backpack, a laptop bag, and enough momentum that he almost didn't stop in time.

"I found it," John said, breathlessly. "I was going to leave you a note, but there's someone in your office. That might be my fault. These days people notice when you reposition telescopes. I only asked for one, but once they found the wisp, they had to be sure. They're moving the Chandra. I have to go now, but I wanted to give you this." John handed him a scrap of paper with a string of numbers on it.

"What's this?"

"Ascension, declination, distance — any astronomer will know what it means, where it points."

"You found it?"

"*You* found it," John insisted. "I have to go. There's a car waiting for me." He squeezed past Sanford to take off down the hall.

"Thanks!" Sanford memorized the numbers as he walked back to his office. The door was open. His visitor had spread large sheets of paper across the desk. He'd opened the blinds and was looking out at the street. Sanford slipped John's scrap of paper into his pocket and found himself knocking lightly on the doorframe. "Hello."

"Dr. Sanford?"

"Yes." Sanford caught sight of a security pass the man was wearing on a lanyard. It was a different color from his own and he had no way of knowing if it was authentic.

"I'm Harry. My friend was on the flight with you."

Sanford relaxed a fraction. "He mentioned you."

Harry beckoned him into the office, pointing at a detail on one of the pages. "Lyndie drew this and said you could tell me more about it."

Sanford looked at the drawing of the sun and planets. There was an arbelos sketched below Neptune. "It's a bit of geometry. A symbol for an idea I have," he said. "And that point under Neptune is where we think the Burst originated."

"Really?" Harry looked at the page with renewed interest. "And what's your theory?"

"It's about interstellar transportation," Sanford answered cautiously.

"Excellent." A phone in Harry's pocket beeped, and he checked the display. "Hatarei," he answered the call. "Now? I'm down the road at post-production. Give me three minutes." He glanced at the clock. "Should we bring Dr. Mir?" Harry disconnected the call.

"I've got a meeting I can't get out off," he said. "But I need you to come to the main production stages to brief us on your theory. Prepare. My assistant will arrange your clearance. She'll be in touch." He left at a brisk pace, dialing his phone before he reached the door.

Sanford stared at the sketches on his desk. He wondered who John had talked to and how quickly the news was spreading. The briefing wouldn't be a problem; he was working on a presentation for the morning meeting.

Sanford turned the page and sank into his seat. Two mated figures were drawn with each node point of an arbelos delicately touching its reflection, and each arbelos filled with a chain of perfectly fit circles. The gaps between the curves were filled with spare pen strokes suggesting finer structures.

"Harmonics," Sanford said. "Oh, my, these are—" He swallowed, pulling his fingers back from the page. The office was empty. The hall was empty. There was no one to show the geometrical flower opening before him, and suddenly he didn't want to share, not before he understood. He impulsively closed the office door and turned on the desk lamp. Uncapping his pen, he opened his notebook to a fresh page and began to copy the drawing.

— « o » —

Wae was dangling from a ladder, holding the rungs with its tail and one hind foot. Estlin sat on the cot, contemplating a nap. Bernie was standing nearby, awkwardly close, and staring at him as though he had three heads. Estlin had offered the short scientist the chair, but Bernie preferred to stand. He said direct observation time was rare and was quivering with excitement despite the complete lull in activity.

"Is it, you know—" Bernie wiggled his fingers in front of his eyes.

"Projecting?" Estlin inferred. "Not at the moment."

Bernie continued to watch him while pretending to focus on Wae. Estlin couldn't believe that he was drawing attention away from an alien.

"Is your nose broken?" Bernie asked.

"No." Estlin wondered whether Bernie had earned his degrees in the library, the lab, or in the field. He had the extra girth that came with a life lost in thought and desk work. "What can you tell me?"

"About it?" Bernie flexed his fingers in a way that gathered tension rather than releasing it. "It breathes and eats through its skin. It can see beyond the visible wavelengths. How much beyond, we don't know. It doesn't like comparative anatomists. That makes sense if it can read us like you say because those guys can't look at a thing like that without imagining a vivisection. We only had two in here, but they lost their lunches. One there." Bernie pointed roughly at the floor beneath Estlin, and then swept his finger back towards the door. "And one out there."

"What do you see?"

"The alien. Blue epidermis, long fingers, prehensile tail, spiky—" Bernie squinted at the enclosure. He gave a resigned sighed. "A dog," he said. "When it does its trick, I see a dog. I know what Harry says. But it's not a lack of imagination — I think domesticated animals are fascinating and exotic in their own way."

Wae raised a hand and tilted it.

"The dog just waved at me," said Bernie. "When I was in here yesterday, we seemed so close to actual communication, only stuck on the surface."

Bernie talked with his hands — dog, waved, here, close, communicate, stuck, surface. Estlin realized he would have had half that conversation without hearing the words.

"What's an ovoid?" Estlin asked.

"Ovoids are egg-shaped, microscopic particles. They're the most structurally complicated flecks of alien we've found."

"Found where?"

"You signed Harry's mutual risk form, didn't you?"

"Probably."

Bernie pointed to the enclosure. "It's being exposed to all the skin and hair you shed, flecks of saliva full of bacteria, fibers from your clothes, everything you exhale, sneeze, sweat, and blink into the room. It's accepting that risk. So, it's only fair—"

"You filter the air." Estlin pointed at the bulky air cyclers mounted above the enclosure.

"We do, but the enclosure isn't hermetically sealed and they were in a park and Harry's truck and on campus." Bernie spread his fingers in a hopelessly expansive gesture. "Besides, we have to accept that there are things that it sheds that our filters aren't designed to catch. We sample the air directly from the enclosure and out here. The ovoids are microns in diameter, big enough that the filters should catch them, but they're still out here."

"Alien bits just floating around?"

"Pretty much," Bernie answered.

"How the hell do you even find micron-sized alien bits?"

"We pull the filters, float everything off them, distill the solids, and catch the stuff on plates. Studio B is full of people examining large glass plates under microscopes trying to distinguish alien materials from dust, pollen and dandruff." Bernie sat in the chair. "Great job. Glad I don't have it."

"But you've found a lot of these bits?"

"Enough," Bernie said. "We send out what we find. Harry wanted them under every type of microscope. Hodges was incoherently excited. I hope Harry calls him back."

"What did he find?"

"I don't know. Neither does Hodges, by the way. Near field scanning optical microscopy uses a beam of squished light to image structures smaller than the wavelength of light. It's hard to interpret the results even when you know exactly what you're looking at." Bernie shook his head. "The spine it gave us was full of complex, highly interconnected structures. The ovoids are even more densely structured — enough so that we can distinguish them from terrestrial bacteria. They seem to be identical, self-contained units. Could be bits of their skin-shell. I'm pretty sure they aren't excrement."

"Nice." Estlin tried not to think of the possibilities.

"They have the technology to get here from another world," Bernie continued. "Maybe I'm an optimist, but I'm hoping that they're smart enough not to bring a transferrable plague with them. Unless, of course, they want to do that because, face it, if you're smart enough not to do that, you'd have to know exactly how to do that."

"You're an optimist?"

"I just wish they'd brought a Babel fish," Bernie added. "The communication barrier is massive. They aren't vocal at all, not even beyond the audible range. We've got infrasonic and ultrasonic microphones in here. The spine-screaming Wae did was the first sound I've heard one make."

"What do you want to ask it?"

"Everything."

"One question," Estlin clarified.

"You'd think the plague question would be a priority," Bernie said. "But I'm settled in my thinking on that; I don't want another answer there, especially not a confusing one. Wait…." Bernie tapped his head.

Estlin's eyes were drawn to the door. He watched the guard turn and open it.

Bernie stopped tapping his head and snapped his fingers. "Got it."

"Hold that thought," Estlin said as Yidge entered.

"Lyndie," she said. "You're wanted."

"No," Bernie said. "You can give us a few minutes."

"Sorry," she said.

"Two minutes," he pleaded.

"You'll have one-on-one time with Wae while he's gone," Yidge consoled him. "The mobile EEG has arrived. Dr. Mir wants Estlin wired up right away."

Bernie was crestfallen. "You owe me a question," he told Estlin.

"See you later." Estlin followed Yidge to the door. "How far?"

"The ambulance is parked by the second gate. Dr. Mir wants to scan you away from Wae before testing you while you're close to it. She'll meet us there." Yidge grabbed a bottle of water from behind the guard's station and handed it to Estlin. She reached into her pocket and retrieved a small envelope containing two pills. "Painkillers for you. Same as before. Dr. Mir says you aren't allowed to be stubborn about it."

Estlin regarded the white pills, wanting to be stubborn because Yidge suggested he shouldn't be. He opened the water bottle and gulped them.

Yidge led the way out of the building, watching him closely. Bright lamps mounted above the door cast a deep shadow at his feet. It was almost dawn. The sky was deep blue, and there was enough light that the quiet lane held a sense of anticipation rather than slumber.

"How's your head?"

"Fine." He'd walked through his previous separation threshold in the building and experienced no pain.

"Headache?" she asked as the next gate was opened for them.

"No."

"Good," she said. "I'm supposed to ask you that question every fifty feet. If you spontaneously report any change, we could have an actual conversation."

"Sure."

"Harry said you met at university," she said.

"One of them. Lakehead. He was finishing his doctorate. I was trying first year biology again," Estlin answered. "I got kicked out of the dorm, and he let me sleep on his couch. It was a memorable term."

"But you didn't finish."

"Harry got his PhD. I got assaulted by a seventy-two year old groundskeeper and expelled." Estlin folded his forearms across his chest, gripping his elbow. He became conscious of the gesture when Yidge noticed it and waved off her attention. "No. Wait. That one was a voluntary withdrawal. The chancellor said that if I stayed, he'd prove that I was illegally releasing squirrels to damage the university grounds."

"How's your head?"

"Fine. I'm good." Estlin felt idiotically happy that his headache might simply have been a headache.

They rounded the next studio and found the ambulance. It was parked, nose first, into a sheltered loading dock. The attendant was leaning on the back bumper, one hand scratching through his cropped black hair.

"You here for the test?" he asked.

"This is Lyndie," Yidge said. "He's your patient."

"You a superstar?" the attendant asked. "I guess I'm not supposed to ask that, or anything else, according to the security guys. Your private doc's been delayed. We've got maybe twenty minutes. Your doctor wants to be here for the scan, so I'll hold off on hooking you up."

"Can we wait inside?" Yidge asked.

"Sure thing." The attendant opened the door.

Yidge climbed into the ambulance, gesturing for Estlin to follow. She tucked herself into the attendant's seat, leaving the gurney that ran along one wall to Estlin. He leaned against it, then sat, surrounded by equipment and concisely labeled cabinets.

"I'll be in front." The attendant partially closed the door as he left.

"Twenty minutes," Yidge said. "Want to catch a nap?"

"No," Estlin answered. "What about you? Harry sent you around the world. Any jet lag?"

"It was an express tour," she answered. "I never reset my watch." She gave him a grin. "You'd think it would blur together, but every flight, every stop was different. And armed escorts the whole way."

"The Americans?"

"No," she answered. "Every country had to protect me and my package from the moment I stepped on their soil until I landed in the next place."

"Harry sent you alone?"

"He put total responsibility onto the host. They knew what would happen if they failed to protect me. All I had to do was carry the spine."

"Dangerous." Estlin wasn't sure he liked the strategy of sending a lamb out under the care of wolves. While it rested on the pretext of self-interest, he knew that underneath it was Harry's assumption that everyone's instinct to protect the helpless was as strong as his own.

"Not really," she said. "Everybody here wants to stay at the center of this. Every country, too. Nobody took any risks." Yidge said. "Did you make progress this morning?"

"Sort of." Estlin wondered how long they'd waited. Not long, he thought, but he was feeling tired. The effect of sitting on a mattress, he thought, even a narrow one. "I saw a shape, but I don't know what it means.... R'member Sanford? He was on the plane—"

"How's your head?" she asked.

Estlin wondered if she'd heard his question or if he hadn't finished asking it. "No headache," he said. "But I'm feeling... a little mushy. Sanford, had a..." he searched for the word, "theory." His head dipped. He looked at his fingers. They were wrapped around the rail at the head of the bed. He flexed them, feeling distinctly detached. "Yidge...those pills. Not the same." The painkillers were definitely having a different effect.

"Why don't you lie down?"

"I think I should—" Estlin started to stand.

"Lie down, Lyndie." Yidge was next to him, pressing him gently back into place. "I'm sorry. This is the only way to get you where you need to be."

The stab of betrayal stole Estlin's breath. He shoved her away, his head spinning.

"Help," he said, not certain who he was asking.

There was a thump near the door and he turned, bracing himself against the wall, hoping to see Dr. Mir or Harry or anyone. Yidge surged forward pressing a hand against his mouth. The door drifted open, the space empty, but there was movement above them. Wae's head dropped into view. It extended itself, dangling from the roof of the ambulance. Reaching through the door, it found a handhold on the roof of the ambulance and swiftly climbed around onto the interior ceiling.

Estlin pushed Yidge away and over-balanced. She let him collapse on the floor in a tangle of loose limbs. Wae was above him with its yellow eyes shining. Estlin could see himself, even as he struggled to keep his eyes open. It was hellishly disorienting.

"Did he drop already?" The ambulance attendant had returned. He climbed into the back and caught sight of Wae on the ceiling. "What the hell? Is that it?"

"Get in," Yidge said. "And close the door."

"Creepy thing. It's like spike-covered vulture." He kept one hand on the door and both eyes on Wae. "Why is it staring at me?"

"We have to go now," Yidge said. "We have to take both of them."

"If they catch me trying to sneak that out of here—"

"It wants to come," Yidge said. "Do you want to try peeling it off the roof?"

"No damn way," he replied. "We'll be searched at the gate."

"It managed the hard part. One gate," she said. "Your equipment blew a fuse. Another ambulance is on the way."

"We can't hide it." The attendant leaned over Estlin. "Not unless we dump him."

Estlin thought that this was all a terrible idea, but his attempt to enunciate that yielded only a thin strand of drool.

"I'll ride with it," Yidge said.

"You're supposed to stay here." The man slipped his arms under Estlin's and heaved him off the floor.

Yidge grabbed Estlin's ankles. Estlin drooled in protest.

"Plans change," she said. "Adapt. It wants to come. It will camouflage itself."

As he was lifted and lowered, Estlin discovered that under the bench seat was a coffin-sized compartment. The attendant dutifully rolled him into the recovery position.

"Don't worry," Yidge said. "You're just going to sleep for a while."

"You aren't invisible," the man complained. "They searched the back before they let me in here."

"Lock the doors. If there's an inspection, I'll hear you coming and snuggle in with Lyndie."

"This is a bad idea."

Estlin agreed. He caught another glimpse of himself. Wae was watching with interest and could see his mind blurring as his potential for movement faded.

"Stop arguing. It's time to go." Yidge dropped the gurney bed back in place, leaving Estlin in the dark, listening to himself breathe.

Chapter Nine

"Post-production?" Stodt asked. The Major General was at his desk, steadily working through a stack of requisitions and reports.

"Progress," Harry answered. He closed the office door, acknowledging Dr. Mir as he took a seat. "I'm bringing a physicist over to brief us. Where's this meet?"

"The boardroom," Stodt said. "That's all the ground we'll give. Handle it."

"I will," Harry answered, pleased to be given free reign. He rose, and Dr. Mir fell into step with him.

"Stodt wants my opinion," she said as they crossed the hall. "Give me time to form one."

Harry nodded and opened the boardroom door for her.

Dr. Imogen Liev sat at next to Dontis. She had a willowy build and precisely bobbed hair. The girl stood behind them, her fingers pulling at the seams on the long sleeves of her white dress. Harry wondered if she should be a part of this meeting at all.

"Sorry to keep you waiting," he said.

"No, you're not," the girl answered.

"Beth," Dr. Liev corrected her charge. She rose to shake Harry's hand. Her pinstriped slacks and tucked blouse accented her angular frame. "I'm Dr. Liev. This is Beth."

Beth's tailored dress made her brown skin glow, but was evocative of hospital gowns. Harry's eyes were drawn to her hands. The skin around her nail beds was worn pink and peeling. Her cornrow braids minimized, but could not conceal the patchiness of her hair.

"Thank you for seeing us," she said. Her words were formal, and she seemed to pull on a cloak of maturity.

You're a child, Harry thought, *you only forget when you have to.*

"I'm fourteen," she said.

Harry had guessed younger.

"You understand why Beth's work will require special considerations," Dr. Liev said. "Especially privacy."

"I refused your request to work directly with Wae," Harry replied. "Did Mr. Dontis not inform you?"

"I assume Major General Stodt has corrected you," Dontis said. "He's a practical man."

"My answer stands," Harry said.

"I'm very good," Beth said. "I can show you."

"We aren't questioning your skills." Dr. Mir entered the conversation. "I know you've traveled a long way."

"I'm not here to visit," Beth said. "I'm here to work."

"New Zealand has a law against having children do dangerous jobs," Mir said. "I believe in this law."

"You need a special person for this job," she said. "God made me for this job."

Dr. Liev stepped forward. "Beth's gifts have been thoroughly documented. Her condition is stable and controlled by medication. I can attest that her talents pose no medical risk."

"Your assurance is meaningless," Dr. Mir replied. "It's our visitor that presents unknown and unknowable risks."

"The answer is no," Harry said. "If you want to appeal, you can make a written submission. I'll review it as time allows."

"We will not be entangled by fruitless paperwork—" Dr. Liev's protest was interrupted by an alarm.

The alarm.

"End of meeting," Harry said. His radio crackled and he bolted for the door with Dr. Mir on his heels.

"Harry, this is Studio C." It was Bernie. "Can you come right now?"

"Coming," Harry responded.

"Any injuries?" Dr. Mir asked.

Harry relayed the question.

"No," Bernie answered. "Not yet."

"What was that last part?" Harry asked. There were strict rules about what could and could not be discussed on the radios. "I want an answer now."

The anteroom was full of soldiers and the door to the enclosure room was open. Harry surged ahead of Dr. Mir. "Bernie!"

"It's gone." Bernie flinched, anticipating Harry's response. "Please don't kill me."

"What?"

"It is gone!" Bernie pointed to the empty enclosure. "I was watching it, and I had a digestive issue. I had to go. When I got back, I swear it was here, but then it wasn't. It's gone!"

Harry checked the room from its corners to rafters. "Where's Lyndie?" he demanded.

"He left earlier. Yidge came and said Dr. Mir wanted him."

"I wanted him?" Dr. Mir threw that concept aside.

"The ambulance for the test arrived. He went with Yidge."

Harry flicked the channel on his radio. "Yidge, where are you? Yidge, report in." He chose a camera with a wide view, stopped the recording, and started skipping backwards through its final minutes. The small screen on the camera didn't offer much resolution, but it was enough. Harry caught a flash of blue. He let the recording play onwards. "It went up," he reported.

Stodt was at the corner of the enclosure, which was visibly damaged. "Where?"

"It came out that corner, climbed to the roof of the enclosure then into the rafters," Harry said. "Fuck. It just left us."

"Did it?" said Stodt. "Where's Hume?"

"Do you think—"

"That it had to leave? That someone gave it a reason?"

"I'll go," Harry said. "I'll find him."

"You won't," Stodt answered. "The gates are locked. Go through the footage. Find out when he left."

— « o » —

The screening hall was empty. The dimly-lit space had theater seating and a podium set in the front corner next to the blank screen. Sanford took a seat. Loose pages with his introductory equations were folded into his notebook. He'd worked and waited for a call that hadn't come. Finally, he'd stretched out on the cot, slept briefly, and apparently, missed another meeting. He wondered what had happened. He wasn't that late, not if the discussions usually ran for hours as Bomani claimed.

"Go find out," he told himself.

He found Sarah at her computer in the office and enquired about the meeting. She looked slightly scandalized, but took another set of her notes to the photocopier for him. Sanford watched the pages slide from the machine and mumbled about jet lag.

"Have you seen John?" he asked.

"He left. Stateside, I think," Sarah answered. "He was reassigned."

Sanford couldn't figure out how to ask if John's news had broken yet, without breaking the news himself. Truly, he didn't know what the news was — all he had was a scrap of paper and a string of numbers. It seemed like the sort of information that needed to be officially released.

"Half the group is gone or going." She gathered the warm pages and pressed them into his hands. "It wasn't much of a meeting. I think they're shutting us down. This might be over before you start."

— « o » —

Estlin was comfortable. He was lying atop a smooth, cool duvet. The mattress was wide and the room was brightly lit. He sat up, sliding a hand through his hair, then down to scratch the stubble on his chin. He felt intact, if fuzzy. A pitcher of ice water was sweating on a tray on the bedside table with a glass waiting next to it. There were two doors, no windows, and no clock. The furniture was ornate and, where one would have anticipated a window, long red curtains framed a tall broad-leafed plant set against a solid wall.

A quiet knock drew his attention to the door. A petit, Asian woman entered with a dress shirt and pants neatly draped over her arm. She was in her fifties, with fine wrinkles extending from the corners of her smiling eyes. The cheerful yellow blouse she wore was beautifully fitted.

"Mr. Hume, I am sorry to disturb you." She opened the wardrobe and hung the clothes, then opened a second door, revealing a small restroom. "His Excellency Ambassador Huo would like to meet with you," she said. "Please dress. I will wait to show you the way."

His mouth was dry and his brain slowly assembled a question as she quietly let herself out of the room. He slid to the edge of the bed and pressed his bare feet into the carpet. He walked to the door, considered knocking, and then tried the handle. It opened with ease. The woman was standing in the hallway, serene and composed.

"Where am I?" Estlin asked.

"You're in the Embassy of the People's Republic of China in Wellington, Mr. Hume."

"Oh, okay." He closed the door, returned to the bed, and poured himself a glass of water. He spotted the small dark dome covering a security camera on the ceiling. The shirt and pants were freshly pressed and his size, which was both thoughtful and disturbing. The dark wood of the wardrobe reminded him of small, closed spaces. He took the clothes into the restroom. Thankfully, there wasn't a camera dome in there. He tried not to think about it, washing quickly and making use of the toiletries precisely laid out in the drawers.

Buttoning the blue shirt, he looked into the mirror. The bruise on his side was ugly. His right eye had a gray bruise under it and his cheek had gained some color around the scrape.

"Okay," he said to himself, then realized the mirror would be the best place to conceal a camera in the tiny room. He returned to the bedroom, ignored the dress shoes placed by the cabinet, found his sandals, and stepped into them.

When he opened the door, the woman was waiting exactly as before. She offered only a small beckoning gesture and led him down the hall. The walls were light green and there were decorative vases in periodic alcoves. They followed the hall to its end, where she opened the door to an oddly sheltered sunroom. The space was full of fresh air and light, but offered no views.

The ambassador was seated at a table. He rose and bowed as Estlin entered. "Mr. Hume, I welcome you and apologize for any discomfort we have caused you." He gestured at the table with an open hand. "Would you like a cup of tea?"

The tea service set on the table with cream, sugar, and short bread reflected the inferred tastes of the guest and not the host. The cups and saucers were rimmed with gold.

Estlin accepted the civilized approach. "Yes, thank you."

"Thank you, Grace." Huo dismissed Estlin's guide with a slight nod.

A lean man entered from the opposite end of the room. He was dressed in black and had balanced features that should have assembled into handsomeness. The expression on his face negated this, narrowing his eyes and mouth. He lifted his chin at the ambassador as though granting him permission to proceed. The elder statesman cooled momentarily, and then he reached for the teapot, lifting it from its china pedestal.

"I was born in the province of Hebei." Huo poured Estlin's tea and passed him the cup and saucer. "The land is much like your prairies with great fields of wheat and a wide sky full of stars. I was fascinated by space, the golden light of meteors, the faint white specks of satellites traveling horizon to horizon, the close and distant moon. But my childhood imagination never carried me this far." The ambassador stirred his tea then set down the spoon. "These events define a new future for all of us. Could you have imagined this as a child?"

"No." Estlin had few coherent childhood memories.

"We did not forcibly relocate them. An invitation was made. One accepted. One did not. We did not know that accepting one without the other would create this alarming situation. Concern for the health of our visitor forced us to bring you here. I am happy that the second visitor took the opportunity to join us. They have been reunited and their health restored."

"So, you don't need me," Estlin suggested.

"I would not say that," the ambassador answered. "China is the world's most populous country, its oldest civilization and a republic of great economic and social strength. I believe our visitors are more informed than one might assume. This embassy borders on Wellington's botanical gardens. The visitors were found less than a mile from here and this may have been their intended destination. Regardless, you must accept that it is their present choice of sanctuary. I wish I could remain their host, but it has been decided that, for the safety of all, they will be relocated as swiftly as possible."

"Where?"

"We do not believe they can be protected here, and the risk of keeping them in a populated area outweighs any benefits. Transportation is ready. It is my hope that you will accompany them to facilitate communication. Our guests should be kept as informed as possible. They should know that the People's Republic of China offers them every measure of hospitality."

"Where are they going?"

Huo glanced at the man standing silently by the door. "I cannot say."

Estlin wondered where the waetapu were being kept. As he thought of them, the room brightened as though clouds had released the sun. It was excessive. He shaded his eyes and found no relief as orange and yellow bands of color spilled through the wall to his left. It was too obvious not to be true.

"It tried to tell me that Waewae was in Wellington," he said. "I didn't understand." He rose, approached the wall, and spread his fingers across the lightly textured floral wallpaper. "They're very close."

The bright ribbons burst into fine beads that bled their color and froze white. The fine white crystals whirled around him with increasing density and speed until the room was obscured by the blizzard.

"What do you see, Mr. Hume?"

"It's snowing."

"Accept our invitation to stay with the visitors. Your skills are greatly needed."

"Where are you taking them?" The swirling flakes coalesced into a white continent. "Antarctica," he said, and immediately wished that he hadn't.

Ambassador Huo's expression darkened. "I need your answer now."

"That's not the climate they chose for themselves."

"Our research stations are both isolated and well equipped. Mr. Hume?"

"No," Estlin said. "You're making a mistake, and I won't support it."

"How unfortunate." Huo stood. "Please excuse me. There are duties to which I must attend. You will return to our guest room and remain there until our visitors are safely moved. Accept my hospitality." He left the sunroom.

Estlin sipped his tea, trying to ignore the snow swirling around him and how he knew the cold of it without feeling cold. The other man stepped through the storm, oblivious to the snow flecking his short black hair.

"What now?" Estlin asked.

The man silently took the teacup from his hands and set it on the table.

— « o » —

Jeanette was condensing her notes into a master list of ships. She'd poured herself a coffee and joined Nia in the lounge. Nia had the TV remote and was compulsively surfing from channel to channel, seeking news reports on the blockade. She had a laptop open and was conducting a simultaneous search on-line.

"Shouldn't you be peeling potatoes?" Jeanette asked.

"This is more important." Nia tapped the remote, returning them to a local channel to watch the news anchor shift the story from the harbor to protests at the American Embassy. "We're restocking the galley," she said. "There'll be apple crumble tonight."

The TV droned about the economic impact of the blockade. The true question behind the carrier's presence in the strait was subsumed by the American focus on their right to be there.

"Have you seen this man?" the news anchor asked. "Estlin Hume, a Canadian on holiday in the Wellington reportedly collapsed early this morning, suffering what appeared to be a severe migraine."

Jeanette looked up from her notes to see a familiar face fill the screen with a "Missing Person" banner across the photo.

"It has been confirmed from video surveillance footage that he left in the ambulance called to the scene," the reporter said. "However, he has since gone missing, having not been admitted to any area hospital."

"Shit," Jeanette said.

"What's wrong?" Nia asked.

"I know him," Jeanette answered, raising a hand to shush Nia as the report continued.

"Concerned that he may have wandered, disoriented from a local emergency room, his friends are conducting a Wellington-wide search amidst further concerns that he may have become a victim of foul play." A second photo of Estlin appeared with an emergency contact number beneath it. "The ambulance which transported Mr. Hume has not been identified, and emergency services, which logs all ambulance dispatches, has no record of the call. Police have deemed the lapse in protocol as disturbing and suspicious."

"I've seen that story." Nia searched her files. "I already flagged it."

"Why?"

She scrolled through the on-line article. "He was picked up on Stone Street," she said. "The captain was in here talking with Bjorn last night. Stone Street is weirdness ground zero. Bjorn thinks there's something there, and that's why all the big ships are in Evans Bay." She looked at the screen. "Why do you think he's here? What does he do?"

"Estlin? I don't know." Jeanette knew he had one uniquely unprofitable talent. She enlarged the picture from the news. "We were in the bio department at the University of Oregon. He lasted less than a year. He dropped out and he dropped me."

"Why'd he—?" Nia curtailed her question as Captain Arnot entered. He'd trimmed his beard and was wearing his dress shirt, his captain's bars shining on the epaulets.

"I've been invited to the Chinese embassy," he announced.

"About the blockade?" Jeanette asked.

"The *Green Meanie* is on its way," he said and pointed at Jeanette. "We're going ashore."

"We?"

"You speak Mandarin."

Jeanette nodded. She'd spent a year dissecting jellyfish in Dalian. Her language skills were not spectacular, but she'd had occasion to practice since joining the crew. "Where's Xin?"

"Xin isn't a freckly redhead who could be mistaken for arm candy," the captain clarified. "I want you to keep your ears open and your mouth shut. Listen, but don't look like you're listening."

Jeanette pushed her chair back and stood. She hated the *Green Meanie.* She'd likely spill her lunch over the side of the RIB, but a part of her just wouldn't say no to the captain.

"Is there a dress you can throw on?" he asked.

"No."

— « o » —

"Sanford, you are working too hard." Bomani leaned against the door to Sanford's office. "Time to go outside for a break."

"I can't." Sanford checked his watch. The morning was inching by. "I'm expecting a call."

"Not on that phone." Bomani lifted the receiver and pointed it at Sanford. There was no dial tone. "They disconnected these or re-routed the numbers. The first day here people kept getting urgent movie calls. The only phones are in the front office. That's who they'll call. You can tell Sarah we're just stepping out."

"I shouldn't."

"You should. We should talk."

"Yes, of course." Sanford looked at his presentation notes. "I'm over-prepared. I just wish I had more from John."

"So do I," Bomani answered. "He left too quickly."

Sanford left everything on the desk and followed Bomani, who was preoccupied and said nothing until they reached the front office. Sanford enquired, wanting to be certain he hadn't missed a phone message. Bomani barely paused to wave, offering a few perfunctory words and pulling Sanford with him.

"John would not tell Jakarta where he was going." Bomani lit a cigarette as soon as they hit the street. "He left so fast, I did not even see him."

"I'm sure we'll hear from him."

"Are you?"

"He has big news."

Bomani caught Sanford by the shoulder. "What did he tell you?"

"That he found our signal."

"He found it!" Bomani smiled broadly. "Good John."

"He gave me a set of coordinates. It sounds like they've pointed some significant telescopes at it. That's where he's gone."

"Where exactly?"

"He didn't say."

"But he's following the signal," Bomani relaxed. "About last night—"

A gray BMW with diplomatic plates zipped up the block, stopping at the curb in front of them. The tinted windows simultaneously rolled down.

"Sanford!" Sergeant Malone was behind the wheel. "I've got another invitation for you." He waved a sheet of paper. "The American attache wants to hear about your theory."

"That's excellent." Sanford felt inordinately pleased with the attention his ideas were receiving. "When?"

"Immediately. I'm your ride to the embassy."

"I can't leave yet. I'm working on a presentation for Harry."

"I know Harry," Malone said. "The biologist. Big Maori guy. When's your presentation?"

"I don't know yet."

"Then there's time." Sergeant Malone reached across to open the passenger door. "You don't refuse invitations from Dontis — he's the president's man."

"Yes, of course." Sanford stepped off the curb, but stopped when Bomani did not follow. "Bomani should come, his mathematical knowledge has been essential. I insist."

"I'll stay." Bomani stepped back to the fence line. "I can cover your talk if needed."

"We can do both together," Sanford suggested.

"Mr. Bomani, come with us. I insist," Malone interjected firmly. "The ambassador will want to meet you."

Bomani nodded, seeming resigned. He raised his cigarette. "I have tried to give these up," he said, taking a last drag. "They are going to kill me one day." He crushed the cigarette and got in the car.

Chapter Ten

A frosted glass dome light was mounted on the finely textured white ceiling above Estlin. He lay on the bed, thinking about small human settlements on an expanse of ice. Isolating the waetapu was understandable, but choosing such a hazardous, inhospitable location didn't make sense. He wondered if staying behind meant that he would literally be confined in the guest room for an indeterminately long period of time. He considered the wallpaper. It was a simple variant of the wallpaper in the sunroom and not very entertaining.

Would there be room service? He hadn't finished his tea, and when he'd returned to the room, the pitcher of water had vanished.

There was a knock on the door. Estlin raised his head long enough to see Yidge enter with a tray in her hands. She was looking young and not evil, her hair in a pair of child-like braids. He let his head fall back on the bed.

"I brought you some water," she said. The short glass jug had several slices of lemon floating in it.

"This kind of hospitality should come with a mini-fridge full of alcohol." Estlin fixed his eyes on the ceiling and refused to feel grateful.

"The ambassador is disappointed." She set the tray on the table and poured the water. "This is not progressing as he'd hoped. I don't just mean your refusal to participate."

"Refusal to participate? Yidge, you drugged and abducted me. I'm planning to hold a grudge."

"This isn't about you," she said. "They're from another world. Don't you want to know why they're here?"

"I think this could go very badly, very quickly," he answered, sitting up.

"That's why we need you. You can figure out why they're here."

"And all will be resolved?"

"You saw Wae jump into the ambulance," Yidge argued. "This is where they want to be."

"Keeping it a secret makes everyone assume something else is happening. This situation is going to blow up."

"Fix it," Yidge said, choosing a glass from the tray.

"I'm not going."

"You want to stay here? If you don't go, it's these walls and that's it."

"How long?" he asked, taking the other glass. He had a headache. He wasn't sure if it was dehydration or an after effect of whatever she'd slipped him. The lemon water was bitter.

"You know where the waetapu are going. Their security is Huo's highest priority. You'll be a guest here until he's certain you can't compromise the situation," she said, as though this was a reasonable, rational conversation.

"A guest," he said. "What happens if I refuse to stay?"

"What do you think will happen?"

"I don't know."

"Consider whether you want to find out," she said.

"I think a hell of a lot of people are looking for me. And when Harry comes pounding on the door, it'll be best that he finds me here." He looked at the empty glass in his hand. He'd finished it without noticing. It wasn't a particularly deep glass. It was short and wide, the sort of glass that looked better with ice in it. The water would have been better with ice. The water would have been better with more water and less lemon. "Why are you doing this?"

"*You said* they needed each other to survive. Harry said it, too," she answered. "During my stopover in Beijing, they showed me footage of Waewae freely climbing over the wall at the embassy here. They asked me to help if I could."

"You trust Huo?"

"No, I trust them," she said. "Harry trusts them. He didn't want them locked up. The enclosure was built like a film set with panels that could be removed for cameras. He didn't tell Stodt."

"Harry didn't want this."

"Waewae wanted to go. It let me see it in the rafters waiting for me to open the door. All I did was open the door and visit with the guards as it closed behind me."

"That's it?" he asked. "A little gesture and you're best friends? It's part of their trick that you trust them — that you want to trust them. It's how they work."

"They've trusted us."

"I bet you think...they smell like cookies." Estlin's raised his hand and stretched his fingers wide. His arm felt heavy, his fingers distant and numb. It was a familiar sensation.

"You want them to live." Yidge took the glass from Estlin's other hand and placed it on the tray. "You have a place in human history. I'm just helping you get there."

"Don't."

"I thought that you understood, that you would accept the opportunity to help once there was time to offer you the choice," she said. "I'm disappointed."

Disappointed was not the word for how Estlin felt. He thought to say as much, drooled on his new dress shirt, tipped sideways, and used every bit of his remaining strength to raise one hand and offer her the finger.

— « o » —

Captain Arnot held the taxi door for Jeanette. She got out and pulled the clip from her hair, letting it loose around her shoulders as she placed a hand on his elbow. A set of ostentatious stairs brought them to the front door. It opened and they were welcomed to the foyer by a woman Jeanette would bet had also been told to listen and keep her mouth shut. She guided them swiftly through the halls, then opened a pair of tall doors to reveal an expansive sunroom.

"Captain Arnot and Dr. Goff," she said in impeccable English, "may I introduce you to His Excellency, Ambassador Huo."

"Welcome." Huo bowed and gestured to seats around a small table that held a traditional Chinese tea service. "Thank you for coming."

"I was surprised by your invitation," the captain answered, "and intrigued."

Their hostess steeped the tea. She moved quietly, precisely filling the small cups, serving first the ambassador and then the captain. Jeanette lightly tapped the table with two fingertips when her cup was filled.

"The icebreaker, *Xue Long*, is here." Ambassador Huo raised his cup as he cut to the heart of the meeting. "The supplies aboard her are essential to our environmental research stations in Antarctica."

Arnot ignored his tea. "The Americans run supplies out of Christchurch. You don't. The *Xue Long* was diverted here. Why?"

"Several of our environmental scientists were here engaged in an analysis of the Antarctic aurora that followed the Blue Moon," Huo answered. "Now, all must proceed southward."

"Why?" Captain Arnot leaned back from the table. "Tell me what difference a day, or two days, will make."

"As you have realized, the *Xue Long* was diverted. It is the time already lost that makes each day critical," Huo said. "The *Xue Long* must go. The captain has no taste for daring maneuvers. He cannot risk damage to his hull or any further delay."

Huo raised his cup again and Jeanette lifted hers in turn. The tea was familiar and yet exceeded familiarity. The cup was a delicate work of perfection.

"The blockade is not ours to break," Captain Arnot argued. "We are committed participants, but this is a local effort. I can't help you."

"The ship will embark today," Huo answered. "If you deny the *Xue Long* exit, you risk many human lives."

"Our protest aims to protect all life from nuclear lunacy," Arnot said. "You have other ships in other ports. Use them."

"The supplies, equipment and personnel are here," Huo quietly, but pointedly answered. "I will make a broad appeal for assistance if necessary. It is a courtesy to ask you first."

Arnot assessed the threat, letting silence fall. Jeanette breathed in the tea and let all tension sink away from her.

"Doctor Goff, would you like more tea?" Huo asked.

"It is very good, thank you." Jeanette dipped her head as she responded.

"As a diplomat, you might expect me to engage with the nuances of language, but I find gestures far more revealing. How one enters a room. How one sits."

Jeanette found herself correcting her posture, straightening herself from the base of her spine. She realized she'd given herself away when she tapped the table in thanks.

"But when there is a difference of culture, there is room for misinterpretation," Huo said, setting his teacup on the table. "Particularly when we succumb to modern pressures and do not give ourselves time to engage, to observe and reflect, to see that there are conversations that don't rest with what is spoken."

"I study marine life. A fish in a tank never behaves as one in open water," she answered. "I've been watching the harbor. It's fascinating."

"The situation defies common explanation," Huo agreed. "These days are mysterious to us all."

"A planned departure would be less disruptive for both parties," Jeanette suggested to both men in the room.

"This was my feeling," Huo answered.

They sipped their tea, aware that Arnot's silence did not signal agreement.

"I understand your commitment, Captain Arnot," Huo continued. "You risked your ship scraping bows with the *Kaiko Maru* this morning. It may interest you to know that the whaler has been re-tasked. Sonagraphic studies will now supersede all cetaceous research."

"Whaling," Arnot corrected.

"Times are changing. I thought that you would support our environmental scientists in Antarctica."

"Your ice breaker is anchored amongst warships. You say the Japanese whaler is no longer a whaler. What if your supply ship has also been *re-tasked*?" Arnot responded.

"I give you my word and invite you to follow the *Xue Long* if you don't believe me," Huo said. "The ship leaves at noon. It will be followed by the trawler *Rong Yu*."

"No," Arnot interrupted. "We won't let a gill-netter out of the harbor."

"It's here?" Jeanette asked. She hadn't seen the *Rong Yu*. It wasn't on her list.

"It has been sheltered in dry dock for repairs to its rudder," Huo responded. "The ship's new owners asked that I engage in this dialogue with you. Their business plan is in jeopardy."

"I will agree to break the blockade for humanitarian reasons," Arnot said. "Profit margins are not my concern."

"Your ship was built for sealing but found a new life. The *Rong Yu* has been acquired by an Antarctic ecotour company. It is small, but international agreements now restrict the size of cruise vessels permitted in Antarctic waters." Huo paused as Grace refilled their teacups in turn. "Grace, please prepare a gift of our teas to send with Dr. Goff," he said.

At this, Grace nodded and silently departed.

Jeanette considered the situation. "If the ship is to be converted, they will have no use of its nets," she suggested.

Huo's surprise was subtly registered. He tapped the table. "I believe the new owners would be willing to cut the nets and surrender them to you. These nets have value. You can ensure that they are neither sold nor disposed of improperly."

"You'll give us the nets?" Arnot paused.

Jeanette willed him to make the deal. International law restricted drift nets to 2.5 mile lengths of indiscriminate, entangling death, but illegal nets ten times that length were still used. The *Rong Yu* was on the Greenpeace watch list.

"If the trawler departs without its nets, we'll let her through," Arnot said finally.

"Will you agree to assume full ownership of the nets left at the dry dock? I do not want our captain to be accused of littering."

"Agreed. Please encourage the *Rong Yu* to ride your icebreaker's wake. Let's keep this as simple as possible."

"So be it," Huo concluded. "Dr. Goff, Captain Arnot, thank you. This has been a productive meeting. Grace will show you out."

Grace had silently reappeared at the door carrying a generous basket of teas. She led them from the sunroom to the entryway. Jeanette accepted the basket and offered her thanks in Mandarin.

"You're welcome," Grace answered. "Your taxi is waiting."

Their taxi was indeed at the base of the stairs. Jeanette examined the contents of the basket as they drove back to the waterfront. A beautiful teapot and cups were nestled in with the variety of tea leaves. She'd seriously scored.

Arnot rolled down his window, letting the street noise into the cab. "Why did he talk about the *Kaiko Maru*? What was that? Half threat, half placating lie. It's not their ship."

"Was it a lie?" Jeanette responded. "Neil, they changed out the crew last night. They had two tenders running back and forth to the dock for hours." The tactics utilized by the departing ship had convinced Jeanette that she'd observed more than a rotation of crew, and that in fact a change of command had occurred. She returned her thoughts to the subject at hand. "Huo cares about the trawler, not the freighter."

"I know," Arnot agreed. "But I don't know why. The trawler is slow — slower than the *Sunrise* — fourteen knots at best. Any ship in the bay could run it down."

"Is that why they'll cut the nets?" Jeanette asked. "To lose weight?"

"It won't make her faster, but with the nets anyone could use an accusation of illegal fishing to stop and inspect the ship."

"What is going on?"

"If I could, I'd follow the *Rong Yu* to find out."

"What do we do with the net?" Jeanette asked, wondering if they'd committed to an obscenely expensive disposal bill. "Incinerate it?"

"We wait for a sunny, slow news day and stretch it from the harbor up the hill to the Beehive," he said, referring to the New Zealand parliament buildings. "Let everyone measure its destructive scale with their car odometers. We use that net to get more of them out of the water."

— « o » —

The receiving room at the American embassy was bright, though the tall windows were shuttered. The dark wood of the antique furniture gleamed, but Sanford found the formal seats uncomfortable. Bomani refused to sit, alternately pacing and standing near the door.

Sergeant Malone had driven them through the embassy gates and into a parking lot beneath the building. He'd led them to the receiving room and instructed them to wait. The man they had rushed to meet was apparently away on urgent business.

"Do you want coffee?" Sanford asked. "We could ask—"

"No," Bomani replied, still pacing.

"Harry asked me to make a presentation in the main production buildings." Sanford folded his hands in his lap, then gripped the arms of the chair again, shifting forward. "Do you think we'll find out what is in Studio C?"

"We won't." Bomani turned away from him, his voice grim and angry. "You should not have insisted that I come, James. I would have preferred to stay behind."

"Nonsense. This is historic and your contribution has been substantial." Sanford had not considered that the man might not want to join him for the visit. He wondered if Bomani had some unfortunate political affiliation.

"We may have just stepped off the pages of history." Bomani shook his head. "I don't know where this path leads. My president may one day wonder what happened to me. We have been brought here in service of your country, not mine."

"This is an international project," Sanford argued. "The implications extend far beyond the interests of any one country."

"Are we are still on the project? When we last met that man, Malone, he had blood on his boots."

"Blood?" Sanford hadn't seen anything, but he wasn't in the habit of looking at shoes. "It was dark. How could you—?"

"I am certain," Bomani said. "He stood with us so the helicopter with the light would not see him. It was looking for a moving target."

"Did you report it?" Sanford asked.

"He checked my ID," Bomani said grimly. "He knew who I was. He knew I had seen him. I surprised myself, Sanford. I did not know I was a coward. I am sorry."

Sanford had no answer for this harsh self-criticism. He wished he had his notebook. They could have distracted themselves with equations, perhaps pushed their work even further.

Sergeant Malone returned with a black bag slung over his shoulder and Sanford's green suitcase in his hand. Sanford looked down without thinking, but Malone was wearing casual civilian clothes — no boots, no blood.

"If either of you have to use the toilet, I suggest you go now," he said. "We're about to fly."

"Fly? What do you mean?" Sanford stood.

"You owe Dontis a briefing," Malone said, "and he's returning to the states."

"We can't leave—"

"Do you need me to clarify? Sanford, you signed a contract. I was witness. Everything you've done since you landed here has been in breach of that contract and potentially in breach of national security."

"I was hired to participate in the international panel."

"You were to serve American interests on that panel, and you didn't attend a single meeting," Malone responded. "Your lack of discretion borders on criminal. You're being presented with an opportunity to redeem yourself. Make the most of it."

"I have no wish to go anywhere," Bomani said.

"You're on American soil without a passport. We have no idea who you are, so you're with us until we can determine your identity and establish that you're not a threat to American security, given the current crisis."

"I have my passport." He drew it from his pocket.

"You said you left it in your desk."

"I was hoping you would not admit me to the building," Bomani confessed.

"Your failure to produce it when it was first requested casts doubt on its validity," Sergeant Malone responded. "It will take time to confirm your identity. Besides, Sanford thinks you're *essential*."

"We can't leave," Sanford protested. "All my work—"

"It's been retrieved." Malone placed Sanford's suitcase at his feet as the heavy thump of an approaching helicopter penetrated the walls. "That's our ride."

— « o » —

Harry threw the file on his desk. The NZSIS had located the abandoned ambulance and torn it apart, finding a customized compartment built to smuggle a person. All bets were that Lyndie had spent time in that narrow box. The forensics report noted no blood nor signs of a struggle were present. This did not reassure Harry.

They had footage of the ambulance rolling out the main gate un-searched. In fact, the driver and vehicle had been subject to far more scrutiny when they arrived. Their absent guest may have contributed to the security lapses. No one had broken in this time, and all suspicions centered on Yidge, who had arranged for the ambulance and vanished with it.

The project, lacking its central subject, was collapsing. A mass exodus of the scientific staff was underway. Case in point, by the time he'd asked another staffer to bring in his new key physicist, the fellow was gone.

Harry sat heavily, then abruptly slapped his desk. He'd forgotten that his personal cell phone was locked in the desk drawer, and it was the one number Lyndie would know. The key to the drawer was in his pocket. He flipped the phone open and scrolled through the messages stopping on a brief text. "Call me. URGENT. Terry."

Terry was chair of the biology department at the University of Otago in Dunedin. She'd invited Harry to move to the South Island, suggesting the pleasure of her company was worth a demotion to sessional instructor. She wasn't wrong, but Harry wasn't ready for that move yet. If anyone wanted leverage on him, Terry was the quickest, sharpest approach. The thought put his guts in his throat as he dialed her number.

"Hello." The sing-song tone of her greeting set everything right.

"It's Harry."

"You sound worried," she said.

"You all right?" he asked, wanting to hear her confirm it.

"I'm fine, but there's a situation down here. We've had a mass migration. I've never seen anything like it. The rabbits have gathered, and I mean all of them, *thousands.* They're all on Long Beach, staring at the water like they want to hop in and swim for it."

"Where's Long Beach?" Harry was up and heading for Stodt's office.

"Northeast of the city at the mouth of the inlet."

"What's out there?"

"Nothing, it's a beach."

"No big buildings? No warehouses?"

"The closest would be a freight terminal in Carey's Bay, and that's five or ten klicks inland from here."

"And they're looking out at the water?"

"Does this have something to with the thing I'm not supposed to know about?"

"Terry?"

"Godwin called. He'd heard some whisper and thought I might have the scoop."

"What's he got?"

"Wild speculation. Crazy tabloid stuff. Easy to dismiss, except that crowd in your harbor has everyone's attention."

"I can't—"

"I know, Harry. You pick up the most interesting jobs."

"You have no idea."

"Well, I'm pretending not to."

"How many rabbits?"

"At least a thousand."

"Could you do me a favor? Could you get out there with a compass and tell me exactly which way they are looking?"

— « o » —

Deep in his subconscious, Estlin was feeling sorry for himself. He could tell because he was dreaming of rabbits. His rabbit friend had died long ago, but he still had a picture of the nameless, white, flop-eared rabbit alone on a deep green lawn. The photo had "Bunny from Uncle Bob" handwritten on the back.

When he was little, he had particularly liked how quiet the rabbit was, not empty quiet, but the kind of quiet you could listen to very deeply. Doctors and nurses and people were so loud that he would bang his head against the wall to silence them, scream to hear himself, and scratch his own skin just to feel it.

He knew that sometimes, when things were bad, his mother brought the rabbit to his room. She would sit and gently stroke its long fur. She would hold the rabbit to touch him.

Estlin was dreaming, and he couldn't wake up. He lay in a field of dry grass with a cactus thorn stuck in his hand and rabbits all around him. He really liked rabbits and, on this one occasion, he let himself miss his mother. He let himself be truly sad about it, and comfort himself, because he was a special boy and even though he couldn't move, he could still pet a thousand rabbits all at once.

Chapter Eleven

"I've got something," Harry told Stodt, closing the commander's door behind him. "You've been tracking the all shipping traffic, right?"

Stodt gestured at the papers piled on his desk. "There have several incidents in the last six hours. Two French submarines, *Le Redoutable* and *Le Terrible*, intercepted the *Xue Long* in international water. The *Redoutable* surfaced too close to the ship or was deliberately rammed. The collision damage was extensive. The *Xue Long* rendered assistance and most of the submariners are now aboard her.

"A trawler, the *Rong Yu*, slipped out with the Chinese icebreaker and continued southward, hugging the coast until it was boarded and searched by an American tactical team in our territorial water. The captain is demanding legal action and compensation for injuries, damages, and the stress of having automatic weapons waved in their faces. The Americans say they were acting on sound intelligence. Neither party has indicated that anything was taken from the trawler."

"Where was that?" Harry asked.

Stodt tapped the map off the coast from Christchurch.

"And it was southbound." Harry checked the times and positions listed.

"Yes."

"They had the wrong ship." Harry flipped through the pages summarizing marine traffic. "Where's the list for Dunedin?"

"Why?" Stodt found the page and slid it across the desk.

"Lyndie was there," Harry answered.

"He contacted you?"

"No. He attracts animals, like squirrels. With squirrels, he doesn't even have to try. For this, he must've been really trying."

"What are you talking about?"

"There are a thousand rabbits on the beach near Dunedin. I think Lyndie was there this morning on a northbound ship. The mouth on the inlet is narrow; it put him close enough to shore." Harry scanned through the responder tracking data and planted his finger on the name of a Chinese freighter, its departure time and course. "Found it." He handed the page across to Stodt. "They ran two ships south, so we wouldn't look at a northbound freighter. The *Lu Hai*. 960 feet. 70,000 tons."

"You're sure?"

"There has to be a connection. A discrete, common domestic flight," Harry said. "We have to act now. The rabbits are going to make the news."

"It's in international water. We can't board."

"Bullshit."

"I'll dispatch the HMNZS *Canterbury* to intercept as a protective escort," Stodt said.

"Pull the ship's agent," Harry insisted, "and search the warehouse. You'll find a connection."

"Even if we find proof—"

"A thousand rabbits!"

"We have to pursue diplomatic channels," Stodt said. "I want you to talk to Ambassador Huo."

"Me?"

"Accuse Huo directly. If he deflects, we conclude that this is the unsanctioned work of a splinter group, and it becomes easier for us to act."

"I'll bang his door for you," Harry answered, displaying all his teeth. When this had started, on his one stop home to gather essentials, he found his grandfather's taiaha in his hand. He'd placed it in his truck, knowing the day would come when he needed a big stick.

— « o » —

A SH-60 Seahawk helicopter was descending into the parking lot beside the American embassy, blasting dust into the faces of those waiting. Bomani did not like the look of it at all. To him, a helicopter was a rock waiting to fall out of the sky. He did not understand why anyone would build a flying machine with no glide capabilities.

Bomani would force himself aboard, rather than being forced. He had no wish to make a scene in the face of history. He could not even curse Sanford because Bomani believed that fate put you where you were meant to be. They were told that the man they were to meet had gone ahead.

A pale, thin woman boarded with a black girl that she pressed in front of her. The girl sat next to Bomani, tucking the white skirt of her dress tight around her legs before buckling her seatbelt. The crewman stowed her small, beige suitcase in a compartment. He turned his attention to his final passenger, greeting her as Dr. Liev. She accepted the man's assistance as she climbed about, but refused to let him secure her leather tote bag. She met Bomani's eyes briefly as she shifted to tuck the bag next to her. The crewman handed out yellow ear plugs and latched the door.

"Have you been on a helicopter before?" Bomani asked the young girl.

"Yes."

"This is my first time."

"They're loud," she said.

"Yes," he agreed. "That is a nice dress."

"I don't like colors next to my skin," she said.

Bomani realized how different the dress was from the visual noise most western teenagers chose. He offered his hand. "I am Bomani."

She considered his hand, then quickly took it squeezing his fingers tightly. "Are you a good man?"

It was not a question Bomani had been asked directly, not for a long time. "I believe that our actions affect every person we meet, even those we encounter only briefly. The sum of all our actions, good or bad, is our legacy."

Beth released Bomani's hand, disappointed with his response. "That wasn't an answer."

"I had a good mother," he assured her. "I choose, every day, to honor her legacy."

"My mother's dead, too," she said flatly.

"Beth," the doctor interrupted, admonishing the girl, either for the subject matter or her willingness to converse with a stranger.

"I am sorry, little one." Bomani answered only the girl.

As the engines cycled up, Beth pressed the earplugs into her ears. Bomani kept his eyes away from the windows as they lifted off. The helicopter hovered, seemed to shift uncertainly as though deciding to stay in the air, and then abruptly rose. He realized that Beth was watching him closely and decided that, for her, he would be unafraid.

— « o » —

The world was thrumming. There was the deep thrum of engines pushing a massive hull through water and another sound that was a color. Estlin looked at the thrum for a long time, until the press of a cold hand distracted him. Yidge was sitting on the floor next to the bunk, stroking his cheek.

"Lyndie?" Yidge withdrew her hand, and Estlin knew why it was cold — there were shining drops of water on her fingers.

"Are you with me now?" she asked.

He blinked. His eyes were hot.

"You've been crying."

"I hate drugs." He tried to lift his hand to wipe his eyes, but it was bound to the bed frame. His hand was splinted, an intravenous line piercing the back of it. His other arm was secured alongside it with a wide-buckled wrist restraint. The room was a cross between a doctor's office and a ship's cabin.

"Do you want some water?" Yidge raised a glass into view.

"Shit. You're kidding." He turned his head aside and pulled at the restraints, trying to get the tips of his fingers onto one of the buckles only to find them locked.

"Don't. You'll hurt yourself."

"I have to pee."

"I'm sorry."

"Yidge!" He stopped himself and knocked the anger from his voice. "That doesn't help me."

The door swung open. The captain entered, wearing his rank on his shoulders. He was short and round-faced, his thin hair combed over the top of his head. Yidge stood and stepped away from Estlin. The captain was followed by the lean-and-mean man from the Chinese embassy. The captain dragged a chair over and sat directly in front of Estlin.

"Estlin Hume, this is—" Yidge was interrupted by the captain. He threw half of their exchange directly at Estlin, communicating with volume and the driving momentum of his words before pausing to allow Yidge to translate.

"The captain has questions," she said. "Who do you work for?"

"Harry."

The captain was not satisfied.

"Who do you work for?" Yidge repeated.

"You saw the contract," Estlin told Yidge. "Harry phoned me. He hired me."

"They know you were working with the New Zealanders. But who else do you work for?"

"No one. I was unemployed when he called."

"You were picked up in a very isolated area. Why?" Yidge asked, this time echoing the taller man.

"That's where I live."

"Why?"

"That's where my house is," he said. "It was an inheritance. Who is he?"

Yidge ignored the question. She slipped her hands under his forearms, gently turning them. "You have unusual scars. These appear to be from defensive wounds."

"They're from a trowel." Estlin looked at the faded marks, remembering when they were fresh and red and drawn closed with fine black thread. "I told you, I was attacked by a university groundskeeper. Twenty-six stitches."

"Please address the captain, not me," she said, waiting for him to adjust his gaze. "Was he charged? Is there a record?"

"He was old. He was sent to a doctor. Everyone thought he'd lost a marble, which he had."

The captain pointed at his head.

"And the scar in your hairline?" Yidge asked.

"It was a splinter. A neighbor knocked on my door with an axe. The squirrels killed her magnolia tree."

She reached out and touched his sternum through the cloth of his shirt. "And this one?"

"Kicked by a camel."

Yidge translated, and the captain laughed. It was not a friendly sound. He asked another gruff question. Yidge reached for the buttons on Estlin's shirt.

"Don't."

She released three of the lower buttons, lifting his shirttail. "The ship's doctor told him that the scar on your side is from a bullet wound."

"It was."

"Another angry gardener?"

"My mother was killed when I was twelve," Estlin answered. "The bullet passed through her and hit me. There's a record."

"I'm sorry," she said, then translated his response for the captain.

The captain shoved his chair back, stood and pointed at Estlin. "Canadian?"

"Yes."

"Prince Rupert. You tell me!" He shot a few words at Yidge seeking an answer from her.

"Describe," she said.

"Describe!" the captain demanded.

"He's been to Prince Rupert," Yidge said, "to the port. Can you describe it?"

"He was there for wheat? Coal? He knows how big Canada is, right?" For Estlin, the port was a dot on a map, where the northern rail line hit water. "Yidge, I've never been there."

The captain shook his head. He took the chair and slammed it against the desk across the narrow room, then left. The other man lingered, asking no questions. He stepped forward to inspect the bindings and scars, then left without a word.

"What was that?"

"Your scars, your skills, the gaps in your work history, and years without a fixed address...." Yidge looked at the closed door. "They think you work for Canadian intelligence or another agency. Canadian passports are popular."

"I'm not going to convince him otherwise."

"I don't think so." Yidge fetched the chair from the desk and sat in it. Estlin ignored her.

"A camel," she said.

"My mistake," Estlin answered, being deliberately obscure. A couple of successful jobs with Harry had inflated his ego. He'd stepped boldly into the wrong field, treated a camel like a horse, and found out that camels don't appreciate lies about water. Apparently, he hadn't learned a damn thing. Estlin twisted his wrists to put his palms toward Yidge. "Where are we going?"

"I don't know," she said.

"Antarctica?"

"I've been in here with you. I offered to act as your translator. I told the ambassador you'd respond better to a familiar face and he agreed."

"You've drugged me twice now. We have a special bond."

"I'm trying to help."

"That's funny. You look like a normal, responsible human being, but your idea of what's helpful is fucking sideways."

"You just need to—"

"Stop. I don't engage in rationalizing conversations with crazy people." He pushed his hands towards her. "I want this needle out of my hand. I want these off." He pulled the restraints taut against the bed rail. "And I want to pee. Make it happen."

— « o » —

The wind yanked Jeanette's hood back and buffeted her ears. She turned off the small video camera in her hand, pushed it into a pocket of her windbreaker, and tried to wrestle her hood back into place and tighten it. The *Arctic Sunrise* had split from the blockade to keep pace with the *George Washington* in its slow circuit of the strait. Jeanette was on deck to collect footage of the carrier and the protest banners billowing in the wind. The carrier was turning again, eastward now, into the wind.

"It's picking up speed," she noted. *Arctic Sunrise* doggedly pursued the American battle group, falling further behind. Jeanette realized that the carrier wasn't turning. It was carrying on out of the strait.

The sense of victory was short-lived as the carrier's air wing roared to life. Jeanette raised her camera as a squadron of snub-nosed aircraft launched in succession. They split away in pairs, heading up and down the coast. A pair of larger, turboprop driven planes followed, each carrying a wide radar dish above their fuselage. She raised the camera further as a helicopter flew directly over the *Arctic Sunrise* returning to the carrier. She didn't catch its number, though the camera might have, but assumed it was the one that had left the ship an hour ago heading ashore.

The *Green Meanie* came alongside and the deck was suddenly alive with crew.

"We're picking up the *Meanie*," Davis, one of the deckhands, told her.

Jeanette stepped back from the rails as Davis swung out the ship's davit, preparing to lift the Zodiac.

"What's next?" Jeanette asked.

"Don't know," Davis answered, dropping a line over the side. "We're following the carrier."

— « o » —

Estlin watched the clock. It was the plainest, cheapest white-faced clock he'd ever seen pinned to a white wall. Yidge sat in the plastic chair at his bedside. Their relationship was at an impasse. The second hand completed another sweep.

"The restraints are locked," she said.

"Pick them, break them, cut them off," he said.

Yidge shook her head.

"Pull the IV."

"It's just hydration."

"It's a needle you can push whatever you want through," he said. "Pull it."

"I could help you with the other part."

It took him a few seconds to realize she was referring to his bladder. He glared at her. He glared until she got up and left. He checked the clock; three more minutes had passed.

The face of it blurred. A new image superimposed itself. The clock hands stretched towards him, turning, spinning time forward. The long arms slowed, stopping at the quarter from and quarter to the hour, widening to create a horizon from which an orange-yellow clock-sun rose.

The sun left the wall. It traced a clockwise semicircle, vanishing below the horizon to the right, rising again from the left after a length of absence. It was a faint and fuzzy light show. The sun rose and fell four times, then froze on the horizon, duplicating itself with different radii in a precisely geometrical way, forming an arbelos. The arbelos inverted with a bright flash.

It was a great answer, Estlin thought, but an answer without a question. He tried to pretend that, without context, the answer was meaningless, but he knew what it meant. Something was coming.

— « o » —

The wind across the deck of the carrier was incredible, but Sanford thought the noise would blow him off it. The deck crew directed them with broad gestures. Sanford followed Sergeant Malone, keeping his eyes on Malone's back and his hands up to shield his ears.

Malone swiftly led them to a door at the base of the tower and through it into the shelter of a narrow room. A crewman latched the door behind them.

"This is Dr. Sanford and his mathematician," Sergeant Malone said. "Do you know where they're going?"

"Yes, sir."

"Good. They need an escort. Have arrangements been made for Beth and Dr. Liev?"

Dr. Liev stood close to Malone, her hand on Beth's shoulder.

"VIP quarters."

"Is my team here?"

"No, Sergeant," the crewman answered. "Major Forester is expecting you."

"I'll take them," Malone said. "Dr. Liev, this way."

"I'll see you later, little one," Bomani assured Beth.

"You don't know that," she answered, pressing her hands together as she turned away and followed Malone to the nearest flight of stairs. She was the oddest child that Sanford had ever met.

"This is wrong, Sanford." Bomani stepped close and spoke softly. "Why would they bring a child here?"

Why are we here? Sanford wondered. The crewman led them from a flight of stairs into a warren of tight hallways and administration offices. The interior of the carrier was utilitarian in the extreme. They passed a series of closed doors and were finally directed into a small room. Three desks were wedged into the oddly angled space while maps, star charts, and data were taped to the walls. Sanford found a familiar face at the center of it.

"John!" Sanford exclaimed.

"You made it!" John Culter greeted them. He'd tied back his blonde hair but was still wearing his equation-covered T-shirt. "I got here yesterday, landed in a C2, thought my eyeballs were going to pop out of my head."

"What is all this?" Bomani asked.

"We're tracking the dust fire," John answered. "We found it. All we had to do was point the right telescope in the right direction. It's growing. The whole group at Livermore is thinking about it, but I told them we needed you."

"What's going on?" Sanford demanded.

"Nobody knows," John answered. "But if there's an energy beam out there, and it's what you think it is, then there's going to be another Burst. Another Burst means another object. The first object landed there." John pointed at a map on the wall where a red tack was planted in the expansive South Pacific.

"Oh! I have more data." He began to gather papers from the nearest desk. "X-ray bands from the bhangmeters on the Vela satellites. They're a network of military satellites monitoring the whole globe. Those detectors lit up during the Burst, freaked the entire defense department. It wasn't like a nuke. But an unidentified signal on that system?" He thrust the pages into Sanford's hands. "They thought it was a whole new kind of bad. And two days later there was a double flash in South Pacific. Again, not a nuke, but it didn't flag as a meteor, either. It was a very different blip. They used the Vela satellites to pin-point the landing."

"Landing?"

"Something came down."

"What?"

"We don't know," said John.

— « o » —

The ship shuddered, its heavy frame emitting an unhealthy groan. Estlin braced himself against the bed rails as the lights flickered and alarms bells filled the halls. He heard shouting crew run through the nearest corridor. The next set of footsteps came and went. He realized that if the ship sank, he'd go under attached to a bed frame. He pulled against the restraints and bellowed against the alarm.

The alarm abruptly shut off. The ships engines were also silent. This was not good. "Eh! In here!" he yelled.

The door clanged open. It was Yidge, panic in her eyes. She flew to the bedside, grabbed the IV line and yanked it out. The tape securing it did not come cleanly, dragging the needle to the side, tearing skin.

"Shit, Yidge!" He twisted his wrists in the restraints, trying to use his fingertips to stem the bleeding.

"Sorry," she said, proceeding directly to the drawers in the sickbay, yanking them open in succession.

"Are we sinking?"

"No. We've been boarded." She grabbed a scalpel from the drawer, tearing the cover from the sterile blade. She returned to the bedside and immediately started to cut through the bindings. "I don't have a key," she said.

The bindings weren't meant to be cut. She dragged the blade across them with ever increasing force until it slipped and sliced into the bedding.

"Careful!" The back of Estlin's hand was bleeding freely.

"Quiet," she said, and resumed her work.

The door swung inwards. They realized in the same instant that Yidge hadn't latched it behind her. She turned, the blade in her hand, and seemed to slip. She hit the bed with alarming force. Blood spilled down her back as she fell further, dropping to the floor. Estlin looked to the door and found the gun. The man holding it was wearing a black balaclava.

Estlin heaved himself back as the man drew a knife. The viciously long blade broke into a serrated edge at its base. The man grabbed his wrist, inspected the bindings and brought the blade against the straps. Estlin leaned over the side of the bed to look at Yidge. Her heart was sending wave after wave of blood down her shirt.

"She's dying," he said. Before his eyes, layers of red lifted from her. The details of the room — the cabinets, the plastic chair, the plain clock on the white wall — all crystallized as a distinctly other awareness entered the space. And Yidge was dying. Her eyes were wide with panic. She was shocked, so shocked to be dying with just enough time to know it. Every effort to heave air into a punctured lung brought a spike of pain.

Estlin couldn't breathe. He knew this death. He'd felt it before. "Help her."

He heard his own strangled voice, and then felt a wave of certainty that she could not be helped from the man slicing through the bindings. A strap snapped, freeing one hand and Estlin was reaching and the waetapu were reaching through him to examine the depth of the red with his eyes, feasting on the flutter of her pulse beneath his fingers.

His other hand was freed, and Estlin pulled himself from the bed, rolling to the floor, no strength in his bones. He raised his hand to her cheek, his hand bleeding because she really did do a crap job of pulling the IV line and she's sorry and in an instant he knows Yidge. He pressed his other hand to her wound and it hurts and he's sorry. He knows it's futile, that the blood pouring from her breast is nothing compared to what the wide wound on her back is yielding and he can hear drums — thunderous, clamorous drums — and he's with her on her mother's lap. The air is filled with living thunder, the heads of the drummers nodding with the rhythm, their faces rising to the light. At the center of it, a small gleaming gong in the hands of a master, the mallet in his hand dancing faster than the eye can follow, the ringing voice of his fingers in the center of the song. Her mother pulls her closer, takes up her hands and claps with them. The sound can't penetrate the drums, but she is still a part of this music, a part of it, and she's never heard anything so big in her life....

And Yidge is gone. The pain is gone and there's only the dark and the Waes drawing the experience through him, feeding on it.

The man grabbed the back of his shirt. Estlin struggled, trying to yank himself from all contact, trying to close the open corner of his mind. His elbows snapped his arms against his chest in a puppet's dance, lifting hard against no resistance, though he felt the weight as he was heaved up and planted on his feet. Red mist filled his mind as the Waes celebrated their discovery of death, soaking in its details with morbid delight. He tried to block the sharp wet pull in his head and failed. He failed until he fell against the nearest wall, which was the floor, and cracked his head against it.

— « o » —

Jeanette woke, feeling as though she'd just turned off the light. The clock betrayed that idea. It was three in the morning, and she was wide awake. *No alarms*, she thought. There was a knock at the door. It was Nia's distinctive, insistent knock.

"Wake up, Jean," Nia called. "The captain wants you."

Jeanette rose and opened the door. "What?"

"Captain wants you on deck." Nia pushed into the cabin. "Get your shoes on."

"Where are we?" Jeanette asked. "Still following the carrier?"

Nia grabbed Jeanette's coat from the closet rail and held it open, sleeves ready. "You have to see this."

Jeanette pulled her coat on over her nightclothes as Nia dragged her up the stairs and outside. Stepping from the dark hallway out into the night, she found the deck eerily quiet. She realized that the engine was silent. They were drifting. The deck lights were off and the dark forms of the crew lined the rail. Nia pushed her forward.

The moon was a ghostly slice of gray. Here, there was no skyward wash of city light to diminish the starscape. The latticework of stars touched the horizon. Over the side, all she could see was the subtle shifting of the brightest stars reflected in the calm water. She realized that the stars beneath them were alive. They were passing through a luminous swarm of cuttlefish. "Nia get the cameras."

"We're recording," Nia answered in hushed tones. "There are so many the captain had to cut the engines."

Jeanette realized that no one was saying anything, that she herself had barely whispered. The cuttlefish were three feet long. She knew they communicated with each other by shifting the color of their skins. When breeding, they converged on an area and cast off their usual camouflage patterns for brilliant displays. The density of the swarm was phenomenal.

"What do they know that we don't?" Jeanette asked herself.

"What did you say?" Neil Arnot said, standing at the rail.

Jeanette hadn't recognized the captain in the dark. "They're big. Sepia apama, I think," she said. "But this is the wrong place, the wrong month for a swarm."

"What would attract them?"

"I don't know." She gripped the rail and leaned over it to watch the smooth movements of the cuttlefish and the colors shifting across their skins. They were holding pace with the drifting ship, riding the surface, dancing for them. Jeanette felt a surge of emotion, so wondrous and powerful that it took her a moment to recognize it as fear. The water darkened as the swarm dove, leaving them behind. A black mass split the water a hundred yards from the *Arctic Sunrise*. Jeanette thought it was a whale breaching, but it kept rising. It was a conning tower, so close they could hear the water rolling back from the body of the submarine.

"Deck lights, cabin lights, spot lights, now!" Captain Arnot broke the silence. "All of you."

"Captain?" Bjorn, with his open query, spoke for the crew. The collective sense of stunned immobility hadn't broken.

The captain was on the stairs to the bridge. "That sub is here to look at us, and we're running dark and quiet. Light up the ship!"

— « O » —

The mood in the production offices was grim when Harry returned from the embassy. His trip had been a waste of time, and he went directly to Stodt. "The great wall of China had nothing to say," he reported. "I had a small altercation with embassy security. You may hear about it."

"Close the door," Stodt ordered.

Harry pulled the door closed, bracing himself.

"Harry, the *Lu Hai* was adrift when the *Canterbury* reached her," Stodt said. "The ship had been crippled and boarded.

There were several injured and one dead. It was Yidge. She was shot."

Harry sat heavily. "They were there."

"The crew of the *Lu Hai* insist that they don't know why they were targeted or who attacked their ship. They say nothing was taken, that the *Canterbury* arrived before the pirates could complete their raid. But they didn't issue a distress call until the *Canterbury* saw smoke rising and initiated contact."

"Who did it?" Harry asked bluntly.

"The attackers had air support," Stodt continued. "The *Canterbury* caught a glimpse of multiple radar contacts then their radar was jammed." Stodt sifted through the pages on his desk. "There are several carriers in the area — the *Viraat*, the *Ark Royal*, the *Asturias*. But the American carrier left the strait two hours ago. It jumped a squadron of Prowlers into the air. They have the capabilities."

"It's them," Harry stated numbly.

"The Australians tell us the *Washington* is heading for the Hawaiian Islands. The Americans say she's returning to Yokosuka. The *Canterbury* will escort the *Lu Hai* into Christchurch. We'll promise not to take the ship apart, and then as soon as she's in port, we'll take that ship apart."

"What's next?" Harry asked.

"We advance a search and rescue team into the field with complete air support. I'll be with them. We'll be airborne in a few hours, and I've arranged a stopover in Apia. It's mid-route and likely our best staging ground. I'm dispatching the *Te Kaha* out of Devonport. You're going. The helicopter is on its way. It'll have to refuel here." Stodt checked his watch. "Grab what you need. I have a car waiting to take you to the airbase."

"Should I contact Yidge's family?"

"Not yet," answered Stodt. "When the *Lu Hai* is in port and her identity has been confirmed by the conventional authorities, we'll contact the Korean embassy. I'm sorry."

"I thought she was born here." Harry knew that Stodt had handled all the security clearances and had interviewed Yidge.

"She was," Stodt answered. "Her parents are Korean."

"This makes no sense," Harry said. Yidge's name had appeared near the top of a short list of potential assistants, already highlighted because of her linguistic skills. She'd worked in Harry's lab for a term, and he'd hired her without question. When that trust was broken, his only thought was that he'd exposed her position by sending her out with the alien sample and her family might have been targeted. Now, he was left with no understanding.

Chapter Twelve

He ran, hooves pounding the earth, his eyes full of prairie and sky. His mouth was dry, his head hurt like heat stroke, and an unnatural vibration had set into the meat of him. The muscles across his shoulders, and from his vertebra to his ribs, were throbbing out of synch with the demands of speed. The earth that had propelled his weight for a lifetime was suddenly gone. The air grabbed him and yanked him down, turning the sky over.

Estlin jerked awake. He felt like he'd left his bones beneath a cliff at Head-Smashed-In Buffalo Jump. The smell of fuel washed away the prairies. Pain sloshed forward and back in his skull with a vomit of memory that surged through the events that had driven him to try to crack his own skull. He'd lost his mind — he must have — head injuries could cripple.

Fortunately, he could feel his fingers and toes, he could remember his name, and the wash of white before his eyes was resolving. His hand was wrapped in fresh gauze. He let it fall aside. He was lying on a cot, the pounding stampede of his dream replaced by the shudder of engines fighting water. A pair of Prowlers were parked facing him, their wings folded up.

"You're on an aircraft carrier." Dr. Imogen Liev was seated on a stool next to him, her tidy professional attire incongruous with the environment. "The *George Washington*."

"What happened?"

"You had a seizure during the rescue," she answered. "We don't know why. How are you feeling?"

Estlin tried to formulate a response, but lost it as doctor pressed a fingertip to one of his eyelids, lifting it. "Liev."

"You remember me." She settled back on her stool, checking the time, her wrist adorned with a watch on a slim gold band.

"Why are you here?"

"I'm the expert on your condition," she answered. "Any nausea?"

"No." Faint orange and yellow spots were floating across Estlin's field of view. He was fairly certain this wasn't a concussion symptom.

"They tried to move you to the sickbay, but the aliens became agitated. It seems you are their pet human. The recovery team found it useful. Transporting them required no persuasion once they were extracting you. Do you want to talk about what happened?"

"No." Estlin thought of the red mist. The invasive image was not meant as an enquiry, but Wae responded. A fine spray of red hit the high ceiling. The splash of color was unfixed from its canvas, tracking with his eyes. The wide beams of structural steel above him, all painted white, reminded him of ribs. "Where are they?"

"Behind you."

"I'm not staying here." Estlin turned to see the waetapu, both of them, hanging from the metal bars of an enclosure. The cage of metal mesh and chain link fencing was built into the corner of the hangar, making use of the existing walls, ceiling and floor. It was brightly illuminated. The waetapu were surrounded by observers, but Estlin knew he had their attention. He tried to pretend he wasn't seeing spots, tried not to respond. "I'm done — with this, with them."

"You're at the center of the most momentous event in human history, and you want to scurry home to your derelict farm?" Dr. Liev was incredulous.

"I'm leaving," Estlin answered, annoyed. He'd moved numerous times without giving the doctor his forwarding address.

"You aren't going anywhere."

"Right." He pushed himself up off the cot. It worked very well, his feet stayed at the bottom of his legs and everything. He turned away from the enclosure and started walking. He stumbled, barely recovered his balance and kept going, blaming the shifting deck for his troubles. This minimal exertion put him into a cold sweat.

"Don't waste everyone's time," Liev called after him.

The walls of the hangar were changing color. He was acutely aware of the number of people on the deck, more aware than he ever was with humans. He considered the risk to them all, just being in a room with aliens that liked the color of their insides. He looked for an exit.

A familiar looking soldier jogged across the hangar deck to fall into step with him, but the brush cuts and fatigues made them all look familiar, and Estlin was focused on getting as far from the enclosure as possible.

"Where are you going?" the man asked.

"Away. I'm leaving," Estlin answered. He was glad his feet were staying beneath him, but they were collecting a lot of the blood he needed for his brain.

"You know you're on a carrier?"

"Am I a prisoner?"

"Of course not."

"I want off." Estlin reached the far side of the hangar and turned to follow the wall, sliding one hand along it for navigation and balance.

"We're in the middle of the South Pacific. There's nowhere to go."

"You have planes." Estlin tripped over his feet, catching himself against a steel support beam protruding from the wall.

"Sit before you fall down," the man suggested. "You want me to call that doctor over here?"

"No," he answered, letting himself slide down to sit on the deck. He looked over at the guy's boots, recognized them and laughed. "You."

"I'm Sergeant Malone. Do you remember me from your flight to Wellington?" Malone crouched next to him and offered his hand. "I've been assigned to your personal security detail."

Estlin laughed harder, which actually hurt. His side hurt, his head hurt, and he was wheezing with laughter.

"Is there a problem, Mr. Hume?"

"Your boots, Malone. You've got a real pair of shit-kicker boots there."

Malone, to his credit, didn't offer any denials. His eyebrows lifted, and he gave a slow nod. "I was careful."

"No, you weren't," Estlin answered. "You brought a gun into a room with an alien that can make you see what it wants you to see."

"I take your point."

"They aren't our little blue friends. They're here for something."

"We're on the same page."

"No, we aren't. You killed Yidge."

"I wasn't a part of the rescue team," he answered simply.

"That wasn't a rescue."

"I was at the debriefing," Malone continued. "Miss Lee had a scalpel. You were bleeding."

"She was cutting me loose!"

"And what was she going to do next?"

"Nothing," Estlin answered. "She wasn't stupid. A half-inch blade can't compete with a gun."

"The risk was unacceptable."

"She wasn't a threat. He fired without warning."

"The risk to you," Malone clarified. "You're the first contact MVP, our only effective translator."

Estlin hadn't thought that he could actually feel worse. His head throbbed sharply. The blood on the walls defied gravity, beading and extending in spikes, surrounding him with red icicles. "I want out."

"I understand, but you need to consider—"

"Get me out of this room. I can't think here. The walls are red."

Sergeant Malone looked over to the where Wae and Waewae were clinging to their cage, their bright eyes fixed on Estlin. "What's—?"

"I'm thinking about Yidge. Because I am. I can't turn that off. And they know that's what's in my head, so strong I can still see it, and they think I want to have a conversation about it, which I don't. And I can't talk to you or to them because it all turns to color and right now everything is red." Estlin covered his eyes. It didn't help. "Please."

"Let's get you out of this room," Malone answered, lifting Estlin to his feet with skill and easy strength. "How far do we have to go?"

"Away," Estlin answered, as they reached a door. He misjudged his step over the knee-knocker and almost went down as Malone pulled him along.

"The ship is a thousand feet long. Is that enough?"

"Half," Estlin answered. "Less maybe," he added, as the door they'd passed through was closed and latched. It already seemed quieter. He wasn't sure if it was the thick metal walls or if the attention of the Waes had shifted. They hiked up the narrow corridor, all opposing traffic stepped aside.

"Okay," Estlin said. "Stop." He leaned against the wall and thought about throwing up. His headache had shifted, tucking itself behind his left eyeball, and pulsing as if it wanted to press it from its socket. He really should have asked Dr. Mir about stroke symptoms.

"Do you want that doctor?"

"No. I'm fine. I mean, I'm terrible, but I'll be fine." Estlin hoped he wasn't lying.

"What happened? How'd you end up on that ship?"

"I met Wae in Wellington—" There was a sharp bang and the wall he was leaning against shuddered. He looked back towards the hangar, fearing the worst.

"That was a plane." Malone pointed up. "You're under a runway."

"I met Yellow-Eyes," Estlin tried to continue, as though the violence of a jet slamming to a stop on the ship hadn't just rattled his bones. "We had a couple of technicolor conversations."

"We know about your ambulance ride. Start there."

"Waewae was with the Chinese. They wanted me. Dr. Mir wanted the ambulance for a test; that was their opportunity. I wasn't given a choice, but Wae followed on its own. I don't know how it got out, but I can guess."

"Guess," Malone urged. "We're real curious about its disappearing act."

"You should be. Don't think you have them contained here. You have to safe this place, starting with that hangar."

"What do you mean?"

"You've got jets in there with engines and guns and missiles." Estlin found himself gesturing wildly. He folded his arms across his chest. "Bad, bad, bad idea."

"You can't just jump in and pull a trigger," Malone answered. "Most ordinance isn't loaded until they're on deck for launch and turning on those birds takes specific skills."

"Has anyone with those skills walked through that hangar since they arrived?" Estlin could guess the answer and continued. "When you broke into the studio—"

"How'd you know it was me? Some psychic whatever?"

"I'm not psychic! Your shoelaces are broken."

Malone looked at his boots. "You saw my shoelaces while I was—?"

"While you were being careful, dancing on my ribs, the alarm went off. It was triggered inside the room, and I bet your man did it."

"What?"

"The guy by the door," Estlin said. "It can trick your senses. Imagine you're by the door and you hear the alarm *before it goes off*. You look at the panel and you see a button to silence the alarm and..." Estlin slapped a patch of air in from of him. "Either Wae flipped the trigger on the door panel from across the room with a wild electrical projection, or your man hit it. Tell me, which is scarier?"

"You don't think—" Sergeant Malone looked back toward the hangar.

"You shot the cameras even though they'd already been disabled. Was that pre-planned or an impulse?" Estlin asked.

"We missed one. I saw it move," Malone said. "Damn. You think it's that good."

"It's that good."

"I have to run that up the chain of command, but we need to talk about what you're doing next."

"Do I get a phone call?"

"When the situation is stable."

"A phone call would stabilize the situation."

"Are you going to cooperate?" Malone asked. "I need to know because they've brought someone aboard who they think has the skills. A girl. I've got a nephew her age, and I have to say, I would prefer to see you do this job."

Estlin thought it ironic that Malone was convincing him to participate by emphasizing the harmful to catastrophic actions being considered. Still, he was compelled. "I'm not going back in there until there are no bullets, no bombs, no fuel."

"That's going to take a minute."

"Good," he sank against the wall. "Maybe I could have a slice of toast? Or a plan? Could we have one of those?"

"I'll see to it."

"When you talk to the captain, or whoever you talk to, tell them that while I was on the other ship, the waetapu suggested...." Estlin didn't want to give information to those who'd spilled blood for it, but whatever came next, he thought it best if the Americans weren't surprised. "I think there's going to be another flash in four days."

— « o » —

The headwind whipped across the deck of the HMNZ *Te Kaha* as it surged across the waves at twenty-three knots. Harry was standing in the wind. The full sensation of movement was the only thing that calmed him. When he went inside, he paced.

The swift intercept course out of Auckland had brought the *Te Kaha* within sight of the carrier. The clear air gave them a view of the *George Washington* from twelve miles out. They lost sight of it when Harry had arrived on the Seasprite helicopter that was now cabled to its platform. The captain had assured him that they were making every effort. He'd explained that no ship could keep pace with the carrier. If it was running flat out, its own strike group couldn't keep up. Like the *Te Kaha*, the American destroyers and frigates would fall behind, particularly as their fuel reserves dwindled. Diesel could not match the unrelenting glow of uranium. Their hope was that the carrier would slow to stay in formation with its protective destroyers.

Harry gripped the rails as the ship heeled over. They were changing course. He waited for the *Te Kaha* to straighten out. It didn't. He realized that they were turning about. He released the rail and found the captain descending the steel stairs from the bridge wing.

"I'm sorry, Dr. Hatarei," he said. "We've been ordered back to Auckland. The air force is taking the pursuit. I'm sure they'll have a seat for you."

— « o » —

Bomani stood apart from the activity of the room, observing Sanford who was leaning over John's shoulder, inspecting images from the Chandra space telescope.

The phone on a nearby desk rang. The yeoman who answered it passed the receiver to John. "For you, sir."

"Yes?" John listened intently, his eyes still on the new images. "They're here. Where?" He wrote a three in the margin of his workbook. "Okay.... Maybe.... Why?" he asked, adding another note to himself. "No, I'd need time. Two hours. At least two hours, at least. Okay? I'll send them." He gave the phone to the yeoman and turned to Sanford and Bomani. "You're wanted for a briefing."

"What about you?" Sanford asked.

"I need to calculate how big the dust fire might be in four days."

"Why?" Bomani asked.

"Don't know," he said, his attention already on the computer.

"Do you have enough data to make that projection?" Sanford asked. "You can't."

"I know, but I have to. I said I would. Look, you're wanted at a briefing. Maybe you'll come back and tell me the reason." John waved at the yeoman who was their minder aboard the carrier. "Can you take them to Ready Room 3?"

"Yes, sir." She turned sharply and proceeded.

Bomani followed Sanford through the maze of blue-floored hallways, lost in thought and trusting the yeoman's lead. He wondered how far from home she was, this young woman in uniform. Her last name, Heron, was written above her breast pocket. Bomani had grown up in Karonga on the shore of Lake Nyasa. He'd seen many herons with their feet planted in water. He considered the sailor, her tightly bound hair, her dark skin and sturdy build. She was a specific sort of bird, one who had taken flight in a box of steel.

"Spirit of Freedom," she said, when Sanford paused to examine the logo painted on the wall. "It's our motto."

"It's a big ship," he said. "I'm quite lost."

"It took me weeks to learn my way around," she said. "The G-dub is 103 thousand tons of fun, over a thousand feet long and twenty-four stories high." She directed them down the hallway, mindful of the task at hand.

Bomani knew the aircraft on board were worth millions of dollars. It changed the tactics of battle when the tools of war were so expensive. He considered it to be a self-driving cycle, where the value of jets justified further spending on defensive and offensive systems, driving their price even higher. "It must be very costly to run an aircraft carrier."

"The strike group has an annual operations budget of approximately 500 million."

Enough money, Bomani thought, to dig the foundation for a school, fill it with bills, set a blaze and keep the fire burning year round. He knew that the true cost of the carrier was whatever it took to make a society believe in the fire.

"It's a floating town, isn't it?" Sanford asked. "With all the crew."

"My XO compares it to a college dorm," she said. "Ship's company is over five thousand," she said. "And we have eleven carriers." The yeoman's words were punctuated with the bang of a jet landing, a sound to which Bomani could not adjust.

It was difficult to think that his own country could power warships. The Americans had stockpiles of uranium, and it was unlikely that they bought any ore from the Kayelekera mine near his childhood home. He tried not to imagine it.

"Follow me." Yeoman Heron led them through another hall to a door with a large three printed on it. The pilot's ready room had high-backed airline style seats bolted to the floor in rows facing a wide screen. The first person Bomani saw was Sergeant Malone. Malone's attention was on a lanky man who was resting in one the chairs. The man's face was marred by bruises. He opened his eyes as they entered, raising a hand to wave.

"Hey, Sanford."

"What happened to you?" Sanford asked.

"It's a long story. I don't get to tell it," he answered wearily. "They want you to explain your theory to me."

"Why?" Sanford asked.

"Ask him." The fellow nodded towards Malone.

"He needs to know," Malone answered.

"You've met, Sanford," Bomani said.

"Only briefly," Sanford said. "On the flight to Wellington."

"I am Bomani." Bomani's offered handshake was met awkwardly with the long fingers of the fellow's un-bandaged left hand.

"Estlin."

"That's about all they need to know," Malone interjected.

"Right." Estlin roused himself to move to a nearby table. He traced a figure on the surface with a single finger. "On the flight, you drew this shape."

"The arbelos," Sanford responded, then took a seat and placed his notebook on the table. "Where to begin? Have you studied any physics? Any math?"

"First year calculus," Estlin answered. "About three times."

"The arbelos is a simple symbol. It's like drawing a semicircle to represent a dam. Imagine it as a reservoir in which you can build energy for a long-range transportation system."

"Long range as in interstellar?"

"Mr. Hume," Malone warned.

There was a collective pause. Bomani took a seat at the table.

Sanford placed the notebook in front of Estlin. "It begins like this." Sanford traced the equations with his finger as he told their story.

After a page and a half, Estlin's attention was drifting. He pressed the fingers of his left hand to his forehead and then his eyes.

"Are you all right?" Bomani asked.

"It's been a long..." he trailed off as though unable to complete the sentence. "I need a more visual explanation — more pictures, less math."

"But the truth is in the math," Sanford protested.

"He lies," said Bomani. "This is all approximation, all representation, and the geometry is perhaps more accessible." He took a pen and pulled a blank pad of paper across the table.

"You know what this explanation needs? Coffee," Bomani said. "Perhaps Miss Heron could help us?"

Heron looked to Malone.

"Go for it," he said.

Bomani put pen to paper. "Can I show you something? It is not in this," he gestured to Sanford's notes, "but where I started learning was with Hopf's fibration. It is a way of mapping from one space to another, transforming a sphere into a torus of circles, for example. But it can also be applied to quantum entanglements." He began to sketch. "I am not an artist, but I find this figure quite beautiful."

It had taken Bomani much practice to draw the figure with clarity, and he enjoyed drawing it now to ground their discussion. He introduced homotopy and the continuous deformation of one function into another in a topographical space. Estlin was progressively more attentive, mostly silent but sitting straighter. He tapped the edge of the page when he needed something repeated or explained a different way. As they reached the true work, Sanford joined in, adding clarifying notes to the margins of each page of his equations.

"You understand this is not about punching holes," Bomani explained. "You continuously transform space, folding until two equivalent surfaces meet each other, and because they are equivalent, where they meet there is no barrier. For an object passing from one of these surfaces to the other it would seem as though nothing had happened, until you unfold."

A klaxon sounded in the room and from the hall. On reflex, Bomani stood, Estlin and Sanford rising with him.

"Sit down," Malone said. "Continue the briefing."

"No." Estlin remained on his feet. "I'm feeling better. They're free. They're close."

Bomani raised his eyes, not knowing who Estlin was referring to, but still looking to the door. He saw a night heron standing on a table on the far side of the room, the feathers on its chest and shoulders standing out like spikes. A second heron was a hovering, like a hummingbird in stationary flight, but its wide wings were extended as though it were gliding. Bomani stepped back. The birds looked at him, their heads tipped with absolute synchronicity, then his vision blurred as though something was shifting within his eyes. The illusion dissipated, and he was presented with an impossible truth, starting with a shade of blue that did not belong on the earth. An alien stood on the table while, above it, another alien gripped the ceiling with wide spread limbs. Both gazed back at him with intelligent eyes.

"Did anyone see them come in?" Bomani asked. His heart was pounding. The aliens were covered with sharp spines, but did not appear to have teeth or even mouths.

"Stay exactly where you are," Sergeant Malone said quietly.

Yeoman Heron appeared in the doorway. The metal carafe of coffee dropped from her hands and clanged against the deck.

"Stay out and close that door," Malone ordered, and she obeyed without question.

Malone glanced at Estlin. "How'd they find you?"

Estlin shrugged. "I'm shiny."

"Shiny?" Bomani asked.

"I don't know why they follow me."

Malone picked up a phone without taking his eyes off the creatures. "CDC," he said.

"Where...?" Sanford sat abruptly, one hand to his mouth.

"They aren't from around here," Estlin answered. "I suggest you leave when Malone offers the chance."

"Located both subjects. Ready Room 3. They've joined Hume." He put down the phone. "Mr. Hume, the commander would like you to ask them why they are here."

"Here? Or *here?*" Estlin asked.

"Just ask."

Estlin snagged the pad of paper. "Bomani," he said and gestured for the pen.

Bomani gave it to him, and returned his attention to the spiny-faced aliens with yellow and orange eyes.

Estlin was sketching the aircraft carrier, his eyes both on the page before him and strangely absent. "They're *here* because I'm here, and they wanted to see more of your floating war machine."

"Will they return to the hangar if you go?"

"I don't know," Estlin answered. "Probably."

"Why have they come?" Bomani asked.

"That's a harder question," Estlin said, pulling his sketch from the pad to start again on a blank page. Bomani watched the scratching pen, unable to discern what was being drawn. Sergeant Malone picked up the other page.

"Wait." Malone placed a hand on Estlin's shoulder. "Wait." Estlin dropped the pen and looked up.

"What do you know about carriers?" Malone asked as he scrutinized the drawing in his hand.

"Planes fly off them," Estlin answered. "That's about it."

"Why did you draw twin flames below the water line?"

"I didn't." He looked at the drawing. "Okay, I did."

"This carrier is powered by two nuclear reactors driving four shafts," Malone said. "Did you know that?"

"No."

"Because from this, it looks like you've seen a schematic."

"That's how they...." Estlin stopped and examined the drawing. "They were showing me that they know where they are. See the three dots? That's us. The rest was just context. I wasn't paying attention."

"We've got a problem. Sanford, Bomani, you're leaving. That door. Go." Malone gestured to the far end of the room.

"But where—"

"*Go,*" Malone ordered. "Stand in the hall until someone comes. Go wherever they tell you to go." He dismissed them and picked up the phone.

Bomani checked his rebellious impulses. Before him was something he'd never imagined seeing, but backing Malone's direction was the warning in Estlin's suggestion that they leave when they could. Bomani placed a hand on Sanford's shoulder. "Come with me."

Chapter Thirteen

Jeanette leaned over the chart table on the bridge of the *Arctic Sunrise*, trying to make sense of the cuttlefish swarm. As she inspected hydrographic maps, everyone else had their eyes on a frigate that was fast approaching on an opposite course.

When its colors became visible, Captain Arnot took the radio. "New Zealand warship to the port side, this is the *Arctic Sunrise*. Good morning."

"Good morning Sunrise," the answer crackled back. "This is the HMNZ frigate *Te Kaha* responding."

"*Te Kaha*, this is the *Arctic Sunrise* reporting a near collision last night," Captain Arnot continued. "A submarine breached within a hundred yards of us. It dived again without making radio contact."

"*Te Kaha* reporting to *Arctic Sunrise*. There is an international sonographic exercise underway. We encountered a Russian Borei last night. There are more submarines in the area."

"Thank you, *Te Kaha*," Arnot answered. "Would this sonographic exercise impact sea life? Could it drive cuttlefish to the surface?"

"*Arctic Sunrise*, could you repeat?"

"We observed a cuttlefish swarm last night," the captain said, loud and clear. "Thousands of cuttlefish were on the surface. We urgently call for you to cease your sonographic experiments and assess their impact on sea life."

Jeanette crossed the bridge to stand with the captain and listen more closely.

"*Arctic Sunrise*, this is the *Te Kaha*. We have a biologist on board. Standby."

"Jeanette." Arnot pressed the radio into her hand. "Talk to them."

"*Arctic Sunrise,* this is Dr. Hatarei, biology professor. What did you see?"

"This is Dr. Jeanette Goff, marine biologist. The cuttlefish swarm was massive, at least one kilometer wide, incredibly dense. The location and surface activity were extremely unusual."

"Which way were they going?"

"They matched our course for several minutes and vanished when a submarine breached alongside us," she answered. "I can give you our heading, but they weren't with us long."

"I'll take every scrap of information available," Harry answered. "Jeanette Goff, are you from the University of Oregon?"

"Yes," she said. "I don't work for the university. I studied there."

"Jeanette, I think we have a mutual friend. Can I speak to your captain?"

"He's listening."

"Captain, the *Te Kaha* is returning to Auckland. I would like to continue on the north-easterly course you are holding. I'd like to jump ship, sir. Permission to board?"

The captain took the microphone. "You're a biologist?"

"Professor of Biology at Victoria University of Wellington."

"Do you know him?" Arnot asked Jeanette.

"No," she answered.

Arnot shrugged and toggled the radio. "Permission granted."

— « o » —

The Waes explored the ceiling, their hands and feet finding easy purchase on the exposed piping. Estlin knew they were watching him. They didn't approach him directly, instead, they followed the paths offered by the ceiling, moving successively closer and further away.

"Subjects remain in Ready Room 3," Sergeant Malone informed the Combat Direction Center, "but Hume indicates they know where our critical systems are — power generation and propulsion." Malone waved at Estlin and covered the mouthpiece of the phone. "Did they make any stops on the way here? Did they visit other levels of the ship?"

Estlin looked at the Waes and painted their paths back across the ceiling to the door through which they'd entered.

He imagined a fragment of gray corridor beyond the door and offered them the colors. The response filled the room, somehow existing in two scales at once, being both the size of the ship and small enough to fit in a single field of view. The Waes traced their path from the hangar.

"They came directly," Estlin answered.

Waewae was traversing the pipes of the sprinkler system. It arrived at a sprinkler head and curled its fingers around it. Estlin thought this was a bad idea and imagined spraying water. Waewae was intrigued.

"Don't!" he shouted as Waewae dropped from the ceiling, swinging its weight onto the single hand clutching the sprinkler head. The plumbing gave way and water poured into the briefing room. "Malone?"

Malone waved for silence. "They've damaged the sprinkler system. No, they are climbing on it." He hung up the phone. "Is this deliberate?" he asked. "A distraction?"

"An accident, sort of. I tried to warn it."

"I'll watch them," Malone said calmly. "Find the shut off valve."

"Right." Estlin tracked the pipes to the valve, and considered how to get to it without getting wet. Wae dropped from the ceiling. It skipped along the backs of chairs, leaping to the catch the valve and pull it.

"That was interesting," said Malone as the shower of water dwindled. "Can you tell them not to touch anything else, anywhere on the ship?"

"Uh..." Estlin tried to think of a way to do that without first thinking about touching the ship.

"Tell them to stay here and sit on their hands."

Estlin did his best. The waetapu were in a particularly responsive mood. They jumped onto an adjacent armchair, folding their fingers together and curling their toes.

"That's better." Malone positioned himself between Waes and the main doors. "You said they would get out."

"Did you think they were contained?" Estlin asked.

The door behind them clanged open. A marine entered, latching the door behind him. He wore a black protective vest, but the holster on his belt was empty. He stepped around the puddle on the deck, stopping once he had a clear view of the seated aliens. "Did they tamper with the ship?"

"No," Estlin answered. Wae's posture and facial markings gave it an innocent appearance. It was resting one hand on the arm of the chair. "Though that one's eating the furniture."

"Mr. Hume, you're looking better."

"You've met Major Forester," Malone said.

"No," Estlin answered.

"I was one of your rescuers," Forester responded. "Sergeant Malone, what part of the containment strategy did you not understand?"

"He couldn't stay in the hangar," Malone answered. "He was seeing things."

"Isn't that your job?" Forester asked Estlin. "If they touched any of our critical systems, if they even walked past them, I need to know."

"They didn't," Estlin said.

"You sound certain."

"I asked them," Estlin said. "That's their answer."

"They came straight here, looking for you?"

"Yes."

"How'd they get out?" Sergeant Malone asked.

"A mistake," Forester answered. "The hangar wall was retracted, damaging the enclosure. They vanished while repairs where underway. Command learned they were gone when one of the repair team asked if the wood pile needed to be moved."

"Hume suggested they could be that effective," Malone replied.

"You should have listened." Major Forester regarded Malone coldly. "Mr. Hume, can you tell me why they are here?"

"No," Estlin answered. "Here or *here?*" While he was asking Forester, he was visually struck by Wae's local sense of *here,* starting with a grid of open boxes, linked by gray channels. The boxes closed and fine red lines crept up the hallways, wiring the boxes shut. "You're securing this section of the ship, placing alarms on the doors and ducts."

"Are you guessing or do you know?" Forester asked.

"You know, so they know."

"The alarms will be relayed directly to the flag bridge, beyond their local manipulations." Major Forester was confident.

Estlin wondered whether the crew beyond the door could install and arm the alarms without making critical mistakes. How many doors Yeoman Heron and others had unknowingly left open to facilitate the Waes movements earlier?

"I want the bigger picture," Forester said. "Speculation is that they chose the South Pacific because it is a safe landing site — unpopulated and undefended."

Estlin envisioned the expanse of water and the waetapu answered. The water bloomed small rings of land, the land bloomed fire, the fires receded and left a faint glow. He saw this over and over again. He saw the bloom of red from Yidge's back. He stood, barely keeping his balance as he backed away from the waetapu. "You're wrong," he said. "They think this is our place of war."

"Why?" Malone asked.

"The Pacific atolls were nuked over and over again, by you, by the French, hundreds of bomb tests. The residues of war are here."

"Why would they land in a battlefield?" Forester's question was interrupted by the phone. He answered it.

"It doesn't make sense." Malone looked at the waetapu, who were lounging in their chair like a pair of contented dogs. "If they're here for reconnaissance, they are capable of complete stealth."

Estlin considered the last two days of his life. "If you aren't from here, you don't know whether our military assets are on land or on the water. You don't know if we paint our warships white or gray. Complete stealth doesn't get you invited to a carrier for a tour."

Major Forester hung up the phone. "The admiral wants them off. I agree with his assessment that they present a risk to the ship. A Greyhound will ferry them to Tutuila. Do you think they can handle a four-hour flight?"

"What's a Greyhound?" Estlin asked.

"Twin engine turboprop logistical support aircraft," Forester answered. "They transport passengers and critical cargo. I need to know that your friends can handle the catapult launch forces."

This was a straightforward concept to project, and it seemed that, during their arrival, the waetapu had observed the runways of the carrier in action. As far as Estlin could tell, the waetapu loved the idea of being shot off the deck. "Best translation," he said. "It is their joy to travel."

"Do they want seats?" Malone asked. "We could modify the cargo pod."

"Will the seats be made of food?" Estlin asked.

"I'll pass the request along," Forester said.

"Where's my team?" Sergeant Malone asked.

"They're en route to Tutuila. They'll secure the airport before you get there. You'll land, transfer the subjects to the C-17 and continue with them stateside." Major Forester checked his watch. "You launch in forty minutes. That gives us time for conversation."

— « o » —

Harry put his trust in the single steel cable, let the harness take his weight, and leaned out into the hot wind driven by the rotor blades of the Seasprite. The harness pinched, and the metal platform below him was rising on the ocean's surge. This was nothing like descending into a forest clearing — a long disused skill that reversed the captain's initial refusal of the ship-to-ship transfer.

The Greenpeace crew had offered to send a Zodiac for Harry, but the *Te Kaha* had been ordered to port without delay. The *Arctic Sunrise* had a green hull decorated with a rainbow rising from the waterline to support a white dove. Dangling from the winch, Harry glanced down at the welcoming yellow "H" painted on the green deck beneath him. The landing pad should have made this adventure unnecessary, but the pilot had vehemently informed him that the platform was not rated for helicopters the size of the Seasprite.

Harry's feet touched the deck, and he crouched, settled and released the cable. He stayed low as the free cable swung above him. His wave to the Seasprite was acknowledged and the cable was winched in as the helicopter rose and turned back toward the *Te Kaha*. The noise and blasting wind from the rotor blades receded, and Harry found himself sitting on the deck with no desire to stand.

Jeanette Goff offered him a hand. Her long red hair was buffeted by the wind, and Harry recognized the smile dimpling her freckled cheeks from a photo that had slipped from one of Estlin's books. She had curves enough to show through all-weather gear, strong hands and enough gumption to be on a ship in the South Pacific.

"Jeanette," he said, keeping her hand longer than needed. "Glad to meet you."

"You said we had a mutual friend," she said.

"Estlin," Harry answered.

"I saw the missing person's report," she said.

"I brought him down to Wellington," Harry said. "We know he was taken by ship. I hope you'll help me find him."

"Captain Arnot wants to meet you straight away."

"Lead on," he said, but found himself touching her shoulder, stopping her. "Jeanette?"

"Yes?"

"I'm glad to meet you."

She nodded and led the way forward up two flights of steep metal stairs to the bridge. The Norwegian captain welcomed Harry and introduced the core of his diverse crew, whose names Harry failed to retain even as they were spoken.

"Thank you for having me, Captain Arnot," he responded.

"I think you have a story for us," Arnot said.

"Yes," Harry answered. "Could we speak privately?"

Harry felt the collective chill in the crew that had just congenially welcomed him. The captain considered his request. He gave brief instructions to the crew and directed Harry to an adjacent room wi th a "We Brake for Whales" poster pinned to the door. Jeanette came with them, and Arnot allowed it, holding the door to a small ready room open and latching it closed behind them.

"Now tell me," he said. "What kind of trouble has a carrier battle group running flat out for home?"

"I can't say," Harry responded. "But I am trying to catch up to the *Washington*. I think it's going to pass through the Samoan Islands on its way to Hawaii."

"You've made a mistake," Arnot answered bluntly. "The *Sunrise* cannot achieve half the speed of your frigate. We won't catch the carrier unless it stops."

"The NZRAF is scrambling aircraft out of Ohakea," Harry explained. "They'll be on Apia within hours. If there's a speck of dirt with a landing strip out here, they'll pick me up."

"What the hell is going on?"

"I can't say." Harry caught the captain's anger and quickly continued. "In Wellington, we were — we are — sharing information. But it was decided — I was part of a decision that we not share the information with six billion people, until we could answer the basic questions that those people would ask."

"There are two people in this room," Captain Arnot replied.

"I gave my word," Harry said. "I signed legal agreements. And I believe this is the best course of action. Everything I know will become public knowledge soon, but it's not my call to make."

Arnot struck him with an unaccepting gaze. "This kindness — where you clutch a secret so we don't know the weight of the truth — it's obscene. Ignorance is a crushing burden. It is the divider between poverty and wealth. The true motive for every restriction of knowledge to the few is *greed*."

Harry looked out the porthole at the expanse of water surrounding them. "What did you see in Wellington?"

"Destroyers in the harbor," Jeanette answered. "Frigates. Breakers. Trawlers. Freighters. Yachts. The American carrier launched helicopters and fighters as it left the strait. They went after something."

"Did they get what they went after?" Harry asked.

"Yes," Jeanette answered. "The helicopters returned in formation, followed by the planes. That's when the race began. What happened to Estlin? Do you think they have him?"

"It seems likely," Harry said. "I need to get to Apia. Ideally, ahead of the *Washington*."

"And what will you do then?" Arnot asked.

"I know where I need to be," Harry said. "If you can get me to an airstrip, I'll have a ride."

"That would take a day and half at best."

"I was hoping for sooner."

"I can't do better," Arnot answered. "And I have no reason to help you. Tell us something. Start with the cuttlefish if you must."

The door sounded with an urgent knock.

At the captain's nod, Jeanette rose and unlocked the door. "Yes, Nia?"

"There's news breaking—" Nia paused to look at Harry, taking a quick breath. "It's not just the web. News networks have picked it up. They say the flash was a space ship — a stealth ship — and that little blue aliens landed in Wellington." She delivered the news with an apologetic gesture.

Arnot and Jeanette looked to Harry for a denial. He let the silence hang, then finally answered. "I can't *confirm* that."

Nia exhaled audibly. "There was a riot at Stone Street," she said. "Someone died."

"Nia, gather the reports." The captain pointed at the door.

Nia's expression clouded, but she obeyed.

Arnot closed the door after her. "You were part of an international response in Wellington," he said. "And you need to get to Apia because the world's dominant industrial military complex decided it should be running first contact?"

"That's a solid hypothesis," Harry answered.

"If I get you as far as I can, will you take Jeanette and keep her with you as a non-governmental observer?"

"I can do that." Harry nodded slowly. "What are you thinking?"

"The naval activity has been so intense Greenpeace dispatched the MV *Esperanza* from Hawaii to investigate. It has been underway for a week, and now it is here." Arnot tapped the map. "It is south of Samoa, but north of the carrier."

"They have a helicopter," Jeanette broke into the conversation.

"What's its range?" Harry asked.

"I'll find out," Arnot answered. "I'll find out if we can get it here, refuel it, hop you ahead of the carrier and set the *Esperanza* on course for Apia."

"Could it fly by the carrier on the way?" Harry asked. "Get a look at it?"

"Unlikely," Arnot answered, his interest obvious. "I'll check the charts."

Chapter Fourteen

There was a stain on the ceiling. Major Forester kept repeating questions, and Estlin couldn't maintain eye contact because the stain above him was growing. At first he thought it was a water mark, a stray splash from the sprinkler system, but the wet shine was a brackish red.

"Are they actually co-dependent or is it a manipulation?" Forester pressed.

Estlin had answered this, but repetition was the mainstay of Forester's interrogation technique. He pursued any variation in the answers and visibly disliked having a subject whose attention was drifting.

"They have complementary...." Estlin wanted to say minds, but the representation seemed more like *nervous systems* or even something broader, as though they kept their memories throughout their bodies. "Wae is a collector. Waewae is also a collector, but in more of a storage way as opposed to a gathering way."

"What *way?*" Forester demanded.

"The Kiwis named them," Sergeant Malone answered. "Yellow-eyes is Wae and orange-eyes is Waewae."

Estlin glanced at the digital clock in the corner. Forester's opportunity to extract and report critical information was slipping away. The red spreading across the ceiling reached the wall and began to creep down it. Estlin glanced at Malone, who was hyper vigilant, watching the aliens and all corners of the room at once. Malone would've commented on the blood beading on the rivets if he could see it.

"I need a break," Estlin said.

"You say they're going to knock out our satellites again," Forester continued, "but you won't say why."

"Sanford thinks the pulse is part of their version of warp speed," Estlin answered.

"What's coming?"

"I don't know."

"Your friends won't tell you?" Forester's gaze shifted from Estlin to the Waes and back again. "Are they scouts for a larger force?"

"I don't know." Estlin had given him the waetapu's answer. They were here as collectors. What that meant was another question, one he couldn't ask because he was on the edge of a post-traumatic stress episode. The sprinkler system was dripping red. Estlin stood, gripping the table edge.

"Malone. Sergeant." Estlin swallowed. His heart was pounding, a living rhythm in his ears. "Was Yidge left where she fell?"

"He needs a break," Malone said. He pointed Estlin towards a chair. "Sit down and chill."

He could hear the small hand gong sounding an alarm through the drums beating in his head. "Does her mother know?"

"I can find out, but I can't find out right now," Malone answered, pressing calm at him with one open palm.

"How'd he get involved with this?" Major Forester asked, then turned the question on Estlin without pause. "What's your angle?"

"Angle?" Estlin was sweating. "I want to keep the cute aliens away from the weapons of mass destruction!"

"We're working on it," Malone answered.

Forester wasn't satisfied. "Are they interested in our weapons?"

"No," Estlin snapped. "I don't know."

"We'll be going soon," Sergeant Malone said. "I like it when you're calm and they're calm *and you're calm.*"

Estlin took the suggestion and tried to quell his agitation. "We need Harry," he said. "He's the expert."

"Not happening," Forester answered.

"What if they want to go back to New Zealand?" Estlin asked.

"You're a lousy liar, Hume," Malone said. "Sit down."

"What's the plan?" Estlin wanted to sit, but the room was getting small. It was time to move. "Are we retracing our steps to the hangar or taking another route? They'll need to know."

"They don't need directions," Forester answered. "We'll take them in the containers we used to bring them aboard. In the hangar, they'll be transferred to a cargo container, which will be loaded on the C2. The deck-side elevator will lift you to the flight deck."

"What was the first part?" Estlin looked to the waetapu. Waewae raised its chin and tipped its head in a gesture resembling a nod as much as a head shake. "They prefer to walk."

The waetapu turned swiftly and started hopping from chair to chair towards the door.

"No, not yet!" he called out, then covered his eyes to block his view of them leaving as he imagined them back in their seats. The waetapu stopped. They considered the situation and presented their thoughts on it as they returned to their seats.

"They accept the flying container. The walking containers don't make sense to them." Estlin got a clearer picture of the hand-carried containers. "You had them in dog crates?"

"It worked before."

"You've secured a path," Sergeant Malone said. "Your men can button the corridor behind us."

"I'm not negotiating," Forester answered. "Tell them how we're going to do this."

"They prefer to use their own hands to carry them," Estlin answered lamely.

"Are you going to force this?" Malone asked. "I want them in a good mood for this flight."

Forester considered it. "I'll make a call."

Estlin tried to take Malone's advice and chill. He sat to encourage the Waes to stay where they were until Forester hung up the phone.

"It's time," he said. "The route is locked. No side trips."

"I'm borrowing this." Estlin pulled Sanford's notebook from the table. No one objected. The waetapu took off toward the door, stopping at Estlin's suggestion.

"Do you want to lead?" he asked Forester.

The Waes held their places on the walls while Forester eased passed them and set the pace.

Malone walked next to Estlin. "Do you know if that's their natural skin?"

"What do you mean?"

"Are they wearing an extra layer? Bio-engineered protection against our environment? Armor?"

Estlin hadn't considered this, but knew there had to be differences in atmosphere, gravity, temperature, light intensity — all the parameters he could think of and all the ones he couldn't. Some compensating adaptation had to be required. "I don't know."

"We don't know much," Malone responded. "The New Zealanders were strict. There were no x-rays, no ultrasounds, no scans, no scrapings. We don't know what they can tolerate and what they can't."

"You want to know how much force can be applied to one," Estlin commented. "You'd be more comfortable if you knew. How much to incapacitate. How much to kill."

"What?"

"You want to know if bullets would work."

"Bullets always work, conservation of momentum, but a bullet can only push what it can hit," Malone answered. "If I can't trust my aim or decision to fire, I don't want a gun. This ride's going to involve rapid acceleration, loud noise, changes in air pressure and jet fuel fumes. I don't think they're fragile, but if it goes wrong and they react badly? The seatbelts won't matter if they convince the pilots that down is up."

At the end of the corridor, a wide door was latched open and layers of thick netting were strung around it to enclose a path to an open cargo container. The double-doored container was six feet high and about as deep. Major Forester stepped aside, as did the crewman at the door, silently leaving the next job to Estlin. He followed the waetapu into the netted corridor. As they walked, the noise of engines above them filled the bay. The Waes covered their elbows.

"Why are they doing that?" Malone asked.

"Because it's loud." Estlin's answer was swamped by the launch.

"What?"

"It's loud!" he yelled.

The waetapu clambered into the container and settled on the seats welded into it. The crewman had followed them. "I'm closing it," he said, trying not to look completely unnerved.

"Okay."

The crewman swung the metal doors closed. Slots had been cut into each of them and heavy metal mesh welded into these windows. He threaded the cable lock at the base of the door, and added a pair of heavy fork seals across the container doors.

"Secure," he yelled.

The netting was released giving Estlin a clearer view of the Greyhound. The wings of the wide snub-nosed plane were folded back. Sunbursts were painted on the outermost pair of its four vertical tail fins and near the nose was an iconic Pegasus logo with "We deliver" written beneath it. Malone led him up the tail ramp. Half the seats had been removed from the aircraft to make room for the cargo pod.

Estlin retreated into the aisle as the crew pushed the container aboard. The waetapu's chariot rattled up the ramp with the bright ringing sound of metal sliding over metal.

"Sit." Malone directed Estlin into one of the high-backed seats in the last remaining row. The rearward-facing seat was equipped with a four-point harness.

"I can't believe this," Estlin said, watching an airman secure the container.

Sergeant Malone took a seat across the aisle. "You asked for it."

— « o » —

"They're going to hurl us off in that?" Bomani pointed at the transport plane turning on the flight deck as its wings unfolded. F-18s had launched in succession, their paired afterburners flaring as they left the deck in a display of improbable physics. The plane beneath him had propellers. "I would rather ride a helicopter."

"They don't have the range," Yeoman Heron answered sincerely.

Bomani did not explain that he was being facetious, that he had no desire to place his trust in either type of flying machine.

"It is quite frightening," Sanford agreed. "The flight surgeon asked me about my heart."

"It's not bad," Heron interjected.

"You've done it?" Bomani asked.

"Once," she said. "I may have screamed a little."

This was not a good answer. Bomani crossed his arms and left the window. He raised one hand to press the backs of his fingers against his neck where the heat of his pulse was rising.

"Bomani!" Beth burst into the room. "You're coming with us?"

"Of course," he answered. "It is good to see you, Beth."

Dr. Liev stood behind her, the leather bag still firmly in hand. Yeoman Heron led them to a room lined with well-used lockers where additional crewman were waiting. One of them pressed a green life jacket into Bomani's hands.

"Why do I need—?" Bomani saw Beth watching him. "Don't answer." He accepted the life jacket and pulled it over his head. "What an ugly green," he said to Beth. "The things we must endure."

Beth curled up her hands and closed her eyes as Yeoman Heron placed the life jacket over her head. The yeoman tightened long straps down to their limits. She checked the life jackets on everyone in the room, handed out ear protection and gestured her goodbyes. A heavy metal door swung open, and Beth's hand found Bomani's. They were closely escorted across the deck. Beth released his hand to be the first to climb the steep steps to the cabin door. Dr. Liev cut ahead of Bomani and directed Beth to a seat near the cockpit. Bomani proceeded down the aisle and found that all the seats were facing the wrong way.

Malone and Estlin were sitting in the final row facing a container strapped into the tail of the aircraft. Bomani could not see into the cargo pod, but he knew what was in it.

"Hello, again." His broad greeting garnered no answer as he took a seat behind Estlin where the wings met the fuselage. He thought it to be a structural strong point, and it kept him away from the few windows. Sanford sat across the aisle in the same row.

Leaning out, he twisted in his seat to look up the aisle. Beth had her hands in her lap. Her fingers moved continuously, driven to express an internal dialogue. Bomani found the tremulous movement of her hands was made fluid and beautiful by her acceptance of it.

"Beth!" he called loudly.

She raised her eyes immediately, almost ahead of his voice.

"Beth, my friend Heron says it is best to scream during the launch, like you are on a roller coaster. It is very helpful, letting the air out of your lungs, especially if it's your first time. So, I want to do it — I'm going to do it — but it will be embarrassing if I am the only one. Will you scream with me?"

"Really?" she asked.

"Oh, yes." Bomani nodded seriously.

"Okay."

Naval Flight Officer McElroy introduced himself, secured the door then walked the aisle, stopping to watch Bomani struggle to mate the buckles on his harness. He took his seat and spoke briefly to the pilots.

The plane taxied an incredibly short distance. The engines roar increased. Bomani pressed himself into the seat, gripping the armrests. The wait was horrendous and then suddenly over. The catapult fired. Everyone screamed as the wheels left the deck.

Bomani did not trust the wings until they proved themselves. When they did not drop into the ocean, he relaxed a fraction, satisfied that his shriek had not been pitched higher than Beth's.

As the plane leveled, Sergeant Malone unstrapped himself and stood, bracing one hand against the cargo pod and peering in through the air holes. Malone looked to Estlin.

"They're very...." Estlin paused in the midst of answering Malone's unasked question. Bomani waited with Malone, tense once more.

"Satisfied," Estlin said finally.

"Good." Malone settled.

"Perhaps you could tell me where we are going?" Bomani suggested.

"Tutuila Island," Malone said.

"Yes. Where is that?"

"American Samoa."

This, Bomani thought, made as much sense as any of it. He let himself sink into his seat, accepting the drone of the engines, accepting that he was going where he was going, and he would know the place when he got there. The sound of the turboprops was complex. His mathematical mind considered the air they sliced through, the speed and lift they generated. Listening carefully, he thought again of the beauty of harmonics. Another complementary sound entered the mix, he would have considered it part of the propellers' song had it not originated from the tail of the aircraft.

"Do you hear them?" Bomani asked.

Malone rose, this time shading his eyes as he peered in at the creatures. "I think they're sleeping," he said. "Estlin?"

Malone turned as Bomani leaned forward, both looking for an answer from their expert. Estlin's eyes were closed, his head was tipped against his shoulder and the headrest, lolling slightly with the movements of the plane.

"Sleeping," Malone confirmed.

"That's amazing," Bomani said, as Malone returned to his seat.

— « o » —

Harry and Jeanette were tucked in an alcove, sharing a window. Captain Arnot had cleared non-essential personnel from the deck as the helicopter from the *Esperanza* approached. Wave action was lifting and dropping the deck relative to the steadily descending helicopter. Jeanette swallowed and turned from the window.

"Tell me when he's down," she said.

"Sure," Harry said and then felt forced to watch the final inches as the helicopter touched down.

The pilot pulled off his headset and unlatched the door while the blades were still turning. The crew rapidly secured the helicopter to the deck, and the pilot hopped out and crouched under the bird, checking each of the cables.

"Let's go." Harry led Jeanette across the deck, climbing the stairs to the stern platform.

The pilot was wiry and deeply tanned. He leaned into the cockpit to pull out a bag and camera.

"I'm Harry and this is Jeanette," Harry said. "Thanks for coming for us."

"Did you know?" the pilot demanded. He shoved his aviator glasses up into graying hair that stood out in all directions. "You knew about the carrier. What else did you know?"

"What happened?" Harry asked.

"I am out there, where there is nothing to see, and the horizon line goes black. I think, *sheisse,* there's a storm I have never seen." The pilot raised the camera he had slung across his shoulder. "I have pictures."

"Of what?" Captain Arnot arrived from the bridge. He'd maneuvered the ship for the landing.

"The American Air Force was stretched across the sky. You can't go around the sky, so I dropped to the water." He held out the camera, scrolling through pictures. "Took these as they flew over."

"How many planes?" Harry asked.

"Do you think I counted? I was busy not wetting myself. Looking for a carrier is idiotic, so I was not looking. It's a big ocean. I never, never should have seen it." He flipped to the next frame and held out the camera. "But there's the mother, the CVN-73. Taking that picture, I get buzzed by a Hornet. The fighter came from behind. The pilot put it on its tail, drifted past me and suggested I fuck off out of their air space. We are not going back that way. We need to be a hundred miles to the left. I have no more range. You must skew your course and get us the miles."

Captain Arnot agreed. "Let's go in," he said. "And set the course."

"I will hit the head. Then, we look at the map."

"How long?" Harry asked.

"You in a hurry?" The pilot rejected the question. "An F-18 walked past me standing on its engines. You are lucky you still have a pilot. You have a dumb pilot." He strode to the cabin door and yanked it open, familiar with the *Sunrise.*

"He have a name?" Harry asked Arnot.

"Wilhem Behnke," Arnot answered. "I'll check the charts and kick the wheel. If the course shift takes too long, you'll be staying the night. We're burning daylight."

Chapter Fifteen

The sound had a shape: an uneven floor, walls and a low, solid ceiling, distinct from trees, overhangs and sky. The others were quiet, resting and digesting, but a twist in his guts had woken him. He released himself into flight. A slight movement, small but sharply defined, caught his attention. He chose his approach, making less sound than the wind. He closed on the flutter of life with absolute precision and swiftly kicked it forward to snap it from the air, crush it with fine teeth and taste its death.

Estlin woke feeling the sharp satisfaction of catching a bug on the wing. It made him want to spit.

He raised a hand to his mouth. He did not remember falling asleep. The cave around him was loud and airborne. The waetapu were awake, but quiet.

"What did you dream about?" Malone asked from across the aisle.

"Bats," he said, and shrugged at Malone's confusion.

Closing his eyes, Estlin listened to the shape the engine noise had in the cabin. He remembered Sanford's notebook, which he'd tucked in a webbed seat pocket. His fingers found it, but extracting it required his eyes. He flipped through the physicist's notes. The diagrams and equations were beyond him, but he kept trying to diligently read them and not simply let his eyes skiff across the pages.

It took him a surprising length of time to realize the curiosity was not his own.

— « o » —

"What's that?" Wilhem Behnke lifted his chin. "To the right. Two o'clock."

Harry squinted into the continuum of bright sky meeting brighter water to find the vessel the pilot had spotted. The co-pilot's seat came with a view that was hard to appreciate without aviator shades. The stopover on the *Arctic Sunrise* had lasted three hours. Beyond the course correction, Behnke had needed much of that time to eat, refuel, do a point-by-point check on his whirlybird and stretch out for a brief nap.

"A destroyer and a carrier," Jeanette said. She was tucked in behind them and had brought her binoculars. "The carrier reads 6111. It's South Korean. The *Dokdo*."

It was a short-decked carrier, designed for vertical take-offs only. Harry could see that the *Dokdo* was alive with small figures, moving with direct, collective purpose. Four white helicopters were winding up, their rotor blades a flashing blur.

"Is that a welcoming committee?" he asked.

"*Shiesse*. What is wrong with you?" Wilhem re-gripped the control stick. "Does anyone speak Korean?"

"They haven't made radio contact?" Jeanette asked.

"Nothing," Wilhem confirmed.

Harry watched the helicopters rise, long banners of white unfurled below them. "Look at that."

"What the hell?" Wilhem twisted for a better view, holding his course and speed. "Are they surrendering?"

"White's a funerary color," Jeanette answered, from behind them.

The sight of the banners billowing in the light made Harry feel the loss of Yidge acutely. He reached for Wilhem's camera, slipping the lens cap off.

"Can I borrow this?" he asked belatedly.

"Go for it."

The camera had a hefty zoom lens and took both hands to lift and steady. Harry located the helicopters in the viewfinder. "There's a marking on the center banner." He took several pictures, hoping the symbol would be resolved.

"It's the *hanja* for judge," Jeanette said. "It's also the symbol for the family name, Lee."

The rising helicopters turned in formation, heading west across the water. Harry kept the camera in front of his eyes, snapping a succession of shots.

"What's out there?" Jeanette asked.

"The Americans," Wilhem answered. "The carrier."

"That's where they're going." Harry wondered if they would attempt to land, invited or not.

— « o » —

The Greyhound was riding through a patch of turbulence. Bomani kept his hands resting on his thighs, fingers spread wide. They'd been descending for too long, rushing to the ground at an unpleasant angle. The wheels touched earth, and he held on as the C2 braked. The plane taxied briefly and finally the engines shut down.

The flight had given Bomani too much time to think and too much to think about. The result was a sort of static of the head, fuzzy ideas disassembling as rapidly as they formed. Returning to the ground did not settle his thoughts, perhaps because he was still trapped in the plane.

Estlin raised a familiar notebook over the seat back. "Can you help me with this?" he asked.

"Of course." Bomani unbuckled his seatbelt, grateful for the distraction.

"Stay in your seats," Flight Officer McElroy ordered from the head of the cabin as Bomani stepped into the aisle.

Bomani sat next to Estlin and compliantly buckled his seatbelt.

"Is that my notebook?" Sanford asked.

"Yes," Estlin answered.

"Can I have it back?"

"Not yet." He placed the book in Bomani's hands. "This page. I don't know what these symbols mean."

"I have tutored many students," Bomani said. He began defining each symbol on the page. As he progressed to what they meant in the context of the equations, Flight Officer McElroy came and leaned over the adjacent seats to speak to Sergeant Malone.

"What is it?" Estlin asked.

"They're extending the stopover here. They want time for a risk assessment and to prepare facilities in Pearl Harbor." Malone glanced at the enclosure. "Is that something they'd want to know?"

Estlin shrugged. "I can tell them. They might already know."

"Go ahead," Malone answered. "I need to go forward for a minute."

Bomani accepted that the lesson was over and waited until Estlin's attention returned to him. "How is it," he asked. "That you learned to speak alien?"

"I don't," Estlin answered. "They do the translating work. I just get what they send."

"And this is direct? Into your brain?"

"I have some experience," Estlin said, "with animals."

Bomani accepted this with a nod, then let himself see this battered fellow with new eyes and realize that perhaps he needed more than the bare acceptance of his presence in the world. He leaned closer. "When I was little, my grandmother told stories of a man she met when she was a girl, a man whose house was full of birds. There were swallows nesting in his cupboards and great white egrets standing on his roof. He was very old and told her that his friends, the vultures would carry him away soon."

Bomani's grandmother had told him this story when he was ten, and he had suddenly realized that she would not go on forever. Thinking of it brought a flood of other memories sharply into the corners of his eyes. "He said that the vultures were poets that did not write. They read their poems into existence, poems that whispered, sang and roared with sweet and pungent scents. She asked how he knew this. He said he could hear them and laughed when she looked in his ears. I imagined such people were so impossibly rare, that I would never meet one."

Estlin offered a little wave of greeting. "My house is full of squirrels."

"Grandma said that the bird house was a wondrous place, but mostly she remembered the stink."

Estlin choked on his own laughter, bracing his ribs. "You have no idea."

Bomani looked into the shadowy holes in the cargo box that dominated the tail of the aircraft. "It's strange. We know so little about what makes an electrical pulse a thought. Imagine the noise of a single, simple action. Reach out to lift a pen. There are signals to the muscles and signals from them, signals from the skin, from the eyes and the ears, constantly repeating and changing. How can they connect? It is incredible, to know what small pulse is the vibration of this machine, what pulse is a word you are thinking of, and what pulse is your memory of the sky that you could not see but thought of as we flew. How can they receive and deliver with clarity through the density of such subtle things?"

There was a buzzing from the enclosure to which Estlin responded. "They like that question."

The sound of the aliens was like a song that resonated in Bomani's sternum and not his ears.

"I have asked them why they are here, but not how they are what they are," Estlin said, his pupils dark and wide. "It begins with their fingers. Not all intelligent species have opposable thumbs."

Estlin began as though reciting from a book, translating the language of the words as he went. "Imagine if the smartest things on Earth were the trees. Long-lived, incredibly intelligent, but able to move only a few inches in a season, extending themselves up or down, left or right. Communicating without sound or gesture, and only with their own kind, only with those they were born amongst."

Bomani had once seen a pine tree releasing surges of pollen to a gusting wind. He'd stopped in the middle of campus to stare at this tree as it had sex with the wind. He'd never seen anything so alive.

"One day, a tree, home to so many bugs and birds and frogs and monkeys, knowing that it can't be heard, still shouts: *Get off!*" Estlin gave this shout its moment of silence. "In that instant, one monkey leaps. If you live a thousand years, you understand how landscapes and species change with time, and what will happen if, for generations, you encourage only the most responsive monkeys to live amongst your branches, to breed there and to drive off all others."

The temperature in the cabin was steadily rising. Sergeant Malone returned to his seat and appeared to relax. Bomani knew that he was listening closely. Estlin's eyes traced and retraced the unchanging space before him, as though he were reading the silhouettes on a distant horizon. Bomani could not help but think of the thorn trees on the savannah. The trees that could scream. When a giraffe broke the leaves of a thorn tree, it warned all the trees that it stood amongst with a scent on the wind. The grove collectively responded by filling their greenery with tannins, becoming unpalatable. This drove the giraffes out across the plains, where they would walk for miles in search of acacia beyond the range of the scream. The giraffes had long ago learned to approach thorn trees from downwind.

"The waetapu became so responsive that they could help the trees in basic ways, bringing water, clearing soil for seedlings, using their free movement to deliver messages," Estlin continued. "Imagine a symbiotic civilization, which advanced until further growth required the waetapu to build more complex things, carry more complex messages. Selective breeding continued, favoring clarity of recall, dexterity and, when it became advantageous, increased independent intelligence." Estlin was as focused as he'd been learning Sanford's equations. "The Waes reached the point where further amplification of intelligence was only possible by merging intellects, combining complementary pairs of minds. By then the waetapu were smart enough to build, in collaboration with the trees, equipment to manipulate genetic codes, smart enough to be living carriers of libraries and databases, smart enough to build space ships.

"The waetapu can receive, store and transmit ideas from other species because they were bred for it. It is who they are. While they served stationary beings for generations, their migratory instincts never entirely left them. Some welcome all opportunities to travel, considering it to be a particularly blessed condition.

"When the trees imagined a way to fold space, it was for the beauty of the equations. They had no desire to leave their earth. When the waetapu came to understand the meaning of the grace knots, the equations the trees had spent hundreds of years solving, they were the ones that were compelled to build. The trees had reservations. It came to the point of conflict, twice over, the second conflict arising when the first test platform surged into the sky and outwards for one hundred years only to be called back, the trees asserting the danger too great if the fold was imperfect. The conflict was resolved when the nsangunsangu learned that the waetapu were willing to spend fifty lifetimes to travel a thousand years to work at a safe distance. Their relationship was forged to its true and present depth, when the waetapu stepped from star to star and found that the nsangunsangu were right. The risks of the fold were so great, that for generations they found only the burnt husks of other civilizations that had tried."

"Nsangunsangu," Bomani said. "That is the Tumbuka word for thorn tree."

Estlin looked apologetic, as though he had stolen something.

Beth tapped on Bomani's shoulder. Engaged in Estlin's strange speech, he had not sensed her approach. There was a gravity to her expression that was unpleasant to see in the face of a child.

"Don't believe him," she said. "He thinks they talk to him, but they are as quiet as stone, as quiet as dead things."

Bomani knew that the creatures were in the container, but now he could see them, their fingers pressed through the air holes. Whether Beth could hear them or not, she definitely had their attention. He knew it.

She addressed Estlin directly. "Imogen says you hear them, but it's your own crazy voice in your head."

"Come back, Beth!" Dr. Liev called from her seat at the head of the cabin. "Come back. You have to sit and keep your seatbelt on."

"Don't think about me like I'm not here," Beth said, focused on Estlin.

"But you shouldn't be. You shouldn't be here," Estlin said, without thought to the girl's feelings on the matter. Beth's expression crumbled.

Bomani could sense the volcanic anger of a child rising. "Beth, you should sit down," he spoke softly.

"I'm right here!" she shrieked at Estlin, stepping between him and the enclosure. "Don't talk to the silence about me." She was pinching a bruised length of her forearm.

"Beth?" Bomani reached out to touch her elbow, gently pressing there.

"How can you sit next to him?" she demanded. "Stop it! Turn it off!"

"I can't. I can't." Estlin looked sickened, he pressed a hand against Bomani's arm. "Please, get her away."

"You're a thief." Beth's eyes were dark, her pupils dilated wide. "He's got drums in his head. How could you steal that!" she shrieked, becoming a creature of teeth and claws, scratching at Estlin's face. He raised his arms to protect himself and she raked her nails down them.

Bomani took hold of Beth's wrists. Hindered by his seatbelt, he feared for her bones as she attempted to wrench herself free. Sergeant Malone restrained her from behind, and Dr. Liev was suddenly there, opening the side pocket of her bag. Her hands made quick work of what she extracted. Bomani thought she was opening a bandaid, until she slapped a patch onto the side of Beth's neck.

"No!" Beth cried, struggling to remove the patch. "It's my turn!"

"Not yet." Dr. Liev crouched in front of Beth, letting Sergeant Malone do the work of restraining her. "This isn't the place. Your time will come."

Beth was settling, a lassitude invading her limbs and manner. "His brain is leaking," she said. "It's all around you. Red mist."

Bomani unbuckled his seatbelt. "I will take her." He did not allow the doctor to argue. He lifted Beth, and carefully turned to carry her through the narrow aisle. Flight Officer McElroy led the way.

"Is it quiet now, little one?" Bomani asked, as he set her in a seat at the head of the cabin. "Is it quiet?"

She gave a slow nod.

"You should have some water." He looked to McElroy, keeping Beth's hands folded in his own. She withdrew them to strap herself back into the seat, her eyes averted, and then rising to meet Bomani's.

"Leave me alone," she said.

— « o » —

Estlin looked at the welts on his arms. Few of the scratches were deep enough to bleed, but the sting of them was an echo from the past. He felt detached, as though his mind was tumbling down a hill.

"What was that?" Sergeant Malone demanded.

"Her medication wore off," Dr. Liev answered. "I was hoping it would last."

"Hoping?" Malone blocked the aisle as Dr. Liev tried to follow Bomani.

"It would have lasted if she hadn't been so overstimulated," she said. "She wanted to be ready to work. Now, she'll be incapacitated for hours."

Estlin snapped back to himself as Dr. Liev's expression of disappointment moved him near to violence. "You bitch."

"She was supposed to tell me," she responded.

"So that was her fault!" Estlin released the straps of the four-point harness. "You're experimenting on a kid!"

"Would you rather she was sharing your childhood? Or worse?" Dr. Liev argued. "Adults with your condition are incoherent. They're lost. They can't tell you if a medication works. If you had tolerated the drug trial, we could've worked together. You wanted my treatments to help children like her."

Sergeant Malone stepped between Estlin and the doctor.

McElroy returned carrying the first aid kit. He planted a hand on Dr. Liev's shoulder. "Sit down and shut up."

"Excuse me?"

"Buckle up. We're moving soon." The flight officer waited for Dr. Liev to obey, then took the seat next to Estlin and opened the first aid kit. "You need to clean those."

Estlin accepted an alcohol swab, which simultaneously cooled his skin and set the scratches on fire.

"It's getting hot in here," Sergeant Malone noted. "Is that a problem?"

"Not for them," Estlin answered.

Chapter Sixteen

Estlin pulled at the straps of his seatbelt and stretched out his legs, impatient and ready to move. The propellers of the Greyhound were finally winding up and the aircraft slowly rolled forward. The volume of the engines increased as they taxied to a stop.

"We're in a hangar," Sergeant Malone explained. He crossed the aisle and planted himself next to Estlin, gesturing to the container. "We'll get off when they do."

Flight Officer McElroy opened the forward passenger door and lowered the steps. The fresh air couldn't break through the heat. As the others disembarked, McElroy lowered the tail ramp and crouched to release the straps securing the cargo pod.

"Welcome to Pago Pago, Mr. Hume." The white-haired Sergeant Pollock boarded via the ramp. "I hear you have a genuine talent."

"I suspect you do more than secure cargo," Estlin answered.

"Ratchet straps are my true calling," Pollock said.

"Who's here?" Malone asked.

"Fleckman has command," Pollock answered. "He's a biohazard man. He would prefer it if we all bathed in disinfectant and spent the next few years in isolation. But Dontis told him to ditch the hazmat suits and take the leap with the rest of us."

"I'm sure that got loud," Malone replied.

"No. It was surprisingly quiet. That man has authority. Fleckman moved the gear and a few of his doctors off the airfield." Pollock glanced over his shoulder. "It might be nothing. Red rubber suits are a recipe for heatstroke here, and everyone thinks the cat's out."

"What's that mean?" Estlin asked.

"The aliens were in a city park," Malone said. "Your buddy, Harry, took them to his university lab, where, as far as we can tell, he didn't even close the windows. The Prime Minister dropped by, met the critters, went to a random public glad-hand event, met with cabinet, then dropped by every embassy in Wellington to issue personal invitations to the first briefing. No one wanted to sideline themselves with a quarantine that would have crippled the government."

"No one wanted a quarantine that would lock new players out of the game," Pollock added. "Fleckman's not happy. Please don't sneeze in front of him."

There was a clang as one of the fork locks hit the deck.

"And Dontis?" Malone asked.

"He has the corner office in the hangar. It's our show, but if he's not satisfied, this could get reclassified as a *diplomatic* operation." Pollock's tone indicated that this was beyond undesirable. "We're operating out of the *Cascade*. I've directed your other passengers there."

"Good," Malone said. "Who set the security?"

"Me," Pollock responded. "The hangar, the fence line, and a patrol farther out. Dewey's on the roof of the main terminal."

"Tell Dewey he's got the ball. These things went for a walk on the carrier, and no one even blinked. We need another distant vantage point."

"There's a hotel roof about a mile from here," Pollock answered.

"Ready," Flight Officer McElroy called out, releasing the last tether on the cargo container.

Pollock left them and took his position on the far corner of the container.

"Sit quiet," Malone told Estlin. "We'll follow."

The cargo pod was on the move, guiding hands sliding it across the metal rollers in the floor of the Greyhound. As Pollock and McElroy carefully shoved it onto the Greyhound's tail ramp, the waetapu popped the door on it and let themselves out.

"They're loose!" Pollock shouted.

The container lurched as all hands let go. It slid free to the concrete as the crew scattered. Malone sprinted down the ramp, leaving Estlin tangled in his harness straps. As Estlin freed himself, he saw the fork locks on the deck, removed by McElroy as he was unstrapping the container. Estlin didn't know how to explain to the waetapu why they should stop doing that in front of the Americans.

"Hume, get out here." Malone stopped, his hands raised. "Tell them.... shit."

When Estlin stepped onto the ramp, the Waes scampered across the hangar to climb the nearest wall and jump into the rafters.

"Stop them," Malone said.

The waetapu settled on the beams above them.

"I think they've stopped themselves," Estlin said.

"Christ. Why wasn't the door secured?" Pollock demanded.

"It was!" McElroy responded.

"You released the locks," Estlin told him.

"I didn't."

"They're in the plane," Estlin said. "Go look."

"You saw it?" Malone asked.

"It didn't register as wrong," Estlin answered.

"Commander Fleckman, this is Estlin Hume," Malone said. "The translator."

"Are they trying to escape?" Commander Fleckman demanded. He had a shaved scalp, bright eyes, and a severity of expression befitting one whose day job was dealing with horrifically dangerous contagions.

"No." Estlin stopped to ask the Waes, to confirm that his instinctive answer was correct. "They like the height," he said because the concept was direct. He struggled with the next layer in detail. "They're less impressed by the building material."

"Get them down," Fleckman ordered.

"Where do you want them?" Estlin asked. "Here?"

"In the container," Fleckman answered.

"But they know they aren't traveling, at least, not right away."

"How would they know that?"

The question came from someone new. Estlin assumed this suit amongst the soldiers was Dontis.

"I told them."

"Why?" Dontis asked.

"That's what I was told."

Malone looked around the hangar, assessing the space. "How long are we here?"

"Until I complete a risk assessment." Fleckman stared at the waetapu who were swinging around the rafters.

"Can we bring them down?" Dontis asked. "Tranquilize them," he clarified, when all eyes turned on him.

"With what?" Fleckman's tone revealed his intolerance of inane questions. "We have no knowledge of their physiology. We don't know what happens if you puncture their skin or if they could survive a forty foot fall."

"And I wouldn't trust anybody's aim," Sergeant Malone added, scanning the rafters.

"What?"

"They can skew what you see," Malone answered. "You're looking up and to our left. He's not. Hume?"

"Maybe if we had a wooden chair or an old ladder they could eat?" Estlin suggested, but he knew the Waes had spent the flight chewing on their chairs and, as far as he could tell, they weren't hungry.

"How did you move them?" Commander Fleckman asked.

"They go where he goes." Malone hooked a thumb towards Estlin. "Get in the box."

"What?" Estlin answered.

"Are you refusing?" Dontis entered the conversation with a distinctive interest.

"Wouldn't you?" Estlin asked.

"Humor me." Sergeant Malone pushed the container doors open. "I need to demonstrate something."

"Humor him," Dontis suggested evenly.

Estlin squinted at Malone, but stepped into the container. Malone closed the double doors and kicked the latch. "Sit down and chill."

"Those have alien gut juice on them," Estlin protested.

Fleckman peered in at the seats. "Do we have a sample?"

"No," Estlin answered flatly and turned to Malone. "Let me out."

"Trust me," Malone said and stepped back.

"Malone?" Estlin slapped the metal door with the flat of his palm. "Hey, hero. When do I get a phone call?" He looked at his hand and considered free-floating flakes of alien and potential new plagues.

Wae climbed halfway down the nearest wall and leapt onto the wing of the Greyhound. Bounding from the aircraft's wing to its tail, it jumped onto the roof of the container, landing with a thump. Estlin ducked. Wae descended headfirst down the face of the cargo pod until it reached the ground, where it unlatched the door, clinging to it as it swung open. Estlin stepped free and looked at Wae, who had climbed to ride the top of the door.

"It does like you," Malone said.

"So, it can work a latch," Dontis said.

"That's right. Latches, locks, interstellar travel — no problem," Malone replied.

"I want the shirt off your back," Estlin said, "for demonstration purposes. Fleckman, you want a sample, don't you?"

"Give him the shirt," Fleckman ordered.

Malone pulled off his shirt, handing it to Estlin, who tossed it to Wae.

Wae wiped its palms on the shirt, leaving a series of glistening slime tracks. It dropped the shirt to the concrete floor, sprang back on the Greyhound, and retraced its steps to join Waewae in the rafters.

"Stop it," Dontis said, far too late.

"That was a wasted opportunity," Fleckman said, approaching the shirt.

"Be careful with that," Estlin said. "It's the active version. The stuff on the chair has been neutralized. They are happy to stay in the hangar until it's time to travel in your big, far-flying machine."

"Our what?"

"The C-17 parked out front."

Fleckman's expression was distinctly pinched. "They stay here."

— « o » —

"Hope you don't mind bunking together." Wilhem held the door to a small cabin on the *Esperanza* open.

Exhausted, Harry was grateful when Wilhem offered to show them to their cabin. Introductions had been followed by aggressive questions from a crew that was not satisfied by his limited answers. The conversation had descended to threats that assistance would only be provided in exchange for transparency.

"In the morning, I'll take you to Apia," Wilhem assured them. "Assuming the weather is fair, which is the forecast. The ship is on course."

"Thanks," Harry said, following Jeanette into the cabin. He closed the door behind them and looked at the bunks. "Top or bottom?"

"I'll go up," Jeanette answered.

Harry pulled his wallet from his pocket and threw it on the desk. "I snore," he warned and after very brief preparations he was in bed. It was Jeanette who turned off the lights, climbing into her bunk in the dark.

"Do they have a space ship?" Jeanette asked. "I mean, of course, but have you seen it?"

"No," Harry answered.

"But you're sure...?"

"Yes."

"You can't blame the captain. It's a massive thing to take on faith," she said. "Even when you make the leap, it's hard to adjust. My mind spins around the idea."

"Mine, too," Harry answered. "Lyndie was good about it. Very quick to engage."

"I haven't seen him since Oregon. It's been years."

"He came to Wellington after he broke it off with you," Harry said.

"Broke it off?" Jeanette's tone argued the point, but she left it to silence. "He talked about me?"

"He wallowed on my couch for days. I couldn't stand it. I put him to work as soon as the stitches were out."

"Stitches?"

"He was fine. I pulled them myself. Eight or nine stitches. It wasn't like Lakehead." At Lakehead, Estlin had phoned him at the lab, needing a ride home from the hospital. "It was obscene how he was pushed out that time."

"Lakehead?"

"He didn't tell you."

"No."

"Well, Oregon wasn't the first. Lakehead wasn't either. When he called to say he was dropping out again, I suggested he visit me. I didn't know he was leaving anyone behind until he turned up two days later."

"I got a good-bye note," Jeanette said. "I'm already gone. Best wishes. Here's a forecast of your shining future without me."

"The squirrels drive certain people bat-shit crazy." Harry answered. "People who've never swung a fist, grab sharp objects and won't be stopped. In Oregon, it was the neighbor."

"Helen?" Jeanette's voice was quiet and full of sorrow. "I went to see if he'd left a forwarding address. She said she'd have the police on him if she saw him again. Her arms were bruised. She wouldn't say what had happened, and he was gone. I thought that I didn't know him."

"She bashed in his door. He escaped through a window onto the roof." Harry found himself thinking about those days more closely. "He took a few good bangs while he was working with me and accepted them like a man who thinks they're his due." The bunk above him creaked, and Harry looked up at it in the darkness. "Jeanette, I don't know more than what Lyndie said, and he didn't say much. But, sometimes a guy runs the numbers wrong, thinks he falls short on some equation for happiness, and lets go of someone he should have fought for." Harry cleared his throat.

"He didn't just leave," she said. "He stayed gone."

Harry had no answer. He kicked the sheets loose of the bunk and rolled onto his side.

— « o » —

"Wooden chairs, as ordered." Sergeant Pollock crossed the hangar floor carrying a scavenged weathered Adirondack chair. McElroy was with him, carrying a second similar chair. The low-slung, reclining seats reminded Estlin of the lake a few miles from the farm.

Pollock had a spare shirt slung over his shoulder. He tossed it to Sergeant Malone as they planted the chairs in the center of the hangar bay. "Anything else?"

"More cameras," Malone answered, pulling on the shirt.

Dontis emerged from the corner office. "There's not much space," he said, "but we have secure communications." Dontis spotted the wooden chairs. "Are they coming down?"

"They like high places," Estlin answered, taking one of the chairs for himself, relieved to have a place to sit. "They'll come when they get hungry."

"When will that be?" Fleckman asked. He'd stayed with Estlin and Malone, working on a risk assessment with his subjects in the rafters.

"No idea."

"On the flight, you talked about their star-to-star transport system," Malone said. "Any clue how it works?"

Estlin shrugged. "Ask your mathematician."

"We want their answer," Commander Fleckman responded.

"It was like a fable. A fragment of history many generations old," Estlin explained. "My impression? It's a dangerous, complicated, energy-intensive thing that took two intelligent species a long time to figure out."

"Why did they build it?" Fleckman asked.

"To explore?" Estlin suggested. "Because they like traveling?"

"This isn't a *Star Trek* episode," Dontis interjected. "Why are they here?"

"They haven't answered that question."

"They haven't answered or you haven't understood?" Dontis asked.

"Both," Estlin admitted. "I think I'm asking it wrong. But it shouldn't matter, considering how they can read us."

"Observer-specific hallucinations," Fleckman responded.

"If they can pick up the conscious and subconscious," Estlin said, "they should catch the question even if I'm falling short on translating it into a visual equation."

"You've asked about their intentions," Malone said. "What about the intentions of those who sent them?"

"What?"

"Let's assume they aren't accidental tourists. They are explorers." Malone pointed at the waetapu. "Who sent them? Who had the resources to send them and why? The tall ships were manned by explorers, but bankrolled by kings and countries. They are here on someone's behalf. Ask them who they speak for, who they represent."

It was a good question, an accessible question that could be broken into pieces. Estlin asked. The answer came back in pieces that he couldn't assemble. "They aren't here to talk to us," he said finally.

"But they like talking to you," Malone countered.

"Yes, I know. That's why it's confusing."

"Who sent them?" Fleckman asked.

The answer was unsatisfying. "They were born to come."

"What does that mean," Dontis asked, "if they have no interest in negotiating with us?"

"They aren't here to negotiate," Estlin answered. On this the waetapu were clear.

"Is that a threat?" Dontis asked.

"No, it's an exact translation," Estlin answered crossly. "It means that they — as in, these two, here in this room — aren't negotiators. It's not their trade."

"What is their trade?" Malone asked.

"Watching, I think. Collecting."

"Like anthropologists or like intelligence agents?" Sergeant Malone settled in the chair opposite Estlin.

"Too subtle," Estlin said. "How would you distinguish between those in a non-conflict scenario?"

"Is this a non-conflict scenario?" Malone asked.

The Waes latched onto the question while Estlin was trying to figure out how to ask it. He saw the certainty of conflict all around him. Waves of color crashed into each other, and a thousand black ball bearings dropped from rafters, sweeping through the colors to crack against the concrete and make it bleed. He couldn't speak. He couldn't explain that in the whirlwind there was no yellow and no orange, that the bullets had fallen from the rafters and not the sky. The watchers weren't here to destroy. They were here to watch. And, of all the things they had seen thus far, he knew what they had observed most keenly.

"What is it?" Malone asked, watching Estlin closely.

Estlin shook his head, twisting around as the image lost coherence and swept itself out, fading to empty air from the far corner of the room to the rafters. The door opened and Dr. Liev stepped into the hangar with Beth beside her.

"Why are they here?" Estlin sprang to his feet.

"You need help," Dontis answered. "We understand how challenging this must be for you with your limited abilities."

"This is a bad idea," Estlin said.

"Why?"

"Really, you need to ask?"

Beth took slow steps with her head back and her eyes on the aliens in the rafters. "They look like polecats. They're built for climbing, aren't they?"

"Is that what you see?" Dr. Liev asked. "Or do you see what they are?"

"I see them," Beth said. "But it's dark in here. It's dark around them."

"Introduce her," Dr. Liev said. "Explain why she's here."

"Why is she here?" Estlin asked.

"To communicate. Like you."

"Better than you," Beth added, dragging her fingernails between her tight cornrow braids.

"We want them to come down, and he's not helping," Dr. Liev told her. "Can you ask them to come down for us?"

Beth asked in a way that felt like falling. Her invitation to plummet from the rafters was so convincing, that the echo of it made Estlin rock back on his heels, trying to catch himself.

"Don't," he said. His protest fueled her confidence, and she pushed harder. The discontinuity in his sense of balance, manifested in true vertigo, the walls sliding as his eyes tried to track with non-existent motion.

"They won't answer," she said.

"They know she's a child," Estlin said.

"Because you told them?" Dontis asked.

"I didn't have to tell them," Estlin hissed. "They won't talk to her. They know she's broken."

"You're broken," Beth hissed at him. "I'm not. There are black spots in your head." She pressed her hands to her cheeks, facing the fluorescent lights above them with her eyes closed. "It's like he's yelling at a door."

Estlin realized that he was pushing against the silence, trying to maintain a connection with the Waes. He stopped. The silence fell with a smothering weight, like sand filling a grave.

"This room is empty." Beth looked at Dr. Liev, alarmed. "It's like you aren't even thinking."

"You can do this," Dr. Liev answered. "Introduce her."

"No," Estlin answered. "If she doesn't leave, I will."

"He's a liar," Beth said.

"We don't know much about you, Mr. Hume," Dontis said. "How did Yidge convince you to help her remove the subject from Stone Street?"

Estlin fixed his eyes on the far wall.

"We have overlooked your involvement, but if you think you can leave before the matter is resolved, you're mistaken."

"The matter," Estlin said. Yidge's face was brought fresh to his mind, the shock in her eyes. He pressed his fingers into the bandage on the back of his hand. The cut from the IV needle throbbed, and he realized that someone, at some point, had washed Yidge's blood from his hands.

"Tell us what happened." Dontis mistook his silence. "Let them tell us. Beth can verify your story."

The story was graphically splashing inside Estlin's head. He was glad the Waes had stolen all the color from the room and hoped that Beth could not see it.

"Come down!" Beth shouted, her hands closed into tight fists.

"You can use her to coerce me into helping you." Estlin told Dontis. "You cannot coerce me into helping you use her. Malone understands the distinction."

"He's not going to negotiate," Sergeant Malone was blunt.

"It's too quiet," Beth said, standing apart from them all, her eyes wide and wet.

There was movement above them and faint symbols materialized in the edges of Estlin's vision. When he tried to look at them directly, they vanished then re-emerged from the corners of his eyes, crawling on the walls. He let his eyes unfocus and glimpsed enough to know what he was seeing. Estlin realized Malone was wrong.

"I'll negotiate," he said. "Send her away, and I'll translate those equations onto paper for you."

"Equations?" Dontis stared at the empty wall.

"It's star math," Estlin said.

"Get her out."

"We haven't tried—"

"Out." Dontis cut off Liev's protest. "Go."

"I need a pen," Estlin said.

"What've you got?" Malone asked.

"It's math," Estlin answered. "I see it. I don't understand it."

"Bring in the mathematician," Malone ordered. "Our translator needs a translator."

— « o » —

Bomani stared at the stars and wished for a cigarette. He was trying not to look at the hangar, but the building was oppressing him. The soldiers had thrown light all around it, and men with weapons stood at every corner and along every length. It was where Dr. Liev had taken Beth a short while ago. Dr. Liev had taken Beth, and Bomani had said nothing.

He'd missed the sunset, reviewing equations with Sanford in a workspace on the C-17. When Sanford nodded off, Bomani had stepped out to stand in the warm night air, trying to dispel the impatient itch in his mind. He wanted another revelation, but the ink marks slept on the page, refusing to rise into any new configurations.

Beth emerged from the hangar. Bomani could tell that she was both crying and trying not to cry. She came to him, stopping when he opened his arms.

"Beth, what happened?"

"It was like an empty cave." Beth folded her arms across herself, showing him every bit of her heart sickness. "People were talking and moving, but it was like they weren't even there. And that man…. He's a thief, Bomani. Don't go near him. He thinks the blue cats are his and no one else should talk to them. He made them blank. He made them blank. He made everything blank."

"I think he wants to protect you, little one."

"He can't protect anyone," she said. "He's already failed and when she fell, he put his hands in her blood and took from her."

Bomani didn't know how to answer.

Dr. Liev emerged from the hangar, agitated and seeking Beth. "You should have waited for me. Thank you, Bomani," she added. "It's ridiculous. The aliens are loose. There's no containment at all."

"You think we should imprison them?" Bomani asked.

"I'm not talking about imprisonment. It's unsafe." Dr. Liev was irate. "They're alien — toxic excretions, diseases, unknown triggers for aggressive or defensive behavior — and we know they can bend our perceptions. It's idiotic to have them roaming free."

"If you think it is dangerous, you should not bring Beth when you visit them," Bomani said evenly.

Dr. Liev crossed her arms, her shoulders notched up. "You're wanted," she said. "Now. In there." She placed a hand on Beth's shoulder and directed her into the C-17.

Bomani stood where he was, all willingness to participate crushed from him.

"Wait," Sanford called, eagerly descending the tail ramp. "They want me, too."

Bomani followed Sanford to the hangar door, considering whether or not he would enter. The door was opened with military precision as they approached. He stepped into the well-lit hangar and found the cargo container resting near the tail of the C2 with its doors hanging open. Estlin was seated near the nose of the Greyhound. He had a pad of paper braced against the arm of his chair and was working deftly with a pen, occasionally raising his eyes to stare at the walls of the hangar. The ever-present Malone waved them closer.

Bomani looked for the two visitors that he knew must be in the room. Sergeant Malone caught his eyes and pointed straight up. The creatures were above Estlin, swaying on the steel beams. This, Bomani found, made it difficult to walk to where Malone boldly stood.

"Look at this," Sanford called. He was leaning over Estlin's shoulder to read what was being written. As Bomani approached, Estlin sank back in his chair. The pen dropped from his hand. Sanford now had a complete view of the page. Bomani stood close to read it with him.

"Oh, my," Sanford said.

"What is it?" Estlin looked at them both.

Bomani lifted the page to look more closely at the equations he had already read. "It's an orchid."

Chapter Seventeen

"**Extraordinary naval activity** in the South Pacific has been linked to an unidentified falling object that splashed down in the region," the BBC correspondent reported. "The Pacific impact occurred two days after an electromagnetic pulse of unknown origin interrupted satellite communications. Meanwhile, substantial troop withdrawals have occurred around the globe."

Jeanette's attention drifted from the report. Wilhem had woken them before sunrise and had spun up the blades of his bird before the pre-dawn light had warmed to color the high-broken clouds. A crewman on the *Esperanza* had given her a laptop with the latest news compiled on it. The extraordinary reports varied only in their degree of speculation. She found herself studying the geometric tattoo on Harry's forearm. His hand was bracing the laptop. They had split the earphones, each slipping one under their headsets. Jeanette checked the file's date and time of the report from Bangkok, which was followed by one from Al Jazeera.

In Oregon, Jeanette had found that Estlin had few friends and all of them were unexpected. During her university days, a party was a room full of students with the same major. On Estlin's birthday, she'd met a beekeeper, a mechanic, and the guy who cleaned the sewers. Harry was another of this difficult-to-define type — Estlin's friends.

Harry nudged her and pointed at a clip featuring a middle-aged man wearing a ball cap. He was being interviewed in a wooded park.

"I've met him," Harry said.

"They aren't aliens. They're cloned Moa birds," the man reported directly to the camera, embracing his fifteen seconds of fame. "They went extinct five hundred years ago but there's enough material around to clone them. They must've injected DNA into ostrich eggs."

Harry snorted, his shoulders shaking. "I shouldn't laugh, but he's a funny one."

"They were the shorter kind of moa birds," the man continued, dropping a hand to just above knee-height. "About this tall with spiky blue feathers."

"When you're around them, they can twist what you see," Harry explained. "They borrow from your imagination and, for that guy, it was all biotech clone-bird army stuff. It's how I knew Lyndie could help. I knew if they were getting into our heads, he could make it work both ways."

"What?"

"He's far better at that stuff than he lets on and not just with squirrels. He once insulted a camel by thinking the wrong thing at it."

"What?"

"I don't know what he said, but that camel was deeply offended. And his convergence range with squirrels is phenomenal," Harry added.

"He never talked about the squirrels."

"Shit. I thought…. Shit."

"He pretended they weren't following him, so I pretended." Jeanette said. "I thought it was pheromones, that by some fluke of nature he had the wrong smell. I bought him new deodorant. I replaced his soap."

"Look at that," Wilhem interrupted. They'd been closing on Upolu Island, but this was their first true view. "Look at that golf course. How long are we staying?"

They flew over the lush green course with its bright sand traps and patches of shade provided by carefully placed palm trees. It was adjacent to the airfield and a row of helicopters were parked on the green. The airport itself had planes of all sizes parked on every inch of grass on either side of the runway.

The tower directed them to a parking lot behind a hangar. Crouched figures wearing orange vests guided them down into the empty lot. A member of the ground crew jogged to the door as Harry climbed out of the helicopter.

"Harry?" he asked.

"That's me," Harry responded. "Where's Stodt?"

"In there." He pointed to the hangar. "Go now."

Jeanette fell into step with Harry, and then realized they'd lost their pilot. "Wilhem?"

"I will explore," Behnke said, pointing to the mixed assemblage of aircraft. "And find out about refueling."

At the hangar door, they met a soldier with a clipboard.

"Where's Stodt?" Harry asked.

"Who are you?"

"Harry Hatarei."

"Who's she?"

"She's with me."

"Stodt's in a meeting," the soldier reported. "Wait here."

The door before them opened and six Samoan officials emerged, each looking more dissatisfied than the next. Harry stepped back to let them pass, then led Jeanette into the office.

"You made good time," Major General Stodt said. "The carrier hasn't arrived yet."

"I don't think the waetapu are aboard. Yesterday, our pilot photographed a northbound convoy of American aircraft." Harry handed Stodt the memory card from Wilhem's camera. They'd copied the images onto the laptop and stowed it on the helicopter. "The question is: are they're still here?"

"All requests to fly into Pago Pago have been denied," Stodt said. "A contingent from the carrier is on that airfield, and there's a squadron of fighters flying patrols out of Ofu. But we've no direct confirmation. There's not enough intelligence to act."

"What do we need and how do we get it?" Harry asked.

"I don't know," Stodt answered. "Give politicians enough time, and they start thinking. There was a riot in Wellington this morning. A crowd decided to go over the fence at Stone Street. One of them landed headfirst."

"I heard," said Harry.

"The newscasters are burning to get the real story, and the internet's a four-alarm fire," Stodt continued. "American Samoa went off-line two hours ago. A transformer blew. It blacked out part of Pago Pago and crashed their hub. That's not a coincidence."

"We need to get over there."

"The Samoans have explicitly forbidden the launch of any offensive from this airfield."

"That's fair," Jeanette said, joining the conversation.

"This is Dr. Goff. Biologist. She got me here. She also observed an unusual cuttlefish swarm. I think the cuttlefish were trying to follow the carrier. Any other sightings? Dolphins? Whales?"

"Nothing I've heard about. You want to tap Bernie to follow up on it?"

"He's here?"

"Find him," Stodt said. "And stay close."

— « o » —

Estlin had to pee. He considered asking for permission or directions, but he knew where the toilet was, and he didn't want permission. He got up.

"Where are you going?" Sergeant Malone asked.

"The toilet," Estlin answered. He tried to ignore Malone, who followed him across the hangar. The door to the restroom was adjacent to the office. There was a phone in the office and Estlin considered fighting to use it, but he had to pee first.

At the restroom, Estlin stopped and blocked the door. "Do you think I'm going to climb out the window?"

"There's no window, and the vents are too small," Malone answered.

"You would know that." Estlin pressed through the door, Malone behind him. "Can't you wait outside?"

"We should talk."

The restroom had a single stall, a urinal and sink. It was close quarters for company. "I actually need to use the facilities. I'm not looking for a private conversation."

"I need to know if you have any special needs."

"Special needs?" Estlin wanted to make a crass remark, but his brain failed to provide one.

"Do you need anything to manage your condition," Sergeant Malone persisted. "Medication?"

"No."

"Do you self-medicate?"

"No. Narcotics and I don't get along." Estlin chose the stall. "Turn on a tap, will you?"

Malone obliged, but Estlin's waterworks would not cooperate. He abandoned the effort. "When do I get my phone call?"

"When the situation is—"

"Don't say it. The might-is-right crap isn't going to fly. The world knows they're here. If someone hasn't tracked them to this inch of earth, they will. Should I look forward to being hijacked by the Russians?"

"You're safe."

"Right."

"Dr. Liev's the expert, and she says you're not rare, you're impossible."

"What?"

"An irreproducible mix of genetics and circumstances built your funky brain. You're a one off, irreplaceable and therefore invaluable. I have your back. You don't have to worry about getting snatched."

"Do you think I have Stockholm's Syndrome? I'm not embracing your protection. You want me to make progress? Let me talk to Harry."

"You'll get your phone call."

"That wasn't convincing, Malone."

"You need something, you tell me."

Estlin considered the urinal. "I need you to leave."

Malone nodded and stepped out. Estlin knew what his life would be like if that pathway in his brain hadn't burned out. As far as he could remember, having a direct link to the rest of humanity offered only confusion and pain. He didn't want his brain unbroken, but he knew every contact with the waetapu was forging new paths and Yidge's death had burned a deep wide channel.

"Special needs," he said and zipped his fly.

— « o » —

Bomani stepped out of frame as Sanford discussed the new equations with the research group at Livermore via a secure video conference directed by Boxley. He'd scanned and sent

Estlin's transcription of the "writing on the wall". He'd also sent his own tidy copy and several pages of clarifying notes. But Sanford had looked at the page and made another theoretical leap, ideas that Bomani was still struggling to understand. He expected to listen to Sanford talk through his theories for their distant collaborators. Instead, Boxley thanked them for their work and closed the connection.

Bomani looked at Sanford and said nothing.

"They need time," Sanford said. "They have to work through the equations themselves. It takes time."

"We need Lazlo Anyos," Bomani quietly replied. "I met him last year. He spoke in Auckland. We went to the pub after, and he went off about hairy and hairless black holes. He knows these equations, and he knows how to talk about them."

"Lazlo." Sanford tasted the name. "I've read his papers. He's German?"

"Hungarian," Bomani answered. "All the crazy, crazy physics guys are Hungarian. I don't know why."

"We can't."

"Can't what?"

"We have to let the team at Livermore figure it out."

"Sanford, I asked one question. One specific question. They didn't acknowledge it. They didn't recognize what the question was. They will not work on it. If they do, if they have an answer, they will waste time thinking about whether they need to tell us!" Bomani felt his temper rising. He saw the refusal in Sanford's eyes. "This isn't an American secret."

"That's not what I said," Sanford answered. "Even if I agreed, you have to know that it's not a choice we get to make. Livermore would have to review—"

"You would let someone else say no for you," Bomani retorted. "Reject the help we need out of pride? Or fear? Do not assume that we can get this right. You are too smart for that."

— « o » —

Harry found Bernie eating a roasted banana. The Samoans were cooking in thatch-roofed fale, grudgingly feeding the sudden arrivals to the island. Woven mats were spread on the nearby grass, and Bernie had planted himself in the shade of a tree. The scientist did not appear to be happy with his banana, though Harry knew the whole situation had him down.

"I need you, Bernie," Harry announced.

"Harry!" Bernie leapt to his feet. "I was just...I was... How did you get here?"

"I got here," Harry answered. "This is Jeanette."

"Oh, hey, hi, hello." Bernie pressed a hand back through his hair. "Want some banana?"

"Jeanette's a marine biologist. Two nights ago she observed a very unusual cuttlefish swarm, drawn by our visitors like the bunnies. Stodt wants you to follow up. Find out if there are other sightings. If the whales are singing a new song, I want to know."

"Okay, okay," Bernie answered. "Cuttlefish? That's interesting."

"Is it?"

"Cuttlefish are *cuttlefish*." Bernie gave the name emphasis, placing his hands a cuttlefish length apart. "Three hearts, blue-green copper-based blood and they are smart."

"How smart?"

"Top body/brain weight ratio of all invertebrates. Think about the processing power required to drive patterns on 200 chromatophores per square millimeter of skin — not just for camouflage but for communication. I don't think there's much radio-tagging work on cuttlefish, though, I mean, they aren't dolphins." Bernie grinned at Jeanette. "I've never understood the dolphin bias. Save the dolphins, eat the tuna. Tuna live longer, swim faster and their brains are—"

"Nobody cares about tuna fish brains." Harry knew how far Bernie could carry a tangent.

"That's exactly my point," Bernie answered. "Think it has anything to do with the bats?"

"Which bats? Where?" Harry asked.

"They haven't turned up yet. Do you think they're coming here?"

"What are you talking about?"

"All the bats left Tongatapu," Bernie answered. "The locals are taking it as an extremely bad sign."

"What else have I missed?" Harry asked.

"Hodges has some *exceptional* results."

"Who's Hodges?"

"The guy with the near-field scanning optical microscope," Bernie answered.

"You've told me what that does, right?"

"It doesn't really matter," Bernie said. "The point is his sample lit up and when he turned off his laser source it kept shining. He sent the data. There's a scan that you have to see."

"What's he doing now?"

"Nothing," Bernie answered. "He lost his sample."

"What?"

"Well, it was very small." Bernie glanced at Jeanette. "It's not the only one to go missing."

"What?"

"Found you!" Wilhem's return spared them any further details. The pilot was gleeful. "It's amazing. Everyone is here. Almost everyone. If you have an aircraft carrier, you aren't here. But Harry, I met a very interesting Russian. He came on a Coaler, an Antonov cargo lifter, and he wants to meet you. He wants to meet you in a spymaster way."

"What'd he say?"

"It was what he didn't say," Wilhem answered. "I have never heard anyone not say things so exactly."

"Where?"

"Far end of the runway."

Harry looked at Jeanette. "Could you wait here?"

"No."

"All right," Harry turned to Wilhem. "Lead on."

"I'm coming," Jeanette insisted.

"I agreed," Harry said.

"Good."

"Unless you want to stay here." Harry turned to Bernie. "Do you have footage of the aliens with you?"

"Everything. I'm reviewing it all. Stodt wants a report."

"I want you to show her."

"But it's…. I can't, can I?"

"I'll stay," Jeanette said.

"Show her all of it," Harry instructed Bernie.

"But—"

"Good-bye, Bernie."

"Okay. Odd migrations," Bernie said. "I'll reassign the bunny team."

Harry followed Wilhem under the wings through the maze of mismatched aircraft. "I might learn more if you hang back when I meet this guy," Harry told Wilhem.

"Not a problem," Wilhem replied.

"What'd he want?"

"You," Wilhem answered. "And he knew to find me to find you. The Antonov 74's have range and airdrop capabilities. The engines are mounted over the wings. Looks awkward, but you can land one on any scrappy stretch of earth and it won't suck rocks into the turbines. See it?" Wilhem pointed down the airfield.

The Coaler's distinctive rabbit-ear engines were easy to spot. The Russian sat on the steps of the open forward door. He was dressed with casual practicality, wearing khaki shorts and a burgundy shirt.

"I'm Harry Hatarei." Harry stepped forward to offer his hand. "You were asking for me?"

"Dr. Harry, the expert on possums and other invasive foreign species. I am Vaska Pepel." He extended his hand, his thinning hair caught by the gusty breeze. "I am lucky to meet you."

"What can I do for you?"

"I must tell you there is a squirrel problem on Tutuila," Vaska said. "Forty-two squirrels were accidentally released yesterday."

"Squirrels?" Harry pressed a knuckle to his lips because he was talking to a spymaster and it would be inappropriate to laugh.

"Strong, fast Russian squirrels," Vaska answered. "A flight transporting them for scientific study had small engine issue and the pilot dropped all his cargo. He thought it would be most humane to miss the ocean. Of course, there is terrible risk when a foreign species is introduced to isolated environment. It can be very dangerous to all the native creatures."

"Very dangerous," Harry agreed.

"The situation must be dealt with swiftly, and you are most qualified to intervene. We have some luck. The squirrels are radio tagged. They landed in the mountains near Pago Pago, but I'm sure they have spread across the island. Recovering them will be difficult. Squirrels do not naturally cluster." Vaska gestured to the activity on the airfield. "You are busy now, but I hope we will soon deal with this danger together."

"Do you know the frequencies?"

"I have tracking equipment. It would be easiest if I give it to you now." He climbed the short flight of steps, reached into the plane and pulled out a knapsack. "I must go, but I wish you luck, Dr. Harry."

He placed the knapsack in Harry's hands.

— « o » —

"The Kiwis were reckless," Commander Fleckman said. He'd called Sergeant Malone to the doorway of the office set against the hangar's wall.

"Yes," Malone agreed.

"No biohazard containment. No containment at all in the end. They knew the aliens could digest cellulose and still kept them in an enclosure made of plexiglass. They may as well have built it out of gingerbread," Fleckman complained. "We know they can break down organics with the touch of a hand. What about metals? Silicates?"

"All due respect, but we've opened every door they've asked us to open," Malone replied.

"Which is a problem. I can't verify that the facilities in Pearl Harbor will contain them." Fleckman's discomfiture was evident. "And, if we believe Hume, they're eager to board our far-flying machine. They want to go stateside."

"I trust his translations," Malone said.

"Half answers," Fleckman responded. "He says they're willing, but why?"

"You'd prefer it if they refused or resisted?"

"Are they cooperating or are we?" Fleckman asked.

"I don't know." Malone looked in the office. Dontis was in the midst of a declarative phone conversation. "But Hume's making progress. We need him and time."

"Everyone wanted this stopover," Fleckman said. "Now they wonder why it's taking so long."

"How long do they think it should take to break through an interstellar communication barrier?"

"Tell me about Hume."

"He can take a hit. He's rolled with this," Malone began. "I don't know how he connects with them, but he does. They respond to his presence and direction. That said; he can only give us the answers they give him."

"Malone!" Estlin's shout rang across the hangar. "Don't! Get it off!"

Sergeant Malone turned and saw Dr. Liev standing with her hand pressed firmly against Estlin's neck. A soldier was in front of Estlin, restraining him through their interlocked arms.

"Let go!" Estlin shouted, pulling vigorously against the arm bar. "Malone! I'm allergic."

Malone sprinted across the hangar as the strength of Estlin's struggles rapidly faded. Dr. Liev kept her hand on Estlin's neck.

"Let him go," Malone ordered. "Now."

The doctor released her grip and stepped back. The soldier waited for Fleckman's approval, then summarily let go. Estlin stumbled away, scraping at the back of his neck with clumsy fingers. Malone pushed them aside to see two adjacent medical patches adhering to the skin.

"I'm removing these," he said.

Estlin placed a hand on his shoulder, steadying himself as Malone picked and peeled the adhesive strips off.

Dr. Liev didn't object. "They release on contact," she announced.

"You..." Estlin said, raising a hand to point at her. "Crap." Estlin's arm dropped to his side.

Malone stepped forward to catch him, taking them both to the floor with barely controlled speed. "Is he allergic?"

"No. He reacted strongly to a test compound years ago. This is different," she insisted. "It's a highly refined variant."

"What does it do?"

"You saw with Beth. It desensitizes them."

"He's out." Malone lightly slapped Estlin's cheek. Estlin's eyes were open but not tracking and barely flickered in response. "Beth was groggy, not unconscious. Why's he out?"

"He was agitated. The treatment works best in conjunction with a sedative."

"Why?"

"We need to corroborate his claim that they are communicating," Dr. Liev answered.

"He gave you a page of space math!"

"Beth will give us another perspective, potentially a deeper, more intuitive understanding, but not if he's blocking or tainting the process."

"You idiot." Malone rolled Estlin onto his side, manipulating him into what he hoped was a comfortable position on the hangar floor. "We could have stepped out."

"They've followed him before," Fleckman said. "We couldn't risk it."

"So you risked this? You deliberately distracted me?" Malone was irate. The waetapu had climbed to the farthest corner of the rafters and were grinding their spines. "Hear that? Good luck getting them to cooperate now."

"I didn't know they would react this way," Fleckman responded.

"I knew," Malone answered. "I've seen it before. They really don't like it when people kick him around."

"You're ascribing terrestrial meanings to their behavior," Dr. Liev retorted, "including human emotions. You don't know what that sound means."

"This is not your science project."

"Your objection is noted." Commander Fleckman ended the discussion. "Dontis ordered it. We need information from as many sources as possible."

"This is a mistake," Malone said darkly. "Expect consequences."

Chapter Eighteen

Jeanette followed Bernie under the wide blades of a Sikorsky helicopter. The tarmac was radiating heat from the equatorial sun, making sweat bead between her shoulder blades.

"I was offered half a desk in the hangar," Bernie said, as they rounded a cargo container, "but there's more space out here and better air flow."

The container had a green tarp tied to the roof on its open side. The tarp was tacked up with poles to create a sunshade. An optical microscope was set on a crate with several laptops stacked next to it.

"They gave me the whole pod, and then added a weight restriction. I had to leave a spectrometer on the tarmac in Wellington. But I've got the basics, and I brought my own tent," Bernie added. "I've got room to share — to spare! — if you need it."

Jeanette didn't respond to the invitation.

"The footage is all here." Bernie pointed at the set of laptops. "And I brought the cameras should we need them. But first you have to see this." He beckoned her to the microscope, illuminated the sample, checked the view and stepped aside.

Jeanette looked into the objective lens, adjusting the focus slightly. "What is it?"

"A little bit of alien."

"Seriously?"

"Look at the filaments. I thought they were structural. Then I noticed the periodic branching, smaller and smaller." He handed her a high-resolution image from a scanning electron microscope. "What does that look like?"

Jeanette saw a series of tiny fiddleheads, but the spirals curled the wrong way for ferns and the coiled fronds had finely structured curls on their edges. She tried to supplant this view with a cellular analogy, but didn't know what answer Bernie wanted.

"We thought these were inert flakes," he continued, "like dead skin cells, but I think they're the key to how they communicate. What if that's a multi-band high-frequency fractal antenna? High sensitivity to electromagnetic fields, I can accept. The advanced signal processing you'd need to interact with a completely foreign brain? That's a ridiculous stretch, but two days ago I met a guy who talks to squirrels."

"Estlin," she said.

"You know him?"

"We used to date."

"Really!" Bernie's eyebrows rose, but he held his questions to complete his thought. "Our space monkey could tell Estlin was coming before he stepped in the room. That's a problem. There's a point where physics shunts it all into the realm of improbability, where the signals we emit are so small that a single distant point of detection — the alien itself — could never catch them. The background noise would be too great. But then I found this." Bernie waved Jeanette closer and peered through the objectives of his stereomicroscope. "Imagine compressing all the components of a cell phone into a particle smaller than a speck of dust — power supply, receiver, amplifier, transmitter. Release these and let them drift where the air currents carry them, each relaying the signals collected through each other all the way back to their point of origin, maybe transforming them from our frequencies," he tapped his head, "to theirs. It's just a thought, but it would explain a lot of what we've witnessed so far."

Bernie yielded space at the microscope. Jeanette saw the wealth of unknown structures in the compact particle, but couldn't assemble the picture in her mind because she was missing the central piece. "Can I watch those videos?"

— « o » —

"They dropped a box of squirrels on the Americans." Harry laid out the contents of Vaska's bag in Stodt's office. There was a Yagi antenna and a multi-channel receiver. The frequencies programmed into the receiver channels were printed on a sheet of paper. He couldn't stop smiling. He believed that Lyndie was alive because he had to believe it. The Russians had the resources to know and the proof was in his hands. "The transmitters on the squirrels have about a ten-mile range. I'll have to go ashore to track them."

"How?" Stodt interrupted.

"The easy way or the hard way," Harry responded. "The Russian damn well said that I should be over there doing the job."

"I need an operational plan."

"I want to pull Jeanette in on this," Harry said. "She's American. Behnke can fly us back to the *Esperanza*. We'll beg, borrow or buy a Zodiac from Greenpeace and head for Pago Pago. They haven't closed the harbor. If we get turned back, I'll power up the receiver as we leave, and you'll hear from us sooner rather than later."

"The gear is likely bugged six times over."

"I don't think I care," Harry answered.

"Harry...."

"I don't need your permission."

"Yes, you do," Stodt answered. "How much did you tell the *Esperanza*?"

"Nothing," Harry said. "The story was breaking on the news. They inferred enough to see the advantage in helping. It'll be harder this time."

"And Jeanette?" Stodt asked. "Are you sure about her?"

"I'm sure," Harry said. "The best way to pretend to be a Greenpeace biologist washing ashore is to be a Greenpeace biologist."

"I'm going to regret this," Stodt said.

Harry didn't offer any false assurances. He packed the equipment. "Whatever happens, it'll get me closer to the situation," he said.

Stodt dismissed him with a wave to the door.

Harry stopped outside the office to refill his water bottle. Leaving the hangar, he decided to find Wilhem and send someone for Jeanette when they were ready for take-off. If she wanted to kick his plan in the teeth, it'd be best if they were already airborne.

— « o » —

Sedatives make it difficult to sustain anger, Estlin thought. He couldn't focus his eyes, but he was consciously trying to keep them open, because he didn't want to leave the hangar. Sprawled on the concrete, he bitterly appreciated Liev's assurance that, despite the swiftly spreading heaviness in his limbs, she hadn't suddenly and unexpectedly killed him. But she was wrong; her 'refined variant' didn't turn off his odd talent so much as shift its frequency. It felt like being caught in an undertow, yanked down to where sap was rising in the grass as worms slid beneath the turf.

The contractions echoed the actions of his finest blood vessels and the ever-moving walls of his guts. He did not like this confusion between what was outside and inside and tried to separate himself from the living carpet. He wanted the faster world of deep breathing creatures. He wanted the rhythm of heartbeats and footsteps. He demanded it. He yelled at the grass and felt the field shudder as though the wind had shifted, as though each blade was turning to follow the sun.

His mind slipped further, sliding into the lagoon to settle on the bottom where he became camouflaged. He took on the color and texture of sand as he stared through the clarity of water at the world above. His presence was noted. He was abruptly forced from this skin and had nowhere else to go.

— « o » —

"Harry! Wait!" Bernie sprinted to him. "Jeanette says you're leaving."

"That's right."

"I need a favor." Bernie dug through his pockets. "Hold still." He placed a hand against the side of Harry's head and poked him in the eye.

"Bernie!" Harry swatted the cotton swab away.

Bernie looked at the swab in his hand. "I missed."

"No, you didn't." Harry blocked the swab's return. "What are you doing?"

"I need a tear drop," Bernie answered. "I think I know how they're swinging the long range communication. It's completely creepy, and I might be wrong, but I'm probably not wrong because I'm very smart."

"What the hell are you talking about?"

"Half the people we sent ovoids have lost their samples. They escaped. So, here's the question: do they float or do they fly?" Bernie bounced on his heels. "They fly, swim, roll, and I think they can burrow. But if they have the option between air and water, they choose water — and we have a nice air/water interface right next to where we keep all our electrical brain juice. I know it's creepy, right? But remember, Estlin? His eyes watered when he met them."

"You think I'm walking around with alien bits stuck to my eyeballs?" Harry demanded.

"It's a theory," Bernie responded. "The ovoids contain structures that I think can catch and relay signals across a massive bandwidth. And they move around, mostly passively, until you try to pin them down for an experiment and then they wiggle away."

"Have you seen them wiggle?" Harry asked.

"Not exactly."

Harry took the swab and pressed it to the corner of his eye. He dropped it into the vial Bernie held. "I don't want to know."

"Yes, you do."

"Bernie, figure it out. And watch your mouth. I don't want to hear any second-hand rumblings about this until you've pinned the details down."

"Got it." Bernie walked away, holding his vial with both hands.

— « o » —

"Where's Beth?" Dr. Liev swept through the seating area on the C-17, passing Bomani and Sanford. Beth was resting in the forward cabin. "Beth, get up. It's your turn."

"I can't. I won't," she answered. "That man—"

"He'll be quiet," Dr. Liev assured her. "I took care of that. Now you can show everyone how good you are."

Bomani blocked Liev's path. "I must come."

"Beth doesn't need any distractions."

Bomani answered with unyielding silence.

"Step aside." Dr. Liev looked for Sergeant Pollock who was at the desk under the forward stairs.

Bomani took Estlin's page of equations from Sanford and presented it to her. "This is a small fragment," Bomani responded. "They were correcting a mistake, a gap, in our equations, our clumsy scratchings. They have more to tell us. If they try, you will need me."

"No interference," she conceded, and Bomani let her pass.

"Sanford, can you call Livermore? Ask them my question again," he said.

Sanford nodded. "It's good how you look out for her."

"Is it?" Watching Dr. Liev guide Beth down the ramp, Bomani could find no nobility in his collusion. He followed them.

In the hangar, the creatures in the rafters were buzzing as they had on the flight. Estlin was on the floor, and his unnatural posture drew Bomani immediately. He appeared to be neither asleep nor awake, breathing evenly, his eyes were open only to the finest slits. Bomani made eye contact with Sergeant Malone, who sat watchfully next to Estlin.

Beth stood in the center of the hangar with her head tipped forward, looking down instead of up. The creatures were suddenly silent.

"They are responding to her," Dr. Liev announced her vindication.

Bomani saw that Estlin's eyes had closed. He looked to Malone, who acknowledged that he'd also noticed. Malone reached out to check Estlin's pulse.

"They're coming down!" Dr. Liev was triumphant.

The waetapu slowly descended, moving like geckos, flat against the wall. Bomani watched them transition onto the hangar floor with the same slow steps. They paid no heed to Beth. Her arms fell to her sides and she bent at the waist, looking at the Waes.

"You will talk to me," she told them.

The waetapu continued, now moving like lumbering sloths. Bomani felt the urge to back away and give them the space, but Malone held his ground, so Bomani did, too. The creatures took positions on either side of Estlin and settled into a statuesque stillness. From their posture, it was a vigil.

"They hear me," Beth said. "I know they hear. I can be loud. Boom, boom!"

Bomani felt her yell between his ears. He refused to fear her. "Hush, little one, hush." He raised a hand, wanting her to stay back.

"No," she said. "It is my turn."

Beth skipped across the floor with small quick steps. The alien with yellow eyes rose on its hind legs, straightening to its full height. Bomani wondered if the light had somehow changed, its eyes seemed darker. The orange-eyed one crouched deeply and started crying with its spines — a sound unlike any Bomani had ever heard. He briefly saw a lioness with her teeth bared.

"Stop, Beth," Bomani said. "Stop."

Beth surged forward, and Bomani moved, too. He knew not what impulse drove him, but he was on his knees sliding to her with his arms spread wide before he knew that she was falling. He caught her, thinking she had fainted, but the word that came from his mouth was *sleeping*.

"She's sleeping," he said with such certainty that he convinced himself.

Dr. Liev was frozen across the room, unwilling to approach the aliens more closely.

"This is over," Commander Fleckman said.

Bomani shifted Beth in his arms to lift her. He stepped back several feet. The orange-eyed alien straightened and turned away from them, focusing its attention on Estlin.

"Put her down!" Dr. Liev protested.

Bomani locked eyes with her. "Do not speak to me."

Fleckman closed the distance between them. He checked Beth's pulse and lifted her eyelid. She shifted in Bomani's arms but did not wake.

"Take her out to the *Cascade*." Fleckman was absolute. "Dr. Liev, I want a word."

— « o » —

Pago Pago harbor welcomed them with a smiling billboard of Charlie the Tuna and the reek of fish from the canneries. Harry had contacted harbor control on VHF and asked directions to Customs. He eased the Zodiac alongside the concrete wharf, their wake rippling through a trapped patch of surface grunge, a mix of plastic bags, detergent bottles and finer detritus. He stepped off to secure the Zodiac, and then stepped back aboard.

"Now, what?" Jeanette asked.

"We wait here. Quarantined until inspected," Harry echoed what harbor control had said. They hadn't been summarily turned away, but this was going to be the tricky bit.

The single customs officer walked out onto the wharf.

"Talofa," Harry said. The greeting was the only Samoan word he knew.

"Where you coming from?"

"Greenpeace ship, MV *Esperanza*."

"Last port of call?"

"Wellington."

"Citizenship?" he asked.

"American." Jeanette offered her passport.

"And you?"

"New Zealand," Harry said, displaying his passport. "I'm just a chauffeur, bringing the lady ashore."

"Purpose of your visit?" he asked Jeanette.

"To get off the *Esperanza*," Jeanette answered. "Domestic dispute with the captain. I'll spare you the details."

The officer examined the passport she had offered him. "No luggage?"

Harry was ready to put both oars in the water. "Captain had her pack, then chucked it all over the side."

"Harry," Jeanette hushed him. She was good.

"He'll lose his job over this one."

Jeanette used a glance to tell him to drop it.

"I'm reporting it," Harry cut back. "We got one bag out of the water. It's radio gear for tracking seals. She's a biologist, see. It's the one bag she had to save." Harry opened the salt-stained rucksack to reveal the gear wrapped in heavy plastic.

"Open it."

"He's lucky he didn't ruin it." Harry worked the knotted plastic open. "If it can't come ashore, I'll get it back to her."

The officer inspected the gear and seemed to accept it. "To land as a tourist, you are required to have proof of exit. If you aren't leaving by ship, you need a plane ticket."

"Can I phone a travel agent?" Jeanette asked.

"Maybe. Usually." The officer scrubbed his chin. "But the airport's closed."

"Why?"

"A cargo plane popped a couple of tires — scratched a groove in the runway. Do you have funds for accommodations and a flight out?"

"Yes."

"Thirty days," he said, stamping her passport and marking in the date. "If you overstay, you'll be fined."

"Thank you." Jeanette hefted her bag to disembark.

"Jeanette, wait." Harry dug out his passport. "Could I spend a day or two here and see her off?"

The officer accepted his passport. "The visa's not a problem." He looked at the Zodiac from end to end. "The boat's a problem. I can grant you thirty days, but only with a cash landing bond."

"Sounds good," Harry said.

"Refuel. Resupply. Don't cross your captain," the officer advised. He pointed at the Zodiac. "If he wants you for theft, you won't be hard to find." He offered Jeanette his hand as she stepped onto the wharf; she looked brilliantly relieved and grateful. "When you've settled with me, you'll have to see the harbor master for a moorage."

— « o » —

Bomani knew that Beth had woken in his arms. "I have you," he whispered as though she were still sleeping.

"I tripped, Bomani." She took hold of him. "I fell."

"I have you."

"They wouldn't talk to me."

"I'm glad, Beth. They are very dangerous. The men they attract are dangerous."

"Imogen said I could help."

She's wrong, Bomani thought and sought a way to express it. "She's very smart."

"Sometimes very smart people aren't very smart."

Beth nodded. She prodded Bomani's shoulder. "You're having dumb ideas right now."

Bomani was thinking that he had Beth in his arms and he should just keep on walking. "I want you to be safe," he said.

"I make you think of your mother."

"Yes," Bomani answered. "I was once a child in her arms."

"I'm too big to carry."

"I will put you down soon," Bomani agreed. He'd reached the tail ramp of the C-17. Beth squirmed in his arms, and he placed her on her feet. "Do you want to sit here for a minute?"

"We could."

Dr. Liev emerged from the hangar. "Beth."

"I'm fine," she said, tolerating the doctor's attentions.

"You should rest," Liev said.

"I'm staying here for awhile," Beth said. "Do you want to sit with us?"

Dr. Liev glanced at Bomani. "Don't leave the ramp. I'll wait for you inside."

Bomani sat as the doctor carried on into the C-17.

"I am fine," Beth said.

"I'm glad." Bomani looked at the runways and thought of how these paved stretches of earth had changed his life. The intermittent flights into Karonga had taught him, from his earliest remembrance, that the world was a place you could go. If not for the runway, he would never have imagined leaving and his life would have been very different.

"You're sad," Beth said.

"Great events press against my sorrows because those I would share them with, who would advise me, are gone," Bomani answered. "But I still hear them. They whisper to me as I think of them."

"How did your mother die?"

The question startled Bomani as did the strength of Beth's intuition. "Her heart faltered, then it failed," he answered. "I was far away. I woke one morning struck with the deepest homesickness."

"Your sister called," she said it simply, trusting him, acknowledging that she'd taken more of the story than he had intended to tell.

"I was at my computer looking at flights when the phone rang. It was my comfort that I could say exactly when I would be home." He remembered that morning with sharp clarity, particularly the rain falling as he had carried his bags to Elise's car. The wiper blades had been left on past need of them, but were the only thing that broke the silence of his leaving.

"There was a bird," Beth said.

"My friend drove me to the airport. A starling struck the windshield of her car," he said. The sound had been sickening. It had closed the door on his hope, forcing him to accept that he would not be home in time. "It was hard, Beth."

"But you went."

"Yes." Bomani tried not to think too deeply of the times.

"You went to dig."

Bomani knew he answered even as he chose not to answer.

"They wouldn't let me go," Beth said. "I was too sick. My uncle took her white flowers. He said they were from me, but they weren't. After, he washed dirt from his hands and remembered. I didn't have to push." She pressed her fist against her forehead. "Her grave was too small. I was so angry. He didn't understand. I thought he had to be remembering wrong, that my mother couldn't fit beneath a stone."

She let Bomani's hand fold over hers. Bomani caught a glimpse of Estlin's limp form on the hangar floor. He wanted to assure her that Estlin would be fine, but could not lie.

"She shouldn't have done that to him," she said. "I didn't ask her to."

"I know."

"He said that I can't help because I'm...." She grabbed her trembling fingers and squeezed them to stillness. "He's wrong. There's something wrong in his head. He's breaking. You will need me."

"I hope not," Bomani said, because he couldn't stop thinking it.

Chapter Nineteen

Flight Lieutenant Verges was on the longest solo flight of her career. Her Harrier carried no ordinance, but its belly was loaded with cameras. Pago Pago would be her final refueling stopover en route to the Royal Navy carrier *Ark Royal*, and her commander had given her full permission to offend the Americans, if needed, to complete her mission.

"RAF 467 this is Pago Pago. Abort approach. Unsafe runway," the air traffic controller responded to her request to land. "Abort approach. Redirect to alternate, Apia, Western Samoa."

"This is inbound RAF Harrier 467, scheduled arrival for refueling. I don't require a runway. Request permission for vertical landing." Verges now had an excellent view of the pair of runways at Tafuna, the lagoon they sided, the nearby neighborhoods, and the mountains farther back.

"RAF 467, go around. Unsafe runway. We have an unsafe runway. Reroute to Apia."

Verges flew over the runway forty feet off the tarmac and slowed the Harrier to a hover-stop in front of the terminal, shooting panoramic footage of the entire area to fulfill her orders. "Pago Pago this RAF 467, requesting permission for vertical landing."

Her conversation was interrupted by a pair of F-18 Hornets overflying the runway so close to the speed of sound that their tails vanished into shock collars of vapor drawn from the air by the pressure drop. Verges transmitted her footage via satellite link as the F-18s rose and turned in formation. There were four more Hornets on the tarmac, along with two C-17s, and a stratotanker.

"Pago Pago, please advise," Verges said. There was a long pause and visible movement in the ground patrol on the fence line. A pair of HumVees, likely brought in on a C-17, were turning toward the terminal. The tail numbers on the C-17 closest to the hangar were familiar, and Verges decided to land alongside it, regardless of whether permission was forthcoming.

"RAF 467, this is Pago Pago. Permission granted."

"Thank you, Pago Pago. RAF 467 descending." She chose a suitably offensive landing site and brought the Harrier down, continuing to taxi alongside the C-17. The stance of her armed welcoming committee suggested that the Americans were unhappy with her arrival. Having guns pointed at her was always worth a little adrenaline. She ran through her shutdown checklist, and then released the canopy, guiding it back with one hand. Climbing from the cockpit, she recognized the career C-17 crewman from Whidbey Island.

"It's a small world," she said.

"I understand you're here to refuel," he said. "Access to this airfield is presently restricted. You will remain with your aircraft."

"Understood. Is Lyndie here, too?" she asked.

"Excuse me?" He was too surprised to keep all recognition from his face.

"Lyndie Hume," she said. "I dropped him off at Whidbey. He flew out on your C-17."

"You're mistaken," he answered. "I'm Sergeant Pollock. The fuel truck is coming. You'll be on your way shortly."

"I'm Verges," Verges said. "I think you remember me."

"Get back in your bird," Pollock said flatly.

Verges held his glare until the staring contest was broken by an urgent voice from Pollock's radio. "Subject moving. All personnel, the subject has left the hangar door. Observe and report."

The soldiers by the hanger had snapped to attention.

"What's...?" Verges didn't finish her question — she couldn't — because something stuck its head out of the hangar door behind Pollock. Its bright colors made her think of tropical birds, but it was an altogether different creature. It clambered through the door on four limbs that bent in odd directions.

"Guns down. Give it space," Pollock said, loud and even.

The creature had spiky blue skin. The spikes had reddish roots and its joints shared that rusty red shade. Its eyes were bright yellow. It crept toward the Harrier on all fours, its manner inquisitive. "Is that...?"

"An alien, yeah," Pollock answered.

"What do we do?"

Pollock lifted his radio. "Distant observer. Dewey? Do you see this?"

"Got it." Dewey reported the position of the creature in feet from the door, his voice traveling through multiple open radios. As it closed on Verges, he added proximity to the Harrier to his litany.

It reached out and touched the bottom rung of the ladder to the Harrier's cockpit. Verges realized that she should have moved much sooner. "We can't let it—"

"Stay where you are," Pollock responded. "Stay calm."

The creature started climbing and Verges had to act. She approached with her hands raised. "Stop. Please stop," she said. "It's not safe."

The bright sun made it hard to look at the creature and Verges froze when it turned to face her. Her eyes were watering. She ducked as it leapt to the tarmac, its joints lightly clicking as it spread the force easily through its fingertips. Shifting onto its hind legs, it beckoning her with a rippling of its odd split fingers then retreated to the hanger door and raised its fingers again.

"Is it...?" she asked.

"I think so," Pollock answered.

"What do I do?"

"It wants you to go into the hangar. I want it to go into the hangar. You're going into the hangar."

"Where did it come from?"

"Fuck if I know," Pollock replied. "Follow it."

Verges took one step. The creature seemed satisfied. It curled its fingers again and proceeded to the door from which it had come. Pollock's distant observer now relayed both the alien's position and hers. She kept a healthy distance between them. The soldiers surrounded the open doorway as she walked through it.

A compact twin-engine navy supply plane was parked in the hanger. Two weathered wooden porch chairs were set near it, and the creature led her to them. A soldier sat in one of the wooden chairs, his profession obvious despite his relaxed posture and lack of uniform. A second blue alien was near his feet, crouched attentively by a man lying on the floor. It was her former passenger, Lyndie Hume. He was better dressed, more bruised and still wearing his sandals.

While the creatures fixed their strikingly colored eyes on Hume, Verges was watched by the other occupants of the room. Soldiers stood in each corner and a stout man lingered in a distant office doorway. No one seemed alarmed by Hume's condition. They all watched and waited.

"What happened?" she asked.

"He's *resting*," the man in the chair answered.

The two aliens fell back a few steps and looked at her with clear expectation. Actually, their eyes swiveled from her to the object of their concern. She approached cautiously, knelt and gently placed a hand on Hume's shoulder.

"Lyndie?"

"You know him?"

"He was my passenger."

"You're that Harrier pilot? Funny."

"Funny?"

"Funny-strange," he said.

She wrapped her fingers around Lyndie's wrist. His pulse was strong and steady. There were sweat stains on his blue dress shirt. When she pressed the back of her hand to his face, checking his temperature, he shifted beneath her touch. "What's going on?"

"He's asleep. Sedated."

"Why?"

"Collective idiocy," the fellow answered matter-of-factly. "I'm Sergeant Malone."

"Flight Lieutenant Verges, Royal Air Force," she said. "They're staring at me."

"They do that," Malone said. "And some people see things. Do you see anything unusual?"

"Two aliens," Verges said. "What do they want?"

"We don't know."

"I mean, right now. It brought me in here."

"Maybe Estlin will tell us when he's feeling better." Malone stood and stretched. The natural gesture seemed out of place. "Do you mind watching them? I'll be right back."

"Wait! Are they—?" She stood.

"Mostly harmless," he said.

The aliens stood on their hind legs and tipped their heads simultaneously, watching her closely. Verges hesitated, then sat. The aliens settled, nodding again towards Lyndie.

"What should I do?" she asked.

"Think happy thoughts," Malone suggested as he walked away. "They can read minds."

— « o » —

Tie line in hand, Jeanette stepped onto the dock. A woman sunbathing on a nearby yacht watched as Harry eased the Zodiac into the last berth in the row. Jeanette tied off the lines, and Harry joined her on the dock, slinging the bag of radio gear over his shoulder.

"French," Harry said, glancing at the yacht as they left the dock. "We aren't the first ones here."

Jeanette agreed. The yacht was similar to the one she'd seen in Wellington. She followed Harry to the road, trying to get a sense of the place. Canneries and reservoirs for water and oil were set into the mountain across the harbor. The peak dwarfed the fishing vessels at anchor. The houses had wide porches and fishing nets spread across the lawns. A white church was the most striking building on the lane. A rosette of stained glass above the entry way was framed by two tall rectangular towers. The indistinct words of a hymn, sung by an untrained mix of voices guided by a piano, floated through the open windows to join the cries of the seagulls. The realization that it was Sunday triggered a far stronger sense of displacement for Jeanette than stands of palm trees and the rugged green mountains surrounding them.

"What now?" she asked. "Rent a car?"

"I'll find a cab." Harry pointed up the street. "There's a bank."

Harry hung back as Jeanette went to the bank machine. As she withdrew her limit, she found herself glancing at the dark panel of glass through which the security camera stared. She turned away, folded the bills into her pocket and emerged to find Harry had wandered down the street and was conversing with the driver of a white and yellow cab.

"I found us a ride." Harry said. "Fofo this is Jeanette."

Fofo opened the door for her. The interior of the cab was worn but colorful. The radio was throwing cheery music through the windows. "Where can I take you, Jeanette?"

"The airport," she said.

"Why do you want to go?" Fofo asked. "Harry says you just got here."

"I'm just planning ahead," she said. "I think this flight's going to cost me."

"The airport is closed," Fofo answered.

"I'll look at the flight schedule if I can't book a ticket," Jeanette said.

"Closed is closed, love," Fofo answered. "I won't waste your money. There's no one can help you there today."

"Can we hire you for the morning?" Harry asked. "To tour us around?"

"This I can do," Fofo answered. "All morning if you like, but I run my Gramma home from church at one."

"Perfect," Jeanette said. "I'd still like to stop at the airport and ask when it will re-open."

"Part of the tour." Fofo started the cab.

"Is there a scenic look-out near there?" Harry asked.

Fofo rattled off their immediate options as they wound southward. Jeanette realized the advantage they'd gained for abandoning the independence and privacy a rented car would have offered.

"We should pick up lunch. For all of us," Harry added.

"There's a KFC out by the airport," Fofo suggested.

The coastal highway offered a series of spectacular views. Jeanette found herself trying to look around every curve, waiting to see the airfield. The windows of the cab were all cranked down, but the air flowing in was hot. There were clusters of pedestrians wearing white shirts that gleamed in the sun. Finally, they got their view. In the distance, a matched pair of military transport planes squatted next to a hangar that was well removed from the main terminal building.

At the turn off, a red squirrel was bounding along the roadside. It had tufts of fur on the tips of its ears. Jeanette tapped Harry's knee and pointed at it. They were going the right way, but they didn't get far. The next turn was blocked by orange pylons spread across both lanes in front of a white truck with a security decal on the side of it.

As they pulled up, a Samoan the size of a linebacker got out of the truck. He ambled over to the cab, hitching his thumb on a belt that was weighted with a radio and holstered weapon. "Airport's closed."

"Liufau, why are you way out here?" Fofo asked.

"Because this is where I am. The airport's closed."

"I told them," Fofo answered, pointing to his passengers. "You going to open tomorrow?"

"Don't know." Liufau leaned over into the back passenger window to address Harry and Jeanette. "The runway was damaged. Fixing it wasn't too bad, but they have to bring in a special inspector. Nobody knows when he's coming yet. See those big birds? You'll know when the airport's open because you'll see them taking off. While they're stuck, you're stuck. That's just the way it goes."

"And everybody gets a holiday, except you?" Fofo asked.

"I'm not complaining," Liufau answered. "I'm getting double time to park out here and turn you around. Go on, Fofo, and don't come back."

"Got it." Fofo restarted the cab and turned it back onto the highway. "There's nothing wrong with the runway. My cousin's a paver. I can tell you for sure it's not that. It's a military exercise. A slew of Hornets buzzed us last night. They rattled my Gram's windows. Most of them went over to Ofu. Eat in or take out?"

"Drive through," Harry said. "We should eat somewhere scenic."

"Most times, you can walk the beach by the airport right out to the point, but maybe not today. If I take you to the ridge, you'll get a view of the lagoon."

Jeanette knew a view of the lagoon meant a view of the runway.

"Sounds good," Harry said.

— « o » —

"Do we know when he'll wake?" Sergeant Malone asked.

"Within an hour," Commander Fleckman responded. "We could force it now if we had to."

"Better to wait," Malone said, satisfied with the time-line. "Someone's going to have to apologize to him."

"Feel free," Fleckman replied.

"It won't mean anything coming from me," Malone said. "What do we do about the pilot? Strange to have that RAF pilot turn up here."

"I think the Brits are pressing all their assets into service," Fleckman said. "They wanted a look at the facilities here and got lucky with the timing. If we were on schedule, she would have missed us. When the *Ark Royal* calls, we'll tell them that their pilot collapsed with heatstroke shortly after landing."

"It beckoned her," Malone said. "Those were some of the most humanistic gestures we've seen."

"They do have a way of getting what they want," Fleckman answered. "I need to know more about Professor Sanford and his history with Hume."

"What do you mean?"

"They were on the flight to Wellington together — your flight."

"The request to get a physicist to Wellington came to us because of the lack of commercial seats," Malone explained. "We knew that having a civilian aboard would help us sell the paperwork we wanted Hume to sign."

"But you chose Sanford."

"We got a short list of suitable academics in Washington State. Sanford was closest and a widower. He was our best bet, but I had a man pursuing the nearest alternate."

"It's too coincidental," Fleckman answered, "that the man with the right theory would be on your flight."

"Are his ideas that different?"

"Did Hume and Sanford talk? Are we getting a delusion-driven echo of theories presented to Hume before he even met the aliens?"

"He doesn't have the background to generate these equations," Sergeant Malone answered. "They were tutoring him on the carrier, starting from the absolute basics."

"It could be entirely subconscious," Fleckman suggested. "Hume could be working within the only theoretical framework he has to describe the phenomenon, thereby giving it elevated importance."

"I understand your reasoning," Malone said, "but it's not my instinct."

— « o » —

Dark forms slid across a forbidding landscape, pressing one by one through walls of blinding heat. The burning earth forced Estlin to his feet. He was standing before he was awake, and falling before he could open his eyes. Hands caught him, but could only guide his fall, and he landed on a girl. He knew it was a girl because she had a certain shape and made a certain sound and held him a certain way when he tried to get up again.

"Lyndie?" She spoke his name with an accent he trusted and kept talking until he settled bonelessly in the shade. He took a second to find his own senses, stop seeing heat, and realize that shade did not make his haven cool.

"Lyndie?"

"Yeah?" He was encouraged to slide to the floor.

"Do you have your brain now?" Verges said it kindly, her hand on his cheek to help him focus.

He tried to work through the confusion of her presence, but the questions piled into each other.

"Huh?" His brain squashed all fine structure from the query, but Verges got it.

"I'm surprised to see you, too," she said.

He looked at the familiar rafters. He was still in the hangar, the Waes were above him and Sergeant Malone leaned into view. Estlin's feelings on that were mixed, so he let his eyes slide back to Verges. Her brown hair fell in layers that complimented the shape of her face. It was a little longer than he'd thought, having assumed that all military barbers were butchers. "How'd you get here?"

"I have a plane." Verges kept it simple. "What happened?"

Estlin didn't know where to start. "I was...uh...they..." He pointed at the rafters, where the waetapu were swinging jubilantly amongst the structural beams. He didn't know what to say about them and let his gesture drop to the Greyhound. He pointed roughly at it with a loose open hand because articulating his fingers was too much trouble. "I flew. And then they...." He scraped a hand across the back of his neck. There was nothing there. "My brain is full of mud. When did you...?"

"Not long," Verges answered. "Your face is bruised."

"He hit me."

"I was careful," Malone responded.

"Careful." Estlin rubbed his neck again. "You said you'd protect me."

Malone crouched next to Estlin, gently tugged his hand aside and checked the back of his neck. "It's a little red," he said. "I pulled those things off right away, but you were already on your way out."

"Liev doesn't care if I suffer collateral damage," Estlin said. "Respond to the threat."

"She got the message. The critters came down," Malone said. "They were guarding you. No translation required."

"They climbed back into the rafters a few minutes ago," Verges added.

Malone straightened. "Need anything?"

Estlin's brain stalled. He couldn't muster himself to demand a phone. Verges had come *with a plane,* and he wanted to lie exactly where he was and admire the view. *I need a pillow,* he thought. He apparently thought it loudly, or said it, because Verges pulled off her olive green flight jacket and folded it into a bundle. She slipped it under his head.

"I'll tell them you're awake," Malone said.

Estlin knew he was something more than awake. "Unhappy," he said. "Awake and unhappy. I had bad dreams, Malone."

"He's gone," Verges said.

Estlin thought that she had really pretty cheekbones. "I have bad dreams, and maybe they have bad dreams." He pointed at the rafters.

Verges followed his gesture. "Is that a squirrel?"

"Aliens," Estlin answered.

"Next to the aliens."

Estlin knew she was right. His brain was getting a little less muddy and there was definitely a squirrel up there. The waetapu were aware of the squirrel, but weren't interacting with it. From the squirrel's perspective, while the waetapu were trying to look like martens, they were definitely not martens. The squirrel was ignoring the pair of not-martens from a safe distance because it had come to see the shiny one.

Estlin decided to lie back and be shiny.

— « o » —

There was an old picnic table at the lookout. Fofo had parked and carried the food to it. Harry stood on the bench seat to take in the wider landscape. The view was incredibly scenic, but ultimately not as good as he'd hoped. From this angle, the terminal building hid much of the hangar and aircraft beyond it.

Jeanette was sitting with Fofo, and struggling with a leg of greasy chicken.

"You don't like it?" Fofo asked.

"I've been traveling with vegetarians," she said.

"Poor thing," Fofo answered. "No wonder you're so skinny."

Harry glanced at his companion, considering the Samoan's opinion. To him, Jeanette was the perfect curvy weight.

The terminal and hangars obstructed the view, but they could see the runways where they projected out along the far edge of the lagoon, and the tail fins of the largest aircraft rose above the buildings.

"Is that a hotel?" Harry asked.

"Expensive," Fofo responded.

"But close to the airport," Harry said. "Maybe we'll go there next."

"I thought you had a boat?"

"I'd love a bath and big bed," Harry answered. He looked further up the mountain. "That's a banyan tree. We should go have a look at it. Banyans grow down from the canopy rather than up from the earth. It's worth the hike."

Jeanette gave him a skeptical look, playing her part. "It's hot."

"Come on," he said. "It'll be worth it for the view."

"All right," she said. "Fofo, want to finish the chicken? We won't be long."

"It's your dime." Fofo helped himself.

A steep, narrow trail took them into the trees. The canopy was a vibrant green while the fallen leaves were baked brown and crackled beneath their feet. The heat made for hard going, but they sweated up to the banyan, where a gap in the canopy gave them another view of the lagoon. The wide base of the banyan was a forest of interconnected trunks. It had taken root on a high branch of a tree and grown to the ground, expanding to smother its host.

Harry dug the radio tracking equipment out of the bag and turned it on. It took him a few minutes to fiddle it into working. It took longer to realize that the first signal he got was a squirrel in the trees above them.

"Do we really need that?" Jeanette asked. "We saw the squirrel at the airport."

"Ten or twelve would make an absolutely convincing report."

"And what does that get us?"

"I don't know."

"If Estlin was out there waving a flag, would it help?"

"I'd jump the fence."

"Maybe that's what we should do," Jeanette answered. "One of us, at least."

Harry read the gleam in Jeanette's eyes. "They're patrolling that fence line. You'd be stopped before your feet touched the ground."

"Could be worth it."

"What?"

"I perturb the system, you watch. Once we call your general, there's no point waiting. If I get snatched for trespassing, I'm still on the other side of the fence. I'll either get to stay there or get kicked to the local authorities and demand a lawyer and an explanation."

Jeanette's enthusiasm did not inspire Harry. He felt a sharp slap of fear. "What if you get shot for trespassing?"

"Unlikely," Jeanette answered. "I'm not looking to take that kind of risk."

"That's exactly the risk you're taking."

"They won't shoot," she answered.

"This is a shoot first, apologize later situation."

"I'll wear a damn bikini if you want. No concealed weapons."

"No." Harry was absolute.

"It's my choice."

"We'll do this together, and we'll use our brains." Harry saw the defiance in Jeanette's eyes. "You try and go around me and I'll get mean."

"Okay," she said. "Are we really going to the hotel?"

"It's three or four stories. Closer. We might get a better view than we have from here."

"And you're going to ask for that? Airport side and a clear look at the runway, please?"

"I don't know," Harry answered. "I'm not a good spy."

"You a spy?" Fofo asked from the shaded trail. He was winded and swiped the sweat from his face with an open hand.

"Shit." Harry fumbled the receiver, catching it roughly against himself before it could drop to the ground. "No, Fofo, I'm a biologist."

"What's that in your hands?" he asked.

"It's just...." Harry utterly failed to think of a reasonable lie.

"It's for tracking squirrels," Jeanette answered.

This, apparently, was the dumbest thing Fofo had ever heard. The tracking equipment chose that moment to emit a shrill whine. Jeanette reached over and shut it off.

"Find another ride," Fofo said, and backed away. He kept one eye on them even as he turned to follow the trail.

"Bugger," Harry cursed. "That was stupid."

"I just wish he'd dumped us closer to the damn airport," Jeanette said. "What now?"

"I guess we make some notes and hike to the nearest phone."

"And then?"

"We find some other way to screw this up."

— « o » —

"We should have corralled them while they were on the ground," Commander Fleckman said.

Sergeant Malone stood square to the commander. He didn't answer because no direct question had been asked.

"You sat next to them," Fleckman continued. "Dangerously close, considering their spines. They could be as toxic as a lionfish for all we know. But that's not my question. Why didn't we surround them with nets?"

"The prerogative so far has been to absolutely avoid the use of direct force," Sergeant Malone answered. "Their defensive positioning around Hume suggested that they would resist confinement."

"That explains why *you* did nothing," Fleckman said. "What about the rest of us?"

"Commander, there's a squirrel in the hangar." One of Fleckman's team stood in the doorway of the hangar office.

Sergeant Malone scrambled to the door and immediately spotted the squirrel bounding across the central H-beam in the rafters. It was a very distinctive red squirrel with tufts of fur on the tips of its ears.

"How'd it get in?" Fleckman asked.

"That's a Russian squirrel," Malone noted.

"Even better," Fleckman responded as he walked across the hangar to where Estlin was idly watching the squirrel.

"What is that?" Fleckman asked Estlin.

"First contact for all squirrel-kind," Estlin suggested.

Malone followed. "Hume, where did it come from?"

"It's not from here." Estlin was slow to answer.

"And I don't think it swam," Malone said.

"No," Estlin answered with his peculiar absent focus. "It fell."

"Get rid of it," Fleckman ordered. "Now."

"I can't." Estlin reclined, adding emphasis to his refusal and provoking an angry glare from Fleckman.

"He attracts squirrels. It's a side effect. He can't control it," Malone supplied. "There are three more."

"Get rid of them," Fleckman pressed Estlin. "You know a way."

"There's a company in San Paolo that sells squirrel repellant," Estlin answered. "But it's expensive, it stinks, and *it doesn't work.*"

Fleckman was not amused.

"This position isn't secure," Malone stated bluntly.

"When was it?" Fleckman grimaced. "Dontis has authorized the flight. We need to get them ready to go."

"To go where?" Estlin asked. "Pearl Harbor?"

Fleckman glanced at Verges and didn't answer.

"You let Liev drug me."

"I was overruled."

"Right." Estlin considered the squirrels above them. "This is where I stop cooperating."

Malone stepped forward. "Your alien friends came down from the rafters and asked us not to drug you again. Even Dontis got the message," he said, though he knew, at best, Dontis would change his tactics, not his objectives.

"Do you know what they think is going to happen?"

There was a darkness in Estlin's words that made Malone look at their visitors. They were dangling by their tails and hind limbs and turned their heads in synch to meet his gaze. He understood why Dontis was keeping to the corner office. The moment was interrupted by Pollock who barreled into the hangar.

"There's a problem," he reported. "We've got snails on the runway."

"Snails?" Malone was lost.

"These are huge snails, a foot long."

"Is this a mass hallucination?" Fleckman asked.

"No, it's a local infestation," Pollock replied. "Giant African land snails. The shells are bigger than your fist and they are everywhere. If they get sucked into the engines...?" Pollock mimed the potential consequences of a fist-sized snail hitting a turbofan. It wasn't an option. "We can't take off."

"Clear the runway," Fleckman ordered.

"How?" Pollock asked.

"Carefully," Malone answered, thinking as quickly as possible. "Consider who invited them. We can use the fire truck and wash them aside, then gather all hands for a shoulder-to-shoulder walk. It's the only way to deal with runway debris."

"How long is this going to take?" Fleckman demanded.

Too long, Malone thought, and didn't answer.

Chapter Twenty

"Did you get the latest pictures?" John Cutler asked, his image moving in fragmented jerks delivered by an encrypted video link.

"Yes, thanks. They're spectacular." Sanford's response was relayed via satellite to the inbound aircraft carrier. "I have questions. Figure six-eight-seven. There's no color scale for the intensities."

"I don't have it either," the young physicist answered. "Not for that one. It's from another source."

"What source?"

"Don't know. Can't say," John answered. "Everyone wants to know if it's bigger than the first one. They want me to tell them."

"How?" Sanford asked.

"They want me to run the numbers back from the Burst signal."

"How?"

"If we could estimate the conversion loss as a percentage of the—"

"Estimate? You'd have to guess your way through the whole equation. What's the point?"

"I know."

"If the power density changes and not the size, it will look the same. There's only so much dust for it to burn."

"I know!" John snapped. "They want an answer, Sanford. You can help me."

"Estlin says they'll have their answer in three days," Sanford responded. "If you answer them now, you'll be judged by your guessing skills. That's not what your degree is for."

"I know." John's image nodded a quarter second behind his words.

"Is Jakarta with you yet?" Bomani asked.

"Not yet. There's a security issue," John said.

"Perhaps you could just send Su the one equation," Sanford replied. "I think his input would be very valuable."

"I can't send anything until the issue is resolved." John glanced over his shoulder. "I have to go."

"Thanks for keeping us updated," Sanford responded.

"I'm glad we've got this link," John answered.

"Bye, John," Bomani called. At the top of the conversation, Bomani had leaned into camera view to wave, and then sat back so as not to crowd Sanford.

"I'll get back to you as soon as I can," John assured them as his image dimmed to black.

Sanford closed the connection, leaving the figure he'd asked John about on the screen.

"It looks like a moth, doesn't it," Bomani said. "With eyes marked on its wings."

"They're beautiful pictures," Sanford agreed. "It is hard to grasp their scale."

"Does it frighten you?" Bomani asked.

"I'm a scientist," Sanford said. "Unknowns are exciting."

"John is stressed," Bomani said.

"It is a little nerve wracking," Sanford confessed, "knowing that something is coming."

"What if it is closer than you think," Bomani asked. "Sanford I have a concern. John said the object hit the Pacific two days after the Burst. It was less than that, only thirty-eight hours. Neptune is very far."

"I have thought about it," Sanford said.

"They can do impossible things. If they have an impossible ship, as swift as light, they could be here in five hours. But, I know they didn't arrive with that speed."

"How do you know?"

"Think of your equations, Sanford. Where does momentum fit in? It doesn't. Maybe they are smarter, maybe we are wrong, but there is no momentum in the work that Estlin gave us, either."

Bomani raised his pen, holding it as an example, an object in space. "Have you ever seen a contact juggler work with a single ball? The ball seems to float in place as it slips from hand to hand. The fold is like that. You would not fire a bullet through it."

"We don't know."

"So, we must consider both scenarios." Bomani slipped the pen back into his pocket. "If they leap from place to place bringing great speed with them, there is no problem. If they sit in a chair as the chair turns from there to here, when they arrive, whatever speed they can achieve, they must first accelerate and then decelerate. Thirty-eight hours, Sanford. What if it wasn't the first Burst?"

"You think we missed one? How could we?"

"What if it had half the power? Or less? John wants to know if it is growing. What if the Burst was the first event big enough for us to notice?"

— « o » —

A fire crew was soaking the runway, but Harry had no idea why. He handed the binoculars back to Jeanette. "Those are marines running the hoses," he said. "They're armed."

"What are they preparing for?" she asked.

"I don't know," Harry answered. "I can't let you go down there."

"We've come this far," she said.

"Yidge died." It hurt him to say it, but he needed Jeanette to understand. "Yidge was my assistant — young, impulsive. When she was a student in my lab, she named possums after comic book heroes." He looked away, down at the distant airfield. "She disappeared when Lyndie did. And she died the following day on a Chinese freighter that we believe the Americans raided. She was shot."

"I'm sorry."

"So am I," Harry answered. "Sorry doesn't cover it. I chose her. I pulled Lyndie in, too."

"Do you think—"

"Jeanette, they have every reason to keep him alive." He leaned against the banyan tree, re-packing the radio equipment. The banyan was so old that the host tree it had smothered had rotted away, leaving a hollow in the forest of banyan trunks.

He knew what he'd risked without thinking, and what he wouldn't risk this time.

"We should go," Jeanette said.

"Yes." Harry led the way down the path with Jeanette a step behind him. As they reached the edge of the trees, he saw the taxi and realized that Fofo had not abandoned them. A police cruiser was parked behind the cab.

"Damn, we're lousy spies," Harry muttered.

"Harry?" Jeanette waited for him to take the lead.

"Let's get on with it." He strode forward.

The constable was standing with Fofo, leaning against the hood of the taxi. "That them?" the officer asked loudly.

"That's them," Fofo answered. "I thought you should meet my cousin, Constable Pao."

"Hello," said Harry.

"Sir, please put down that bag," Pao directed.

Harry complied. His attempt at a disarming smile was defeated by the scar that turned one corner of his lips. "There's been a misunderstanding," he said.

"My cousin says you arrived this morning," the constable said. "I'd like to see your passports."

With a glance to Jeanette, Harry surrendered his passport and she followed suit. The officer examined them with a few short, sharp glances. "Fofo says you're tracking squirrels."

"Yes, sir."

"That's interesting because there are no squirrels here," the officer said. "Not until today. It's illegal to introduce a foreign species to Samoa."

"We didn't," Jeanette assured him. "They aren't ours."

"But you have equipment to track them."

"I'm a biologist," Harry said, "a possum expert. I heard about the squirrel problem."

"That's interesting." He closed their passports and tucked them in his pocket. "Tell me about the submarines."

"What submarines?" Harry was rattled by the change in topics.

"Did you come from one of them?"

"We're off the Greenpeace ship *Esperanza*," Jeanette answered.

"I didn't see your ship in the harbor."

"We came in on a Zodiac," she said.

"Interesting," he said. "You arrived when the submarines surfaced. If you were on the water this morning, you must've seen them."

"We didn't," Jeanette answered. "Maybe we were already in the harbor meeting with Customs."

"Look out there." The officer pointed out beyond the lagoon. "See them now?"

"Yes, sir." Harry could see four black towers. From the officer's questions, he assumed they weren't American subs. That made it an even more unusual gesture with one or more nations raising their subs, foregoing stealth to display their presence.

"But maybe you weren't looking that far out. Fofo said you were interested in the airport."

"This is a misunderstanding."

"I don't think so," the constable said. "Dr. Hatarei, I was given your name half an hour ago with instructions that, if found, you were to be delivered to the airport. How does that sound?"

"About right," Harry said.

"It seems unusual to me," the constable said. "But the instructions were clear." He opened the back door of the squad car. "Leave the bag. I'll take care of it."

Harry obeyed, got in car and slid across the seat to make room for Jeanette.

"This is going to be interesting," he said, and received a withering glare.

"I don't understand the squirrels," Fofo said. "Think they mounted little cameras on them?"

Officer Pao swung the heavy door shut and went to cautiously check the contents of Harry's bag.

— « o » —

"Are you feeling better?" Verges asked.

"Not really." Estlin rolled from his side onto his back. He was thirsty. His skin felt hot and tight. Malone had gone to check on the snails, leaving Verges to watch over him. "I'm tired."

"What's going on?"

"Aliens," Estlin said.

"How'd they get here?"

"Plane." Estlin pointed at the Greyhound. He knew it wasn't the answer Verges was looking for, but it was all he had.

"And you were with them," she said.

Estlin nodded. "I met them in Wellington. Got snatched by the Chinese and ended up on a freighter. The Americans raided the ship. They killed a girl named Yidge Lee. Can you remember that name?"

"Yidge Lee," Verges said.

"Yidge Lee, assistant to Professor Harry Hatarei of Wellington," Estlin said. "Please remember."

"I will," she answered.

Verges watched the squirrels and the aliens move through the rafters, keeping a respectful distance from each other. "They seem enamored with you."

"The squirrels?"

"The aliens."

"I'm a useful curiosity," he answered. "I translate for them, but they can project images at anyone. I'm not that special."

Verges disagreed. "They were watching over you when I arrived."

Estlin wondered what exactly had happened while he was making friends with the lawn. Beads of color floated through the rafters in answer to the question he hadn't consciously asked. Bright orange swirled into yellow. The colors split into two half-empty vessels, falling away from each other.

"They're bonded to each other — co-dependent," he translated for Verges. "They were separated in Wellington, and it diminished them. I met one while it was alone and acted as a substitute."

A flicker of blue rose from him to meet the open yellow form, folding against it. The yellow spun with its flaring blue skin, its orbit taking it across the path of an orange sun. The orange and yellow spheres twirled around each other on elliptical orbits like binary stars, until the orbits collapsed and the suns merged their power.

The blue was displaced, but remained attached to the yellow, flowing out like a sheet pegged to a clothesline. The blue shape inverted, shifting not to black but to a profound absence of color, a translucent gray space that drained color from the yellow wherever the two forms touched.

"While I was more quiet than sleeping, less quiet than dead, Wae felt the separation. I thought — it thought — that once they reunited, I wouldn't be needed. It shouldn't have felt anything."

"What do you mean?"

"Wrong species," Estlin said, pointing at himself. "There shouldn't be a lasting connection with me."

Wae corrected his species bias, showing him the depth of bond that their kind forged with the nsangunsangu — a bond known to all but those born to travel. The vibrant blue filled the room, billowing like a sail tethered to a dense yellow form. This time the points of contact connecting the two forms failed one by one. The sheet of blue flailed free, falling to the concrete where the color bled from it.

"What happens now?"

"Bloodshed." A gleaming darkness of broken forms filled Estlin's mind. At the center, an attentive orange-yellow eye turned like the lamp of a lighthouse, drawing in the darkness rather than dispelling it. "They are here to watch."

A million glimmering stars filled the room. The starscape was like a sandstorm that suddenly froze, so the steady light of stars became distinct from fine flecks of light jumping between them. The view shifted to follow the path of a single falling speck, which landed in the center of the floor like a glimmering grain of sand. The walls and rafters twisted towards it. The floor groaned, stress fractures snapped the concrete and the edges ground against each other as the entire structure fought to fold itself towards this single point. The illusion of the floor heaving skyward was so strong, Estlin reflexively tried to catch himself.

Verges grabbed one of his hands. "What is it?" She caught his other flailing hand, but her grip couldn't break the certainty of his fall into a crushing point of light.

"They think I'm going to die."

"What?"

"They came to stand at the center of the storm, to observe, to catch an image of us so deep and clear...." The speck had swallowed all it could. The dense matrix expanded and began to transform itself over and over, each permutation showing a new face. "There's an equation."

"It's a test?" Verges' anger colored her words. "Do you know how they are going to strike? Or when?"

"No, that's not it." Estlin was missing something. The waetapu were swinging through the rafters with loose-limbed abandon. "They aren't expecting a bolt from the sky. The conflict will be ours. Bullets on the ground. They think I will fall in the crossfire, and they may regret my demise," he said. In truth, he knew he might be confusing uncertainty or self-concern for regret. His connection to Wae was an unpredictable complication.

"Forget it," Verges answered. She assessed the hanger with new eyes, evaluating obstacles. "I'm not cannon fodder, neither are you."

The hanger door opened, and Malone entered with Pollock who was pushing a pallet jack. Malone kept his eyes on the Waes as Pollock closed the door behind them.

"Hey, Hume, how are they doing?" Malone asked as he slipped the jack under the cargo container. "Hume?"

"They're fine," Estlin answered.

"Good." Malone cranked the jack a couple of times, bringing it just to the point of contact with the container while Pollock unlatched the doors and swung them wide open. "Call them down."

"No," Estlin said. "We need to talk. I can't come with you."

"You are not having a tantrum now," Malone answered.

"Tantrum?" Estlin felt a surge of raw anger. Blood was rushing to his face.

"Get your head in the game," Malone said. "You're tired, and it's making you stupid. Get this job done. Sleep on the flight. If you want, we'll have a king-sized bed waiting, and you can fall into it when we land."

"They'll go with you," Estlin argued. "You don't need me."

"There are jobs you stick to until they're done."

Dontis emerged from the corner office. "Sergeant Malone, how soon will they be ready?"

Malone stepped close, his voice low. "Do not pull this shit now."

"Is there a problem, Sergeant Malone?" Dontis barreled across the hangar.

"No problem, sir. Hume's bringing them down," Malone answered. "You can do this. They'll stand on their heads for you."

"No," Estlin answered decisively.

Verges' planted her feet, but did not rise from the seat opposite him.

"If you want them, you have to agree to leave me behind," Estlin spoke directly to Dontis. "I'm done."

"We appreciate your help, Mr. Hume, and you will be compensated for it. But this is not the place for negotiation."

Estlin shook his head. "I'm not negotiating. I'm finished."

"That's regrettable," Dontis answered. "But you are far from my primary concern. Bring them down. It's time to go."

Estlin's negotiating position abruptly slipped as the waetapu clambered down the wall. The pair leapt to the floor together and bounded across it, stopping at his feet to stare at him with open expectation. He refused their company, refusing to embrace his own demise. They folded their bodies forward, their eyes never leaving him, then rose and ambled to the cargo container. He wanted to warn them, but they were here to ride the whirlwind and had chosen their hosts.

The waetapu climbed the frame of the container to sit on top of it as a pair of shadows followed the expected path into the cargo pod. Sergeant Malone diligently secured the door while Pollock carefully filmed the action of his hands on each lock, watching the camera's view screen.

"Very good," Dontis said, once the doors were secured. He walked to the container and peered in at the figments as he lifted and checked each lock. "Sergeant Pollock, notify the carrier. I want our escort in the air." Dontis left the hangar.

Malone turned on Estlin, standing over him with his arms crossed. "What are you playing at?"

"Not playing. Will Dontis let me stay behind?"

"You want to stay here?"

"I'm overdue on the *Ark Royal,*" Verges countered. "He can ride with me."

"You have no fuel." Malone was blunt.

Estlin wondered what the waetapu were planning. Would they leave without him or only send their figments. "I can't go with them."

"Why not?"

"You can leave me here."

"What did they say to you?"

"Nothing," Estlin said. "This is going to end badly, and you know it."

"Oh, for fuck's sake." Sergeant Malone twisted to look over his shoulder. "Where are they? You looked over the container. Where are they?"

Estlin dropped his eyes to the floor. "Malone, I can't."

"They fooled Pollock's camera?" Malone waited for an answer.

"Pollock was focused on you securing the locks. It's definitely locked."

"But they aren't in it?"

"They'll go," Estlin insisted. "They said they'd go."

"Where are they?"

"On top," Estlin answered. "I just, I can't—" Estlin coughed roughly, feeling wretched. "I can't go with them."

"You're scratching." Malone stepped forward and yanked Estlin's shirt front. "Shit."

Estlin looked at the red blotches rising on his belly. "Aw, hives."

"You sure?"

"Drug allergy. I told you."

"We aren't going anywhere. Fleckman's going to lock us down," Malone scrubbed his face. "And Dontis will lock you down for manipulating him."

"But they—"

"You watched. Pollock!" he yelled across the hanger. "Pollock, I need Fleckman over here and antihistamines from the *Cascade*. And I want you to review that tape, all of it, from the first frame, because they aren't in that cage."

"What?"

"You heard me. Go!"

— « o » —

Bomani sat with Sanford as he typed his notes, transcribing the handwritten equations that had already been scanned and sent out.

"This is ridiculous," Sanford complained. "How can they not have a basic equation editor installed on any of these machines?"

"We're going to fly soon, aren't we?" Bomani said.

"Seems like they wanted to leave an hour ago," Sanford answered, glancing up as Dontis boarded the plane. "Where do you think we'll go?

Dontis went directly to Dr. Liev. "Mr. Hume has withdrawn his services," he said. "I've never met a more shiftless, unambitious man."

"His early intellectual development was severely limited by his condition," she answered. "I doubt he truly appreciates the situation."

"Fortunately, the aliens are contained," Dontis continued. "We'll fly them first. You'll follow with Hume. Make sure that he is fit to travel. We can't afford another of his calls to the animal kingdom."

"What about Beth?"

"We may yet need her."

As Bomani stood to protest, Sergeant Pollock ran up the ramp. "We've got a problem," he said, yanking the first aid kit from the wall. "Sanford, get off that computer, now." Pollock threw the first aid kit at Bomani. "Open it," he said. "You're looking for antihistamines and the epi-pen. Estlin needs them."

"Why?" Bomani cracked open the kit and began searching.

"What's going on?" Dontis demanded

"Hume's turning another color and Malone says the subjects are loose."

"They escaped?" Dontis said.

"We never had them." Pollock plugged the camera to the computer and skipped the disk back to the start, speeding through the frames.

Bomani had the antihistamines, and Dr. Liev pointed at the yellow cylinder of epinephrine mounted prominently in the raised lid of the kit.

"There," she said.

Bomani grabbed it, turned and pressed both into Pollock's hands. "What's wrong with Estlin?"

"Allergic reaction," Pollock answered and glanced at Dr. Liev, "to your drugs."

"He can't know that," she said. "He's had days of direct exposure to the aliens."

"He's covered in red splotches," Pollock said. "Come diagnose him."

"Your commander needs to quarantine that hangar," Dr. Liev responded, "and call in his reserve biohazard team."

Sergeant Pollock paused the video playback. "They aren't in the container."

"I saw them—" Dontis stared at the video. "Tell me they are still in the hangar."

Pollock looked at Dontis. "I'll find out," he said, and was gone as quickly as he'd come.

— « o » —

Sergeant Malone watched Estlin try not to scratch. The red blotches were now visible at the base of his throat and the backs of his hands. "It's spreading."

"Hives go everywhere," Estlin answered.

"Stop scratching," Malone suggested.

"Right." Estlin interlocked his fingers. The gesture of self-restraint lasted a few seconds..

"Any other symptoms?" Verges asked.

"No," Estlin answered. "Stop looking so worried. I've survived Dr. Liev's medicine before."

"She said this was a different drug," Malone said. "A variant."

"Right."

"What a mess," Malone said.

"You have no idea," Estlin answered.

"They think he's going to die," Verges said.

"Verges!" Estlin protested.

"That's what they told you."

"Not like this," Estlin answered. He raised his eyes to Malone's. "They think there's going to be a conflict, and I won't be safe when the bullets start flying."

"Did they tell you to stay behind?"

"No, they expect me to accept my short future." He leaned his head back and closed his eyes briefly. "Our softly written memories die with us. But, for them, death is the transition from a shifting pattern to fixed one that survives in collective memory."

"And how does that work?" Malone asked.

"Wae gave us one of its scales." Estlin's fingertips were tapping the air, tracking the beats of some invisible conversation. "That scale was a copy of the scale beneath it, built on a master structure at its root. Yidge carried it around the world, watching it be destroyed a fragment at a time. The obliteration of a life record writ more completely than we could ever imagine."

Malone could imagine it too well — scientists dissolving a hard drive, learning only what elements went into its construction.

"To be collected by them is to rest in the library of another world — kept as a static pattern, coherent enough to speak to the librarians and all who come to study, but never to give a new answer unless a new question is asked." Estlin was silent for several long seconds, his damp eyes looking through Malone, tracing and retracing the space beyond him.

"Okay," he said with quiet certainty, and sank into his seat, all tension draining from him. "Will it hurt?"

This question chilled Malone to the bone.

"Lyndie?" Verges reached for him.

"No," he said. "Lay your head down."

Malone watched as Verges responded, settling to her knees, then stretching out to rest her head on her hands.

"What are you doing?" Malone demanded.

"They should all lay their heads down," Estlin suggested quietly.

"Don't!" Malone shouted. "Hume!"

Estlin's gaze remained distant.

"Stop." Malone's reach fell short as he slipped to his knees, his muscles remembering the way down. "Don't."

"It's okay," Estlin said.

"It's not," Malone said as he placed his head on the ground. "Whatever they are asking, don't agree. Don't do it."

"They want me to live," Estlin said, his irises fine bright rings around an infinite black. As the darkness swept out from them, Malone felt betrayed, but only for a moment.

Chapter Twenty-one

Bomani woke gasping, his cheek against the metal deck of the C-17, his lungs trying to force strength back to weak, sleeping limbs. The attack had come from within, forcing a physical surrender before blacking out his thoughts. He heard Sanford's snore, but knew the man wasn't sleeping. Rising to his knees, Bomani saw Dontis and Dr. Liev folded against each other on the deck. Beth was limp in her seat, her eyes closed.

Bomani rose and gently shook Sanford who remained unresponsive. There was no movement beyond the gaping tail ramp, but he knew that answers were waiting in the hangar.

"Don't go." Beth hadn't moved but her eyes were on him.

"I have to, little one. I have to. Stay here." Bomani took her hand and waited for her reluctant nod. He did not want to leave her, but would not bring her with him either. "Stay safe."

He descended the ramp cautiously and found Sergeant Pollock lying on the tarmac halfway to the hangar. Bomani ran to him and took the medicine from his hands. The soldiers at the hangar door were also unconscious. He knocked, then turned the knob and sent the door drifting open with a single push. "Hello?"

"Bomani." Estlin stood in the center of the hangar. Red splotches marred his pale skin, and he seemed perfectly lost. Verges and Malone were asleep at his feet, and Commander Fleckman was slumped against the distant office doorway.

The waetapu were perched on the cargo container and watched Bomani closely. Their spines were lying flat, making them look smaller, but he knew how great their power was and what they'd done. Bomani caught Estlin by the shoulder and pressed the pills into his hand. "Pollock said you needed these."

Estlin accepted the packet, checked the label, and tore it open. He dry-swallowed the pair of pills. "Pollock?"

"He's lying on the tarmac with all the other soldiers. How has this happened?"

Estlin hooked a thumb towards the waetapu. "They hit the sleep button — hard." He looked at Malone. "He's not dreaming."

"This is unnatural, Estlin. It is wrong," Bomani said. "However many sleep, more will come. Do they mean to escape?"

"No. They'll ride that crate to wherever the Americans want them." Estlin was agitated. "I think they're trying to help me. I want to leave. Do you want to leave?"

"I will not leave alone," Bomani answered. "Where would you go?"

"It's not safe here." Estlin pressed his palms to his eyes, pushing tears aside.

"I know." Bomani accepted this truth. "Are you going to swim or fly?"

Estlin turned in place. It was clear his frustration was subverting his ability to speak. "Crawl," he said. "Under a rock? Into a ditch?"

"You do not need company for that," Bomani said. "Your gift is yours, but—"

"Don't say it."

"I took those beautiful equations and did not thank you."

"You are ruining my escape."

"I'm sorry."

"Stop being so fucking sincere," Estlin snapped.

The Waes clambered to the nearest edge of the container, leaning forward to watch them, using their tails to defy gravity. Bomani could not tell if they were fascinated by the argument or invested in its conclusion. Estlin was silent, but the tight flexing of his wrists and hands betrayed an internal argument.

"Do not double team me," Estlin called over his shoulder. He met Bomani's eyes. "If they shoot me, I will haunt you." He shook the pent up energy from his limbs and crouched next to Sergeant Malone. "Should we wake him?"

Bomani knew this was a bad idea, but Estlin pressed one hand against Malone's shoulder with a manner of direct concentration.

"He's going to be pissed," Estlin predicted.

Malone's fingers flexed as he woke. The slight movement was followed by a sudden strike at the hand on his shoulder. He grabbed Estlin's wrist and pulled him forward. Estlin fell over Malone, struggling to keep his own weight from breaking his pinned wrist. Within a second, Malone had Estlin's throat in the crook of one elbow and his other arm locked across the back of his neck. Estlin struggled briefly, and then surrendered.

"What did you do?" Malone demanded.

"Everyone's asleep, Malone," Bomani said.

"If you twitch the wrong way, I will drop you. Do you understand? Do they?" Malone kept the pressure on Estlin's neck, giving him no opportunity to answer. "What's going on?" he asked Bomani.

"I woke and everyone was asleep," Bomani answered. "I could not wake them. Everyone on the plane. Everyone outside. The aliens did it."

"You told them to do it." Malone spoke into Estlin's ear. He gave Estlin half an inch of breathing space.

They told me, Estlin wheezed.

"They asked you," Malone insisted. "You agreed. Why?"

"I want to live," Estlin answered.

"Good luck," Malone answered. "What's the plan?"

"We are not strategic thinkers," Bomani interjected. "That's why we woke you."

"You woke me?" Malone asked.

"Yeah," Estlin answered.

"Why?"

"I'm stupid."

Malone slid a set of keys to Bomani's feet. "Unlock the container. Get those doors open."

"Malone!" Bomani protested.

"Don't screw around," Malone said, compressing Estlin's throat. "They go in the box, right now. Ask nicely."

Bomani picked up the keys and unlocked the doors, but Estlin refused. His struggles renewed.

"Get them in there," Malone insisted, momentarily giving Estlin enough air to reply.

"No."

The waetapu simultaneously leapt from the top of the container to ricochet off the ground and into the cargo pod where they hunkered behind the chairs. Bomani considered this a very bad sign. Malone released Estlin, leapt to his feet, and grabbed one of the container doors swinging it closed.

"Something's coming," Estlin said, still gasping on the floor.

"No shit," Malone answered.

— « o » —

Constable Pao tapped the horn of the squad car as he braked to a stop at airport roadblock. Harry glanced at Jeanette and looked through the metal-reinforced plastic barricade that separated them from their driver. The airport security guard, Liufau, remained in the truck parked blocking the road, his head resting face down on the steering wheel. The grass was rippling in the breeze, but there was an unnatural stillness to the scene. As Pao leaned on the horn, Harry hoped Liufau was sleeping on the job.

Liufau shook himself awake and stumbled from the truck. "Hey, Pao, was I sleeping?"

"We need in, Liufau," Constable Pao responded. "Move the pylons."

"The airport's closed," Liufau replied. "It's really closed, Pao. No exceptions, not even me."

"I have Mr. Exception in the back seat. His name is Hatarei."

Liufau looked into the police car and waved at Harry. "Talofa! They noticed you," he confirmed. "After I turned them around, the marines had questions. I'll call it in." He walked back to his truck.

Pao swiveled in his seat. "If your name could get you in, why were you turned around?"

"I didn't introduce myself," Harry answered. "The timing wasn't right."

Liufau hung up his radio and returned from the security truck, one thumb hooked on his belt. "There's no answer. I can't let you in unless I get an answer."

"You going to stop me, Liufau?" Pao pressed. "I was told to deliver him."

"This is my job, Pao," Liufau argued. "You have to wait here. They do not like company."

"Move your truck," Pao responded.

"I can't. I'm not obstructing your authority, man," Liufau hastily explained. "This is a special situation."

Pao got out of the car and put himself nose to chin with Liufau. His next words were quiet and direct and forceful enough that Liufau stepped back.

Harry looked across the airfield. Liufau's call in hadn't summoned a response. There was no movement at all — except distantly — there was an object flying at the airport. It didn't move like a jet. It was close and yet too small for Harry to identify. He knocked on the back window and shouted through it, waving at the sky. "Something's coming."

The unidentified object rapidly approached. Harry couldn't resolve it until he realized that there were two objects and their trajectories became clear.

"Get down!" he shouted as the first missile smacked the runway. A cloud of earth churned upwards. He felt the thump through the frame of the squad car as he pulled Jeanette into the foot well. The explosion was immediately followed by a second blast.

— « o » —

Sergeant Malone flattened Estlin and bodily protected him as the impacts rattled the hanger. He measured the scale and proximity of the explosions from their sound and the vibration that reached them through the earth. Silence followed. When Estlin squirmed, Malone pressed an elbow between his shoulder blades. "Wait."

"Those were bombs," Bomani said. "Why?"

"Everyone has eyes on us." Malone released Estlin. "Someone saw our men go down."

"Beth." Bomani jumped to his feet and ran.

Malone followed him to the hangar door which had slammed inwards and was now drifting on its hinges. Bomani ducked low as he ran through the doorway without slowing down. Malone stopped at the shattered doorframe and peered out. Smoke was rising from the main and secondary runways. The soldiers at the door were still asleep, their skin dusted with fine earth.

Malone sprinted back to Estlin. "Wake everyone now!"

Estlin scrambled across the ground to place his hand on Verges' forehead. He released his grip and shook his head. "I can't."

"Do it!" Malone shouted.

"I can't!" Estlin shouted back.

"You woke me." Malone snapped.

"They did!" Estlin pressed both palms to Verges cheeks. "They aren't helping. Their focus isn't here. It's starting."

"What?"

"We can't stay here." Estlin stood, spinning in place, looking for a way out.

Sergeant Malone planted himself in front of Estlin. "We aren't leaving them."

"I'll carry her—"

Malone clipped him with a swift blow to the jaw, following through to barrel him to the ground. He grappled Estlin into a hold. With his free hand, Malone pulled black plastic binders from his hip pocket and looped Estlin's wrist, caught his other hand and secured them together behind his back.

Estlin spat curses as Malone dragged him to the cargo container. He hauled on the doors, letting them slam together. A second cable tie allowed him to secure the door while simultaneously pinning Estlin's hands to it.

"Are they in there?" he demanded.

Estlin glared at him.

"They're here," Malone said, scarcely caring if they weren't. "You stay. They stay."

He ignored Estlin's shouts as he jogged away. He knew the man couldn't appreciate the level of shit that was descending on them. On his way to the C-17, Malone tapped Pollock with his foot. There was no response, which wasn't surprising considering the man had already slept through a missile attack. A pair of F-18s cracked across the sky. Helicopter gunships would soon follow. Malone ran up the tail ramp of the *Cascade*.

Bomani was crouched next to Beth trying to convince her to take shelter in the hangar. "It is the safest place," he insisted.

"I doubt that," Malone interrupted. "Beth, I need you to wake everyone. Right now."

She looked at Bomani.

"Estlin can't do it." Malone looked into Beth's wide, dark eyes and hated himself. "But you're stronger, aren't you?"

"I'm stronger," she said, and opened her hands, the ever-present tremor still in her fingers.

"Start with him." Malone pointed at Dontis.

"Don't." Bomani placed his hand over Beth's. "We can leave, together, right now."

"There's nowhere to go," Malone insisted. "A fire storm is on the way. We need to secure this airfield."

"There's another answer!" Bomani responded.

"Not for me. Wake him. Wake them all."

Beth placed her hand on Dontis' cheek, bending down until their noses almost touched. Dontis shuddered, and his eyes sprang wide.

"Get away from me," he growled, slapping her hand as he grabbed the nearest seat and pulled himself to his feet.

"Sir, we have a situation," Malone said.

"Get her away from me." Dontis unleashed his hatred with each word.

Bomani took Beth's hand and obliged.

— « o » —

Harry held Jeanette wedged in the rear footwell of the squad car as hot air swept through the open driver's window. He raised his head. Pao and Liufau were on the ground, pressed tight against Liufau's security truck. Clumps of earth pelted down, and thick dust drifted on the breeze, sinking towards the lagoon. The main and secondary runways were cratered at their centers. The strikes were precise, delivering heavy, highly localized damage. Harry yanked on the squad car's disabled door handle. He slapped the window. "Pao!"

Jeanette cautiously extracted herself from the footwell. "Harry?"

"Missiles," he answered, raising his eyes to scan the sky.

Pao yanked the car door open. "Who's firing at us?"

"One of the subs?" Harry guessed. The impacts had supplanted what he'd seen of the inbound missiles — the trajectories he'd observed were fixed on their destinations, not origins.

"Get out of the car."

Harry obeyed and Pao closed the door behind him, trapping Jeanette in the backseat.

"We aren't spies." Harry protested, raising his hands. "I'm a biologist."

Pao pulled handcuffs from his belt. "Who's firing at us!"

"That wasn't a pot shot." Harry was rattled but starting to assemble information. "They hit the runway. That's all. They won't risk hitting the hangar or the aircraft."

"Who?"

"Everyone was in Wellington. Everyone." Harry knew he'd have to lay out the situation. "I don't know who has the balls to fire at you, but there are forty-eight countries with planes on the ground in Western Samoa. There are submarines and warships in your waters." He locked eyes with Pao. "Do you watch the news? The moon lit up. There was a splash in the Pacific. An alien wandered through a park in Wellington and now it's here."

"Bullshit." Pao spat the word at him. Distant sirens sounded.

"I met it. It was my job to take care of it. You think I'm a liar?" Harry had Pao's full attention. "I could spin a better lie. It's here. Whoever blasted the runways is trying to keep it here."

"There's no answer from the marines," Liufau interrupted. "No answer from the terminal."

"When the army arrived, what story did they give you?" Harry engaged Liufau. "You've seen something, haven't you?"

"It's big, Pao," Liufau said. "The marines were pointing machine guns at teenagers out on the rocks last night. They've got guys camped in the ditches in full camouflage."

"I'm going," Pao decided. "They stay with you. Keep the road blocked."

"You were right," Harry insisted. "Bringing me here, you got it exactly right. Don't botch it now."

Pao looked at Harry, then opened the back door of the squad car and waved at Jeanette. "Get out."

"Harry?" Jeanette called out in question as she cooperated with Pao, who immediately caught her wrist and closed a handcuff around it. Liufau kept both eyes on Harry and one hand on his holster.

"He can help you," Jeanette insisted.

Pao led Jeanette to Liufau's truck and threaded the cuffs through the side mirror before closing it around her other wrist. Pao turned from her and pressed a key into Liufau's hand. "Keep everyone back. If there are more strikes, evacuate." He pointed to Harry. "You're with me."

— « o » —

"How is this better?" Estlin yanked at the bindings. There was no give, except in the skin of his wrists. He twisted to put one shoulder to the container, trying to shift some of his weight from his hands, exploring with his fingers. "You need to tell me what the fucking plan is!"

They were going to get him killed, and they weren't even paying attention. It felt like they'd wrapped their minds into each other and blocked him out. He pulled, twisting his hand, broadcasting the hurt at them. He needed help. The squirrels had gathered in a ring around him, shaking their tails, looking for the threat.

"If you were wolves, no one would mess with me," Estlin told them, wondering if there was any way to use their protection. He directed their attention to the plastic straps binding his hands. "Can you gnaw through these?"

The squirrels responded with collective enthusiasm, but continued to gaze at him from a respectful distance.

"Now would be good."

A young squirrel took a hesitant step forward.

"You can do it." Estlin tried to press it into direct action. The squirrel took another step, but it had already figured out that he wasn't offering food.

A door clanged and the squirrels skittered away. Estlin couldn't twist far enough to see around the side of the container.

"Police! Police, coming in!"

"Over here!" Estlin yelled, sagging against the container. He wasn't sure if the Waes deserved thanks for his changing circumstances considering their broader culpability. "Help."

"Lyndie?"

Estlin borrowed the color-blind perspective of the young squirrel and saw two figures moving cautiously into the hangar. "Harry?"

"Come out, now! Hands where I can see them."

"I can't," Estlin answered.

"Lyndie!" Harry ran to the container, passing the police officer, who shouted after him. He arrived, grinning broadly. "Where are—?"

"In there."

Harry peered into the container. "Both! What happened?"

"The Waes put everyone down for a nap. They thought it might help, which, I guess it did." Estlin twisted and wiggled his fingers. "Could you please?"

"Damn." Harry leapt back from him. "What's wrong with your skin?"

"Drug allergy. I promise. A gift from Dr. Liev."

"Sorry. Everyone's been dead scared of alien pox since they arrived." He pulled a pocketknife from his boot.

The police officer with Harry was young, but moved with practiced authority. He crouched next to Verges, checking her pulse. "Drop that knife," he ordered. "He stays exactly as found."

"Pao, this is the most nonthreatening knife you have ever seen." Harry closed the short blade and placed the knife on the floor. "You need to look in this container."

Pao maintained his distance, focused on Verges. "What happened here?"

"They're asleep."

Pao tapped Verges cheek. "Bullshit. Who's in charge?"

"Harry is."

"Wrong answer."

"Then they are," Estlin responded, lifting his chin towards the container at his back.

"Who hit the runways?" Pao demanded.

"I have no idea," Estlin answered. "But the world is flipping out because there are aliens in the box behind me. And it turns out their job is to watch us flip out because they're here."

"What?" Harry interrupted.

"First contact generates conflict, and if you hang around to observe the conflict, you get a great data set for study," Estlin answered. He looked at the rafters, wanting to see the sky. The squirrels on the roof ducked and scattered, but he still snagged a view of the Hornets roaring overhead. "It's their job to watch the meltdown that's going to happen because they are here. So, I want to not be here. I would like to not watch this from as far from here as possible. It's time to go."

"I'm cutting him loose," Harry said.

"No, you aren't." Pao moved to look in the container, his hand on his gun. "I don't see.... Oh, shit."

"Aliens," Estlin said. "The blue kind."

Pao looked at Estlin. "Who are you?"

"They don't speak English," Harry answered. "I hired him to translate."

"Thanks for the job, Harry." Estlin raised his chin, displaying his most recent bruise. "I'm serious about the imminent conflict. We need to get out of here."

"And go where?"

"Anywhere." Estlin snatched another view from the roof. It was hard to recognize extremely distant objects. The squirrel assumed it was seeing birds out over the water, a lot of birds.

"Helicopters," Estlin said. He craned his neck, which, being the wrong neck, had no effect on the view. He nudged the squirrel on the roof, wanting to see the whole airfield. It dropped back to all fours and made a quick jump turn. That's when he saw her. She was sitting on the sloping metal — a ghost, dressed as she was when she'd died.

"Oh, fuck," Estlin whispered. He shrank from the vision, giving up his view of the sky only to find her standing before him in the hangar. Yidge was looking right at him with her hands at her sides. "Harry...?"

She was her own source of light, growing brighter until the glare should have washed away the details of her hair, her hands, her eyes, but instead they burned clear.

"I see her," Harry said.

"She's dead," Estlin said. "Harry, she died."

"I know."

Estlin turned his head aside and squeezed his eyes shut. This opened the image even more. He could see the bone beneath the skin, the bullet against the bone. He opened his eyes and let the angel burn him.

"You're dead," he said, his eyes hot and wet, though the fierce glare was from the rising from the wrong end of his optic nerve. He felt Pao backing away, fighting the impulse to run while, at Yidge's feet, Verges was awake.

— « o » —

"She's dead," Beth said.

To Bomani, nothing could be more apparent. The woman in the aisle was wearing her own blood but stood without pain. She spoke to them without lungs or voice, her lips moving silently. He could not understand her, and it disturbed him to his very bones to look on one so completely visible and completely absent.

Beth was next to Sanford. She had not touched him, but he was awake, his eyes fixed on the apparition moving amongst them. Dr. Liev, too, had risen and was clinging to the nearest seat.

"How is she here?" Dontis asked, choking on his own voice.

"They stole her," Beth said. "When she died, they stole all of her. They're thieves. They're waiting for us to die."

— « o » —

Jeanette leaned against Liufau's truck. She took a breath and dropped her shoulders, trying to suppress the fight-or-flight imperative that had her heart pounding. A fire engine had arrived in a succession of vehicles belonging to volunteer firemen. They were now clustered at the truck, jumping into their kit as the fire chief grabbed pylons from the road, hurling them aside. There was no word from Pao or Harry, and the argument between the fire chief and Liufau was escalating.

"Move your truck!"

"Pao said to wait here." Liufau held his ground.

"Get that truck and that girl out of the road," the fire chief insisted. "If you don't move, we'll move you."

The columns of smoke from the runways were dwindling. Jeanette could understand why one wouldn't immediately rush to a place where bombs had fallen, but there was no movement at all on the airfield. "Where's the other truck?" she asked.

"Which truck?"

"The airport fire truck," Jeanette answered. "Bright yellow. It was out there an hour ago. Where is it?"

"She's right. They were hosing down the runway." Liufau was staring at the airfield. "The marines were there, too."

"I don't see anyone," the fire chief answered.

Jeanette's focus shifted from the runways to the empty road before them where a dead woman stood, beckoning to them. Jeanette had always thought of ghosts as faint wisps in dark places, but the woman was standing in the full sun. "Do you see her?" she asked.

There was a sense of explanation in the woman's eyes but no sound from her lips. She reappeared, closer, raised one hand before her, open to Jeanette, and stretched her other arm out behind her to point at the hangar. Then she was gone.

"Did she—" The fire chief pressed his hand against his chest.

"I'm going," Jeanette said, ignoring the bindings on her wrists. "You saw her. I have to go."

"She pointed at all of us." Liufau used the key from his pocket to released one of the cuffs. He pulled it free of the mirror bracket, but kept his grip on it. "Can I leave her with you?"

"What? No!" Jeanette turned to the fire chief, even as he accepted the open end of the cuffs as though it were a leash.

"It's my job," Liufau said. "And I'm going to do it. I don't argue with the dead." He walked around the truck and got in behind the wheel.

"Wait," the fire chief called, pulling Jeanette with him. He leaned in the open passenger window. "Roll the windows up," he said. "Close the vents. If you get any whiff of bad air, lean on the horn and turn around. Getting on the radio comes third. Don't get out of the truck unless you see walking, talking people over there."

"You think it was a chemical attack?" Liufau looked back at the airfield.

"It's too quiet." The fire chief frowned. "And I just saw a ghost. We've got a carrier out there. They have the gear and skills for whatever this is, but if there are people that need help now—"

"You got it," Liufau answered. He rolled up the window and started the truck.

— « o » —

Sergeant Malone watched the insubstantial Yidge fade away, his eyes straining to hold her in view.

"I met her." Sanford sat in the aisle way, stunned. "Is she—?"

"She died two days ago," Malone answered.

Pollock stumbled up the ramp. "There's a dead girl out there."

"Did she say anything to you?" Malone asked.

"Couldn't hear her," he answered. "The sky is full of birds. We have air support coming hot and heavy, and there are *birds*. The seagulls are screaming."

"Sergeant!" Dontis recovered his voice. "Call for a helicopter. I want a Seahawk to evacuate key personnel."

"What?" Malone demanded.

"They're twisting our perceptions," Dontis responded. "Decisions made within their range of influence cannot be trusted. This airfield will be quarantined. Report to Fleckman and secure the hangar."

Malone exchanged glances with Pollock and turned on his heel. He jogged from the ramp to the tarmac. The guards at the hangar door were on their knees. Malone hauled the nearest one to his feet.

"Keep your posts," he ordered and continued into the hangar. Fleckman was upright and surrounded by his staff. Verges was blocking his view of Estlin, and the hangar population had increased.

"Commander!" Malone announced himself.

"Malone, report!"

"The aliens dropped all of us, right to the end of the runway," Malone answered. "Both runways were bombed.

Dontis would like you to know he plans to rabbit and quarantine the airfield."

"I'm quarantining the island," Fleckman answered. "No one leaves."

"Air support is inbound," Malone continued. "They'll drop ground support at least a mile back from the blackout line and contain us from there. The apparition, if you saw it, was Yidge Lee. She was killed on the *Lu Hai*. And that's Harry Hatarei, New Zealand's *first* first-contact guy. I don't know how the hell he got in here."

"Officer Pao found him on the mountain with a radio antenna." Fleckman introduced the cop next to him with an off-hand gesture. They both regarded Hatarei who was crouched with Verges, his complete attention on Estlin and the aliens. "He's our problem now. Pao is returning to the civilian checkpoint to coordinate with our forces. The security perimeter will be expanding. Residential areas will be evacuated. I'm going to get on a radio and clarify the situation. Keep the chaos to a minimum."

"Yes, Commander," Malone answered, and Fleckman left him with the cop.

"Aliens," Pao said.

"Our security will escort you out," he told Pao, "and explain why you won't be talking about what you've seen here." He conveyed that order to a marine with a single gesture and went to check on the aliens. They were where he'd left him, or at least they appeared to be contained. Harry Hatarei was supporting Estlin, who was slumped against his restraints, looking significantly worse for wear.

"What happened?" Malone asked Verges. "He was conscious when I left him."

"Cut him loose," Harry responded. "Or I will kick your ass out your ear."

Chapter Twenty-two

Estlin's pulse was throbbing in his fingertips. Someone was holding his hand, their thumb stroking his palm. It was confusing, this comfort as he woke on a hard floor painted with the acrid smell of jet fuel. A concerned squirrel advanced to sniff his pillow.

"No squirrels on the bed," he mumbled and tried to blindly push it off with the back of his other hand. The squirrel leaned into his touch.

"Harry?" Verges called quietly.

The squirrel was sent away with a snapping of fingers. The waetapu were apologizing, creating a rippling blue surf that responded to his slightest movements.

You should be sorry, Estlin thought.

"Lyndie?" Harry's fingers were on his ear.

Estlin opened his eyes. "Don't pinch me."

"There you are." Harry clapped his cheek. "Good."

Verges helped Estlin sit up. Her flight jacket was folded in her lap. Estlin recognized his pillow and the press of her thumb, now on his shoulder, supporting him. Verges released her grip as soon as Estlin took notice of it.

"What the hell was that?" Harry asked, crouching close by with Malone standing behind him.

"They were trying to communicate without me." Estlin covered his eyes with one hand. There was white at the center of the black, like a burned-in sunspot. "They were pushing to get you to see what you didn't want to see. The wattage on that was brain-damage high."

"Yeah, you went a bit gray," Harry answered. "I thought it was the subject matter."

"That, too."

"Could you ask them not to do that?" Malone suggested.

"They know," Estlin answered.

"Was that Yidge?" Verges asked.

Estlin met her eyes and didn't have to answer her any further. "What'd I miss?"

"We saw her, briefly," Harry answered. "Then she just faded out."

Pointless, Estlin thought and was suddenly horrified by the fate the Waes had expected him to accept — realizing fully what it meant to be collected by them. He pressed his spine against the container and got his feet beneath him. Verges gave him room, but he had to shake Harry and Malone off his elbows.

"Don't help me," he snapped, pointing at Malone. There was more than one ring of bruises around his wrist.

Malone stepped back with a casual shrug. "You didn't encourage them to mess with us this time?"

"No." Estlin's response was bitter, his head was throbbing. The noise from low flying fighters was rattling the light fixtures. The rippling blue from the Waes had vanished. He peered through the barred windows of the container door. The Waes were perched on one of the chairs and regarded him with interest. "Don't blink at me. You heard Harry. What the hell was that?"

The Waes were unresponsive. Estlin tried to push the question at them, but trying to re-envision Yidge was immediately painful. He couldn't think of any other way to ask. He couldn't think what meaningful answer they could offer. He gave the cargo container a frustrated shove and spun away from it.

"Where are you going?" Malone asked.

"To the fucking bathroom." Estlin pressed the back of his hand to his nostrils and was unsurprised to find a trace of blood. "And you can stay the fuck out here and watch them while I'm gone."

"You've really pissed him off," Harry told Malone.

Estlin stopped himself and leaned against the container window again. "Stay," he said, not caring if they listened, and stomped away. Harry was a half-step behind him. "I can hold my own dick, Harry. You need to deal with these people. Sounds like the fucking sky is falling."

"There's a job I want," Harry replied sarcastically. "You're all right?"

"Spectacular," Estlin answered.

"I'll do what I can." Harry waved at Malone. "Can you tell your air support to turn down the noise? It's not helping."

"F-18s," Verges told Estlin, still following him. "A squadron."

Estlin tried to glare at her, but it became an apologetic grimace.

"Trust me. I'll wait outside," she said. "I've got nothing better to do."

Estlin pushed through the bathroom door. The sink was rust stained, but the water was cool and clear. He leaned over and tried to calm the fuck down because he'd hit the point where he couldn't think without swearing. He drew a deep breath, raised his head and found Yidge in the mirror. He leapt back, fell over his feet and landed on his tailbone, slapping the tiles with his hands, too late to catch himself. "Fuck!"

There was a knock on the door.

"Stay out," he yelled, adding, "please." From the floor, he couldn't see Yidge anywhere in the room. He got to his knees and raised his eyes above the sink level. She was watching from the mirror, asking questions with silently moving lips.

"That hurt." He got to his feet, faced the mirror and resisted the impulse to twist away to search for Yidge in the empty room. Her reflection was fully animated and seemed to have a lot to say. "Stop talking, Yidge. It doesn't work."

The look of consternation on her face was pure Yidge. "You know your name?"

She nodded.

"You know you're dead?"

She nodded.

"Are you *you* or are you them?"

She raised both hands palms forward because it was a stupid question.

"Are you a puppet?" he asked, but he knew, even as she shook her head, that while she was less than who she'd been, she was still more than that. "I'm sorry, Yidge."

She tipped her head, another question on her lips.

"I'm sorry," he said, and tried not to see her disappointment as he stepped away from the looking glass. Verges was waiting for him at the door.

"You all right?" she asked.

"All right." He considered the words as he walked directly to the cargo container.

Harry stepped into his path. "What is it?" he asked.

"Them," Estlin answered. He slapped the metal door of the container twice. "You want to talk to me, then *you* talk to me."

"You want to calm down?" Malone asked.

"No." Estlin slapped the container again, hurting his hand. "Explain. Or I will walk away."

He maintained his grip on the container as colors expanded from it, brightening the entire hangar bay. "Light show," he said, noting that Harry, in particular, was brightly illuminated. "They are glad to see you, Harry."

"What're you seeing?"

"Light," Estlin answered. "Stars. I think they've been here before."

The scale of time involved was so vast that the Waes used a change in the sun's position in the galaxy to mark it. The story began with quiet clarity, as though the waetapu were drawing a giant canvas across the head of a pin, following the traces of history to a specific point. "It's been a long time, but they are not too late."

"They've been here?" Harry said.

"They saw a flash, the sign of others reaching," Estlin answered. "They came and found darkness. The fourth planet had burnt itself to dark. This world was alive, but no one here wanted to talk of the stars."

"Lyndie, you're not making sense."

Red ash filled the sky. Estlin gripped Harry's arm. There was no softening of the memory, no comfort in the depth of history. It was a memory living in the present tense. "This was the first time they had seen the flash of life. They'd traveled for generations and seen many places where life had burned to silence. They saw the flash and came with care and speed and expectation. The horror of arriving to greet a civilization that had advanced far enough to reach for distant stars only to be consumed by a single failure.... They are travelers, and this is where their path changed. It was this horror that convinced the nsangunsangu to share the grace equations."

"The unsangsang?"

"The very smart trees of another world," Estlin explained. "Trees that imagined how to fold the space between the stars. Here is where they decided the knowledge should not be theirs alone."

He raised a hand to hold back Harry's questions. There was too much color. The room was transformed into a kaleidoscope, many-angled shards of every shade flared bright and were folded into nothingness.

"Sharing brought new sorrows," he said. "Where they gave light, the dark still followed — so many types of darkness, brought so many ways. Swift ends for civilizations that would not have walked the stars on their own."

Estlin was dizzy. The complex information pressed into his brain in a rapid swirling dance, with events presented in a way that was both simultaneous and sequential. He wasn't sure if sorrow was the correct word, but each unique equation that nullified itself was a loss and these intellectual losses were mated with physical negatives. While periods of dark/cold could be accepted or even embraced as part of natural renewal, progression towards an infinite dark/cold was terrifying. "They studied every civilization that accepted their gift to learn where the light would remain and where it would sharply fade. At first, they studied without selection. All received the gift and outcomes were compared to predictions, until the predictions became useful."

"Lyndie, take a breath."

Estlin's vision cleared. He saw Harry. Malone and Verges stood close behind him. Estlin gave them the last of it. "They came to gather information for the prediction. But we saw the Burst and understood — or at least began to imagine. Bomani and Sanford have started to work it out. A few pages of math and their prediction no longer matters. The idea is already here. They know our impatience. They know that in a thousand years, without the gift, we would still build. We would engage with the danger. And this is the first place, the place where they cannot allow history to repeat."

"By history, you mean extinction?" Verges asked.

"Yes," Estlin said. "This was a different world when they visited. Think cretaceous."

"You're suggesting they were here 65 million years ago." Malone was incredulous.

"I might be off by a few million years. Same difference," Estlin answered. "They came to watch us die for their data set. But the fight you've been fixing for since they arrived is no longer necessary. That nap you just took was them trying to put the brakes on, but now they believe their attempt to interrupt events was...incorrect. So, either we stop ourselves or...." Estlin trailed off. Yidge's ghost was sitting on the arm of the Adirondack chair. No one was taking any notice of her. "I think my brain is leaking."

"We're about to have a lot of company," Verges said, pointing skyward. The cacophony of helicopters and other aircraft was rapidly increasing. "What should we do?"

Nothing, Estlin thought, then shook his head. The Waes weren't offering any answers and inaction hadn't saved him yet. "I'm going outside."

— « o » —

"I'm going outside," Beth said quietly.

Bomani heard her. Dontis' shouts were ringing from the cockpit. He seemed unable to reconcile his expectation of privileged authority with the report that American ground support would work in from a wide perimeter and no airlift to safety was in the forecast.

Dr. Liev was livid and directing her anger at Sergeant Pollock. "I have a child in my charge. She must be protected. Anything less than immediate evacuation is unacceptable."

"Why are you telling me?" Pollock responded, turning to climb the steep steps to the cockpit.

"Missiles." Sanford remained in his seat, shell-shocked. "Someone fired missiles at us. We're at war."

Beth slipped her hand into Bomani's. "Come with me?"

"Where?"

"Outside."

Bomani nodded and stood. He had hesitated before, when Estlin had presented the opportunity. He would not make that mistake again.

Sanford placed a hand on his wrist. "Bomani?"

"We're leaving."

"They won't let you go."

"Stay safe, my friend," he replied and let Beth's slight hand lead him to the tail ramp.

— « o » —

Estlin paused at the hangar door, shielding his eyes against the sunlight. Hot wind swept across the airfield, bending the grass, and the verdant mountains were gathering wisps of cloud. Gulls circled and thumping rotor blades heralded the approach of heavier flyers. He closed his eyes and felt the Waes drawing the sensations through him. The air tasted of dust. The soldiers at the door raised their guns and fell frozen into the gap between orders and reality.

"Stand down." Sergeant Malone's directive was exact and immediately obeyed. "Hume, get back inside."

Estlin ignored Malone. He crossed the taxiway to the grass. The helicopters circled close, crowding the sky.

Above him, radios were active, and the Waes were listening. The new arrivals were delivering assistance whether it was welcome or not. The Americans were unhappy with the incursions into their airspace, but weren't ready to shoot their allies yet.

Estlin chose a single helicopter and pointed directly at it. "Land." He whispered the suggestion and lowered his hand. The white helicopter hovered as the pilot considered this gesture that defied all the chatter on his radio. "Land," Estlin insisted, pointing at the ground. "Land."

The pilot obeyed.

"Stop," Malone ordered.

"Lyndie, this is a bad idea," Harry suggested.

"They're here," Estlin argued. "Do you think they're turning back?"

F-18s cut through the airspace aggressively, but maintained the prescribed distance between the hot wash of air from their engines and the helicopters.

Malone stepped in front of Estlin. "You are not a strategic thinker."

Estlin pointed at a helicopter wearing desert camouflage and Cyrillic text. He gestured clearly. "Land."

"You can't—"

"Land." Estlin waved broadly. "All of you."

Twelve seagulls dropped to the ground his feet, forcing Malone and Harry to step back. Estlin found it hysterically funny, seeing himself as a small figure surrounded by birds. He didn't care if the antihistamines had wiped all sense from him or if he'd simply snapped. He raised both hands, waved at a South African helicopter hovering overhead and directed it downwards. "You. Land."

"Lyndie, what are you doing?" Harry demanded. "Is this them or you?"

"Stop," said Malone. "Or I'll stop you."

"You won't," Harry answered, placing a hand on Estlin's shoulder. "I understand what you're trying to do but—"

Harry was interrupted by a blue-footed booby. It dove into the scene, forcing him to step out of the way. The bird landed awkwardly with its wide wings raised as it almost fell over its own feet.

"Beth, get back in the plane!" Dr. Liev shrieked. She was on the tail ramp of the C-17, unwilling to step from it. Beth crossed the tarmac with Bomani.

"She can't be here," Estlin protested.

"You're making a mistake." Beth was angry. "The sky isn't yours to call on."

"Really?" He waved a hand at the birds surrounding him.

"That's them," she said, pointing at the hangar, "making you loud."

"I don't care."

"That's why you have to stop," Malone said. He turned to Bomani. "Take her inside."

"You're tired," Beth told Estlin. "You should sleep. That place where they pressed, I know where it is now."

Estlin thought she was going to execute her simple threat, but then Beth tilted her head and looked to Malone.

"Who's Dewey?" she asked.

"Sniper," Malone said. He grabbed Estlin's shoulder. The seagulls scattered into the air, the flock turning around them. The ungainly booby was beating its wings, considering take off. Estlin watched in a detached manner, not realizing that the perspective wasn't his own until he saw himself fall.

"Down!" Malone shouted as the cloud of crying gulls turned upwards.

Estlin was down, crashing to the tarmac, his hip and jaw striking so hard that he felt disoriented even with his face against the ground. Malone and Harry dropped alongside him. He felt the blood pouring from Malone's arm where a bullet had torn away a strip of skin. "That hurts." Estlin raised himself slightly.

Malone swept an arm out, grabbed Estlin's head and pressed it to the tarmac. "Stay down," he snarled.

Soldiers on all sides of the hangar shifted into fighting formation. Those nearest to the hangar door moved forward, placing themselves into the line of fire. Pinned as he was, Estlin could still see far more of the situation than should have been possible. Harry was crouched low, eyes up and ready to move. Bomani was sprawled on the ground, folded almost completely around Beth, holding her tight and hiding her from view.

"What hurts?" Malone asked, his hand still pressing on Estlin's skull.

"Your arm," Estlin answered, cataloguing other pains. His shins hurt, and he realized he was on the ground because Malone could kick faster than he could shout.

"Hume! Were you hit?"

"No," Estlin answered quietly.

"No extra holes?"

"No."

"You are an idiot."

"I know." Estlin glanced over to the rooftop of the distant terminal building, tracking the view he'd glimpsed back to its source. It was farther away than he'd thought, impossibly far. Fleckman was shouting through all the open radios, but it was Beth's ecstatic whisper that Estlin heard.

"They're listening," she said.

The blood had the waetapu's attention, and they were singing with interest. The crowd of minds that Estlin had welcomed to the airfield was singing back. He'd brought them down, and they all had bullets waiting to kick in their palms, shed their jackets and fly. Now, he wanted them all to get back in their machines and climb with the birds.

"They're advancing," Harry said.

Malone rolled himself deftly into a seated position, a hand pressed tight against the gash on his arm. "Fucking friendly fire."

"He was aiming at the booby," Estlin offered.

Malone looked at him as though he'd lost his mind.

"The bird. The one that wasn't a seagull," Estlin clarified. "He was ordered to wing me."

"I took a bullet for a booby?" Malone stopped abruptly. "How do you know that?"

Estlin didn't answer.

"I don't like this," Malone muttered. "They can't have that kind of range."

— « o » —

Sanford was pressed against the window mounted in one of the emergency doors of the C-17. Dontis had been evicted from the cockpit, but remained upstairs engaged in a voluminous argument. Outside everyone had dropped to the ground, covering their heads. Sergeant Pollock slid so quickly down the steep steps from the cockpit that Sanford thought he'd fallen, but he'd landed on his feet and sprinted out of the aircraft.

"They're shooting!" Dr. Liev shouted as Pollock bolted down the ramp.

Dontis descended from the cockpit level.

"The helicopters are landing," Sanford relayed from the window on the emergency door. "They have guns. What do we do?"

"Get away from the window," Dontis answered gruffly, marching down the aisle, stopping at the top of the ramp. "Make a choice," he growled at Dr. Liev and punched the ramp controls.

She turned in alarm as the ramp rose beneath her feet and scrambled into the belly of the aircraft, gesticulating wildly. "Beth is out there!"

"If you lost track of your charge, that's on you," Dontis replied.

"Bomani is with her," Sanford offered.

"He dragged her away from me!" Liev snapped. "This is his fault!"

— « o » —

"Bomani, go now!" Sergeant Malone yelled.

Bomani picked up Beth and ran for the hangar.

Sergeant Pollock dropped into a crouch next to Malone, having sprinted to them, clutching a medical kit. "Dewey's very sorry," he said, inspecting the wound on Malone's arm. "It's not deep. Deal with it inside."

"What was that?" Harry demanded.

"Miscommunication," Pollock suggested.

"My ass," Malone answered. "Where's Dontis?"

"On the *Cascade*. There was some confusion."

"He thought he could prevent things that had already happened?"

"You could say that," Pollock answered. "He's trying to set a quarantine that won't include himself, and the *international aid* descending on us alarmed him. Fleckman has the airwaves now. He's instructed everyone to stay with their rides. Our forces are staging from a football field two miles from here."

"What are we doing?"

"Holding the airfield," Pollock answered. "Fleckman wants you inside."

Hot wind was billowing across the tarmac, the breath of idling helicopter engines. Estlin realized that the new arrivals were converging on the hangar, contrary to instruction. He wondered whether his odds for survival had improved.

Harry leapt to his feet. "I'll go talk to them."

"You have no authority," Malone responded.

"Would you like them to stay out of the hangar?"

"Go," Malone answered. "Pollock, go with him. Keep Fleckman informed."

"Harry?" Estlin rose.

"See you later," Harry answered.

"Go back inside." Malone pointed at Estlin. "Go."

"You, too," Pollock added as he followed Harry.

"Right." Malone rolled to his feet, one hand pressed tight across the graze. He gestured for Estlin to precede him and glanced over his shoulder to where Harry was holding back the advancing forces with his open empty hands.

Chapter Twenty-three

Another formation of helicopters flew over the roadway, descending behind a distant tree line. Jeanette sat with Liufau in the shade of his truck. Her wrists were cuffed together in front of her. The big security guard hadn't made it to the airfield as soldiers had sprung from the grass to stop his truck, sending him back to the firefighters to "stand-by" and wait for further instructions.

"They're landing on the football field," Liufau said.

A squad car emerged from the airfield with its lights flashing. It was waved through a new military checkpoint after a brief stop. Liufau got to his feet. "That's Pao. We'll get answers now."

As Constable Pao pulled up, the firemen and Liufau gathered around him.

"We're pushing the perimeter back," Pao announced. "Liufau, close the highway. Go up the road and throw your pylons down. This is a military situation. A state of emergency has been declared. We need an orderly evacuation of the immediate area."

Pao tapped Liufau to follow him and split away from the firemen to approach Jeanette.

"Where's Harry?" Jeanette asked.

"He's where he wants to be," Pao told her. "You and I are going to have a talk later. Well, you'll talk, because in the interests of National Security I can't say a goddamn thing about what I saw in there." He held out his hand, and Liufau dropped the handcuff key into it.

"Keep her with you," Pao told Liufau as he released the cuffs.

— « o » —

A doctor from Commander Fleckman's team had pulled two stitches across the gouge on Malone's arm and thrown a dressing on it. After that, he'd been left to babysit Estlin, who was so tired and withdrawn that Verges couldn't draw him into conversation. The RAF pilot was pressing a palm full of water to the back of her neck. She'd gathered several water bottles and settled with Estlin, joining him in quiet isolation. Malone wondered if she would soon be displaced by more recent arrivals.

"Sergeant, you're wanted." A young yeoman directed him to the corner office. She'd arrived with the reinforcements as the carrier deliberately dumped crew who'd had direct exposure to the aliens ashore.

"Commander Fleckman?" Malone paused at the office door.

"Have a seat," Fleckman said.

Malone closed the door behind him. "Who hit us?"

Fleckman didn't answer.

"Whoever hit us sent teams in with that flight of angels," Malone said, because it's what he would have done.

"I've given the Brits access to the terminal building and shipped everyone else to the Rainmaker Hotel," Fleckman responded evenly. "We're siphoning fuel from the helicopters to avoid unexpected departures."

"We're staying?"

Fleckman nodded. "The squirrels are constantly triggering alarms, particularly around the hangar. It makes the optical fencing useless."

"I'll speak to Hume. He can't send them away, but maybe he can bring them closer," Malone suggested. "Get them inside the perimeter and keep them there."

"He's slipping."

"I think he had a badly-timed moment of self-interest."

"You're generous," Fleckman responded.

Malone disagreed. "He was having an allergic reaction to drugs designed to alter his brain chemistry. That was our mistake. It bit us in the ass."

"His skills are a form of untreated mental illness." Fleckman continued. "We need to ensure that everyone placed in direct contact with the aliens is absolutely reliable."

Malone's derisive snort was not appreciated.

Fleckman crossed his arms. "We've over invested in a single avenue of communication."

"No one else has made any progress."

"No one has been offered the opportunity since they got here," Fleckman noted.

"Beth."

"An ill-conceived, unscientific effort," Fleckman answered.

Malone's mind was on another track. "On the flight, Beth was violent when Liev's medication wore off," he said. "She was angry and impulsive. Did the doctor warn you about side effects?"

"We'll be pursuing less subjective options soon."

— « o » —

Harry was overbaked, and he wanted to get back to the hangar before anyone decided he could be sent away with the others. He'd stepped into the chaos with grand intentions and wound up assisting the Americans as they shuffled everyone off the airfield with an alarming speed. Sergeant Pollock was assembling a master list of all the new arrivals.

The soldier assigned to the next area was standing in the thin shadow of a RNZAF Seasprite — the helicopter Harry had ridden in two days ago. Wilhem's Greenpeace bird was parked nearby, but Harry decided not to draw attention to it. "Where's this crew?" he demanded, pointing at the helicopter.

"They were transported to the hotel," the soldier answered.

"Get them back."

"I'm not authorized to do that, sir."

"Where's your list? I need to know who was aboard." Harry snatched the scrap of paper from the soldier. Bernie's name was at the top of it.

"Pollock!" he yelled loud enough that Pollock came bounding over from another helicopter. Harry held out the list, pointing at Bernie's name. "That's my assistant. If you want to know how they flattened you today, you'll get him back here. He's figured out their long range communication trick."

"Bats. Big bats." The soldier with them raised a hand to block the sun as the eight brown fruit bats flew over. Sergeant Pollock stepped away from the helicopter to watch the swooping, diving cluster of bats fly towards the green peaks.

"All the bats left Tongatapu yesterday," Harry said. "Flying foxes. The locals think the volcano is about to belch, but I knew you were in the area."

"How many bats?" Pollock asked.

"Hundreds? Thousands?" Harry guessed. "Bernie will know."

"You think they're coming here?"

"Soon," Harry answered. "See that dark patch of sky?"

"Shit," Pollock said. "How the hell will we deal with that?"

"Ask Lyndie," Harry answered. "He speaks bat."

— « o » —

"I don't speak bat," Estlin protested.

"Harry says you do," Sergeant Malone answered.

"I worked one job with him," Estlin said. "One barn. One group of bats. Once."

Verges was listening closely to the entire exchange.

"The bats are coming," Malone answered, "because you played pied-piper on the flight here. This is your problem to fix."

"What?"

"They're flying rats. Turn your mojo on," Malone answered. "You dragged them from their island, send them back."

"I didn't—" Estlin silenced himself to listen to a rustling in the back of his mind. "Crap. You're not kidding."

"Okay, we're going outside."

"Not without an umbrella," Estlin answered. He'd been hit by bat shit before.

"We're going outside because you are not bringing them in here," Malone said. "We don't need any more wildlife in the rafters."

"It doesn't work the way you think," Estlin said. "I can't just yell at the sky."

"You did earlier."

Estlin stifled a childish retort. He didn't want bats in the hangar either, but he didn't know how to stop them. What alternative could he offer them if he could even connect? As his mental gears ground to a halt, the bats swept over the building in a hungry flurry of beating wings.

"They aren't stopping," Estlin said. "They won't stop here."

"Good," Malone said.

Estlin couldn't read Verges' expression, but could guess what she was thinking. "I didn't do anything," he said. "They're hungry. They're going into the mountains for fruit."

"Bat whisperer," Malone said.

"No, that's not—" Estlin realized he was being provoked. "Anyone could read that from their flight path. It's basic behavior."

"Says the man in the windowless room," Malone responded, satisfied.

— « o » —

Jeanette was literally hiding in Liufau's shadow. She stood one step behind him wearing a baseball cap borrowed from his truck, watching another convoy of Hummers arrive from the airport. She dutifully looked for Harry in the crowd of people deposited at the highway roadblock. The highway had become a transfer point, where airport arrivals were transferred to buses manned by immigration officers. Jeanette had learned not to drift more than a foot from Liufau. Any distracted step left her presence open to question and drew the question of whether she should be sent on with the others to the hotel that Liufau called the Ratmaker. The hotel was under renovation and its unoccupied space had apparently been commandeered and secured.

Wilhem had walked by earlier without giving Jeanette any sign of recognition. She reminded herself to be glad that Harry was still on the inside then spotted another familiar face. "Bernie?"

"Jeanette! You made it." Bernie bounced in place. "Where's Harry?"

"At the airport."

"Oh, good," said Bernie. "Did you see the bats?"

Jeanette pointed at the hillside where the bats were moving through the fruit trees.

"Wow," he said. "That's going to be a real kick to the ecosystem."

"Dr. Bernard Springer!" A soldier standing next to the first Hummer shouted.

"That's me," Bernie said to Jeanette. "That's me!" Bernie scrambled back to the Hummer and dug his passport out of his pocket. "That's me," he said.

The soldier glanced at the open passport. "Get in," he said. "You're wanted back at the hangar."

"Thank you!" Bernie exclaimed. "Nobody's happy about being sent out here. The team I arrived with—"

"Just you," the soldier said.

"Bernie!" Jeanette interjected.

"This is Dr. Goff," Bernie said. "She's also a biologist and—"

"No," the soldier said.

"I'm sorry, Jeanette."

"Don't be sorry," Jeanette responded. "Do something."

Bernie twisted his fingers together as he considered and abandoned multiple points of argument. "Dr. Goff has been working with Harry Hatarei. She knows Estlin, *the translator*. She and Estlin were *close friends*." Bernie was so unsubtle it was almost comical.

"Get in the vehicle, Dr. Springer."

"Tell Harry that I'm here," Jeanette said.

— « o » —

Harry watched a HumVee follow the airport access road to the hanger. His frank conversation with Commander Fleckman had been surprisingly productive. He'd been granted access to the hangar. Harry didn't care whether Fleckman was angling to use his diplomatic leverage or his friendship with Estlin, or just wanted the bucketload of alien secrets he'd promised. He was where he needed to be, and now all he had to do was wait for the assistant he had so forcibly demanded. The HumVee pulled up, and Bernie was frantically waving at him from the back seat.

"Bernie." Harry held the door as Bernie hopped out of the HumVee. "I just traded everything you know for a sandwich."

Bernie was nonplused. "How'd you get here?"

"I got here," Harry answered. "You're going to give a briefing. What you know and what you've guessed."

"But—"

"We need everyone to settle. I think the quarantine will help, and they'll accept the quarantine if we give them solid reasons for it."

"But—"

"As we're all up against it, I suggested they bring in the guy who figured out how they're communicating." Harry clapped a hand on his shoulder. "I want a list of everyone who attends your briefing. Don't agonize over minutia; just throw the information at them. After that, I'm putting you in charge of the sandwiches. Have you got a credit card?"

Bernie nodded with much trepidation.

"The Americans have closed the airspace. Your equipment is in Apia. You have time, and we have no supplies. Phone the local grocery."

"Harry?"

"I want you to stand next to a table of fresh food and talk to everyone who turns up," Harry said. "Find out what we've missed. I've got to go. Estlin and both Waes are in that hangar. I've been away from them for too long."

"Harry, wait!" Bernie called after him.

"What?"

"Jeanette's stuck out there," he said. "She wanted me to tell you."

"Okay."

"Okay?"

"You told me," Harry answered. "Sandwiches, Bernie. I like roast beef."

The soldier at the hangar door admitted Harry. The Waes were contained. Estlin and the pilot, Verges, were seated against the far wall. Harry noted that they had tucked the two reclining chairs together and each was canted towards the other for conversation. When he'd met Verges earlier, there had been little time for introductions. The question of how she'd ended up in thick with the Americans remained, but he appreciated the concern she'd shown for Estlin.

"Words are overrated," Estlin said. "They are as dull as they are precise. Think of the places music or dance can take you — the concepts that can be conveyed and how you understand them from within to a degree that is impossible to capture with a collection of words. This is all dance and music."

"I don't understand how you make sense of it," she said.

"Bees dance," Estlin said, "to communicate flight paths — directions, distances, rewards. We watch the dance and try to understand. The other bees don't watch the dance, they join the dance, they feel it. If you feel it with them, the leap to understanding is much shorter."

Verges swung a considering gaze in Estlin's direction.

"It's just an example," Estlin said. "Bad example. I don't really listen to bugs."

Harry decided to step in before his friend ruined any chance he had with the pilot. "Bernie's here," he said. "He's going to give a briefing, then he'll probably come poke you in the eye."

Estlin's quizzical expression at Harry's obscure entry to the conversation was not without shades of annoyance. "You were gone a long time."

"Transforming chaos into order," Harry answered. "And they had to decide to let me back in here. I interrupted you. Bees?"

Estlin ducked his head. "I'm too tired to think," he said. "And Fleckman wants me to keep my mind to myself for awhile."

"How's the rash?"

"Great." Estlin scratched the crux of his elbow in response to the question. He caught himself and stopped. "Thanks for asking."

"*Can* you keep your mind to yourself?" Harry asked.

"They've been quiet."

"Do they mind being locked up?" Verges asked.

"They've broken out before," Estlin answered.

"The cage seems small once you've seen them in the rafters," she said. "Do they need anything?"

"*Anything* is difficult to visualize. You have to work from specifics and try to open it up."

Harry caught the look in Estlin's eyes. "I think you're breaking the rules."

"It's Verges who is asking," Estlin answered as he took her hand. "Specifics."

"Food. Water. Bedding," she said. "They go still. They put us to sleep. But do they dream?"

"That's another question," Harry said. "Lyndie?"

"The air is sufficiently moist," Estlin answered. "The chairs could sustain them for weeks. I think, if we gave them rope, they might build elevated beds, but it's not a priority."

Harry turned his attention to the Waes and felt he should have greeted them properly. "In Wellington, they always rested in high places."

"They've missed you, Harry," Estlin said and went silent.

Sergeant Malone casually crossed the hangar floor from his chair by the cargo pod. "He's breaking the rules, isn't he?"

"Rushing, rushing, rushing to get here," Estlin said to Harry. "And then you went for a walk with someone."

"That's right," Harry said. "I hiked up the ridge to get a look at this hangar."

Estlin looked at him like his words were made of color and took time to decipher. Harry waited.

"You went to see an old quiet one," Estlin said, finally, surprised. "Harry, did you visit a tree?"

"The banyan?"

"I think they want to meet it."

"No," Malone said. "Tell them no. Make sure they listen."

Chapter Twenty-four

Bomani clapped his hands as he viewed the feast. Cold cuts for sandwiches were laid on a table set in the shade of the C-17's wing. A cooler on the ground at the end of the table contained bottled juice wedged into rapidly melting ice.

"This is brilliant," he said. "We have not been hungry, but there was nothing fresh. Who must I thank?"

"Harry wanted sandwiches." The answer came from a short man, who was spreading mustard on a bun. "I phoned the grocer."

"I will thank you, then." Bomani snatched a bun and considered the sliced meats. "I am Bomani."

"Bernie." Bernie's eyes left the table. "That's the biggest snail I've ever seen." The snail was climbing one of the wheels of the C-17. Bernie left Bomani to get a better look. "You don't think it could crawl up the table legs do you?"

"You must protect the lettuce," Bomani said.

Bernie immediately fetched a big leaf of lettuce. "Do you think it would let me feed it?"

"Bomani!" Dr. Liev cut into the conversation. Apparently, her luggage had arrived. She wore a fresh white blouse, dress slacks and a wide-brimmed hat. "We have to get Beth away from here, across the island, if not off it."

"My objections failed," Bomani answered. "What has changed?"

"Do you know how the aliens manipulate us?" Dr. Liev exclaimed, anger adding color to her pale cheeks. "They release bugs into the air. Tiny germs that are like wireless microphones that transmit what we're thinking."

"Dr. Liev—" Bernie interrupted.

"Everyone on this airfield has the right to know," she continued. "Bomani, they are gathering our thoughts right now and tampering with them."

"We found free floating alien cells," Bernie clarified. "I think they contain active structures that collect signals and transmit them back to the waetapu. But they aren't germs. We've seen no evidence of self-replication and no one has had any immune response."

"You have a hundred micrographs, a handful of spectra and a hunch," Dr. Liev responded. "The only thing you are certain of is our exposure."

"The ovoids definitely spread across wide areas surrounding the critters," Bernie confirmed.

"Very interesting," Bomani said. "An expanded sensory system has obvious defensive advantages, but this could be something more. Estlin says they evolved in symbiosis with vast tree-like creatures."

"I haven't heard anything about trees," Bernie said.

"He said the creatures have a natural relationship with a species far larger and far more static than they are," Bomani answered. "To communicate with a species that thinks or speaks with structures that are hundreds or thousands of times bigger than oneself must require very special adaptations."

"Like a method to capture signals on a massive scale and re-encode them," Bernie said. "Perfect. The cells they use are broadband receivers, but the signals they relay between themselves are at several specific frequencies."

"This is aggressive, infiltrating, corrupting technology," Dr. Liev argued. "There is nothing natural about it."

"Our clarity of sight would be incomprehensible to a worm," Bomani said. "A shark can smell blood from miles away. It's a disturbing adaptation, but not unnatural. In fact, it reflects the shark's fundamental nature. If the transfer of knowledge is fundamental to the Waes, isn't this reassuring?"

"Listen to your own analogies!" Liev snapped. "Are we worms? Are we wounded fish, bleeding our weaknesses into the air for them to collect? Until these signals are blocked, none of us will be safe."

"That won't be easy," Bernie said, snatching a bite of his sandwich. "Might be impossible."

"Electromagnetic signals can be blocked," Liev responded. "Whatever their frequency range, thick metal will smother them."

"It'll be a real problem if they have adaptive relay systems." Bernie kept his eyes down on the table.

"You're relying on guesswork. I've studied this," Liev answered. "I've run tests. Beth can't read anything through an open metal screen. It may take more with the aliens, but a steel vault would stop them. I guarantee it."

"I mean, yes, *temporarily*," Bernie conceded. "But ultimately a Faraday cage won't work because the ovoids are mobile. Eventually, one or more would penetrate the walls and then that one point could transfer signals from all the ovoids within the cage to those outside it and vice versa."

"You're guessing." The doctor's indignation darkened into an even more severe outlook. "I wonder if your reflexive submission to the situation is a consequence of exposure to this alien pixie dust." She turned and left them.

"Everyone is guessing," Bernie muttered. "We should all put on steel goggles, Bomani, and stumble around blind."

"Our expectations for the future are broken," Bomani answered. "We are already stumbling blindly. It is very dangerous."

"She thinks I've been compromised," Bernie answered, shaking his head as he built himself a second sandwich. "Harry said to brief them — maybe to prove that I'm useful? — but they don't want us here. She'll give them a reason to throw us off the island."

"The planet is an island," Bomani answered. "Where would we go?"

Bernie took a deep breath and pressed his fingers together. "Every time I think I'm past the panic phase, I have these moments."

Bomani offered a shrug of acceptance and examined the fruit piled in bowls on the table. Among the bananas was a large green-skinned melon that he did not recognize. "What is this?"

"Breadfruit," Bernie answered. "My mistake or the grocer's joke. It needs to be cooked."

Sergeant Pollock emerged from the C-17. "Bernie. You're Bernie, aren't you?" he said. "Commander Fleckman wants you."

"But I'm eating," Bernie answered, lifting his sandwich like a shield.

Pollock took the plate from Bernie's hands. "We'll bring it."

"I'm supposed to watch the table."

"Too bad," Pollock answered. He directed Bernie to the C-17 and stepped aside to take a radio call. "Bomani, you're wanted in the hangar."

Bomani, too, pointed at the sandwich on his plate.

"It'll keep," Pollock answered. "You know the way."

Bomani left his plate on the table. He considered grabbing a banana, but found the breadfruit in his hands. It was the size of a football and heavier than he expected. He tucked it under his arm and proceeded to the hangar.

The Waes were scampering around on the floor when he entered. Estlin sat between them with a big pad of paper in front of him.

"Did they escape again?" Bomani asked.

"It does keep tourists out of the hangar," Estlin answered.

"I was summoned."

"Sorry, Bomani, that was me," Estlin said. "They want me to draw what I see, but I suck."

Bomani looked at Estlin's efforts at perspective drawing and agreed. "What is it meant to be?"

"A name. I was trying to cross-section it to show more details," Estlin continued. "I didn't have crayons when I was a kid."

"I didn't learn until later." Bomani sat next to Estlin. "And more drafting than drawing. Technical pictures." He planted the green fruit on the floor and reached for the pad of paper.

"What's that?"

"Breadfruit."

Estlin reached out and rolled it around before lifting it. "Hefty," he said. "Do you mind?"

"It needs to be cooked," Bomani said as Estlin rolled the fruit off to the Waes. They converged on it. The yellow-eyed one examined it closely, spread its fingers and rested its palm against it.

"It's funny how they do that." Bomani refused to think closely about the purpose that had emerged from his own seemingly random choice. "It's quiet in here. That is good, better for everyone."

"More cameras, fewer people."

"And your squirrels have come."

"They're Russian," Estlin answered. "The Russian's air-dropped squirrels to find me. It's kind of funny." He said it without humor, frustration dominating his features as he resumed work on his drawing.

"This is a name?" Bomani asked.

"Malone gave me a list," Estlin said. "He wants their specific symbols for things. I thought this would be a good place to start, but it's hard. Complicated. I see more than I understand." He shoved the page towards Bomani. "They pulled Verges out of here. The British wanted to debrief her. Do you think she'll come back?"

"If you ask for her, maybe." Bomani picked up the blue crayon. "How can I help you?"

— « o » —

"We appreciate your opinion, Dr. Hatarei, but these experiments are more advanced than the efforts made in Wellington. You weren't invited to debate their efficacy." This rebuke came from the speakerphone centered on the desk.

Harry had been summoned to Fleckman's office for a conference call about alien communication methods. His critique of the hypotheses presented for testing had not been welcome. "I understand how you leapt from Lyndie's descriptions of visual communication to your test design, but *he's not using his eyes.* The Waes will use whoever is in the hangar to see and interpret the images you project."

"We are aware of the issues," the reply came. "That's why we are asking you to remove the key obstacle to this experiment."

Harry had missed the introductions, and it annoyed him not to know who was dismissing him from the conversation. "Okay, mate. I'll get on with that," he said. He got a nod from Fleckman and left the office without a further parting word.

"Bizarro land," Harry said as he closed the door behind him.

The hangar was as he'd left it. The Waes were at rest. The ubiquitous soldiers were keeping their posts. Sergeant Malone was sprawled in one of the deck chairs while Bomani and Estlin worked on their drawings. A folding table had been found, and they each stood at it, leaning over wide pads of paper. They had arrived at a method by which Estlin's rough sketches and descriptions were redrawn by Bomani with greater skill and clarity.

"Spherical?" Bomani asked, pointing at a misshapen detail in Estlin's drawing.

"No, it's elongated."

"One to two? One to one-and-a-half?" Bomani reached out to Estlin's page, adding adjacent shapes stretched out to varying degrees.

"That one," Estlin answered. "The surface is smooth and bright, but just under the skin there's dark layer. It's textured, like rice." He sketched the detail, then grabbed a purple crayon and added a film to one of his rice grains. "Furry rice, if you look at it closely."

"Got it," Bomani said, returning to work on his own page.

"What are you working on now?" Harry asked.

"The name, still," Estlin answered. "There are a lot of details."

"We should show some of these to Bernie when you're done," Harry said. "They remind me of the ovoids. Bomani, do you have enough to work for awhile? We're taking a break."

"May I take all of these?" Bomani asked.

"Go for it," Harry said.

"There is software for creating three dimensional shapes," Bomani told Estlin as he gathered papers. "Perhaps, we can do this more efficiently."

"What's up?" Estlin asked as Bomani left the hangar.

"The egg-heads want to run a remote communications experiment," Harry said, turning to shout across the hangar. "Malone, we're going out!"

"Wait," Malone responded, rising to join them.

"What kind of experiment?" Estlin asked.

"Projections of geometrical shapes. I laughed at the demo," Harry answered briefly. "And they think you'd invalidate the experiment. They're right. Even if you could shut down the mind trick, I see the potential for disruptive giggling."

Estlin directed a death glare at him.

"It's a light show," Harry continued. "Television-for-babies style. I can't see any harm, and you need a night off," Harry said. "Fleckman wants us out. So, we're going to be bunkmates in a tent somewhere."

"We're going outside?" Estlin was processing the concept slowly.

"I'll check the arrangements," Malone said. "Sounds good, though. I'm supposed to lie down for a few hours."

"Get your own tent," Harry called after him.

"Bunkmates," Estlin said.

"I've missed you terribly," Harry responded. "In Wellington, I was too trusting. Lesson learned. How much have you slept?"

"Do periods of sedation count?" Estlin asked.

"No."

"There's a tent?"

"Several tents," Harry answered. "We get one."

"Okay." Estlin headed for the hangar exit.

"Do you need to tell the Waes that you're going?"

"They know," Estlin answered.

Malone stood with a group of soldiers just beyond the hangar door. He waved at them and pointed at a tent on the tarmac to their left.

"I think we're bunking over there," Harry said.

"Estlin!" The jubilant call came from the opposite row of tents on the grass to the right of the hangar.

"Jeanette's here," Harry announced. "Did I tell you that Jeanette's here?"

Estlin tipped back on his heels, perilously off-balance as Jeanette dashed over to them.

"How are you?" she asked. "Harry had us chasing squirrels around the island trying to find you."

"She helped me get ashore," Harry explained.

"Then he ditched me at the gate."

"Sorry for that," Harry answered. "It's been hectic."

"They tried to shift me off to a hotel with everyone else. I had to sign a contract with the Department of Defense to get in here. Can you believe it?"

"No," Estlin answered literally.

"I'm reviewing footage for them," she said. "Bernie's equipment arrived. He brought his own tent."

"We're going to get some rest," Harry responded.

"You talk to squirrels!" she said, entirely focused on Estlin. "And now aliens! And you didn't tell me."

"You guessed," he said.

"I guessed wrong," she said. "I thought it was a chemical attraction, not psychic."

Estlin flinched. "You knew I was the problem. The squirrels kept knocking the power out at her place," he added to Harry.

Harry had roomed with Estlin long enough to know that squirrels and power lines could have a mutually detrimental relationship.

"We had a few candle-lit dinners." Jeanette's buoyancy was lost on Estlin, who was sinking in the opposite direction.

"You wanted to move," he said forlornly.

"I wanted to move in with you," Jeanette said affectionately.

"Oh."

Harry could tell that Estlin had not considered this possibility. "Lyndie hasn't had any sleep," he said.

"I'm glad you're okay," she said, reaching out to take Estlin's hands. "This is an incredible opportunity. I hope you don't think that I'm staying for the wrong reasons."

Estlin nodded mutely.

"Good night," Harry said firmly.

"Good night," she said.

Harry watched the awkward seconds during which Estlin's distant demeanor stalled her impulse to embrace him.

"You are tired," she said. "Get some rest. We're just over there."

"Good night," Estlin managed as they parted.

"Let's go," Harry said. "Tent on the left."

"You told her," Estlin said.

"It came up," Harry answered.

Estlin shrugged, still confused by the entire conversation. "Am I right to think, in this context, that I'm the wrong reason?"

"You really can't read your own species." Harry snagged water from a table set next to the tent as he lifted the entry flap. The tent was eight feet high and eighteen feet long. A pair of chairs were just inside the tent and a lamp illuminated the four cots set further back.

"Just us?" Estlin asked.

"I hope so," Harry answered.

"The moon's going to flash again." Estlin proceeded to the furthest cot. "The Waes told me a few days ago. I don't know what else I need to tell you — everything, eventually — but there's going to be another burst. Did the Americans pass the word along?"

"I hadn't heard," Harry said. "But I've been out of the loop. When?"

"Soon. Tomorrow? I've lost track of time." Estlin sat heavily on the cot. He kicked off his sandals. "I need a shower."

"True." Harry handed him a bottle of water. "It can wait until morning."

— « o » —

A generator was humming next to the equipment tent and several extension cords had been snaked through the walls. Bernie was surrounded by lamps and monitors, his computers still booting up.

"We've got power!" Bernie stated the obvious with enthusiasm.

Jeanette took the seat next to him. Seeing Estlin standing on the tarmac, seeming a thin shade of himself, had shaken her.

"They want three complete copies of the files. It's dumb, and it will take hours, but—"

"It's fine. It'll get me oriented," Jeanette said.

"That's a week of footage from Wellington and they already have all of it!" Bernie said. "We gave it to them day by day —

nothing edited, nothing withheld. I told them that, and I got laughed at. That was after I was abused for having all the data with me, because anyone could have rolled me for it. When I suggested that generating copies would be a waste of your time, they threatened to take everything. You understand the irony?"

"Maybe the left brain isn't talking to the right brain," she said. "You released everything, but maybe they don't have it."

"It would be typical," Bernie said, "for them to have a security analyst deciding what footage behavioral biologists should and shouldn't see and distributing edited recordings." He settled, seeming appeased. "Use two laptops for file transfers and pop the third for your work. It's a lot of high res footage. Once the external hard drives are hooked up, they won't need your attention."

— « o » —

Harry wasn't sleeping. The tent on the airfield wasn't a quiet sanctuary and Estlin was restless. The creak of him shifting on the cot was familiar enough that the sound of it rebounding unburdened was obvious. "What are you doing?"

"Going for a walk," Estlin answered.

"You haven't slept."

"Yeah, I'm tired." Estlin shrugged and continued on his way.

"Wait." Harry scrambled from his cot to put himself between Estlin and the tent door.

"What?" Estlin was confused by Harry's efforts to waylay him.

"You need to put your shoes on," Harry said.

"Oh." Estlin turned slowly, went to his cot, and stepped into his sandals.

"Where are we going?" Harry asked.

"Out," Estlin said.

"Where do you want to go? Back to the hangar?"

"No," Estlin said. "The beach."

"What beach?"

"Island," Estlin said. "Grass, runway, grass, beach."

Earlier, on the ridge, Harry had seen where the rocky shore gave way to a narrow strip of sand. "It's dark," he said. "I don't think they'll want us out there."

"Is it cloudy?"

"No," Harry answered. "How's your head?"

Estlin shrugged and wandered to the tent door.

"We're going to be popular," Harry muttered. He wanted a flashlight, but instead grabbed the blanket from his cot and threw it over his shoulder as he followed Estlin.

Chapter Twenty-five

"Mr. Hume cannot leave the airfield."

Estlin unwound his fingers from the chain-link fence and realized that the soldier's reproach wasn't directed at him. Harry was deftly picking the padlock on the gate.

"Where'd you learn that?" Estlin asked.

"My Dad used to lose the shed key every other week," Harry answered. "Got it." He hooked the open padlock on the fence and pulled the chain from the gate.

"I'm ordering you to stay on the airfield."

"Tarmac." Harry flipped his thumb up to point back over his shoulder, and then pointed forward. "Beach. And you've locked up the whole island."

"You will stay on the airfield."

"You sound sincere," Harry responded. "But you let me pick the lock."

"I wanted it open," the soldier answered. "If he's clinging to the fence, we need to search the beach, don't we?"

Estlin checked his hands. He wasn't clinging to the fence, but the chain-link had marked his palms. He remembered crossing the runway, but it felt like the runway was still before him, waiting to be crossed. "They're coming," he said.

The soldier turned to see the creatures gliding low across the field. "Bats," he said.

"Not bats," Estlin said.

The Waes bounded across the grass, took the fence in single stride, and leapt down the other side without slowing.

"That was quick." Harry peered into the darkness. "Where are they?"

"Up a tree," Estlin said.

Two soldiers pushed through the gate and followed the tracks in the sand. Their flashlight swept up into the palm leaves and they shouted their success as they spotted their targets.

The soldier who had remained to block the gate raised his radio. "This is Dewey. Wake Malone. The subjects have left the airfield. They're up a tree on the beach." He lowered his radio, ignoring the immediate back-chatter.

"Did you know they were breaking out?" he demanded.

"How would I know? I wasn't in the hangar," Estlin answered. "They kicked us out for some kind of test."

"Are you with us now, Lyndie?" Harry asked. "The way you drifted over here, I don't think you were the one navigating."

"They do not get to stay out here," Dewey said. "Hume, tell them to return to the hangar immediately."

Estlin looked at the Waes, tried to ask nicely and translated the key images in their response. "Tree. Water. Leaves. Light," he said. "They like the tree. They want to stay."

"So you say."

"That's right," Estlin snapped, suddenly recognizing the man opposite him. "That's what I say."

"Get them down, now."

"You know what? It's my night off."

"You think you're funny?" Dewey shot back. "You think this is an island holiday?"

"Should I thank you for not shooting me?" Estlin responded. "Did you lose your roof-top for hitting Malone or for missing me?"

"For missing," Dewey answered, tracking the Waes as they leapt from one treetop to the next.

"Lyndie, what are they doing?" Harry asked.

"The moon's going to flash," Estlin said. "They want to watch."

"You been keeping secrets, Hume?" Dewey pointed his flashlight at Estlin's face.

"I told you! I told you days ago!" Estlin raised a hand to block the light. "You want them down? You ask."

"Try me," Dewey said. "They jumped from the rafters when you took a turn, didn't they? How much would it take?"

"Right." Estlin stomped away from the palm trees, kicking the sand all the way to the water's edge. He stopped himself there, resisting the unexpected urge to plunge into the water. He turned and found Harry had followed him. There was enough light from the runways to silhouette the rocky outcrops bordering the short stretch of beach.

"You're funny when you yell," Harry said, spreading the army blanket out on the sand. "Want to sit down?"

"No." Estlin felt like he was about to fall backwards into the water. He took a step towards Harry.

"Sit down." Harry said, waiting expectantly until Estlin wordlessly conceded. "I've never seen them move so fast," he said. "Did you know they'd join us out here?"

"I didn't know I was out here," Estlin answered. "You opened the gate."

"You were clinging to the fence," Harry said.

"I am losing my mind." Estlin let himself fall back against the blanket.

"I thought sleep would help with that."

"No rest for the wicked." Estlin considered the depth of the sky. The sun had fallen below the mountains, but had not surrendered yet. The sky was a breathless dark blue, carefully holding each of its brightest stars. "I want to see this."

"I missed the last one," Harry said. "Wrong side of the planet. You sure it's tonight?"

"They're sure," Estlin replied.

"A satellite. There." Harry pointed at a steadily moving speck of light. "And one more." He raised a hand to wave. "We're popular."

"They've changed the sky," Estlin said, his eyes on the stars. "Imagine what's up there? We've always imagined, but its different now."

"Everyone's holding their breath," Harry answered, "waiting for the future. Dontis expects a warship to swoop from the stars, smack us from existence, and take the planet."

"You talked to him?"

"I talk to everyone. Your prime minister yelled at me today." Harry pointed at the distant lights on the water. "There's a Canadian frigate out there. I met the guys they sent ashore.

The Americans promised they could talk to you, then bumped it off the schedule. I had to assure your PM you weren't a hostage. I'm not a liar. It's the wrong word, isn't it?"

Estlin didn't comment. A pair of squirrels scampered across the sand. He decided to allow them on the blanket.

"Alien abductee," Harry said, and was startled from his snorting laugh by the silent arrival of the squirrels. "We need beer. You need to start taking advantage of your position," he suggested. "Make demands."

"Like beer?" Estlin asked. The squirrels maintained a respectful distance. For once, Estlin wanted them closer. "I should send them home," he said. "But they're familiar." He wondered if this was cruelly self-indulgent given the unrelenting heat. Verges had filled bowls of water in the early afternoon and set them out around the hangar.

"You doing all right?" Harry asked.

"Yeah." Estlin closed his eyes. "No one's hit me for hours. It's very unsettling." His grin was fleeting. He considered the Waes in their tree. "They're no longer interested in our inevitable conflict. How does that make it any less inevitable?"

"I wish you wouldn't say stuff like that," Harry answered.

"It's dangerous to be around me," Estlin said. "Yidge was.... It was a mistake. The bullet that bounced next to me today could have hit anyone."

"You think you own this trouble?" Harry anticipated what Estlin couldn't quite say. "I found them. I'm not leaving. The business with Yidge—"

"Will always be one of their first indelible memories of us," Estlin finished flatly. Harry said nothing, but Estlin could read every emotion in his eyes, including raw anger.

"Imagine descending from the stars to provoke a schoolyard fight," Harry said, "to see who throws into the scrap and how they purport themselves. It's...disappointing."

"What happens reflects us, not them," Estlin said. "It's not about them manipulating us into a fight."

"You said it was their job to kick off a conflict," Harry responded.

"It's not what they do. It's what they are. They can sit in a tree or borrow bow ties and go speak to the United Nations.

We're going to freak out about it." The urgent survival instincts that had driven Estlin through the day had faded to a strange philosophical detachment. The galaxy was populated; therefore meeting one of the neighbors was inevitable. Every historical example of first contact between cultures he could think of had come with a clash. "They're here. That's the trigger."

"Now, I really want a beer."

"I don't know a thing about politics, but this is a game changer." Estlin grimaced as their conversation was overwhelmed by jet engines. The snub-nosed fighters overhead were distinctly louder than the F-18s. Their engines made an extra grating, rattling noise, like rocks in a blender. "Every civilization is structured. Competitive groups naturally try to maintain their positions or advance. Their arrival applies an immense pressure. How the stress is translated through a civilization depends on its structure, and therefore reveals it."

"So, we're going to wallop each other over this, no matter what?"

"I should ask for danger pay," Estlin answered.

"From who?"

"The prime minister?"

"Mine or yours?" Harry answered. "The Canadian here — Fredericton? No, that was his ship. He could stare down a bear. I knew that if you didn't meet him today, you would tomorrow. God, I've shifted onto island time."

The starlight shimmered on the ocean. Estlin found the dark as fascinating as the light and, in that darkness, movement that broke the rhythm of the wind and waves caught his attention. He wondered if the Americans had military divers out there, in addition to the sailors and submariners.

"Harry—" Estlin stood, certain that something was about to crawl from the depths. "Maybe we shouldn't have crossed the fence."

The waetapu descended from their branchless tree while two more of their kind crawled from the water. The skin tones of the new arrivals brightened from deep-water black to match the sand at their feet before shifting to a familiar red-tinged blue. They matched the Waes in size and shape, but moved differently. Their toes and fingers were webbed and their tails were wider.

Dewey, admirably, kept their security escort back. "Malone's on his way. Do we need to—"

"Give us a minute," Harry said. "Lyndie?"

The Waes offered him an unfolding view of their motives, like boxes within boxes.

"What do you know about cuttlefish?" Estlin asked.

"They're tasty?" Harry was very focused, despite his glib answer.

"Not funny," Estlin said. "Something's wrong. They say the cuttlefish are being unreasonable."

"They're talking to the cuttlefish?"

"I think so," Estlin answered. "They may have spoken to them before. The dinosaurs came and went. The cuttlefish remained. The waetapu were here when the world was changing. Who did they talk to?"

"Cuttlefish?"

Shifting iridescent patterns flowed across the scaled-spiked skin of the new waetapu. It was an incredible, complex affirmation. The Waes painted the sky with bright images, representing the cuttlefish with a thin rippling fringe as the story began.

"This pair was sent to the water, but the cuttlefish mistake their purpose," Estlin explained. "They want to hire the waetapu to exterminate the two-legs."

"Lyndie—?"

Estlin tried to wave him off, but Harry caught his hand.

"No," Harry said. "You have to keep talking."

"The waetapu tried to explain, but something was lost in translation," Estlin answered shortly. "The cuttlefish are still trying to negotiate."

"Because we eat them," Harry said. "We can stop."

"No." Estlin tried to pull his hand away from Harry. A series of grim visuals convinced him that this wasn't the issue.

"Keep talking."

Estlin pulled his attention back to Harry. "If you were a cuttlefish hoping to hire an exterminator, what would you offer in payment?"

"If I were a fish, I'd sell the land," Harry said.

"They do not borrow from the earth," Estlin said. "They offered what is theirs, what they value and what we and the dolphins value of them. They offered their own flesh and bone. They think the waetapu won't negotiate because they are vegetarians."

"That's disturbing," Harry said.

"Yes," Estlin agreed. The cuttlefish were dancing in the shallows, and all their flesh was for sale, because they'd leapt ahead in their understanding of the Waes purpose.

"The cuttles prefer to deceive and avoid," he said. "But they understand the waetapu can see the future, that their observation of our conflict would yield a predictive model. They want to know whether man will fail, whether cuttle will fail. They want to have their conflict with us."

"Mr. Hume, back away from the water." Dewey's tone was quiet but heavily armed.

"They want.... That's a bad idea." Estlin turned to the Waes, who were suggesting that he dive into the conversation in a very literal way. He tried to be as blunt as one could be when conversing with dancing figments of color, telling them he would not swim with a swarm of angry cuttlefish. "No, thank you."

Sergeant Malone charged onto the beach, stopping when he saw the new arrivals. "Estlin," he said breathlessly, "you've got new friends."

"They crawled out of the water," Dewey reported.

"I want to go back to the hangar," Estlin said.

"That's an excellent idea," Malone agreed. "Will they follow?"

Estlin asked, trying not to impose an answer by imagining it. The new aliens didn't answer, but their skins darkened to match the moon lit sand as they lumbered into the surf.

"Is that a no?" Malone asked.

"They were very quiet," Estlin answered. "Our two are staying." He started walking as Harry shook sand from the blanket and slung it over his shoulder.

The Waes bounded toward the hangar with renewed vigor.

"Tell them to slow down," Malone said. "Let's take this easy."

The Waes paused in the same instant, twisting to face Estlin, before looking at the circling aircraft.

"It can't be a coincidence," Harry said. "They crawled from the water while everyone was staring at the moon."

"I still want to see the flash," Estlin said.

"Lyndie, you missed it."

"What?" He looked up. The moon seemed perfectly normal. He always saw the silhouette of a sleeping rabbit curled among the craters. "Why didn't you say something?"

"You were busy," Harry answered. "It only lasted a few seconds. I'm sure someone took a thousand pictures of it."

"Not the point."

— « o » —

"That is so sexy," Bernie said, leaning over Jeanette's shoulder, planting a hand next to her notebook.

Jeanette released her pen, curling her shoulder inward.

"Your notation!" Bernie clarified, pointing at the pages before her. "The way it distinguishes between moving and held gestures."

Jeanette paused the playback on her computer screen and set her pencil down. Each camera caught different details. She was reviewing the footage from Estlin's first sessions with the Wae. It was hard to remain detached while watching Estlin drop as though someone had punched him in the head. Bernie lingered. She knew he was fixated on a glitch in an entirely different data set.

"Yes, Bernie?"

"There's a problem with the cuttlefish," he said. "An inconsistency."

"Wrong place, wrong time," Jeanette agreed. "But the aliens have induced several migrations."

"Not like that," he argued. "In Dunedin, they drew rabbits to the beach. They flew over Tongatapu and the bats followed. Here, we have squirrels and snails. Apparently, Estlin pulls in squirrels all the time and with the snails — I think that's what happens when you tranquillize a squirrel magnet."

"The cuttlefish were following the carrier," Jeanette said. "Estlin and the aliens were aboard."

"But where did they come from?" Bernie asked, arriving at the point of confusion. "In every other case, the Waes were within a mile of the animals drawn." He slid a map across to Jeanette, pointing at his own notations. "The carrier's route. Your route. And the cuttlefish were here." He tapped the map. "I know telemetry studies are limited," he said. "But there shouldn't have been a swarm out there for them to attract."

"The footage doesn't capture it," Jeanette said. "There were thousands."

"Maybe it's not a mystery." Bernie dropped into the nearest chair. "Or, it's a mystery, just not one of ours."

"Excuse me, sir," Yeoman Heron spoke from the corner of the tent. She'd been assigned to the quarantine zone because of her direct exposure to the aliens on the carrier. "The cuttlefish are here."

"Where?" Bernie asked.

"By the beach," Heron answered. She pointed at the radio receiver in her ear. "It was just reported."

"I need to see this," Bernie said, jumping from his chair.

"No, sir. Dr. Springer, you need permission." Heron raised her radio. "Stay here. I'll ask." She stepped out of the tent.

"Cameras," Bernie said, slinging equipment into a backpack. "What else?"

"Batteries. Light," Jeanette said.

"I know." Bernie dug under his cot for a heavy-duty flashlight. He slapped it against his free hand, testing its power. "The cuttlefish are here." He waved the light across the roof of the tent before flicking it off.

Yeoman Heron returned to the tent. "A jeep's on the way."

"Perfect," Bernie said.

"Cuttlefish," Jeanette said. "You'll love this."

Yeoman Heron stepped in, blocking the doorway. "Sorry, ma'am, we need you to continue to do what you're doing." She pointed Jeanette back to her work.

"But I saw the first swarm," Jeanette said.

"Migrations are his assignment, not yours," Heron responded.

"I'll take pictures," Bernie said, slinging another camera around his neck. He left the tent quickly without meeting her eyes.

"Great. Perfect. I'll stay here," Jeanette said to herself, and then dismissed her own complaint. She'd spent the afternoon watching people being herded away from the airport. Now, she had access to multiple hard drives full of footage. She wound back the recording she'd been viewing and froze the image of Estlin as he entered the studio for the second time. He looked like he'd just fallen out of bed. The fluorescent lighting wasn't doing him any favors, but he had a near cinematic intensity of presence. *Wide eyes,* she thought, feeling voyeuristic because his expression was so open and unguarded. It was remarkable considering the circumstances.

"I'm missing something." She rewound the recording, abruptly minimized it, and chose a wider view from a completely different angle.

— « o » —

Sergeant Malone had set a direct path to the hangar and wanted a slow steady pace, but the aliens were dawdling, bringing the whole procession to a crawl. The HumVees idled behind them, their headlights illuminating the parade.

"Is the extreme air support necessary?" Estlin asked. The low altitude flybys were creating an incredible, conversation-killing din. Wae looked particularly prickly, its spikes standing tall.

"Are they concerned?" Malone asked.

"I am," Estlin responded.

"Not what I asked."

"The bats are not happy."

"Are bats ever happy?" Malone asked. The bats above them were flying so erratically that he had to agree — they did not look happy. The aircraft weren't far above them. Their details were obscured by the dark, but their running lights were enough for Malone to see their distinctive profile. "Prowlers."

"Prowlers," Estlin said. "Intercepting signals?"

Malone didn't answer. He tried not to think about the Prowlers. He didn't want to even guess why they were up there as he stood next to the mind-reading aliens. The greenest looking crew he'd ever seen had entered the hangar with a load of equipment an hour ago. Malone was sure that they didn't have the slightest clue what the true experimental objectives were, and that was entirely the point.

Estlin laughed. "Imagine shining projections on the hangar walls trying to get a response from the alien projections."

"The illusion blinked out as they crossed the runway," Malone responded.

The Prowlers were flying low, slow and dirty. Sergeant Malone realized that someone who wanted to attempt to disrupt the alien projections could consider this an opportunity. Specifically, people prone to bad fucking ideas, who would prefer to try this while the aliens were far away, standing next to someone else. He tried to stop thinking about it, but couldn't as he considered the many ways it could go wrong.

"All stop," Malone shouted. "I want radio contact with distant observers, now."

"What is it?" Harry asked.

Estlin turned, searching the airfield. "They're here."

"Where?" Malone asked, as though he knew what the hell Estlin was talking about. He tracked Estlin's gaze and found, lumbering across the grass towards them, a pair of shadows that brightened from black to blue.

"The fishy ones," Harry said. "I thought they'd gone."

"Hume, what do they want?" Malone asked. Then he exchanged glances with Harry, and they both shut up because Estlin's eyes were doing the glazed shudder-flutter that said he wasn't listening.

Chapter Twenty-six

It was an invitation, conveyed through a vision of dark fathoms of ocean. Strands of rippling light illuminated rocky outcrops teeming with life. The ocean floor was littered with the wrecked frames of steel and wooden ships, and he could tell that they were trying to tempt him with the familiar. Estlin refused, conjuring a field of bright yellow canola flowers, glowing beneath a vaulting prairie sky.

His field was swallowed by a chasm of water as solid as a cliff of rock. He countered with wild grass forcing roots into hard dry earth, trying to reclaim a curving gravel drive. Intimate caves were offered, their mouths jeweled by anemones fondling the currents with bright fingers. Estlin adamantly refused, reaching out to grip an aging deck rail that he conjured so vividly that the white paint flaked beneath his palm. He planted his feet on the deck of the farmhouse and would not let water flowing around his ankles pull him from his home. He walked to the porch door, placed his hand on the handle and found his fingers pressed against nothing. Wind swept across the airfield. The Waes were close, but the other two had vanished.

"Want to tell us about the show?" Harry asked.

"I was…. It was an argument. I think," Estlin answered. "About swimming."

"Did you win?"

"I didn't lose." Estlin considered the tumultuous images, certain he'd missed something. "But I don't think they conceded, either."

"Can we get them back inside?" Malone broke into the conversation.

Estlin looked at the hangar and brightened the path to the door. The Waes considered his query as the Prowlers flew over, one following another, each only a few hundred feet above the runway. Gray lightning split the sky, arcing across the surface of his eyes and bursting into color — all colors at once until there was only red. "Harry!"

He'd seen red before, but this was different, a chaotic visual static — mechanical, not emotional. Through the blizzard of red, he saw Harry clutching his eyes. A blinded bird turned into the distant hangar wall and broke its neck. He fell with it.

"Shut down!" Malone shouted. "Shut down!"

Estlin tried to shield his burning eyes as a profound darkness fell across the airfield. He could smell blood and felt it on his fingers, slicker than tears.

— « o » —

Bernie's weight hit his seatbelt as the driver panic-braked. The formless gray that had blanked out his vision was replaced by a red snow, through which he could see the vehicles clustered on the runway a few hundred yards away. He unbuckled himself and threw open the door of the jeep. A pilot drifted on a chute as his sixty-million dollar ride fell into the ocean. The other Prowlers peeled away from the island, and he knew what had happened.

— « o » —

Harry blinked, pinching the bridge of his nose. The migraine strobes of color had stopped. Estlin was down, but moving. Malone was shouting orders, trying to triage the situation. The red-out had encompassed the airfield.

"Lie still, keep your eyes covered." Harry pressed one hand to Estlin's shoulder and hated himself for what he had to ask. "Are they okay?"

Estlin didn't answer.

"I don't see them," Harry said. "Are they here?"

"That was bad." Estlin released his eyes but kept them closed and pressed his fingers into the ground. "Very bad."

"Stay down."

"Harry!" Bernie sprinted directly to them. "I'm sorry. I didn't know." He pointed his flashlight at Harry's eyes. "You're okay. The burns to the sclera are pin-points."

"Explain," Harry growled, noting that Bernie's eyes were also marked.

"I told them a vault wouldn't work," Bernie announced, profoundly apologetic, waving his hands in frustration. "I was trying to stop them from doing something stupid!"

"Bernie!"

"They tried to jam the signals that interconnect the ovoids," he explained, pointing at the sky. "But the signals transmit information and *energy*. Jamming doesn't block transmissions, it swamps the frequencies with noise. I think they zapped the power receivers on the ovoids and burned them out."

"That was an experiment?" Harry was furious.

"Oh, shit." Bernie caught sight of the blood on Estlin's eyelashes. "Do we need an ambulance?"

"Back off and be quiet," Sergeant Malone interjected. "Estlin, where are they?"

"You are fucking joking," Harry answered.

"Have you missed that we are two aliens short of having two aliens here?" Malone snapped. "He's the only way to get them back, and you know it."

"You did this." Harry jabbed the air with a finger barely uncurled from his fist.

"I am not arguing with you." Malone dismissed Harry. "Estlin?"

"You've just blasted their mechanism for communicating with us." Harry crouched next to Estlin. "What do you expect him to tell you?"

"Hume!" Malone shouted. "Where are they?"

Estlin turned his face to the ground. "Too much noise."

"You won't find them unless they want to be found," Harry said. "Good luck with that."

"Pollock!"

"The stretcher's coming," Pollock said. "We lost a Prowler."

"I heard. I saw," Malone said.

"And the bats are going crazy," Pollock added.

"We're leaving," Harry said.

"You're here at my discretion," Malone answered. "Adjust your thinking or you'll wake up on another island."

"American diplomacy at its best."

"This is not my fuck up, but it is my problem," Malone responded. "I'm getting them back. He's the only beacon we have. I'll strap him to the hood of a HumVee, if I have too." Malone turned away, barking orders across the airfield, directing the search.

"Bernie," Harry beckoned his assistant and pointed at the ground. "Plant yourself here. Stay with him. I'm going to go punch someone in the face."

— « o » —

Bomani looked into Sanford's eyes found they were speckled with fine flecks of blood.

"Bomani, your eyes." Sanford stared at him, seeming unable to explain further.

"Yours, too." Bomani blinked tears from his burning eyes. "Are you all right?"

Soldiers jogged passed, saying nothing, called to service while still shielding their reddened eyes. Dr. Liev was bent over a pocket mirror, pulling down her lower eyelid with one manicured fingernail.

"It had to be done," she said. "They were controlling us."

Bomani was sickened by the realization. "You've hurt all of us," he said.

"An unexpected side effect, but the damage is minor." She snapped the mirror closed. "Inconsequential."

"You've hurt us," Bomani insisted. "More than you know."

"Not me," Beth said, disappointed.

Bomani turned and took her by the shoulders to inspect the clean whites of her eyes. They had so little knowledge of the visitors. The future had become so uncertain it could easily blacken the mind, but Beth's eyes were clear. He felt such a depth of faith and peace that he had to embrace her.

"Protect the young," he said.

"Their listeners were reduced to dust," she said. "You should go."

"I'll stay with you," Bomani answered. "I'm happy here."

"Go." She punched his shoulder from within his arms, and then folded against him to speak softly into his ear. "He's going to need help."

"Beth?"

She released him, pushing away. "I don't need you." Closing her hands into fists, she averted her gaze and left him.

She stomped over to Dr. Liev to sit, folding herself into the shape of a petulant child.

"They've ruined this," Sanford said. "Haven't they?"

Bomani had no answer.

"I'll stay," Sanford assured him. "Do what you can."

Chapter Twenty-seven

Bomani was a breathing ghost. The living world swirled around him as he walked across the airfield. Soldiers stepped together through the grass an arms-length apart, searching with flashlights. The chaotic vortex of bats above them was echoed by squirrels and snails on the ground. Bomani did not feel the push of alien direction, except perhaps the persisting calm that had arrived as he left Beth.

In the distance, Harry was nose to nose with Sergeant Malone. Beyond the pool of bright light thrown by the vehicles, Estlin stumbled through the grass with one hand covering his eyes. The aliens were ahead of him, moving in a way that made Bomani imagine a pair of search dogs eagerly pulling on their leads. They dashed ahead when Bomani approached.

"I'm here, my friend." Bomani said.

"Bomani." Estlin dropped his hand and looked at him, his eyes a frightening red.

"What can I do?" Bomani asked.

"My head hurts." Estlin shielded his eyes. "I've fallen behind."

"Then we should catch up," Bomani answered. He took Estlin's free hand and brought it to rest on his elbow. "Close your eyes. Give me a direction, and I will guide you."

"I don't want to sleep," Estlin complained, forcing his dazed eyes to focus.

"That is good," Bomani answered. He knew they would not be returning to the hangar. "I think we are about to break the quarantine."

"I want to go home." Estlin gripped Bomani's arm.

Bomani did not want to deny or deceive Estlin. "We should catch up first," he suggested. "Which way?"

"The water is too far," Estlin said.

"Walk with me," Bomani answered. "We will go slowly. You'll manage." Bomani knew he was wrong as soon as he said it. He reflexively twisted to catch Estlin's full weight. It was a struggle. His awkward grip did not hold, and he had to let Estlin slide to the ground.

"Or I could carry you." Bomani set his stance, pulled Estlin across his shoulders and lifted with his knees. His eyes were drawn to the shadowy trees, where the grass of the airfield yielded to sand and water. "If I am shot for this, I will haunt you."

Bomani kept his eyes on the grass, placing his feet carefully, moving steadily towards the fence surrounding the runway. He found an open gate. The soldiers stationed on either side of it swept their lights into the darkened palm trees, then left their posts, chasing the wind into the trees. Beyond the gate, footprints had churned a path through the sand to a place of surging, living water. Bulging-eyed squid were sliding body-over-body in the shallows. They jetted away when Bomani's feet touched the water. The energy of the water dissipated, and it settled to glassy stillness, creating a smooth path of moonlight.

"Estlin, it would be good for you to wake up now." Bomani shifted Estlin's weight across his shoulders. "If you could wake and perhaps tell me what will happen next?"

The water before Bomani fused into a solid shape, a thick plate that was the blue of ancient glaciers. The plate sank, but its surface remained dry as curved walls grew continuously from its edges. The structure was the length of a man and reminded him of a coffin as much as a canoe.

"Could you wake him?" Bomani asked the water and sand. "It would be much easier if he was awake. This should rest on his faith not mine."

There was no answer.

Bomani stepped into the water, continuing until he was knee deep. He deliberately pressed his leg against the side of the ice-like vessel and found that it was both solid and as warm as the water in which he stood.

"I hope this is the right thing," Bomani said, lowering Estlin into the water sled. "I'm sorry if it is not."

— « o » —

"They won't risk it," Pollock said.

The airspace had been cleared despite Malone's demands. Submariners were retrieving the downed pilot. The EM pulse associated with the moon flash had glitched the most sensitive spy satellites, delaying all intelligence from orbit.

Malone decided to return to the organic approach. He threw his radio to Pollock. "Keep asking," he said and turned to Harry who was glaring at him with his teeth bared. "Hume can find them."

"No chance." Harry's stony visage did not shift.

"You can help, or you can leave," Malone answered.

"The bats are messing with drone surveillance," Pollock reported.

"Bernie!" Harry shouted.

Malone followed Harry's gaze to where Bernie was crouched at the edge of the runway. "Where is he?"

"I thought I saw them, but—" Bernie directed his flashlight at the grass. "The snails are pairing up. We could be facing a population explosion."

"Where's Lyndie?" Harry asked.

"Oh, no," Bernie turned in place, searching.

"Hume!" Malone bellowed.

"He was here!" Bernie argued.

"You think it's an illusion?" Malone asked. "That he's here — they're here — but we aren't seeing them?"

"The ovoids burned," Harry said. "How can they still be working?"

"Maybe you didn't zap all of them," Bernie answered. "Maybe they aren't all active. If redundant ones go dormant or if some operate on different frequencies—"

"Is that possible?"

"I don't know!" Bernie answered, sweeping his flashlight back and forth, still searching for Estlin.

"Go back to your lab," Malone ordered. "I want an answer."

— « o » —

Bomani had abandoned Estlin. He walked from the beach to the grass to the runway, knowing he would soon be stopped. He lacked the will to conceal his actions, even by lies of omission, though he knew the Americans might string him up for everyone's failings.

"Bomani!" Bernie jogged along the edge of the runway. The scientist was rushing, alone, back towards the hangar. He directed his flashlight at Bomani's shirt. "The bats got you. More than once."

"Very unlucky," Bomani agreed, pulling at his shirt to survey the damage. "I don't have a spare."

"Jeanette thinks we should raid the airport gift shop," Bernie said. "Or I should. But I need a shower, not a shirt. We're on the equator. You'd think access to showers would be a priority. Not a *priority*-priority, next to the aliens, but up there with food and toilets. Can you believe how hot it is here in the middle of the night?"

"Yes," Bomani answered. "I have not met Jeanette."

"You'll like her. She's smart," Bernie said. "I have equipment in one of the tents. They want me back there, so I can look at the ovoids and find out what their big zap did. You can help! The more eyeballs around for me to sample the better. I just need a few tears. You've been in the hangar today, yours should be really good," Bernie assured him.

"I will help however I can. You will figure this out?"

"I have ideas. They demand answers, and then send me *walking* back to the hangar," Bernie complained.

Bomani shadowed Bernie back to the tents. He did not receive any attention from the security forces until he was acknowledged by Yeoman Heron, who recognized him from the carrier. She pulled the canvas door to Bernie's tent open for them.

"You have to see this," Jeanette said as they entered, pointing at her computer screen.

Bernie glanced at the screen long enough to register the image. "I've seen it." He continued to his microscope and flicked on the lamp. "This is Bomani. You can show him."

Bomani dutifully watched the recording on her screen. It showed one of the aliens dropping off the plexiglass window of a cage in a wide, empty warehouse. Estlin stepped into frame shortly thereafter.

"It reacts before he enters the room," she said. "Some of the other angles show it better."

"I reported that as it happened," Bernie said, harvesting one of his own tears. "It's how we knew Estlin was the real deal."

"You noted a distance," she said. "Eight meters before he entered the room."

"Sounds right," Bernie agreed, his attention on the microscope slide. "Got it." He refocused as he increased the magnification. "These are definitely toasted."

"But the ovoids give them far greater range," Jeanette said. "It knew he was coming long before he reached the door. I can show you."

"Oh, shit." Bernie left his microscope. "I am so stupid."

"Watch its fingers and its eyes." She switched to a close-up of the alien on the plexiglass and rewound it. "There." She paused the recording. "It knows he's coming. I reviewed the audio log for the control room. Confirmation that he was on his way was acknowledged by you six seconds later." She let the tape play out. "Now, here's where it gets excited."

"Because he's close," Bomani said.

"He's more than close," Jeanette said.

"He's in primary contact range," Bernie said.

"Exactly," she said. "I think that's when he crossed from indirect contact relayed by ovoids to direct contact. They have an inherent range."

"Estlin's gone," Bernie said, dejectedly. "When they blasted the ovoids, the Waes vanished. Everyone was searching for them. Harry was yelling at Malone. And then Estlin was gone."

"Gone where?" Jeanette asked.

"Gone, gone." Bernie flicked his fingers apart to indicate a magical vanishing. "They sent me back here."

"Where's Harry?" she asked.

"Looking," Bernie answered. "Everyone's looking. Except us."

Bomani looked at the stripes of slime across his shoulder. "Jeanette, do you know where I might get a fresh shirt?"

— « o » —

The Brits thought they were running the airport terminal. Harry was no longer welcome in the hangar, so the Americans had dropped him at the luggage bay to face off with a Brit who wanted to see his passport. It was a reminder that he'd have to track down the cop who had snagged it. The terminal building was bright and open and eerie. There were enough British soldiers in the building for Harry to know they had not been invited to join the search for the aliens. Verges, the RAF pilot, and Bomani were sharing a table in the small food court. They looked at Harry expectantly as he joined them.

"Estlin?" Verges asked.

"He's gone," Harry said.

"They're still searching," Verges responded.

"He's gone," Harry assured her. "Look at the squirrels."

Harry had found the change in their demeanor obvious once he was willing to see it. There were two squirrels in the terminal, begging crumbs from the soldiers at the other end of the food court.

"There is no pull on them," Bomani observed. "No direction." His shirt was emblazoned with a swooping eagle clutching a staff and club, the icon from the Samoan flag.

"Nice shirt," Harry said.

"It's clean," Bomani answered with a shrug. "You need food. I've eaten. I'll find something for you."

— « o » —

"I lost him twice," Bernie said. "I was supposed to be watching him both times."

Jeanette was lying on a cot. She'd balanced a monitor on one of the chairs and kept her eyes on the footage.

"It's like being the crappy storm trooper," he said. "I must have a weak mind."

"An open mind," she suggested.

"You don't have to be nice to me," Bernie said. "I mean, I appreciate that you are nice, so maybe it's automatic." He closed his laptop, but didn't turn to face her. "Not everybody can be Han Solo. I knew that as a kid, so why pretend? But I envied the guys who played the storm troopers. How cool would it be to have that anonymous bit of fame? Now, space-monkeys have arrived, and I don't even want to be in the movie."

— « o » —

Bomani watched Sanford study the fresh signal data from John, new ideas spilling into his notebooks. The C-17 was hot and quiet. Bomani needed to sleep before he could look at the new spectra, but he feared his dreams would drag him to the ocean's bottom. So, he sat with Sanford, who was fixated on a flicker in the numbers, an anomaly that none of them were even certain was real.

"Do you think they'll find them?" Sanford asked.

"Not here," Bomani answered.

"I hate this," Sanford said. "The answers were here, and we drove them away."

Bomani said nothing, fearing that if he spoke, his culpability would be apparent.

"They want me in Livermore," Sanford continued. "Boxley offered me a job in his think tank. He said I could have my own little piece of the puzzle."

Sanford's bitterness was not lost on Bomani. He knew that if Livermore was next, he would not be invited. "I should go to the hotel," he said, "where they sent Beth."

"They'll clear everyone out soon." Sanford turned the pages over to stare at their stubborn white backs. "I feel selfish. We need everyone working on this, but Livermore? The size of that place makes me feel irrelevant. It's like my ego is too big and too small at the same time and if I refuse — if they let me refuse — I think the door will slam so fast I'll be buying my own ticket home."

"Would that be so bad?"

"No." Sanford considered it. "Teddy hates it when I'm away."

"Teddy?"

"I have a cat. I didn't want a cat, but my neighbor died and I inherited an angry cat. It yelled at me for weeks. I thought he was deaf. Then I thought it was so stuck in the past that the present would never measure up. But the past wasn't the problem."

Bomani realized that he knew nothing of Sanford's family. The man had not spoken at all about his life beyond his work. He knew where Sanford lived because he knew where he worked.

"I lost my wife," Sanford said, immediately raising a hand against Bomani's sympathy. "We had good years, more time than expected. She fought cancer twice, but after that...there were cupboards in the kitchen that I didn't open. I decided that a widower only needs one pot. But one day, I brought home a fish. I cooked rice and fish and the cat danced. It wasn't the fish, you can rake fish from a can any day. He loved the preparation, the anticipation. I dug into the drawers for Millie's recipe books." Sanford paused, pressing his fingers against his pursed lips. "She'd written in the margins. Little notes. Added ingredients. Flavors I had to find again."

It was bread that Bomani missed. Bread from dough pressed flat by his mother's hands. "You are making me homesick."

"Sorry." Sanford adjusted his reading glasses, turning the page to face his equations. "I should learn this while I can."

"You don't work for your ego, Sanford," Bomani said. "You work for those moments of true realization, when you suddenly see what the rest of us have missed. Whatever jobs you are offered, you should work wherever you think you will be most effective."

"You're still leaving," Sanford said.

Bomani nodded. "This will be a temporary parting of ways," he said. "I'm inviting myself to your house in Seattle. I will bring fish. I will meet your cat and enjoy your cooking. And I will bring my skills to your science."

"Very good." Sanford stood and took Bomani's hand firmly, as much joy as Bomani had ever seen in his eyes.

"This is not an idle threat," Bomani insisted and pulled Sanford into a proper embrace. "We'll meet again. Travel safely, my friend."

"You, too."

— « o » —

Harry watched a gray Sikorsky rise from the airfield. It was too far away to pick out the marks identifying its country of origin. It didn't matter. Everyone was leaving, one flight at a time. A pair of widely spaced Prowlers flew alongside the helicopter, sweeping it with a strong EM field as a final follow-up on similar decontamination conducted on the ground.

Harry had moved one of the wooden deck chairs out into the shade of the C-17. He had no access to any of the intelligence being gathered, but could judge from the methodical activity on the airfield that there had been no revelations.

Verges arrived, handing him a bottle of water as she opened one for herself. "I've added my name to the departure queue," she said. "Orders."

"My flight was delayed until tomorrow," Harry replied. "I delayed it — threatened to strand myself if it left sooner. There's no logic to it. He's not here. How far do you think they took him?"

"They value him," she said. "They were protective."

"We see what they want us to see," he said. "That's their game. Their motivations are as alien as they are."

"They thought we might kill him," she said.

"They came to watch us kill and die," he answered. "We should all go home."

"You're hopeful," she said. "So, don't pretend you aren't."

"Thank you," Harry said. "For having his back while you could."

"This is every bit of contact info I have." She handed him a folded sheet of paper. "I want to hear from you."

— « o » —

The prairie grass whispered a quiet warning of approaching winds. The stars were bright and the white night-sun was full. A flash stroked the yellow grass. He rose from a crouch to his full height then quickly climbed the nearest hill for a proper view. A distant storm was flinging lightning into the ground. It was so far away that there was no sound. The sky above him was clear. Only at the edge of the storm were the stars vanished by the clouds. Each bolt burned its complex shape into his eyes and offered a glimpse of distant land usually obscured by the heat haze of the day. He wondered whose homes were built there. How many ears were filled by the roar of the light?

Suddenly, he was at the center of the storm, as though the earth had abruptly shifted and the expansive thunderheads stayed exactly where they were, roiling with power. The grass surrounding him yielded, bending low to the ground in fear. He scrambled down the hill and dove into his home. He bolted downward, the passage to his bedroom wrapped and held by the roots of the prairie grass. In the small room, the home that he had built, that had held him safe through three winters; he hunkered, wondering if the rain would come or if his world would burn.

— « o » —

"I've got something," Bernie said. "It emerged from the Pacific and flowed through the Rockies like a storm."

Harry examined the sequence of weather radar images Bernie had spread across the table. "Because it's a storm?"

"The Pacific tsunami sensor net picked up an eight inch unusual surge just as this storm boiled up out of nothing," Bernie said. "But, the interesting part is not where the storm started, but where it ended up." He handed Harry a satellite photo.

"Holy shit," Harry said. "How'd you find this?"

"The weather channel," Bernie said. "The storm path was wrong."

Harry fixed Bernie with a long hard look.

"Terry contacted me," Bernie added, "with some albatross telemetry. It pointed me in the right direction."

"You said there were no anomalous migrations," Harry said. "You sent me into a meeting to say that we had nothing."

"Three birds," Bernie answered. "It wasn't a migration. She had three birds five hundred miles further north than they've ever been. It wasn't enough to report."

"Now, it is."

Chapter Twenty-eight

Darkness gave way to formless light, and Estlin woke with his eyes already open. He was cold. The rain blot on the ceiling looked different. He wondered if his patch job on the roof had failed. He wondered why he was lying on the hard-wood floor, then stopped wondering because the Waes were asleep on the closet shelf and Yidge was sitting at the end of his bed.

"Hallucinations are bad," he said, and tried to ignore her nod of agreement. He pressed an elbow to floor and levered himself up, his bones aching. He ignored Yidge and looked into the closet where the Waes were curled together. "Make yourselves at home," he suggested.

"They like your place," Yidge answered. "It's tasty." She seemed far more solid than when he'd last seen her.

"You're not you."

"I know."

He rubbed grit from his eyelashes and looked at the dark dust on his fingertips. "My eyes were bleeding."

"Do they hurt now?"

"No."

"Good." Yidge stood and stretched. She was wearing a sundress. The light through the window was dancing on the wall in a very unusual manner. There were water drops on the glass and the sky was a deep cloudless blue.

"How'd they fix your voice?"

"A bit of technology." She held out an object the size and shape of a marble. It was the color of her skin. "They use these to manage memories like me."

He walked to the window because something was wrong with the sky. Two meters out from his window, the air ended in a vertical wall of rippling blue. He knew he wasn't dreaming. "Yidge? Did you hijack my house?"

"You wanted your home." She appeared confused by the question.

Estlin's throat constricted. He pressed his fingers to his eyes, preventing tears, finding his tolerance for upheaval ripped from its foundation. "Where am I?"

"Home."

He did not want to clarify the question. "My house was attached to a particular patch of Earth."

"Yes."

"I didn't want it moved."

"Oh," Yidge said. "Your home is home. Not hijacked."

Estlin recovered his breath and pointed mutely at the view.

"The cuttlefish accepted your offer to host the first conversation," Yidge answered. "A significant amount of water was required to accommodate their collective."

"The cuttlefish are here?"

"Yes."

"In a giant puddle of ocean." He peered into the blue and saw shadows moving through the light. "Oh, shit! You didn't drown the neighbors?"

"The water is on your land," Yidge assured him. "Above it, actually. The support field follows the terrain, leaving room for life below. The waetapu have assisted with this."

Estlin pressed himself to the window to peer out. The water didn't touch the grass and, to his left, a narrow column of air extended off the corner of the porch. This key hole offered a view of the closest tree. "How many cuttlefish are here?"

"One thousand three hundred and sixty one."

"And they want to kill us?"

"No," she answered. "They are predators, but you are not prey."

"Good."

"You misunderstand." Yidge joined him at the window. "Their collective does not want to consume you, but the idea of having your species exterminated by a third party has just entered their consciousness."

"The Waes refused," Estlin said, seeking confirmation.

"The cuttlefish have accepted the refusal and regret the wastefulness of their proposal, particularly as the Waes have clarified their interest in the observation of conflict, not the direct practice," Yidge answered. "But the cuttles know that there is life amongst the distant points of light and, if they ask, they will find creatures that would appreciate our meat, perhaps even basic life forms that would not suffer from regret."

"How considerate." Estlin backed away from the window. He paced the room and knocked on the frame of the closet door. The Waes didn't even twitch. "How can they sleep?"

"They rest in memory," Yidge answered. "They are preparing in their own way. The cuttlefish are enjoying the view. They asked that conversation be delayed until dark."

"I'm translating?"

"The Waes are not here to negotiate or mediate," Yidge answered. "You will speak to the cuttles. They will watch."

"This is a bad plan. I can't do this."

"Should I help you prepare?"

"Prepare!" Estlin squeaked. "What do I do? Apologize? Promise a new future?"

"It is the new future that they fear," Yidge answered. "They've been here since the depth of memory. Millions of years compared to our thousands."

"We've made some mistakes."

"Understatement." She offered him a ghost of a smile, but there was sorrow in her dark eyes. "The poison spilling from our nests does not concern them. They trust their resilience far more than ours. It is the new danger that drives their consideration, the danger presented by the Waes. If we accept technology that could, by incompetence, be the end of all living water, they must consider the threat and respond to it."

"I can't do this, Yidge. It can't be my job."

"You agreed to meet them here."

"No, no, no! I will get us kicked off the planet," Estlin answered. "In my life, attempts to negotiate have always ended in eviction. I'm a hopeless liar. I can't promise that we won't pursue the stars. And, as a species, I doubt that our days of doing stupid things are behind us."

"Your pessimism is troubling."

"I'm outnumbered!" he retorted.

"This was not meant to levee advantage to the cuttles. You stood alone in your invitation. They recognize this difference in your species. We can delay if you wish to stand with a thousand of your own when you speak."

"No," he answered, horrified by the thought.

"The Waes did not think numbers would enhance your clarity," Yidge answered. "This is a first conversation. It is best for you to speak for yourself unburdened by greater responsibility."

"Right." Estlin answered flatly. His eyes were watering. Unable to identify which emotion was driving the tears, he chose to blame the grit and dragged his fingers across his eyelashes. "Besides, there's only one bathroom."

He looked around. The blue sheets on the bed were untucked and the light blanket had fallen partly to the floor, thrown back by his rising in the night. "Okay. One conversation," he said and got into bed.

"What are you doing?"

"Lying down," he said. "I have time."

"You slept on the journey," she said.

"Sedation doesn't count." He pulled up the covers and let his head settle on the pillow. "I'll sleep, I'll shower, and then maybe I'll have beans on toast." Estlin imagined himself in the kitchen with the can opener and the flaming stovetop. Yidge was watching him, though he wondered if she had eyes at all now or just the illusion of them. "Please take yourself and your marble somewhere else while I sleep."

"I'll go," she said. "But I'll stay here." She held up the marble and set it on his bedside table. It flattened into a coin and changed color, matching the dark wood. "Sleep well."

He closed his eyes and felt the tension that had coiled each of his muscles. It felt as though the bed was moving. The house sounded wrong. It smelled wrong. It was too cool for August. He wondered where the birds had gone, whether any were trapped beneath the water or if they were flying through it in bubbles of air.

He rolled to his side drawing the blanket close around him. He thought about having a nervous breakdown, but knew that breaks from reality were far from restful. Besides which, Yidge was right. He didn't need to sleep.

He flopped over again to stare at the ceiling. There was no rustling in the attic. It was profoundly wrong. "Damn it."

The phone hummed to life, vibrating against the bedside table. He startled, clutched the bedding, and tried to ignore it. A tap on the window compelled him to sit up. A black squirrel was on the windowsill, balanced on its hind legs with its hands against the glass.

His life had always been absurd, occasionally to the point of cruelty.

"Don't even think about it," he told the squirrel and gave in to the phone's persistent thrumming. "Hello?"

"Oh, good! You're home. He's home!" Harry declared enthusiastically. "Lyndie, are they with you?"

"Harry?"

"Are the Waes with you?"

"They're asleep in my closet," Estlin answered. "Could you ask everyone not to blow up my house?"

"No one is even thinking about it."

"Right. Tell them that blowing up my house would be an extremely bad idea."

"What's happening?"

"The cuttlefish are here, a lot of them, in a giant puddle floating above my yard," Estlin answered.

"That's water?" Harry exclaimed. "I've got a satellite picture — thought it was a huge shiny space ship."

"I think the status quo is about to have its ass handed to it."

There was a pause. "Everyone would like us to stop talking on this unsecured line," Harry said finally.

"It's the only phone I have."

"Sounds like there's a way to locally catch your signal and keep it off the public network," Harry said. "It'll take a bit of time. I'm coming to you."

"Where are you?"

"Still in Samoa, but I know someone with a Harrier," Harry answered. "She says nine hours."

"Bring beer," Estlin suggested.

Harry laughed. "See you soon."

Epilogue

"Tomorrow?" Harry demanded a better answer.

"If you don't want to ride with us, you can always stick out your thumb," Sergeant Malone replied. "When the flight is confirmed, a helicopter will shuttle us to Ofu. Pollock's coordinating it. Complain at him if you want." Malone walked away through the open-walls of the tent.

Harry was roasting by the hangar on the airfield, his wings clipped. The Harrier had been grounded by a proclaimed lack of aviation fuel. His quick exit had been replaced with the promise of a seat on an American flight sometime the next day. He was furious, but his own air force could do no better.

"They say you are the famous Harry."

Harry turned to find the Russian from Apia had entered the tent.

"I am Dr. Pepel. Expert in the sea cucumber." He offered Harry his hand, greeting him as a stranger. "I did not think you would still be here."

"There are holes in the runway," Harry answered. "It's limiting my options."

"Yes, those big birds are stuck, aren't they?" Pepel pointed at the two C-17s. "The craters break the runways almost perfectly in half. I come with the helicopters to help, and I am sent to a hotel." Pepel shrugged. "I don't complain. The bar was open, and there were many rumors, ridiculous whispers, like Americans bombing themselves."

"What do you think?"

"It is not my field. If the French did it, they get caught. The French always get caught. If it was someone else?" Pepel turned his hand in the air. "Comme ci, comme ça. Maybe the French are still caught, and someone fixes their submarine."

"Where's your helicopter, now?" Harry asked.

"It left this morning when the others did. But you stayed."

"Yes."

They were interrupted by aircraft engines. Harry stepped from the tent and looked up, shading his eyes to see the An-74.

"This is my ride," Pepel said as the distinctive cargo plane overflew them. "Runways are for sissies."

The Coaler banked to approach the airfield and dropped its landing gear. It planted its wheels on the first inch of runway and stopped in one quarter of the space available, throwing up a cloud of dirt.

"Do you have any room?" Harry asked, elated. The An-74 was already turning to face the water.

"There are seats," Pepel answered, "but would you believe where we are going?"

"Will the Canadians let you land that in a field?"

"Do you think we will ask?"

```
            *
           * *
          * /\ *
          */*\ *
         * //*\\ *
```

About the Author

Claire McCague is a writer, scientist, and folk musician who fabricates nanostructured materials by day and spins words into scripts and books as the stars rise. She lives and doesn't sleep much in British Columbia.

Claire McCague has spent time playing with focused electron beams, femtosecond laser beams, neutron beams and plain, old X-rays. She has a doctorate in chemistry, achieved explicitly to support her arts habits, and spends her days trying to save the world through development of nanostructured materials for sustainable energy conversion systems. Claire performs regularly with the Sybaritic String Band and her plays have been featured in festivals across Canada.

— « o » —

If you enjoyed this read, please leave a review.

Need something new to read?

If you enjoyed The Rosetta Man, you should also
consider these other EDGE titles:
~ ~ ~

Milky Way Repo

by Mike Prelee

Running a starship repo company isn't easy or cheap. It's just
an endless string of fuel costs, ship maintenance, legal red tape,
unhappy debt bailers, shady associates and uncooperative
dock officials from one end of the galaxy to the other.

Nathan Teller owns and operates Milky Way Repossessions,
a company that tracks down and repossesses starships. And
although he's only managing to break even on his debt, he
wouldn't trade it for anything. (His ex-wife holds that against
him. No surprise there.)

When Nathan and his crew successfully steal a freighter
from the clutches of a particularly tenacious and corrupt dock
official, he earns the respect of their high profile employer.
Opportunity seems a sure thing.

Nathan should be happy. But when that lucrative job op
turns into a ransom delivery for a starship crew being held

hostage by a cult, he suddenly finds himself pursued by a self-immolating loan shark hell bent on collecting a gambling debt.

How will it all turn out? You never know. Especially when Nathan and his Starship repo agents are up against a cult and the mob...

Praise for Milky Way Repo

The debut novel of Mike Prelee is a very entertaining Sci-Fi/Noir, with vivid, likable characters and a fast pace. He's got a great handle on plot and a knack for drawing you into the story. For fans of fast-paced space adventure with a smattering of crime drama mixed in, this should do the trick. I finished it in two sittings. High praise for sure. I would definitely read a sequel (or two).

— marc a. gayan

Milky Way Repo is a nice, light but exciting read. With just enough action and even a bit of romance and comedy, I definitely recommend this read to anyone who enjoys a good sci-fi/blue collar space opera.

I gave Milky Way Repo 5 stars because it provided me with a short, albeit adventurous, fun and light hearted escape for a few hours. It is well written, with well rounded characters and a wonderful storyline.

I have to say that Duncan was my absolute favorite character. Officially starting a Duncan fan club!

— Chaelsie Jenyk

~ ~ ~

The Genius Asylum

by Arlene F. Marks

The truth is out there...

Earth Intelligence and Space Installation Security each think Drew Townsend is working for them. They're wrong.

Sent undercover to set up a covert intelligence operation on Earth's remotest space station, Drew Townsend finds himself managing a crew of brilliant mavericks, making friends with the most feared warriors in the galaxy, and feeling more at home in the controlled insanity of Daisy Hub than he ever did on Earth. Then he learns the truth about his mission there, and it's time to choose. In the coming interplanetary conflict, which side will Daisy Hub be on?'

Like the clues of a cryptic crossword, each book set in the Sic Transit Terra universe contains a puzzle – perhaps a riddle, perhaps a maze or an anagram – and in each case, the answer to the smaller puzzle brings the reader and characters one step closer to solving a much larger and more important one. The Genius Asylum is '1 Across' – it initiates a multi-book story arc that addresses one of the great mysteries of life: Why are we humans the way that we are?

Praise for The Genius Asylum

"The Genius Asylum starts out on Earth as something that looks like a crime story, but it then quickly describes a world of interstellar travel and alien alliances. After the first act concludes, the story's complexity starts accelerating and

doesn't slow down, and you'll find yourself drawn into the world, needing to know what comes next. It is an excellently written story that provides the framework for the series that is to come, and I'm looking forward to reading the rest of it."
— Chris Marks, reviewer

I thoroughly enjoyed this Sci-Fi Brainteaser. Very well written with incredible plot twists and turns. We've got a very intelligent double agent as the main character and an intriguing support cast. I was thankful for the planetary history at the beginning as it was helpful in understanding the different organizations mentioned throughout the novel. The Author has a witty way of expressing viewpoints, clearly has put a lot of thought into the storyline and created edge of your seat suspense and mystery! Admittedly, I was confused about the title of the book until about halfway through reading it but it makes perfect sense now. I highly recommend this absolutely unforgettable installment and can't wait for the next.
— Stephanie Herman

~ ~ ~

For more Science Fiction, Fantasy, and Speculative Fiction titles from EDGE and EDGE-Lite visit us at:

www.edgewebsite.com

——<<<>>>——

Don't forget to sign-up for our Special Offers

——<<<>>>——